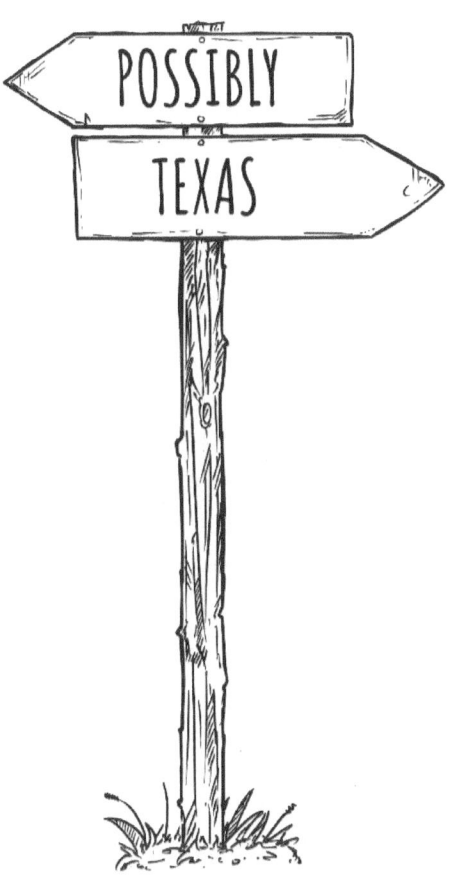

POSSIBLY

TEXAS

A Novel

By: Chase Connor

Book Cover Designed By: Allen T. St. Clair
©2020-2022 Chase Connor; The Lion Fish Press

Published By:

The Lion Fish Press
539 W. Commerce St #227
Dallas, TX 75208

www.chaseconnor.com
www.thelionfishpress.com

AUTHORS' NOTE:
This is a work of fiction. Names, characters, places, and incidents either are the product of the authors' imagination or are used fictitiously, and any resemblance to actual persons, living or dead, business establishments, events, or locales is entirely coincidental. None of this is real.

E-book ISBN 978-1-951860-30-1
Paperback ISBN 978-1-951860-31-8
Hardback ISBN 978-1-951860-32-5

Also by Chase Connor

LGBTQ+ YA Books

Just a Dumb Surfer Dude: A Gay Coming-of-Age Tale
Just a Dumb Surfer Dude 2: For the Love of Logan
Just a Dumb Surfer Dude 3: Summer Hearts
Gavin's Big Gay Checklist
A Surplus of Light
The Guy Gets Teddy
GINJUH
When Words Grow Fangs
Sending Love Letters to Animals and Other Totally Normal Human Behaviors

LGBTQ+ New Adult/Lit Fic/MM Romance

A Tremendous Amount of Normal
The Gravity of Nothing
Between Enzo & the Universe
A Straight Line (w/ co-author J.D. Wade)

LGBTQ+ Magical Realism

Possibly Texas

LGBTQ+ YA & MG Fantasy

A Million Little Souls

A Point Worth LGBTQ Paranormal Romances

Jacob Michaels Is Tired (Book 1)
Jacob Michaels Is Not Crazy (Book 2)
Jacob Michaels Is Not Jacob Michaels (Book 3)
Jacob Michaels Is Not Here (Book 4)
Jacob Michaels Is Trouble (Book 5)
CARNAVAL (A Point Worth LGBTQ Paranormal Romance Story)
Jacob Michaels Is Dead (Book 6)
Jacob Michaels Is… The Omnibus Edition (all 6 JMI books and CARNAVAL)
Murder at the Red Rooster Tavern (Book 7)

Erotica

Bully
Briefly Buddies

Audiobooks

A Surplus of Light: A Gay Coming-of-Age Tale (narrated by Brian Lore Evans)
Between Enzo & the Universe (narrated by Brian Lore Evans; Tantor Media)

Translated

Between Enzo & the Universe – **Spanish**
A Surplus of Light – **Spanish**

Anthologies Contribution

Magis and Maniacs: And Other Christmas Stories (Frank, A Christmas in Pajamas, A Surfer's Christmas, and *The IT Guy)*

Kindle Vella

Tricked: The Men of Briefly Buddies (serialized/episodic continuation of *Briefly Buddies*)

Dedicated to:

All the butterflies who managed to forget they were once caterpillars. The desert tortoises who gaze up at the moon and hope. All of the artists who open the doors and invite the sunshine inside.

Contents

Act I

Act II

Act III

About the Author

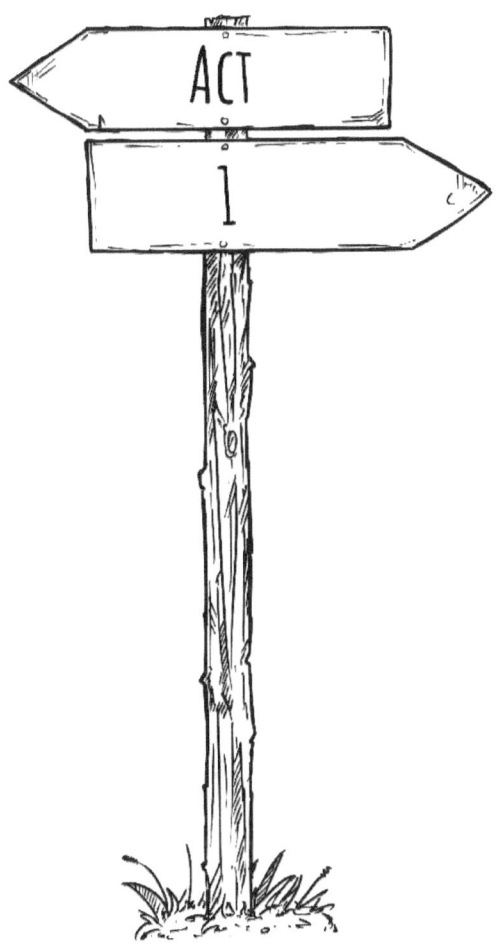

TWO MILE-
TRAIL

My shoes aren't a dusty brown; they're actually black. Dust from the dirt road I'd walked along, while also trying to drag my suitcases behind me without them toppling off of their wheels, was the reason for the color. A backpack was strapped tightly around my chest. So, with its weight, trying to drag two suitcases, and walking along a dirt road that some municipality forgot to pave, it wasn't the best day of my life.

They were new kicks my mom bought for me when we were stuck in Tuscaloosa. The shoes, I mean. A few months before, the alternator went out in her car as we were driving from Atlanta to New Orleans, and Tuscaloosa, unfortunately, was where it happened. Not that Tuscaloosa—or Alabama itself— is all that bad, but it's definitely not a place where you want to find yourself stuck. Especially when none of the mechanics in the entire town can get the specific part needed for your mom's car in less than four days. Also, when all your mom can afford is to get a room at a motel just off the interstate and pay for sparse meals created from what she bought in a vending machine, it's not what you might think of as a glamorous situation.

Now that I think about it, my mom might have lifted the shoes from a store.

She said she bought them for me, though.

Not that traveling with my mom couldn't be exciting, or even glamorous, at times. It's just that Tuscaloosa, staying in a roach infested motel for a week, and living off of snack cakes and beef jerky the entire time, isn't ideal. We'd certainly had better times, traveling together. Like, one time, when we were in Savannah, and my mom was performing in this big theatre there, she met some guy who owned a hotel. Within minutes, my mom had convinced the hotel-owner-guy to put us up in one of his best suites for the entire three months we were in town. We'd even get free room service from time to time.

That place had the best hash browns and sausages at breakfast. Lots of cheese and grilled onions for the hash browns. The sausages were always crispy on the outside and soft and juicy inside—fried to heart attack perfection.

Like all things with my mom, the Savannah hotel suite was only temporary. Three months later, the job was over, the hotel owner realized my mom wasn't looking to settle down, and we were back in the car after mom placed a few phone calls.

My mom is an actress. Not one you've ever heard of, though. Well, I guess she's more than an actress since she'll do almost any job necessary to keep us in gas, food, and lodging. And sometimes a new pair of kicks. Mostly, she chases jobs across America. A play in a theatre here. A commercial shoot near the Gulf of Mexico in Louisiana there. Voice-over work that has to be done in a sound booth in L.A. Circus lost their magician's assistant? Call my mom! If she's not busy, we'll be there as soon as possible. Do you need a blonde-haired, blue-eyed woman who looks closer to twenty-five than her actual forty years of age to do your boat show? Call my mom!

She's kind of a jack-of-all-trades when it comes to acting jobs. No job is too big or too small, though most of them are pretty small. One time she did puppet shows at a theme park

2

in the Ozarks for not much more than minimum wage. That's called "scale," apparently. That job wasn't so bad, though. For me, I mean. Mom hated it, but we got to stay in a decent motel that provided fresh towels each morning, had cable, air conditioning, and a swimming pool that was actually kept clean. And it was all free. The owner of the theme park also owned the hotel, so mom was able to charm him into free accommodations as well.

That's another thing my mom can do well. Charm people. Especially men.

Almost every guy in America who owns a theatre, production company, hotel, or any place to perform, really, has had me call him "Uncle so-and-so."

I'm not stupid. I'm sixteen. I know these men aren't my uncles and I know my mom doesn't really give a damn about any of them. Well, maybe she likes them all well enough, I guess, but she likes what they can do for her more. If a man can provide a job, some place to live—especially for free—or a decent meal, my mom can like him.

I'm probably not making my mom sound great.

But since she was the reason that my new—well, newish—kicks were dusty brown instead of black, my back was hurting, and my suitcases kept bumping violently into my knees, I didn't really care. That was kind of my mom's M.O.

Not considering how her decisions affect me, I mean. Gotta make my son live off of junk food out of a vending machine for a week? Sure. What's that hurt?

There was a time we had to pack up in the middle of the night and leave our motel in Chattanooga because she had pissed off her boss at a theatre.

Another time, she made me hide lunch meat inside of my coat at the convenience store down the street from our motel in Memphis because all we could afford was bread. And it's hard to make a good sandwich out of just bread.

More than once she's forced me to busk when she couldn't find a job—and I can only play, like, three songs. I can't even sing all that well. And she'd never get the permits for busking when they were required.

Run like hell if you see the cops, she'd say.

I've run like hell a lot.

It's hard to scoop up a coffee can full of coins and loose bills, a guitar, and run from the police, let me tell you. But I've managed every time.

I've been running like hell since I was probably, like, twelve-years-old, I guess? Twelve was when my mom thought I was old enough to be dropped off somewhere to busk on my own while she went out looking for jobs or made calls about jobs. She'd drop me off somewhere and tell me she'd pick me up at a specific time. In case I had to run from the authorities, she'd give me a "rendezvous point" where she would look for me if I wasn't at the busking site. She said if I wasn't at the busking site, and I wasn't waiting at the "rendezvous point," she'd call the police station to see if I'd been picked up. She never explained what she'd do to get me out since it was rare that we had enough money to pay fines. And, I mean, would they have even taken me to jail when I was that young? Do kids get taken to Big Boy Jail or somewhere else?

It's the twenty-first century. Surely, Child Protective Services would have been called, right?

Fortunately, and somehow, miraculously, we'd never had to find out what happens to twelve-year-old boys whose mothers dump them on a street corner with a guitar and an empty coffee can. I know how to run like hell.

Being dropped off is exactly why my shoes weren't looking new as I dragged my suitcases along behind me on the dirt road and they wobbled on their wheels with each miniscule bump they encountered.

Two-Mile Trail.

That's what the sign off of the highway proclaimed the name of the dirt road to be. It was really just some trail, though. A couple of cars could pass by each other on the dirt road— but just barely. As I mentioned, the road wasn't paved, and it wasn't in the best condition, so I couldn't imagine anyone would actually want to drive on it. Especially if their car was new. Or *newish.* Like my shoes. They'd just end up with a different colored car and possibly a flat tire. If it was raining, forget about it. Two-Mile Trail had to be a mudhole when it rained. Any normal car would probably get stuck quickly and easily. And good luck getting someone who knew where the hell Two-Mile Trail was to come tow you out.

I couldn't help but think that there had to be a better way from the highway into town than Two-Mile Trail. Surely, there had to be a paved road on the north side of town. Or the west. Something besides Two-Mile Trail that would lead into Possibly.

That's where I was headed on foot—instead of in my mom's car—Possibly, Texas. We had left our motel in Dallas when the sun was just starting to come up. Mom talked a lot as she drove, but ignored anything I said in response. She was a woman on a mission.

Since it had been lunch time, and I had been walking along Two-Mile Trail, my stomach got super pissed at me. My head wasn't too happy, either.

It was a sugar crash. My diet hadn't been great for months.

The fact that it was early June—in Texas—and I was walking along a dirt road, dragging two suitcases, sweating like a sinner in church, probably didn't help either. Between the heat and my body wanting some real food, it was no wonder I felt like crap. Furthermore, the fact that the road I was lugging my suitcases along should have actually been called Twelve-Mile Road, made things worse. Of course, if my mom hadn't been such an inconsiderate jerk, none of that would have mattered.

When she had seen the sign off of the highway, which we flew by in the car, she had hit the brakes, done a uey, and eased up parallel to the mouth of the road. We sat there for several moments, eyeing the dirt road proclaiming to be Two-Mile Trail, and I found myself wondering why mom wasn't turning the car down the road that would take us into Possibly.

It doesn't look like an easy drive. My mom had muttered. *But Jack told me this is how you get to town.*

Again, I found myself waiting for mom to turn the car down the dirt road.

It's only two miles... She had said finally. *That's pretty close.*

Next thing I knew, I was standing on the side of the highway, my backpack strapped on, and my two suitcases standing up beside me. Mom had quite literally tossed me from the car.

I's not far. You've walked further. Just follow the road and—BOOM—you're in Possibly, Jordy. She had announced brightly through the car window, though her eyes were glistening.

Jordy.

My name is Jordan. Mom calls me "*Jordy.*"

I hate it.

But I hated it more when she dumped me out of the car and told me to make my own way from the highway into

Possibly—all through the freaking window of the car—and then drove off happily, waving as she left me there on the side of the road. That's my mom. Leaving a sixteen year old on the side of the highway with his backpack and two suitcases on wheels to walk two miles down a dirt road so that she can get to Vegas quicker. I guess that's all you really need to know about her. That, and the actress thing.

When I had started walking along Two-Mile Trail, mostly dry, grassy fields rolled outwards from each side of the road. After what I guessed was the first mile of the trail, trees and lush green grass started to appear. When the trees and green grass appeared, somehow, the walk became less miserable. The trees weren't close enough to the road to provide any shade, but they somehow made it seem a little less sweltering on the road. After a few minutes of having trees and lush grass as my view, I started to hear music off in the distance. Well, something that sounded like music. It was kind of indiscernible.

There was something familiar about it, though, and that's why I thought it was music. It sounded like a song I'd heard before. However, ahead of me was a bend in the road, and all I could see was trees. I couldn't tell where the sound was coming from or why someone was playing music out in the middle of nowhere.

Even in the middle of the day, it was kind of creepy. I mean, who goes out to the middle of nowhere, on some dirt road, to play music?

My steps became slower and shorter and my hands clutched my suitcase handles tighter as I made my way towards the bend in the road. What would I possibly do if I rounded the bend and found some banjo-picking weirdo sitting on the tailgate of his pickup truck, half of his teeth missing, and a smirk on his face? I mean, I could've run like hell—which, we've established, I can do well—but I would've had to dump my suitcases. Besides my backpack, they held everything I owned. Back the way I came on Two-Mile Trail was the only direction I could've run unless I wanted to venture into the trees. I didn't know the woods. I could've easily gotten lost. A country bumpkin—probably with fewer teeth than brain cells—a banjo, and a pickup truck, probably knew the woods well. He would've easily caught me. I would have been tied up in a cellar in no time. Having to walk down a dirt road to some tiny town in the middle of nowhere would've been the least of my problems then.

Some guy wanting to make you his teenage bride and then use your skin to make an area rug is definitely the worst way the day could have ended. I had thought to myself.

As I drew closer to the bend that cut through the trees to the left, or a westerly direction, the sound grew louder and clearer. It was a country song—*I thought*—that sounded familiar. Of course, it easily could have been a song playing on a truck radio. *The truck radio of the country bumpkin with missing teeth.* Even though the sound was familiar, and most likely a song being played, it didn't comfort me much. Sure, the sun was out, and it wasn't like I couldn't run away if I found myself in a dangerous situation, but being out in the middle of nowhere by myself, the song was just eerie. Who would be playing a song out in the sticks? Since I'd walked away from the highway, I hadn't seen a single sign of civilization, so hearing a country song playing out in the woods was odd.

My fingers tightened around my suitcase handles as I continued my sweaty march along the road, determined to make my way around the bend. If some weirdo jumped out of the trees, I'd swing one of my suitcases at him. My suitcases contained everything I owned. Having one or both knocked up against your head would easily lay someone out.

But this is Texas, Jordan. What if the weirdo has a gun?

My heart began thundering in my throat as I followed the road along its curve, wondering what I'd find coming into view. When I had turned along the bend in the road, the sound became clearer, no longer blocked by the trees. I had been right. The song was familiar. I'd heard it a million times when we were in places like Nashville and Memphis—where country, bluegrass, and all things Americana reigned. It was *Then I'd Be Satisfied with My Life* by Tiny Tim.

There wasn't some weirdo sitting in a beat-up pickup truck playing the song on his stereo, though. No weirdos were in sight, actually. Along the right side of the road, my eyes landed on a waist-high pole sticking out of the ground, a speaker attached to the top of it. The song was coming from the speaker on the pole. The sight made me falter a bit, but when I looked further up the road, my eyes landed on a river…actually, more of a creek. A wooden bridge, just wide enough for one car to cross at a time, spanned the width of the creek. Just beyond sat Possibly, Texas. Having walked down the dirt road with nothing but trees and grass to look at for the last several minutes, the sudden appearance of the town out of nowhere was unnerving. Everything looked normal, though. Well, as normal as small-town Texas can.

Sensing that I wasn't in danger as I had imagined, I loosened my grip on my suitcase handles and my knuckles gave a sigh of relief. Approaching the radio on the pole, I still felt uneasy—*because who sticks a radio on a pole on the side of road just outside of town?*—but with the town in view, I easily swallowed my concerns. At least what passed for civilization in the buttcrack of Texas was just over the bridge. I could probably scream for help if I did find myself in danger. Tiny Tim crooned a final time about being "satisfied with life" and the music faded from the radio as I stood at the side of the road, suitcases in hand, staring across the creek at Possibly. When a voice poured from the speaker, I nearly came out of my skin. My fingers jerked and both of my suitcases tipped over, sending clouds of dirt billowing up from the road where they landed.

"You've been listening to AMOR, the most popular radio station in Possibly, Texas. All day long from 6am to 6pm." The gravelly male voice announced.

Ah. It's a local radio station. I chuckled nervously to myself as I knelt to pull my suitcases out of the dirt once again.

"That was Then I'd Be Satisfied with My Life *by Tiny Tim. Next up—*Then I'd Be Satisfied with My Life *by Tiny Tim!"*

I rose, suitcase handles gripped tightly, my eyes locked on the speaker. Surely, the man hadn't announced that he was going to play the same song they had just played. *Right?* And 6am to 6pm is not all day long. *Right?*

Tiny Tim's voice poured from the speaker, warning people to never hit their grandmas with a shovel, proving that the radio DJ hadn't been lying about his intentions. For obvious reasons, I couldn't get my feet to move for several moments.

"What in the crap?" I actually mumbled out loud as I stared at the speaker.

I'm not sure how long Tiny Tim's *Then I'd Be Satisfied with My Life* is, but that's how long I stood there, gripping my suitcases, sweating and staring at the speaker. Once again, the song faded away, and the radio DJ's voice replaced it.

"You've been listening to AMOR, the most popular radio station in Possibly, Texas. All day long from 6am to 6pm," he said.

I waited.

"That was Then I'd Be Satisfied with My Life *by Tiny Tim. Next up*—Then I'd Be Satisfied with My Life *by Tiny Tim."*

Even with Possibly just down the road and over the bridge, clearly in sight, my feet didn't want to move at first. What the heck was going on with the radio station? Playing the same song three times in a row? And not even a recent, popular hit. Tiny Tim was their choice to play three times in a row. That was just odd.

Welcome to Texas. I thought to myself.

"Ooooookay." I rolled my shoulders.

Apparently, AMOR in Possibly, Texas had a limited number of songs to choose from each day. Instead of contemplating what was wrong with the people over at the radio station, why they put speakers on poles, and why they had chosen Tiny Tim of all artists to play, I commanded my aching feet into motion once again. Even though I had newish shoes and the walk into Possibly hadn't actually been that far, my dogs were barking. I just wanted to sit back and kick my feet up—preferably after kicking my shoes off. Of course, just getting to Possibly was one part of the problem. Finding the right house in town was the other part. For all I knew, I would soon be living under the wooden bridge I had to cross to get into town.

My feet carried me along the last stretch of the dirt road towards the bridge as my mother's words rang in my head. *Jack's house is to the northwest of the town square. Look for the graveyard and then head left. You'll find it. If you start seeing housing developments, you've gone too far. He's in Possibly proper. You can't miss it. Jack will watch over you. I love you forever! Bye, Jordy!* That was when she started waving out of the car window as she drove away down the highway. Vegas—and getting there in a timely manner—was more important to her than making sure I got to Possibly.

11

Okay. So, walking through a small town in Texas in the middle of the day is probably one of the safest things you can do. As long as you don't look too liberal or anything. But I hadn't been in Possibly since I was a little kid. I couldn't even really remember the place—I was just trusting that as fact since my mom had said so. I didn't know the layout of the streets, where anything was, or any of the people. I didn't even really know Jack. Finding his house—and kind of meeting Jack all over again—was going to be odd. What was I going to say to the guy? I mean, communicating with him was difficult as it was, but we were virtually strangers. And I was expected to march up to his front door and say: *"Hey, it's me. Jordan. Mom said I should come stay with you because I'm cramping her style or something? Got an extra bed?"*

The further I walked away from the speaker on the side of the road, the quieter I expected Tiny Tim's voice to get. It should have faded off into the distance, yet it seemed to get louder the closer I got to the wooden bridge that spanned the width of the creek. Initially, I thought I had to be going crazy. First, the phantom music that I heard along Two-Mile Trail, then the odd speaker-radio-thingie on the pole on the side of the road, then the music was getting louder the further I got away from the speaker. Possibly, Texas—as my mom had warned me—was…*different*. She didn't really elaborate on what she meant by "different"—I mean, she didn't mention any people with horns growing out of their heads or who carried around wolverines as pets—but there had been a look in her eye when she had said it.

The music grew louder as I grew closer to the bridge and it finally dawned on me that the town sign was staked into the side of the road a few yards before the creek. When I approached it, still dragging my suitcases behind me, I realized why the music had not faded away. Another speaker was attached to the lower third of the pole that held the town sign. The fact that there might be poles with speakers attached to them all throughout town, playing the local radio station, suddenly dawned on me. I didn't know if that was creepy or charming.

I let my eyes move from the speaker up to the sign.

Possibly, Texas. Pop. 712.

So…a small town. *Miniscule.*

Also, the town name "Possibly" and the state name "Texas" were on two different arrow-shaped, wooden signs. One was pointing to the left; one was pointed to the right. Neither pointed towards town. Both looked as though the wood had seen better days, but the names looked like they had been painted recently. Obviously, sign upkeep was of paramount importance in Possibly. I found myself imagining that one of the seven-hundred-twelve people in town was on sign duty, going around and making sure the paint was fresh. That's how new the paint looked. It was also obvious that the signs had been painted by hand, so I imagined my suspicions about a town sign painter were not that far off from the truth.

Why is one sign pointing one way and one pointing the other?

Just as I began to contemplate the mysteries of sign design in Possibly, movement by the bridge caught my eye. I turned to find a man—well, maybe a teenager, since he didn't look much older than me—walking across the bridge from Possibly in my direction. He wasn't looking at me. His eyes were down as his feet *clop-clopped* on the wooden boards of the bridge. He looked…*forlorn?*

Watching as he traveled across the bridge, I wondered if he was going to walk along Two-Mile Trail to the highway. Maybe his mom was waiting to pick him up? Mine dropped me off on the highway, so maybe his mom was the type to pick him up on the highway? However, my thoughts were interrupted by the sight of him stopping halfway across the bridge. He placed his hands upon the railing along the side, then he hoisted himself, climbing the handrail until he was standing upon it precariously. The wooden rail was just wide enough for a man to stand upon, but not for long. No one could keep their balance that well outside of a circus.

I watched in horror as the teenager threw his arms out wide and looked up at the sky. A moan-like scream poured forth from his mouth:

"*Emmmmmmmmmiiiiiiiiiiily!*"

Then he was falling off of the bridge and into the creek below.

I gasped in horror and ran towards the bridge, the suitcases bumping and jolting on the road behind me. They weren't rolling so much as bouncing on the wooden slats. My feet made their own *clop-clop* sounds on the wooden planks as I raced across it and to the spot from where the guy had leapt. I let go of my suitcases' handles and put my hands on the rail, looking over to the creek below.

He's probably dead. I thought frantically. *There's no way the water is deep enough. He probably cracked his freaking skull open and is floating on the water, bloody and dead!*

Over the side of the bridge, I did find the teenager floating, but he looked fine. He was swirling his arms at his sides, his legs kicking to help tread water. He was simply...*floating*. He wasn't dead or hurt. At least not physically.

I watched as the teenager pursed his lips and a plume of water shot out of his mouth like a fountain, sailing in an arc into the air above him, before losing its game with gravity and splattering back onto the guy's chest. The teenager continued to paddle his arms and legs as he floated there, fully dressed, his eyes closed, as the sun beat down on him lazily.

What the crap is his problem?

"Are you okay?" I braced myself against the handrail so I could lean over and shout down at the teenager, a mere ten feet below.

"Fine." Came his response.

"Did you hurt yourself?" I shouted again.

"Fine," he said. "Just need to think."

For a few moments, I considered asking the teenager what his freaking problem was—why he had flung himself off of a bridge into the creek below. Did he have any common sense? Did he need help? Did he need someone to talk to? Should I call an ambulance? Instead, I found myself deciding to let the teenager have a moment to himself. Obviously, the dude was going through…*something.*

"Uh, okay," I responded. "Uh, hope, uh, you're okay and stuff?"

"Fine," he said.

That annoyed me. Tiny Tim was singing about being satisfied with life, my suitcases were laying in a dirty heap on the bridge, my feet ached, the sun was sweltering, and this guy was looney tunes. Like, Bugs Bunny taking a wrong turn at Albuquerque crazy.

I watched for a few more moments as the guy floated on his back, treading water with lazy kicks from his legs and flaps from his arms, fully clothed, and completely insane.

Who the crap is Emily? Isn't that what he screamed before he jumped off of the bridge like a freak?

Contemplating what would make some weirdo throw himself off a bridge—which I quickly determined was over enough water and not high enough that anyone could really harm themselves—was pointless. I reminded myself that I was in the panhandle of Texas. Weird stuff was bound to happen. If I looked up and saw an opossum driving a Big Wheel over the bridge, sipping a bottle of malt liquor, I wouldn't have been surprised.

Finally, I pried my eyes from the teenager floating in the creek and knelt down to snatch at the handles of my suitcases. Moments later, my now dusty brown shoes, and the wheels of the suitcases, were *clop-clopping* over the other half of the bridge. I found myself already mightily annoyed with Possibly, Texas. The sound of my shoes and the wheels on the wood slats, the weirdo who leapt off of the bridge and scared the crap out of me, the dirt road that probably ruined my shoes, and Tiny Tim's high-pitched voice, were giving me a headache. Of course, some of that was still probably attributable to the heat and the sun beating down on me.

Hopefully, Jack will have indoor plumbing so I can have a glass of water—if that's not too much to ask for in Possibly.

When I reached the other side of the bridge, finding that the roads in Possibly, though narrow, were actually paved, made me feel a little less grumpy. At least the wheels of my suitcases could actually perform their job. Everything else that I found on the other side of the bridge made me feel…*confused.* From the other side of the bridge, I was pretty sure I could see most of downtown Possibly, and what I saw was *different.*

To my right stood an old two-story clapboard house, painted teal, with red shutters affixed to its windows. However, it wasn't a house. The sign out front proclaimed it to be the post office. To my left, further down a street that curved off of the one I was on, was a gas station. But I didn't see any cars. Or employees. Straight ahead sat an honest-to-freaking-goodness pirate ship. The Jolly Roger even sailed from a mast that reached for the sky above it. A quick glance let me know that the ship had been converted into a shop of some kind, and a few people walked in and out as I stood there, staring like a simpleton.

Further on, just down the street from the pirate ship, was what looked like a mosque or holy temple of some kind. On the other side of the street sat two identical buildings, that could have been homes or businesses, as well as what looked like a very small reddish-orange circus tent. At the end of the street that the post office, pirate ship, and mosque were on was a street that ran perpendicular to it. Four simple looking, one-story houses lined that street, though I wasn't sure if they were homes or businesses. If I squinted a bit, I could see that on the street behind the one with the pirate ship there were other businesses and what looked like...*train tracks?* Off to my right, and much further down the creek, I could see a big red barn. I assumed that was simply a barn, but this was Possibly, Texas. Maybe it was a church?

I didn't see a graveyard. That's what mom told me to look for when I got to Possibly. Scanning the town around me, I couldn't image that I had missed it. There wasn't all that much to see in the downtown area of Possibly, after all. My aching feet told my brain to just ask the first person I saw if they knew where the graveyard was in town. It would be a lot quicker than walking around like an idiot until I just happened to stumble upon it.

My hands clutched the suitcase handles firmly and I marched towards the pirate ship. Hopefully, whichever person I found to ask actually lived in town and wasn't just visiting. Then again, from what I could see, I couldn't imagine anyone visited Possibly unless forced. Like a teenager whose mother dropped him off on the highway and said: "*Good luck!*" I mean, essentially.

As I approached the massive pirate ship, plunked down in the center of town, I realized a swinging glass door was set in the side of the hull. A sign over it proclaimed the establishment to be *Starbuck's*. Not Starbucks, but *Starbuck's*. From the smells wafting out of the place, I could tell that the pirate ship was actually a coffee shop. The other thing that immediately got my attention was the man—or what I assumed was a man—standing to the side of the entrance in a green-screen suit. Like the kind used to do special effects in movies. The suit covered every inch of his body, including his face and his head, but certain *things*—around the waist area—led me to believe the person in the suit was male.

"Hey," I said as I approached, "can you tell me—"

"You can't see me." The man cut me off.

"What?"

"I'm invisible today," he said. "I'm part of the hull."

"You're part of the—"

"Shhhh!" He hissed. "Hulls can't talk. Maybe waves slapping against them make some noise or something, but they can't *talk*."

I just stood there, dumbfounded.

"Crap." The man groaned.

Then he was reaching up and snatching off the green hood that covered his head. Golden curls and the sun-tanned, freckled skin of a guy not much older than me appeared.

"I ruined it, didn't I?" he asked, golden flecks in his brown eyes sparkling in the sun. "I shouldn't have said anything, right? If you're being a hull, you're a hull. Hulls don't talk. I talked. I'm hopeless, man."

"Wh-what?"

"If you're going to be a hull, you *have to be* the hull, right?" he explained. "Everyone always tells me, *'Levi Lee, you have to commit. If you can't commit, don't bother!'* And here I am talking to you."

"I'm sorry?" I giggled nervously. "What is going on?"

The man—Levi Lee—frowned at me for a second, his eyes wandering over me before landing on my suitcases.

"Oh!" He jumped suddenly, a smile splitting his face. "You're not from here, are you?"

"No?"

His chest bowed out proudly. "Levi Lee, my good man. Performance artist and all-around handyman."

His hand shot out. Against my better judgment, I reached out and took it.

"That explains nothing, but nice to meet you," I murmured. "Levi Lee?"

"That's me," he said proudly once more. "Now, the specials today are Café Mochas and Red Eyes. Personally, I'd stick with the mochas. Chocolate hides a lot of sin and coffee tastes like sin to me. Of course, I probably shouldn't say that to a customer, but—"

"Look, Levi Lee?"

"Yes?" He smiled brightly.

I didn't get a chance to ask my question. A gunshot rang out nearby and my instincts kicked in; I dropped my suitcases and got low, throwing my arms around my head to protect it. When I looked up at Levi Lee, he was just staring at me quizzically, the lime green hood clutched in both hands in front of him. *I prayed he would hold it a little lower to cover…things.*

"What is going on?" I barked.

"What?"

"The gunshot?" I asked frantically, glancing up and down the street as I crouched in front of the coffee shop next to him.

"Oh." Levi Lee chuckled. "That's Wyatt."

He gestured vaguely towards the end of the street in the direction of the mosque-like building. I uncovered my head just enough to glance around Levi Lee's body in the direction he had indicated. A man, dressed like Yosemite Sam—blue jeans, chaps, plaid long-sleeve shirt, ten-gallon hat, with a handle-bar mustache to boot—was strolling up the street towards us, gun in hand. It was hard to tell at such a distance, but it even looked like the gun was a six-shooter.

"His timing's all off," Levi Lee said, as though this explained everything. "You'll get used to it."

"What?" I looked up incredulously.

"He had a stroke." Levi Lee gestured for me to rise, and I slowly obeyed, using the hull of the ship to brace myself since my knees felt like jelly. "His timing is off but he's harmless."

I watched cautiously, keeping Levi Lee between myself and Wyatt as the weird man marched down the street, swinging his gun. He passed within a few feet of us, paying us no mind, then turned on the road that went down towards the gas station.

"Don't go buying any candy, Wyatt!" Levi Lee hollered, making me jump. "You know it gets you all riled up!"

The crazy man with a gun and no timing—raised a hand in the air, a single finger rising to respond to Levi Lee's demand. Levi Lee laughed.

"Grandy won't sell him any candy anyway." Levi Lee waved a hand in Wyatt's direction.

"I'm pretty sure I'd give a guy with a gun anything he asked for," I muttered.

"He's harmless," Levi Lee repeated.

Obviously, I was in a town full of crazy people. People who jumped off of bridges into creeks after screaming some girl's name. Guys who did performance art in green screen suits outside of a coffee shop that looked like a pirate ship. Men who felt shooting a gun randomly was a perfectly okay thing to do. And then there was the radio station DJ who really, really, *really* loved Tiny Tim. I could still hear the song playing, but it seemed to be coming from multiple directions. Apparently, my theory about several speakers littered throughout town had been correct.

Where is Jack's place?

"Levi…Lee?" I asked.

"Yes, my good man?" He beamed.

"I'm looking for a graveyard."

"You don't look like you need a graveyard yet," he quipped. "You've still got plenty of years left in you, I'd think. If you want 'em."

I paused. "Right. Yeah. The graveyard is supposedly close to a house I'm trying to find."

"A marker!"

"What?"

"A landmark." Levi Lee expounded. "One of the steps on your journey!"

"Sure. Yeah. Okay." I agreed to avoid further discussion. "A landmark. I need to find the graveyard."

"Well, it's never in my interest to keep a man from his quest," Levi Lee said importantly. "Bend of the Road Graveyard is just over there. Just beyond AMOR."

AMOR? AMOR!

"The radio station?" I asked, looking in the direction Levi Lee was pointing. "That green building between the two yellow buildings?"

"Precisely! Just walk through the trees there. You'll see the tram—"

Ah. They're tram tracks. A tram? In Possibly?

"—and just keep walking past the buildings. Behind AMOR, you'll find Bend of the Road Graveyard."

"Thanks." I reached down to grab the suitcase handles. "Thanks a lot."

Levi Lee bent at the waist, performing a grand bow.

"Anything for a fellow searcher and traveler," he stated grandly.

I looked at him, my eyes darting to his waist area again.

"Maybe a pair of shorts to complete the outfit?" I suggested as I walked away.

Levi Lee glanced down for a moment, shrugged, and then he was sliding the lime green hood back over his head. When I made my way around Starbuck's, and through the cluster of trees, I found the tram tracks. I stopped for a moment, looking at the wood and iron tracks in front of me. A glance to the left and then to the right let me know that the tracks were no more than forty yards long. They started near the end of the street and ended near the creek. Which was where the tram was sitting. Squinting a bit, I could see what I guessed was a conductor sitting at the front of the tram, reading a book, his legs kicked up. The tram itself was not much more than a small train that one might find at an amusement park that people rode for a few tickets.

Why does Possibly, Texas need a tram? Especially one that traveled along a single street that was no more than half a football field long?

The sound of metal against stone jerked me to attention once again, pushing all thoughts of the tram from my mind. My eyes darted around, looking for the source of the noise. Due to the fact that the street wasn't that long, I quickly found the person making the sound. Some guy, dressed in a plaid long-sleeve shirt, bib overalls, work boots, and a straw hat, was taking a pickaxe to the middle of the street. I nearly shouted out, wanting to ask the man if he was allowed to be tearing up the town's roads, but then my eyes landed on the police officer, dressed in his uniform blues, leaning against one of the front walls of one of the businesses. He was watching the man with the pickaxe, not concerned in the slightest.

If he doesn't care, then I don't care. I thought to myself.

Upon closer inspection of the man with the pickaxe, I saw that he was tearing up a part of the road that was much different than the far left and far right ends. Different colored bricks had been placed in the paved road in front of the businesses. Reds, blues, greens, oranges, yellows, purples, pinks—all the colors of the rainbow.

Is this man installing rainbow-colored bricks in the freaking middle of the street?

As I stood there, my hands still gripping my suitcase handles, the cop's eyes landed on me from across the road, and he smiled. He reached up and gave me a friendly wave. Anxiously, I let go of one of the suitcases' handles and waved back. When the officer's attention went back to the man with the pickaxe, I grabbed the suitcase handle and hurried across the road. Within moments, I was passing between AMOR and whatever business was to the left of it.

A few seconds later, I was on a street behind the businesses, and there was the graveyard. Although, it wasn't much of a graveyard. One, there wasn't a church nearby—which is what makes a place of burial a graveyard instead of a cemetery. Two, there were maybe ten headstones—or less—and two weeping willows. Additionally, the "graveyard" was just a patch of land between paved roads. It looked like the town had sprung up around it and the roads laid so that they didn't interfere with the dead.

At least I found the graveyard. I thought to myself. *I have to be close to Jack's place.*

I walked across the road to the graveyard and turned to the left as my mom had instructed. There was a road on both sides of the graveyard, but both seemed to go left and meet briefly before splitting and winding around another copse of trees. At first, I wasn't sure if I should take the road that went to the left of the trees or the right of the trees. However, I could see a three-story clapboard house, a dingy brownish-yellow with a red roof that a chimney jutted out of, off in the distance.

Even though I was in Possibly, Texas—of all places—I couldn't help but smile.

That has to be Jack's place.

I took off at a jog, my suitcase wheels bouncing on the paved road as I made my way towards the house. Less than a minute later, I was letting my suitcases rest at the base of the steps up to the front door, making sure they didn't topple over. Then I ascended the stairs and took a deep breath. The main door beyond the screen was shut, obviously because of the heat of the day, and the screen door seemed to be closed and locked tightly as well.

Maybe he's not home?

My feet were killing me to the point that I couldn't even think about whether or not Jack was home. I lifted my hand and knocked on the door, tentatively at first, then increasingly louder until I knew I would be heard wherever he was in the house. I stepped back from the door, just in case Jack decided to swing it open without looking. I didn't want to get pushed off of the steps. Crickets chirped in the grass around the house.

Birds sang in the trees nearby. Tiny Tim sang his melody. A gunshot went off in the distance.

Finally, I heard footsteps coming from inside of the house. When the front door opened, and a face appeared through the screen, I knew that at least I had found the right place.

Jack looked exactly as I had remembered when I drew upon my oldest memories.

Even if it had been a long time.

A STARRY NIGHT

J ack stood, his face framed by the screen in the wooden door, his eyes squinting out into the bright afternoon sun, taking me in as I waited on the steps. His raven black hair was still even darker than mine; that type of black that almost seemed to be tinted with blue or purple. Dark eyes peered out from his hooded brow as he looked me over. He knew who I was, so that wasn't the problem. It's not that I had known Jack enough, or been around him enough to read him, but I felt as though he couldn't believe how much bigger I was since the last time he had seen me.

Slowly, Jack reached over and unlatched the screen, then he pushed it gently outwards, giving me a chance to turn my body in just the right way to avoid being hit by it. I grabbed the edge of the screen and held it open and stared up at the man. He was almost as tall as the doorframe; his hair nearly brushed against the top of the frame. Gruffly, he crossed his arms over his chest and moved to lean against the doorjamb as he looked down at me.

I thought Mom had called him?

The smell of something cooking on the stove inside wafted outside, around Jack's lithe body—something like chili maybe? Always a great meal for summertime in Texas. Regardless of the heat and the meal Jack had chosen, my stomach grumbled at me. I would have been willing to eat anything Jack offered from his pantry or fridge. I'd had nothing to prepare me for the day and I was starving. And I was so thirsty.

"It's me," I said. "Jordan?"

Jack just stared down at me for a moment. Then he gave what looked like a salute.

"Hi," I said. "Mom said she called you. Uh, she said she told you I was coming to stay? I mean, if that's okay. Well, I mean, I really can't walk back to the car. She left me out on the highway. I walked down Two-Mile Trail to get here?"

The corner of Jack's mouth turned up slightly. He was amused. Did he find it funny that I had walked through town to get to his house—or was he amused thinking about what a jerk my mom was and always had been?

"She's on her way to Vegas," I explained, my finger digging into the screen door as I stood there. "I mean, I can call her on her cell if you don't want me here or something. But it might take her a while to get back here."

Jack stared.

"If she is even willing to come back."

Jack was smirking again.

"So," I said, "is it okay if I, uh, stay here or whatever? Mom said it was cool, but I can tell you might not have known I was coming. I can figure something out I guess if—"

Jack's hands started to move. I watched for a moment.

"My sign language skills are pretty rusty, Jack." I stopped him. "Can you...nod or something?

Jack rolled his eyes, then disappeared from the doorway. Since he hadn't waved me in or indicated that I should follow him, I kept vigil on the steps, waiting for his return. As suspected, Jack appeared in the door moments later, a small notepad and pen in hand. I waited, holding onto the edge of the screen door as he clicked the pen and began to scribble. A

27

few seconds later, he looked up at me and turned the notepad so I could see it.

In block letters, it said:

Margie just dumped you off on the highway?

I snorted. "Yeah. She goes by Marlena now. More exotic, I guess?"

Jack smirked and started scribbling again.

She didn't even drive you into town to make sure you got here safe?

I sighed and looked up at him. There was no point in answering. I just shrugged.

Again, more writing. Then the notepad was turned for me to read again.

Margie didn't call. You can stay.

I nodded. "Okay."

Before I could turn around to grab my bags, Jack was writing once again.

Your room is the same. Upstairs. You've gotten bigger.

He gave me a tight smile when I looked up from the notepad.

"I guess I've eaten a lot."

Jack wrote one more note.

Need help with your bags?

"Nah," I said once I'd read the block letters. "I dragged them all the way from the highway and into town. I can carry them up a few flights of stairs. Is there food?"

Jack didn't lift his notepad or write anything. He waited for me to grab my bags and turn to the stairs again, then he gave me a nod. He motioned to the top of the house and my bags, then gestured that I should come back downstairs. Apparently, once I got my bags up to my old room—and by "old," I mean a room I didn't even really remember ever sleeping in—Jack meant for me to come downstairs for lunch.

As I ascended the steps into the house, Jack stepped to the side and reached out to hold the screen open for me. I squeezed past him into the cool darkness of the house. Air conditioning immediately hit my sweat dappled skin and I felt cooler immediately, as though icicles were prickling along all of my exposed skin. Jack closed the screen and latched it, then the door, while I waited just inside the house in the dark living room.

"Keep most of the lights off to save electricity?" I was only teasing a little.

Jack turned away from the door to give me a shrug. The kitchen light was on—obviously so he could see well enough to make lunch—and a single lamp was lit on an end table at the end of the sofa in the living room.

Jack's house wasn't extravagant, but it had a middle-American charm to it. Plain tile in the kitchen to the left, tan carpet in the living room. Plaid couch, recliner, flatscreen T.V. that was probably a little too big for the room. Unassuming and functional drapes to block out the hot Texas summer sun. A kitchen table that looked like it had been bought from a diner that was going out of business—with chairs to match. Dark woods that would have looked better in a different decade.

The house was three stories altogether, from what I could remember. First story—the one we were on—was the living room, kitchen, half-bath, and screened in porch off of the back of the house. The second story was two bedrooms and a full bathroom. Then there was the third floor—where my old bedroom was, nestled into what was almost an attic, with an attached three-quarter bathroom. Toilet, pedestal sink, cubicle shower. Just enough for a teenage guy to get by.

Everything was impeccably clean, though, which said a lot for a virtually single man living on his own in a rural town like

Possibly. Jack was dressed and groomed well, his house looked clean enough to eat off of the floor, and he had air conditioning. The guy seemed to have his life together for the most part. From the smell coming from the kitchen off to the left, it seemed he knew how to cook well enough to get by as well. Maybe staying with him for a while wouldn't be so bad?

Jack reached out and tapped me on the shoulder. I had been too busy looking around, refamiliarizing myself with the house to even remember he was there. He gestured upwards when I turned to look at him, repeating his instructions to put my bags up before lunch.

"All right," I said. "Uh, third floor, right?"

Jack nodded.

"Okay," I replied. "I'll be right back. Uh, the food smells good."

Another nod from Jack and then he was heading into the kitchen. I made my way to the stairs at the back of the living room, and headed upstairs, my two suitcases bouncing on the stairs behind me with each step up. I could hear Jack banging around in the kitchen when I got to the second floor. Though I wasn't sure where the memory came from, I felt that the second-floor hallway smelled the same as I remembered. Something like Pine Sol and…*wood?* I stood at the landing to the second floor for a moment, breathing deeply and looking around.

At the end of the hall was where my mom's and Jack's bedroom was. The bathroom was just outside of the door and to the right. Carpet lined the hallway and it looked to have been vacuumed recently. Curtains had been drawn in the second floor as well to help keep out some of the heat so that the air conditioner would be more efficient. Though it wasn't quite as cool on the second floor of the house, it was still much nicer than it had been outside. My sweat was already drying up and I felt a lot less lightheaded as I looked around the house.

As I ascended the stairs up to the third floor, I could immediately tell that I wouldn't want to spend time in my room during hot days if I could avoid it. Though it wasn't oppressive, it was still much warmer on the top floor than it had been on the first and second stories of the house. When I pushed through the door at the top of the stairs, I realized that Jack had not come into the bedroom to close the drapes in the room. I let my bags stand by the door and stripped off my backpack, letting it rest atop the suitcases.

Across the room from the door was a double bed, nestled perfectly in an alcove—the wall on either side making the headboard and footboard of the bed—with a dormer window above it. Summer light was pouring through the glass, turning the room into a greenhouse. I found the light switch by the door and flipped it on, then went over and quickly pulled the drapes shut across the window. I had to crawl up onto the bed and perch on my knees to reach the drapes, but I finally got them shut, effectively blocking out the sun. Even with the overhead light on in the room—all bare board walls and wooden rafters with wooden slat floorboards—the room was dark without the natural light.

I scootched around on my knees on the bed and plopped down on the edge, glad to let my feet have a rest finally. A quick glance around let me know that other than needing a good dusting and sweeping, the room had been kept fairly clean. The bedding might need to be laundered, since I wasn't sure how often Jack cleaned the sheets in an unused attic room, but it looked good enough for my first night's sleep in the house.

Along the wall to my left was the old desk Jack had dragged up to the room for me when I was a small child. If the memories suddenly flooding my brain were, in fact, true. Something I could use to play with my action figures or use to draw and color. On the other side of the room was a squat bookshelf which still contained books for a kid much younger than sixteen years old. In the corner next to the bookcase was a chair that maybe one of my buttcheeks would fit into if I tried.

I'll have to see if I can bring a different chair up here.

I bounced off of the bed and kicked my shoes off, leaving them in the middle of the floor. My socks felt wet when the cooler, inside air hit them. Of course, I had probably sweated a gallon—a lot of it from my feet—so that was probably the reason. I padded across the wooden floorboards to the backpack atop my suitcases and unzipped the front pocket. The cell phone I extracted was nothing new or fancy, but it worked. Well, it worked when it was charged. One glance and a tap of the screen let me know it had died sometime between leaving the motel that morning and arriving at Jack's house.

I dug around in my backpack for the charger, and with the phone and cord in my hand, I searched the walls for an outlet. Finally finding a socket beside the desk, I plugged in the charger and connected my phone, then laid the device on the desktop. It would have plenty of time to juice up while I had some lunch. Maybe by the time my belly was full and I had cooled down, I would be able to text Mom and let her know I got to Jack's okay—and that he had actually let me in the house even though she *hadn't* called him in advance like she said.

All thoughts of what had or hadn't been done got pushed out of my head when I felt my stomach grumble again. Even two floors away, my nose picked up the scent of the food Jack had been cooking when I arrived.

Leaving all of my belongings behind—which I never did on the road, but I felt safe to do at Jack's house—I ventured out of my room once again, slapping the light switch off as I went. The smell of the food seemed to be searching me out, filling my nose and beckoning me downstairs with each step I took on the stairs. The banging around I heard on my way upstairs was gone and I could hear Jack shuffling around in the kitchen, finishing up lunch. When I got downstairs and made my way through the living room into the kitchen, I found Jack getting a couple of bowls out of the kitchen cabinet. A large serving bowl full of...*something*...was sitting on the table.

When Jack closed the cabinet and turned, his eyes landed on me and he nodded. He pointed at the kitchen table and then at the living room. Then he shrugged.

"Uh," I said, "we can eat wherever you want. I'm used to eating in the passenger seat of Mom's car or on a motel bed most of the time, so either choice will be downright fancy."

Jack grinned and his face contorted like he had tried to laugh. I just smiled. Finally, he motioned at the table and indicated I should have a seat. So, I slid into the closest chair and waited. While Jack began ladling something out of a pot on the stove into the bowls, I leaned over and peered into the serving bowl on the table. Sliced cucumbers, tomatoes, and purple onions with some type of vinegary dressing. It looked refreshing. And healthier than anything else I'd eaten in a long time.

Jack finished filling the bowls with the ladle and made his way over to the table. He set a bowl in the spot across from me and then put one in front of me. He padded back over to the cabinets and retrieved the paper towel roll and a couple of spoons, then grabbed his notepad and pen. When he finally slid into the seat across from me, I looked down and confirmed that chili was what he had cooked for lunch. However, it looked homemade. Lots of kidney beans, black beans, tomatoes, and peppers. Big hunks of meat. My stomach grumbled again.

When Jack held a spoon out to me, I accepted it gratefully, and immediately dug into the bowl of chili before me. I didn't care that it was the southside of Hell outdoors—I was starving and in an air-conditioned house. The chili would be great. As I shoveled the first spoonful into my mouth, Jack rose from the table again and got two more bowls out of the cabinet, along with serving utensils. When he came back to the table, I was scarfing down chili, so he took it upon himself to load a serving of the cucumber salad into a bowl and pass it to me.

Then he was up and filling a glass of water at the sink before setting it before me. When he finally sat down to enjoy his meal, I was tipping the glass back, swallowing the cool drink as quickly as I could. My stomach was begging me to fill it with everything. I could barely breathe since I was shoving food into my mouth and pouring water down my throat as quickly as I could. I hadn't realized how thirsty and hungry I was. For several minutes, I shoveled food into my face—both the chili and the salad—and drained my glass of water.

Jack gestured at my empty bowls and glass when I was done and I was sitting there across from him, practically panting.

"Um, yeah." I was embarrassed. "Can I have more?"

Jack nodded and gestured that I should help myself.

So, I got up from the table and went over to the stove to refill my chili bowl, and then I filled my glass at the tap. When I sat down across from him again, I didn't dig into my food like a starving animal. I ate like a sensible human being.

Jack watched me throughout my quest to stuff myself, but once I slowed down, he let his spoon rest in his bowl and reached for his pen. I had just finished filling up my other bowl with more of the cucumber salad when he turned the notepad for me to look at it.

How is Margie?

"Fine," I said. "I guess. She's still being an actress. We were in Dallas this morning. That's where we stayed last night. I guess she thought she had a lead on a job there, but as soon as we arrived yesterday, she made a call and found out it fell through."

Jack began writing in his strange block letters again.

"When she said she had called you," I continued without waiting for him to finish, "I figured she did that last night or something. Or in the middle of the night while I was sleeping, I guess? When she woke me up at butt-early-thirty this morning, she said she was going to drop me off to stay with you, and then she had to get to Vegas because she was going to be in a show. One of the casinos or something?"

Jack finally finished writing and turned the notepad to me.

She have a new boyfriend?

That question bothered me. I was staring at the block letters my stepfather had written on a notepad—a man my mother was still legally married to—and he was asking if she had a boyfriend. Of course, he knew my mother as well as I did. He didn't even look hurt at having asked the question. It was just a question.

"She's had a few," I answered, picking at my salad and avoiding his eyes.

I saw Jack nod out of the corner of my eye. He set the notepad to the side and grabbed his spoon from his bowl. We ate the rest of our meal in silence. Not that silence was rare around Jack—but I didn't try to fill it.

Jack didn't touch the notepad again until we had finished lunch, cleaned up the plates and table, and put everything away. Once that was done, he went to the table and wrote down another question. This time he was slower, as if hesitant to write whatever he was going to write. Finally, he picked the notepad up off of the table and held it up to me.

Your last name still Burke?

Burke. That's Jack's last name. The same last name mine was changed to when I was a toddler and my mother had married Jack.

"I'm still Jordan Burke," I answered.

Jack's eyes lifted and he looked at me for a moment before nodding and setting the notepad back onto the kitchen table. He walked past me into the living room and sat down in the recliner heavily. Then he grabbed the remote off of the end table and flipped on the T.V. He looked over and gestured at the sofa, indicating that I should join him. I really wanted to just excuse myself to my room, but what else did I have going on? I shuffled over to the sofa and plopped down, pulling one leg up underneath me. Jack found a marathon of some old sitcom playing on a network channel and we watched in silence. The minutes turned into hours and we both found ourselves curled up on in our respective seats, not exactly uncomfortable with the silence, but not quite sure what to do with it, either. Jack didn't fetch his notepad, and I didn't really say much other than a random comment here and there about the show.

When night fell and bedtime crept closer, the sitcom marathon ended on the channel he had selected, so he flipped off the T.V. and reached into the air, stretching for the ceiling.

36

Jack indicated that he was ready for bed and pointed at the stairs, letting me know he was planning to go up and turn in, so I just gave him a nod. Sleep sounded good. There was nothing else to do—and neither of us had ever indicated that we had been hungry for dinner when it rolled around, so bed was our best option. It's not like we could have stayed up painting each other's toenails and having a heart-to-heart.

Well, we could've, but Jack didn't seem the type to be interested.

Jack went about making sure everything was in order and the lights were shut off as I made my way to the stairs. Before I got to the second-floor landing, he was ascending the stairs as well. As I was making my way up the second flight, Jack had made his way to the second floor, so I gave him a wave over the banister—which he returned—and rushed up the last few steps to my room. I didn't bother turning on the light in my room. I shut the door and immediately stripped down, not caring that I hadn't washed the sweat off of my body yet.

Over at the desk, I stood there in my boxers, and checked the glowing blue screen of my phone. No missed calls. No missed texts. I had intended to text Mom to let her know that I had arrived safely. But she hadn't bothered to check on me. Pettiness got the best of me, and I decided that she could just worry about me until the next morning.

If she's even worried.

When I crawled onto the bed, I knelt at the window and swung the drapes open, thinking that sleeping under the stars and moon would be nice. When the drapes were open, I finally realized that my bedroom faced Possibly, and I could see the whole town from my window. Although, at night, everything in town was closed. Not even a streetlight shone in the distance, just black tree-shaped blobs and boxy outlines of

37

buildings met my eyes. If I squinted hard enough, I could make out the moon shining on the creek surface in the distance.

I had started to pull back the musty blanket so I could crawl into bed, but something caught my eye off in the distance. On the northeast side of town, along the river, my eyes landed on a large boxy black shape in the distance.

Is that the barn I saw earlier?

I watched through the window as what could only be described as laser beams emanated from the roof of the large building. My eyes grew wide with wonder, unsure of what was going on inside of the barn that would produce the colorful lights. Was it a dance club at night?

Gently, I slid the middle window in the dormer up, letting in the fresh night air. My eyes stayed on the barn in the distance and the laser-like lights shooting out of the roof. The summer night hadn't kicked up much of a breeze, but it carried a tune upon it. Something, way off in the distance, sounded like a song.

Night club. I nodded to myself. *Maybe? Levi Lee's probably there, dancing in his green-screen suit, trying to impress all the ladies with…things.*

I listened to the sound for a moment, wondering if I could figure out which song was playing over at the barn, but it was too far away. Eventually, I gave up and closed the middle dormer. I pushed back the covers and laid on the stale sheets. Jack's washing machine would have to be used the following day, but one night on stale sheets wouldn't kill me. Even with the air conditioning doing its best, my room was stuffy. So, I laid there in my boxers and let the moon shine its cooling blue light down on me through the window as the stars blinked their soundless lullaby. Before I knew it, everything ceased to be.

THE MYSTERY OF SHIRLENE

The washing machine on the screened-in porch had seen better days, but it was still capable of washing my bedding. Jack was working on some project in the yard as I stuffed the sheets and blanket into the washer and added soap. After considering how long it might have been since the sheets were washed, I tipped the detergent jug and added a little more.

When I'd woken up as the sun was rising—the open drapes on the dormer window allowed the sun bring me back from the dead early—Jack was already eating breakfast in the kitchen. Actually, he was eating cereal out of a bowl as he stood at the sink. He didn't use his notepad when I had stumbled down the stairs groggily, but he gestured at the shelf containing cereals, waved at the fridge—generally gave me the idea that I should help myself. Apparently, breakfast was not a "sit at the table and eat together" meal. By the time I had poured myself a bowl of cereal and found the milk in the fridge, Jack was done with his bowl and had set it in the sink to soak.

He dashed off through the living room and screened porch to the backyard before I had even had a chance to pour my milk.

Was he regretting my presence already?

I sat at the kitchen table and ate slowly, waiting for my body and brain to catch up with the day. Afterwards, I washed mine and Jack's bowls and put them in the draining rack, then went back upstairs for a shower. Fresh clothes, some deodorant, brushed teeth—I finally found myself ready for the day. A glance at my phone let me know that Mom still hadn't tried to text me, so I left it on the desk. I wanted to text or call her and tell her I was okay, and to make sure she was doing fine, too. But something resolute in my gut refused to let me.

Instead, I stripped the sheets and blanket off of my bed, took the pillowcase off of my pillow, and ventured back downstairs, cradling the bundle carefully as I went down the steps. Before I bothered using the washing machine, I had hollered at Jack through the screens in the porch, asking if it was okay to use his machine. He had simply waved a hand in the machine's direction, so I took that to mean it was okay.

I turned the dial, pushed the start button with my thumb, and the machine came to life with a jolt. After a few moments, I realized that the machine was going to work—it was just loud as hell. Hopefully, I had done everything right so that Jack's machine wasn't destroyed by my bedding. When I opened the screen door on the porch and stepped down into the yard, I got a better look at what Jack was doing. A long oak table, probably long enough to seat twelve or more people for dinner, was set out in the yard on a tarp. It looked as though it had once been painted—*who would do that to such lovely wood?*—but Jack had stripped it and sanded it down to the wood grain once again.

Some type of electric cutting tool was in his hand and he was carving grooves in the wood of the tabletop, his back to me. So that I wouldn't startle him, I rounded him in a wide arc, making sure he saw me coming towards him. He wasn't deaf—obviously—but if he started up the tool as I was walking up to him, he wouldn't hear me approach. Then he might spin around and gouge me with the tool on accident. You don't make it to sixteen years old without knowing a little bit about staying out of the way of tools that could accidentally be used as weapons.

Jack's eyes caught mine and he paused, the bit in the tool against the wood.

"I didn't see a dryer," I said.

Jack gestured across the yard.

I turned to find a clothesline on the other side of the yard— metal cords strung between two T-posts that had been painted a sky blue.

Really?

"Okay." I shrugged. "Uh, what are you doing?"

One of Jack's eyebrows raised and he glanced down at the table, then back to me.

"Yeah," I said. "Working on the table. What are you doing to it?"

Jack set his tool down and started to make movements with his hands before remembering that sign language was mostly pointless with me.

"Want me to get your notepad?" I asked.

Jack shook his head in frustration and reached into his pocket. He extracted his phone and held it up so I could see it.

"I don't have mine on me. It's upstairs," I said.

Jack still unlocked his phone and tapped away at the screen. I waited patiently, wondering if he had heard anything I said. Did he realize he didn't even have my phone number? Even if I had my cell phone on me, I'd never get the text. When Jack finished tapping away, he held the phone out for me to look at the screen.

I leaned over and read his screen.

I need smokes and the mail.

41

"Cigarettes?" I asked.

He nodded.

"You shouldn't smoke."

Jack just stared at me.

"Okay. Fine. Where are they? I'll go get them. I'll go out to the mailbox, too."

Jack shook his head. Then he was looking down at his phone and tapping away at the screen once again. A moment later, he was holding the phone out to me.

Post office doesn't deliver mail. Can you go get it? You can stop at Grandy's for cigarettes.

"I mean," I said, re-reading the screen, "I can go get the mail. I know where the post office is. Not that it'd be hard to find in this town. But I'm only sixteen, Jack. I can't buy cigarettes. Okay, I've bought cigarettes before. Lifted some beers once in Memphis. But…something about this town tells me that it won't be so easy to lie about my age or steal."

Jack frowned disapprovingly. I shrugged.

Another round of tapping and the phone was in my face once more.

Don't steal. I'll text Grandy to let him know you're coming and you're my stepson. He'll let you have the cigarettes.

"Okay," I said.

Jack typed away on the phone again.

Tell Sofia who you are. She'll give you the mail.

"Who's Sofia?"

A few moments later: *Postmaster.*

"All right," I said. "Uh, I don't have any money. For the cigarettes?"

Jack laid his phone on the table and reached into his back pocket. I expected him to yank out a wallet and fish out a few bills. Instead, his hand simply reappeared with a twenty. So,

Jack kept cash loose in his pocket. We all have our quirks. Jack eyed me warily as I leaned across the table and took it from his hand, as though I'd get far on twenty bucks. I slipped the bill into my front hip pocket and Jack picked up his tool once more.

"Uh, I'll be back soon? Town doesn't seem that big. From what I saw yesterday, I mean. So…I'll be back soon?"

Jack didn't even look up at me as he started working on the table once more. A slight nod of his head was his only response. I had made it to the corner of the house when an idea struck me.

"Hey," I hollered over my shoulder to Jack.

He looked up at me.

"Mind if I, like, buy a soda?" I asked. "Just a twenty ounce or whatever. Nothing major. Mom didn't give me any cash when she dumped me."

A jerky nod of Jack's head, even though he was already looking away, let me know that I had the all-clear to purchase a drink for my troubles. Jack was a tacit guy—if not by choice—but he wasn't half bad.

The walk back into town wasn't as horrible as the day before since it was a bit cooler. I was still dealing with Texas in summer, but the temperature was bearable. Of course, it was mid-morning, so by the time noon came around, it was possible I'd be a puddle of sweat. As I sauntered down the road towards the graveyard, a gunshot rang in the distance. Instinctively, I jerked and ducked, wanting to avoid gunfire, before I realized that the weird guy who looked like Yosemite Sam was probably being crazy again.

What was his name? Wyatt?

When I hung a right at the graveyard, towards the center of town, and AMOR and the other buildings alongside it came into view, I heard an odd mechanical scraping sound. At the corner of the street AMOR sat upon, and where I'd seen the guy digging up the concrete, I realized I had missed the street sign on my way out to Jack's the day before.

Liberty Lane.

Apparently, the radio station sat on a street whose concrete was slowly being dug up and replaced with rainbow-colored bricks, and it was called "Liberty Lane." Fair enough. Not important information, but information either way. When I turned right onto Liberty Lane, headed towards the creek, where I could see the teal clapboard house that was actually a post office, I realized where the mechanical scraping sound was coming from.

The tram was inching along the tracks and the conductor was holding the steering lever, looking ahead officiously as the tram rolled down the tracks towards me. My feet slowed and I came to stand at the end of Liberty Lane so that I could watch the conductor and his tiny little tram. It took less than a minute, but finally, the tram reached the other end of the tracks and stopped to my right. The conductor slid the gear shift into place, turned off the tram, kicked his feet up, then grabbed his book. A few flicks of his finger, which he moistened with his tongue, and the conductor had found where he'd left off. He went about reading his book, pretending he hadn't just seriously driven the tram forty yards before calling it a day.

Of course, the tram only ran the length of Liberty Lane. Unless he wanted to throw the thing in reverse and go the other way, he was out of track.

Why in the world is there a tram that just goes up and down one street that takes less than a minute to walk at a leisurely pace?

With the sight of the conductor reading his book without a care in the world, I knew there was no point in trying to figure things out. Between Levi Lee, the guy who jumped off the bridge, and Wyatt with his gun—I already knew everyone in town was crazy. The tram conductor just cemented that theory in my mind.

It dawned on me that I had been so caught up in watching the tram that the rest of the world had seemed to melt away and fade into the background. *Who Do You Love?* by Bo Diddley was playing on the speakers the radio station had staked up around town. In fact, I was close enough to AMOR that I could see its storefront. It looked pretty innocuous—not at all like a lunatic was in charge of the place. Then again, most lunatics do all they can to avoid detection, including living and working in "normal" places.

My focus shifted from the conductor, his reading, and the tiny tram, and I listened to the song playing throughout town. It wasn't so loud as to distract anyone from what they had to do as they went about their day, but loud enough that you couldn't help but notice it playing. As the minutes ticked by, the song came to an end, the last chords fading on the gentle summer breeze.

"You've been listening to AMOR, the most popular radio station in Possibly, Texas. All day long from 6am to 6pm," the radio DJ announced. *"That was* Who Do You Love? *by Bo Diddley. Next up—*Who Do You Love? *by Bo Diddley."*

So, this was a thing in Possibly? The radio station played a different song each day and they played it for twelve hours? Didn't the citizens of the tiny little town get tired of that crap? Who wanted to hear the same song on repeat for twelve hours a day?

Another gunshot went off in the distance.

I only jumped a little.

Instead of waiting around to watch the conductor read or to listen to another round of Bo Diddley, I took off down Liberty Lane towards the teal clapboard building by the creek. As I mentioned, the road wasn't long, so I made it quicker on foot than I would have had I jumped on the tram and asked for a ride. Before I knew it, I was coming up on the backside of the building, rounding the side, and approaching the front door. Brown, heavy wood, just like the door on a house, greeted me at the front of the post office.

At first, I felt odd opening the door and letting myself inside since it looked so much like a private home. However, I glanced over at the sign near the door that proclaimed this was indeed the post office, and the hours were from "6am to 6pm." My hand found the doorknob and I pulled the door open, a blast of frigid air slapping against my skin as I stepped into the building.

AMOR's song of the day was playing somewhere deep inside the building—towards the back up more upstairs. The front room looked like it had once been a living room, except postal lockers had been installed to the left of the door, all along one wall. A few more were across from the door, along with shelves that held mailing materials and paraphernalia.

The wall alongside the lockers and shelves across from the door seemed to be absolutely covered in papers and flyers pinned up with thumbtacks. Every piece of paper looked vaguely the same at first glance. Probably people advertising odd jobs or services. It was probably integral to have side hustles when you lived in a town like Possibly and the nearest big town was at least thirty minutes away.

To my right, I found a large wooden counter, almost like one you'd see in an old timey train station. Pens attached to chains stuck up from the counter and a round, matronly looking woman with a smile that could light up a room stood behind the desk. She wore an honest to goodness postmaster's hat, which was perched precariously atop a bundle of black hair. The woman didn't look quite old enough to be called "old," but she looked *older.*

"Well, hello there," she greeted me. "This is something new."

"I'm sorry?" I asked, shaking my head to clear my thoughts.

The air was absolutely frigid in the post office. Instinctively, I wrapped my arms around myself and turned to approach the counter.

"Sorry, hon," the woman said. "I'm going through the change of life. If I don't keep it cold in here, I'd burn up."

Well, that was information I didn't need to have. But it explained a lot.

"O-oh," I stammered, "yeah. No worries, ma'am. I just came to pick up the mail."

"Well, I don't recognize you." She leaned against the counter as I approached the other side and I got a clear view of the shimmery blue powder over her eyes and the pinkish hue of her lipstick. Crow's feet decorated the corners of her mouth and eyes. But her eyes sparkled with a friendly spirit. The nametag on her chest proclaimed her to be 'Sofia Salazar.' "You new to town?"

"Uh, yeah," I said. "I mean, I'm new, but I'm picking up mail for Jack Burke? I'm Jordan Burke. His son—*step*son."

"Well, I'll be." The woman clapped joyfully. "You do look like him!"

"*Step*son," I repeated blandly.

"How's Jack doin'?" the woman asked as she bent down, disappearing behind the counter.

47

"Are you Sofia?" I finally asked, though I had seen her nametag.

"One and the same." Her muffled response drifted over the counter.

"Oh, okay," I said, still hugging myself. "Uh, Jack's fine. But I just got here yesterday. He said to tell Sofia, the postmaster, to let me have his mail. So, that's why I'm here."

Sofia—the postmaster—stood up from behind the counter, a couple of envelopes clenched in her hand.

"Not much today, I'm afraid," Sofia said. "Hardly worth the trip down here—*Jordan*, was it?"

"Uh, yes, ma'am." I reached out and took the envelopes from her. "It just takes a few minutes to walk from his house to here. I mean, the town isn't...*big*...is it?"

Sofia slapped the counter and cackled.

I just grinned tightly, wondering if Sofia was like Wyatt and would produce a gun to start shooting up the place like a mad woman.

"A truer statement's never been stated." Sofia agreed. "Possibly proper—whatchu see when you cross Susurrus Creek is about what you'll get. You gotta drive out a couple miles past Jack's place to find most the people around here."

"Oh?"

"Most Possibilians live in the housing developments out on highway 12," Sofia continued, straightening up her counter as she prattled on. "About a hundred of us actually live here downtown. Some keep to themselves, though, so don't bother goin' 'round countin'."

"Okay."

"The planning board doesn't really allow for much development down here by the creek anymore," Sofia said. "They don't want to ruin the natural beauty of Possibly."

"Makes sense, I guess?" I shrugged.

"I'm sure Jack's told you all about it," Sofia flitted her hands in front of herself. "In his own way, of course. I'm probably wasting your time."

"No," I said, though I didn't really feel like hanging around to chat, "it's no big deal. I guess it's good to know about the town I'm staying in, right?"

Sofia grinned widely.

"Right."

"Well," I said, "uh, thanks."

I shook the envelopes at her gently.

"Anytime, Jordan," she replied. "I always have Jack's mail set aside, so you just come right in and I'll have it ready for you."

"Thanks," I said again.

Sofia gave me another smile and she was back to straightening things under the counter—probably other stacks of mail waiting on Possibly residents to pick up. As I turned and stepped away from the counter, my eye caught the wall of tacked up flyers, and I was compelled to see what exactly people did for odd jobs in Possibly. Sofia continued to work behind me as I shuffled over to the wall to check things out.

To my surprise, the first piece of paper my eyes landed on was a letter.

"*Dear Shirlene,*" it said.

Not wanting to get into other people's business, I tore my eyes away and looked at the paper next to it.

"*Dear Shirlene,*" that one said.

The next paper was addressed the same way. And the next. And the next. My eyes flitted around and I quickly determined that the entire wall was plastered with letter's to "*Dear Shirlene.*" Why were there a bunch of letters to some woman named

Shirlene pinned up, absolutely covering one of the walls in the post office?

"Tragic, isn't it?" Sofia's voice came from right beside me.

I jumped and turned to find her standing next to me. Apparently, as I had been checking out the letters, she had rounded the counter to look over the letters as well. Her blue eye-shadowed lids were focused on the wall of letters, sadness etched on her face.

"I'm sorry?"

"The letters," she said.

"They're all to…Shirlene?"

"Yeah." She sighed dreamily. "We get a new one every few days. Well, a few times it's been a week or two between letters, I guess."

There had to be dozens if not a hundred or more letters tacked to the wall. There looked to be more than one layer of them.

"Shouldn't you, like, deliver them to her?" I asked the obvious question. "Instead of plastering them on the wall for everyone to read?"

"Well, that's the thing," Sofia said. "There's not a single Shirlene in Possibly. Someone has been writing her love letters for over a year—maybe two now—and she doesn't even live here."

"Can't you send them back?" I asked as I leaned in to look more closely at a letter.

My heart beats with a desire it feels will never be fulfilled; only Shirlene can quench its thirst.

Definitely love letters. Somewhat spicy love letters.

"They never arrive with a return address," Sofia explained. "They're always addressed to 'Shirlene.' I'm hoping Shirlene will eventually show up to claim them. Maybe she can make heads or tails of everything. Right now—well, they're just up there waiting."

"Should you have even opened them?" I asked.

Wasn't that, like, a federal crime? Opening people's mail?

"Oh," Sofia waved me off, giving me a nudge on my shoulder, "they're not sealed when they arrive. They're just slipped through the mail slot like that."

I looked closely at the letters. None of them seemed to have ever had a fold crease. Someone had been writing love letters to Shirlene and had simply been sliding the page into the mail slot—hoping Sofia would help them find their owner.

Odd.

"When I say they're addressed to 'Shirlene,' I mean the opening lines of each letter," Sofia continued. "But so far, we haven't been able to figure out who she is or where she may be. I guess we've all just been enjoying reading about the love this person has for her."

"Oh."

"I want to meet the woman who inspires such devotion." Sofia sighed dreamily.

"Yeah," I said, "uh, it seems like the guy who wrote the letters is, uh, obsessed."

"Or gal." Sofia nudged me.

I turned to find her winking at me.

I smiled. "Yeah. I guess 'or gal.' But isn't there a signature at the bottom of the letters?"

A quick scan of the letter in front of me, then the letters on either side of it told me that the sender intended to keep their identity private. Sofia saw me looking for the answer to my question, so she didn't bother responding.

"One day," she was sighing dreamily again, "we'll all know who Shirlene and her mystery admirer are—and hopefully they'll fall madly in love."

"Maybe."

I didn't know what else could be said about the letter, Shirlene, or her mystery guy-slash-gal. So, I held the letters up and jiggled them at Sofia once more. With a nod of my head, which she returned, I headed for the door. When I stepped outside into the warm June air, and I was closing the door behind myself, I glanced over my shoulder to see Sofia still staring up at the wall wistfully.

People get so caught up in love stories. I thought. *Especially unrequited love stories.*

The people of Possibly were getting stranger and stranger. Everywhere I went in the tiny little town I seemed to encounter another person who didn't quite have their head screwed tightly onto their neck. My mom used to describe flighty or airheaded people as being "*a taco short of a fiesta platter,*" and the people of Possibly were helping me to better understand that saying.

I probably should text or call Mom later.

"*EMMMMMM-ILLLLLLLLL-EEEEEEEE!*"

I clenched up at the sound of a guy screaming from the direction of the creek. I turned just in time to see the same teenage guy from the day before standing on the handrail of the wooden bridge, his arms spread out wide. Then he was falling backwards.

What is going on here?

My eyes darted around, looking for any other person who might have just witnessed the insane teenager jump off of the bridge for the second time in two days. A flash of neon green caught my attention and I realized that Levi Lee was in front of Starbuck's again, pretending to be the hull. When he noticed that I was looking over at him, he began to wave happily. Or, it looked like a happy wave—arm held aloft, swinging about lazily.

Levi Lee must have realized that he had broken character once again, because he suddenly stopped, froze in place, then dropped his arm to his side.

"*Shit.*" His voice drifted over from the pirate ship.

"Sorry!" I hollered back.

"*It's all right! I'll get the hang of this!*"

Quickly, I gave him an encouraging wave before glancing over at the bridge. There was no point in checking on the teenager. Obviously, Levi Lee had seen the events unfold as well, and he didn't seem concerned. Besides, the teenager was becoming a pro at jumping off the bridge. He was probably fine.

The envelopes that I still held in my hand got folded in half so I could stuff them in my back pocket, and I took off down the road to Grandy's Auto. It was less than twenty yards away, directly down and west from the post office, so there was no chance of getting lost. Of course, everything in downtown Possibly seemed to be *"just ten or twenty yards away,"* so if you got lost in Possibly, something was wrong with you.

Within a minute, I was walking up to the front of Grandy's—three pumps, an air compressor, some squeegees—your standard small-town gas station. The building itself looked to be just big enough to have a check-out counter, a few shelves for snacks, and a few coolers for drinks. The place looked fairly modern from the outside. The pumps accepted debit and credit cards and all of the equipment looked new. Around the metal awning that went over the pumps, and was attached to the brick building, all of the paint looked fresh.

Maybe the designated town sign painter comes by Grandy's?

Outside of the store, on two cinderblocks stacked on top of each other next to the front door, a man was sitting, staring off into space. Dusty blond hair and a beard of the same shade that was trimmed neatly to his face made him look young. However, the crinkles around his eyes and mouth let me know that he was probably older than I thought. The fact that he was wearing bib overalls with no shirt underneath, and I could see a sprinkling of gray hairs on his chest, confirmed that thought. In fact, that's what the man was focused on while staring out at nothing. He was lazily scratching at the hairs on his chest as he stared and sat.

I'm sixteen years old, so I'm not, like, the most experienced person in the world. However, I've travelled enough with my mom across the country to know when someone should be treated politely, yet given some space. So, I gave the man a nod—just in case he noticed me—before stepping past him to open the door and go into the store. He didn't seem to notice my greeting. He just kept scratching at his chest and staring.

Fine by me.

Inside of Grandy's, I had the exact opposite experience I'd had in the post office. Everything looked modern, nice and clean, but it was stifling warm. There were a couple oscillating fans hung from the all four corners of the room near the ceiling, *'stirring the stink around,'* as my mom would have said. However, it didn't seem that Grandy had turned on the AC. I could see vents in the ceiling as I strolled through the tiny store, but they could have just been for heating purposes, I supposed.

As I had suspected, there were exactly two coolers in Grandy's Auto. And he didn't really keep a variety of drinks stocked. What he had, there was a lot of it, but the choices were limited. Coke, Sprite, Mountain Dew, and something called

Mello Yello. There wasn't even a forty ounce of beer in sight. In fact, there wasn't any alcohol in sight—which was kind of strange for a gas station.

I selected a Mountain Dew—because, caffeine and sugar—and I shuffled over to the check-out counter tucked away in the corner next to the door. When I had entered, I hadn't seen Grandy or anybody working, but I assumed they'd hear customers enter and come check things out. Maybe they were in the bathroom or something?

"Hello?" I asked of no one.

A glance in the direction of the bathrooms off the back of the place let me know they were unoccupied. They were just closet-size rooms and both doors were open. I could have easily seen if someone was in there…*relieving themselves.*

"Uh…Grandy?" I asked again.

I'm not sure how long I stood at the check-out counter, waiting patiently for Grandy to show up because I hadn't brought my phone with me, and there didn't seem to be a clock anywhere in the store. The fact that all I wanted to do was buy a soda and a pack of smokes for Jack—which, I suddenly realized, I didn't know which brand he smoked—frustrated me. A guy having to wait so long to make a seven- or eight-dollar purchase was annoying. Without any other option, I set the Mountain Dew on the counter and walked back to the front door.

"Hey," I said to the guy on the cinderblocks as I cracked the door, "do you know where Grandy is? Or someone who works here?"

"I'm…Grandy," the man responded slowly.

He didn't look away from whatever he was staring at, and he didn't stop scratching his chest.

"Oh." I frowned. "Okay? Well, uh, I'm ready to check out, sir."

"Whatchu... tryin'... to... buy?"

I glanced over at the counter where my soda sat.

"Uh, a twenty-ounce Mountain Dew," I said. "And I'm supposed to pick up some cigarettes."

Grandy, the chest-scratching sky-watcher seemed to think on this for a moment.

"You...Jack's...boy?"

"I'm his stepson."

"Grab... him... a... pack of... them... Marlboro Reds," Grandy's drawling answer came. "Shorts... none... them... fancy... things."

"Okay?"

"Then... come... on... out... here."

Wow.

Possibly, Texas. Possibly this was the strangest damn place I'd ever been to in my entire life. Instead of asking Grandy further questions—it didn't seem a great day for that—I went back to the check-out counter and grabbed my soda. I searched the rack of cigarettes behind the counter and found a pack of Marlboro Reds. I wasn't sure if he liked the hard back or soft pack, so I went with the hard pack. Better safe than sorry.

When I got back to the door, I pushed it wide and stepped back outside to deal with Grandy. He, as expected, was still staring and scratching. I wasn't even sure he was actually seeing whatever he was staring at in the distance. A quick glance over my shoulder provided a view of grass and trees beyond. Nothing all that interesting.

"How much do I owe you?" I asked, turning back to Grandy. "Just the soda and smokes, please."

"You... just tell... Jack... to get... me... next time," Grandy drawled. "I ain't... feelin' like... I want... to... run... the register...today."

Is this guy okay?

"Are you okay, sir?" My thought slid right from my lips.

Grandy, as though suddenly realizing I was there, turned his head to look up at me. His eyes were nearly white they were so gray. I almost jumped; the color was so startling. It was actually kind of spooky. I'd never seen anyone with eyes so gray.

"I'm fine," Grandy said. "I just... feel... like thinking... today."

"Um," I fiddled with the bottle and cigarettes, "I don't want anyone to think I stole these."

"Nah," Grandy said and went back to staring out at nothing, his fingers scratching at his chest again. "Won't...nobody think...that."

"Yeah. Okay." I stepped back from him. "Um, I'll tell Jack right when I get home that he needs to come pay you soon. Okay?"

"Oooookay," Grandy drawled.

Instead of asking Grandy if he was okay again—he'd *said* he was fine—I turned to leave. Getting away from Grandy, his creepy eyes, and his sauna of a store sounded better than trying to get him to act normal.

"You... ever... think about how... caterpillars turn... into... butterflies?" Grandy's voice stopped me.

Turning back to look at the man sitting on the cinderblocks, clad only in bib overalls, who was staring out at the world like he was lost, I suddenly felt sorry for him. He looked a little misplaced, a little frazzled—okay, *a lot* frazzled—as if he was going through it. I mean, he didn't even feel like doing his job he was so perplexed by life. Obviously, something wasn't right with him. Besides, someone who asked a question like that was obviously a little…*not right.*

He was probably just lonely. And insane.

"Um, no sir," I said. "I guess not?"

"I just wonder… if they… ever… miss bein'… caterpillars is all."

I stared at him. He stared out at nothing.

"Maybe when they change into butterflies they forget?" I shrugged.

Neither of us said anything for a few moments. And I was about to turn to leave, but then Grandy's face lit up with a smile, though he kept staring out at nothing and scratching at his chest.

"Yeah," he drawled. "Maybe… they… can… forget. I like… that."

"Yeah." I nodded slowly, inching backwards. "Um, thanks. I'll tell Jack to pay you."

Grandy didn't answer so much as nod slowly as he continued to stare. So, I took that to mean that our transaction, or lack thereof, was done.

I hate to admit it, but I walked away from Grandy's a little more quickly than was typical for me. In fact, it might have actually been fast enough to call a jog. When another gunshot went off in the distance—somewhere in the direction of the post office, my speed turned into what could have been classified as a full sprint. In fact, I sprinted down to the corner of the street, hoping to put plenty of space between Grandy's and me—and Wyatt and his gun.

At the end of the street, my sprint turned back to a jog, and finally, I slowed to a walk. A glance over my shoulder proved that Grandy had not followed me like some psychopath and Wyatt wasn't chasing me down with his gun. Stopping at the corner, I stuffed Jack's pack of cigarettes into my hip pocket with the twenty I needed to return to him, and started to twist off the cap of my soda.

Seconds later, greenish-yellow deliciousness—*if that's a way to describe something delicious*—was sliding down my throat as I held my head back and gulped soda from the green plastic bottle. I savored the citrus-y soda, both tart and sweet at the same time, letting it roll around in my mouth briefly before swallowing it down. The back of my nose was tickled by the carbonation and my cheeks sucked in from the tanginess as my salivary glands went into overdrive.

Typically, I'm a Dr. Pepper guy—especially whenever I've been in Texas—but there's something about the crisp, sweet, slightly sour taste of Mountain Dew when it's hot. I'd probably be drinking a lot of Mountain Dews while I was in Possibly. If Jack wouldn't mind bankrolling my habit, anyway. As I pulled the mouth of the bottle away from my lips and screwed the green plastic cap back on, a flutter of bright orange fabric off to my right caught my eye.

A soft breeze had blown down the street, slapping at my back and cooling my neck. When my eyes landed on the orangish-red miniature circus tent on the corner of the next street over, I realized that the wind had made the tent flaps flutter. The breeze blew softly, yet persistently, and the flaps continued their flutter. Inside of the tent was dark, seemingly illuminated by a single, weak, source of light.

I could just make out a woman sitting at a table in the center of the tent. She seemed to be wearing a dress made of heavy, dark fabric. A shawl was draped around her shoulders, and long tendrils of heavy brown hair hung from her head. As I stared, not really paying attention to what I was doing—you know, staring at a stranger like I was Grandy the Weirdo—the woman in the tent raised her hand. She waved a long-fingered hand at me, but it was more like a flutter of her fingers, not a real wave. Then she smiled—an almost knowing smile, as though we shared a secret.

The last of the Mountain Dew I had been holding in my mouth slid down my throat like a stone as I realized how weird the woman and her tent were. In her dress and shawl—not to mention all of that hair—sitting in the middle of a canvas tent set out in the sun during summer in Texas, she had to be burning up. But she looked perfectly content and cool. The breeze picked up and my shirt tail ruffled around my waist. Somewhere, to my left, I heard a tinkling of...*bells*?

My head whipped around to look for the source of the noise, but all I saw was woods off to my left. A dirt pathway led off from the end of the road towards the trees, disappearing into the woods. The tinkling sound peppered the air as the breeze continued to blow down the street. When I looked away from the noise coming from the trees, so that I could check out the lady in the tent once more, she was no longer fluttering her fingers at me. Instead, she seemed to be gesturing towards the woods.

'*Scat. Go check it out.*' her gesture seemed to say as she continued to smile knowingly at me.

My head turned back and forth from the lady and her tent to the grouping of trees. The breeze continued slapping against my back, a refreshing breath of air that, combined with the slug of Mountain Dew, made me feel downright cool in the summer sun. For a moment, I wasn't sure if I wanted to wander over— cautiously, of course—and talk to the lady in the tent, or if I wanted to check on the tinkling noise coming from the woods.

Neither option seemed all that safe or wise. However, when I realized that the woman was no longer gesturing for me to go to the woods, and had turned her attention to something on her table, I made my choice. I turned left onto the dirt path and headed towards the woods. I'd already walked along Twelve—I mean, Two-Mile Trail—so, what was one more dirt trail in two days? The breeze tapered off a bit, but continued to blow through town, and the tinkling sound from the woods continued.

As I strolled along the dirt path, trying to be cautious, yet brave, the tinkling sound grew louder as the trees grew closer. Moments later, I was within the trees, their branches towering over me, providing a cool shade, as I strolled along the path. The tinkling sounded different within the dark, cool confines of the woods. Well, not different, I guess, but…*well, different.* Because it didn't just sound like "tinkling" anymore. It sounded like a lot of different things.

There was the tinkling sound, but also what sounded like pieces of glass tapping against each other. Hollow wooden logs bonking together. Metal on metal. The click-clack of stones being slapped together gently. When I reached the end of the dirt path, I found that it had led from the street in town to a clearing in the middle of the small wooded area, no larger than was needed to place a building the size of the post office.

It wasn't the noises coming from all over the woods that startled me suddenly when I found the clearing, though the myriad sounds coming from the trees was unusual. At the end of the path, I found myself stepping aside and ducking behind a tree, out of sight, because someone was in the clearing.

On the other side of the grassy area of the clearing stood a boy, and though his back was to me, something about him made me assume he was probably about my age. He was a slender, wispy guy, with long limbs that looked like they could reach up to the tops of the trees, though he didn't look like he was much taller than me. Dark brown hair that was cut close to his head greeted my eyes, as did the strange camouflage cargo pants he was wearing. Well, the pants weren't so strange, other than it was summer and they weren't the coolest choice.

It was the black fabric around his waist that draped down, almost like a skirt, which flowed with the breeze that blew through the clearing. A simple white tank top was the only other thing he wore. He didn't even have on any shoes. At first, since his back was to me, and he seemed to just be staring into the woods at the other side of the clearing, I felt concerned. Maybe a little scared? But then I realized he wasn't looking at the trees, but what they held.

The source of the tinkling and other noises.

In the trees on the other side of the clearing, and even on the sides of the clearing, I found the source of the noise that beckoned me down the dirt path and into the woods. *Windchimes.* Windchimes of all shapes and sizes, all made with different materials, swayed and jangled in the breeze. Some of the chimes looked fairly traditional—metal chimes hanging from strings that were attached to a piece of wood. Some had chimes made from shards of glass. Or bottle caps. Or bamboo. One of the chimes appeared to have old antique iron keys hanging from it, clanging dully in the breeze.

I was so distracted by the sounds and sights around me, that I almost didn't notice when the boy in the camouflage pants and skirt turned away from the trees and began walking back towards the dirt path. I ducked back further behind the tree I was using as a hiding spot, letting the shadows of the woods swallow me up, yet I continued to peer around the tree at the dirt path.

The boy drew closer, walking along the trail back towards downtown Possibly. As he got closer to my hiding spot, I could hear his humming over the breeze and the windchimes. *Who Do You Love?* by Bo Diddley was his choice of tunes. Obviously, he was an AMOR fan. I watched as he traveled along, first noticing that he was barefoot, his toes kicking up dust on the trail. Just as he passed by, I realized that his hair was brown from the back—and even a little in the front—but some of it was white.

It took a moment for me to realize that the white in his hair was in a triangle shape, jutting up from his hairline to a point that jabbed at the crown of his head. Even stranger, the white of his hair was mirrored by stark white skin that was in the shape of a triangle, jutting down his forehead and ending in a point between his eyebrows.

A birthmark, maybe?

I stayed behind the tree, keeping myself in hiding as I spied on the boy walking by. He hummed and walked by jauntily, a placid smile on his face. He didn't look left or right, so there wasn't a chance he saw me. His eyes looked to the path ahead as he hummed his tune and practically skipped away, his skirt fluttering around his pant legs. My eyes followed him along the path, away from the clearing, then he was gone, swallowed up by the light at the other end of the trail that popped out into Possibly. And the breeze settled. The chimes stopped tinkling.

What was up with this town?

THE GRIEVING WOMAN

AMOR had already snuck into Jack's house the following morning. I didn't even have to walk over to downtown Possibly to know that the song of the day was The Animals' version of *It's All Over Now, Baby Blue.* When I tumbled down the stairs and into the kitchen, still in my boxers, though I'd thrown a t-shirt on, the song was playing. Jack wasn't in the kitchen, but he'd left the radio on by the sink. I ventured over to check it out and found a note next to the radio from Jack, telling me he'd be "out back" working on a "his project."

Jack's big, odd block letters looked like he was screaming. I'd have to explain to him that, like texts or emails, he should turn off the All Caps. The radio DJ was announcing that the song was going to play—*again*—as I was digging the carton of milk out of the fridge. And I was diving into my first bowl of cereal by the time the song had started.

I sat through two rounds of the song, which was just long enough to eat my breakfast, then I washed up my dishes, got a drink of water, and turned the radio off. With the sudden absence of the music, Jack's house was quiet as a church. There was no ticking of a clock up on a mantle. No sound of a T.V. playing. No cars driving by on a freeway outside. People weren't down the hall raiding a vending machine. The ice machine in the vending area wasn't kicking off and on. No sounds of kids screaming, laughing, and splashing in a pool in the courtyard.

It was so unlike my existence for the last decade.

It felt…*lonely*.

I wondered what Jack thought of the quiet. He couldn't talk, but he could hear.

Did he ever feel lonely there on the edge of downtown Possibly?

What did he do with no one to talk to each day? I mean, there was no one to talk to him so he could write back responses. There probably weren't that many people in Possibly who could do sign language, either.

Did Jack just hang around his house and do his wood-working, ignoring the world unless he needed his mail, his cigarettes, or groceries?

Standing in his kitchen and contemplating how quiet Jack's life must have been, the lack of noise was suddenly deafening. But also, overwhelming. I found myself dashing through the house, out through the screened-in porch, and into the yard, mildly panicked. Jack stood from his position leaning over his table project, a carving tool in hand, as I barreled down the stairs.

My eyes were probably wide with panic, my breath was coming in gasps, and I was still in my pajamas. Jack probably thought I'd gone crazy.

He eyed me for a moment, then set his tool down on the table and turned both palms up and held them parallel to his chest, slightly moving them back and forth.

What? I knew that one.

"Nothing," I said, suddenly very aware of how freaked out so much quiet had made me. "Just, uh, coming to see what you were up to, Jack."

A moment passed before Jack made the "OK" sign, but his facial expression said, more or less, *you're a bit odd.*

Jack started to pick up his tool, but he stopped long enough to pat his thighs, then point at me. I looked down.

Oh, yeah. I was in my boxers.

"Who's gonna see me, Jack?" I asked. "There's, like, seventeen people in this town, and they're all dodging Wyatt's bullets."

As if he somehow heard me, Wyatt's gun went off in the distance.

I both wanted to laugh and scream.

Jack shrugged. *Fair enough,* he seemed to mean, because he picked up his carving tool and went back to doing whatever he had been doing to the tabletop. From what I could see just a few paces away, he was carving grooves—almost like tunnels—along the wood of the tabletop. Twists and turns, running from one end to the other. Why someone would pay for a table that had been gouged all to shit was beyond me, but that was Jack's job. He made and restored furniture. Whatever he thought was best.

Instead of standing there like a stalker, staring at Jack as he carved the table up, I found myself wanting to stretch my legs and shake off the rest of the sleep that clung to my brain. Jack's backyard was pretty much the field that surrounded house and a grove of trees several yards from the backdoor. Basically, property that probably belonged to the City of Possibly, state or federal parks, but proximity to his house made it Jack's backyard.

I found myself walking through the yard, back and forth, one side to the next, still in my bare feet. So early in the summer, the grass was still green and lush, early morning dew clinging to it. It was like walking on freshly cleaned carpet that hadn't dried all the way. A mist still clung to the ground of the wooded area behind Jack's house, but I was sure once the sun rose more within the hour, it would burn away.

When walking around the backyard of Jack's property didn't seem to shake my feelings of being overwhelmed by the quiet of the house, I headed to the front yard. Maybe a change of scenery, even so subtly, would help? I paced back and forth in the yard, not caring that anyone might wander by and see me in my boxers. Back and forth, my bare feet slid across the dewy early morning grass as I tried to calm myself down.

Being on the road for so long had turned me into someone who found silence unbearable. I hadn't lived anywhere so quiet in a long time. There was always people's voices or the sound of movement and life all around me all day long. Even at night, while drifting off to sleep in a motel bed, I could hear life going on around me. At Jack's, even in the middle of the morning, it sounded like I was living in a tomb.

You've only been here, like, a day and a half, Jordan. Calm down. I thought to myself.

How could less than forty-eight hours unnerve me like it had? Sure, sudden changes in people's routines and lifestyles could kind of make them go nutty for a bit—but usually it took more than a day and a half to sink in and really get to them. In fact, I had felt myself going crazy in the span of minutes just standing in Jack's quiet kitchen.

Maybe I should have left the radio on? I thought to myself.

Maybe that would be the solution—leaving a radio or T.V. on at all times. At least until I had adjusted to life around Jack's place. If I talked to Jack and explained that I was used to noise all of the time, he'd probably let me keep the radio in my room—or wherever I was in the house. And if I wasn't in the house, I'd just have to make sure I was with Jack. Listening to him chip away at a wood-working project would keep my mind off of the quiet.

Just as the thought of how to solve my problem entered my head, I looked up as I was crossing the yard once again, and movement near the graveyard down the road caught my eye. I paused, my toes wriggling in the slippery grass, wondering what could have possibly been moving in the graveyard to catch my eye. I stood at the edge of the yard, squinting as I peered down the road.

It's All Over Now, Baby Blue was drifting on the morning breeze from downtown Possibly.

For a few moments, all I could see was the handful of trees and the headstones shadowed by their sprawling branches. However, just as I was going to turn around and go talk to Jack about all of the quiet, I saw movement again. A gasp nearly shot from my mouth as a dark figure moved out from under the shadows cast by the trees.

A person swathed in a black cloak, complete with hood, stepped out from under the tree, moving through the mist that hung in the graveyard like that at the back of Jack's property. I watched as the dark figure approached a headstone, their face shadowed by the hood over their head, and stopped to stare down at the stone monument. No breath or sound escaped my lips as I stood rigid, watching the cloaked figure just stand there, staring down at the headstone. My heart was thundering in my chest as the person stood still as death right there in the mist. My mouth felt like a desert and my palms were suddenly sweaty.

Then, as quickly as they had appeared from the shadows cast by the trees, they slipped back into the shadows and disappeared. My heart felt like a hammer against my breastbone as I turned around, nearly slipping in the grass, and raced to the backyard. Jack was still chiseling his patterns in the table when I slid to a stop at the other end of the wooden project.

"There's some weirdo in the graveyard, Jack!" I gasped as I slammed my hands down on the table.

The jostling my slap created made Jack look up at me, annoyance suddenly etched all over his face. He dropped his tool and signed "what" again.

I took a deep breath. "Somebody," I said, "in a black hooded cloak is in the graveyard! Acting like a freaking weirdo!"

With a roll of his eyes and a shrug of his shoulders, Jack reached for his tool again, brushing me off—which really pissed me off.

"Damnit, Jack!" I slapped the table again, which made him scowl at me. "Why is some weirdo in the graveyard this time of morning in a cloak looking like the Grim Reaper?"

Jack dropped his tool on the table, a resounding "clunk" filling the air. He began patting at his pockets, first his shirt pocket, then his hip pockets, before his hands moved around to the seat of his pants. Finally, he found what he was searching out. He motioned me over impatiently and began flipping through the notepad as I was rounding the table.

I waited patiently for Jack to write his thought.

People have the right to mourn whenever they want, Jordan. His odd block letters had said.

"Nah." I waved him off. "This person was a grade-A weirdo. They, like, appeared out of the shadows, then disappeared again. It. Was. Freaky."

Jack scowled and began to write again.

"Oh, forget them." I stopped him. "What about that Wyatt guy and his gun? Or the weirdo, uh, Levi Lee outside of the coffee shop? He pretends he's invisible. And Sofia? At the post office? She needs a Danielle Steele novel stat. Grandy? I think his parents are inbred. Some guy is digging up Liberty Lane while the cops just watch, some guy keeps screaming this girl's name and jumping off the bridge, and the radio plays one damn song *all day long*. This town is majorly weird, Jack."

Jack held a finger up gruffly, his mouth twisted up in frustration, then began to write again. Once more, I had to wait for Jack to give me a response to my multiple questions. Or non-questions. They were really just observances. Finally, Jack was shoving the notepad in my face again.

Just because people are different than you doesn't mean there's something wrong with them.

Jack waited for me to have enough time to read the paper, then he shoved it at me again, his way of saying I needed to read it again. A few moments later, he threw the notepad down on the table and glared at me. He reached up and wrapped both hands around his throat loosely as he scowled.

I felt like shit immediately.

"Jack," I said, "man, I'm sorry. I didn't mean that people who are, uh, different than me, uh, are weird. You know I didn't mean anything by that."

Jack's hands fell from his throat and he snatched up his tool. His eyes went back to the table as he started to violently chip away at the tabletop. The scowl didn't leave his face, but Jack was taking his anger out on the table instead of me.

"Jack," I said, "come on, man. You know I didn't—"

Jack stood up from working just long enough to wave me off.

Get out of here!

That's what his waving arm told me. I didn't need expertise in sign language to understand his intention. I wanted to stand there and try to explain myself further to Jack so he wouldn't think that I thought that *he* was weird, but I knew that would only make things worse. The way his mouth was curled up in a scowl, the hurt in his eyes, I knew that I needed to walk away.

So, I did.

"Sorry, man," I muttered as I walked towards the front yard once more.

The only sound that reached my ears was the scraping of Jack's tool on the table and the sound of *It's All Over Now, Baby Blue* in the distance.

Back at the front yard, I risked a glance towards the graveyard again. The mist was dissipating and no hooded figure was in sight. So, I climbed the front steps to the house and let myself back inside. My feet carried me on auto-pilot up the two flights of stairs to my room. I grabbed my phone off of the desk on my way to the bed and fell onto it.

My room was already getting warm.

And I didn't have any messages from my mom.

I opened the text messaging app to tap out a message to her.

Come get me! Jack already hates me. Why did you leave me here in this crazy place?

But I stopped myself. Mom wouldn't turn around to pick me up. She had left me in Possibly because I was cramping her style anyway. She had offloaded me on Jack—my stepfather I hadn't seen in a decade—because…I didn't know why. Life had been okay on the road. Maybe not great; but it was okay.

I started to tap out a message again. Just to ask if she was okay.

There was no signal.

At least that made me feel a little less crappy.

Maybe Mom hadn't messaged or called because my phone hadn't been picking up a tower in the armpit of Texas? It wasn't that she had already forgotten she had a son.

MY FRIEND, THE MOON

Before being ditched in Texas to live with Jack, I'd never really done something like sit in bed and stare out the window at the moon and stars. I'd never sat in the dark of my mind and the silence of my loneliness, thinking about my life. My life—my every day existence—was full of noise and movement. The sounds of the road and theaters and motels were my constant companions. I never really had friends to talk to—not even via text. I never really stayed anywhere long enough to meet people my own age. My friends lived in the T.V. or on the radio. Or maybe, for a single day, some kids I swam with at the motel swimming pool.

Those friendships were fleeting. If they were even friendships. They were just one lonely boy searching out temporary companionship from other kids who had some other city or state to be in the following day. Except they were going somewhere new on vacation or back home. Sooner or later, when I left a motel, it was so Mom could move us into a new motel in a new town where she had found work. I'd never know for how long.

After a while, at least, once I stopped being a stupid kid with stars in his eyes, I realized that trying to make friends was pointless. Eventually, I stopped trying to play Marco Polo in the pool with other kids who were staying for a night or two. I stopped talking to kids I saw at the vending machines. I stopped trying to be friendly with the kids who lived near the motel who walked by on their way to the corner store or to the movies…or wherever kids with a permanent home go to have fun. I started to think of myself as a desert tortoise.

Desert tortoises live on their own in the desert. Naturally. They only meet up to mate or to share a burrow during hibernation. Even when a momma desert tortoise lays eggs, she digs a hole, lays the eggs, covers them, and leaves them, rarely ever to return. The hatchlings, no bigger than a quarter, are on their own from birth. Sink or swim. Maybe one day they'd share a burrow during hibernation if ever their paths crossed again. My mom and I hibernated together at night at motels, but otherwise, I was on my own. We shared our burrow. But I spent my days in the desert alone, wandering, foraging, and waiting for another hibernation period. Night time was good. Sleep was good. Because I wasn't alone then. Usually. Sometimes Mom spent the night with one of my "uncles."

Yeah. I'm sixteen. I know what they were doing.

But that was me. A desert tortoise.

No real purpose other than to exist, forage, hibernate and, eventually, maybe one day help to perpetuate the species.

Then I'd have someone to abandon like I'd been. Make someone feel as rotten as I did most of the time, though I didn't know it. Okay. I did know it. I just never had time to sit in the quiet and think about it much.

And I never had anyone to share that thought with when it popped into my head. So, not only did I discover I was a tortoise, I only had myself to share it with when I discovered it. That's the true definition of loneliness.

When you get good news, who do you call first?

I didn't have an answer for that.

I had me. The tortoise.

Up in my room on the third floor of Jack's house, I had the time and quiet needed to really think about life. I found myself that night, sitting cross-legged on the bed in front of the dormer windows, staring out at Possibly. The inky outlines of downtown in the distance, standing quietly as the stars and moon shone down placidly. Shadows are usually black, right? With the moon and stars shining brightly, and no light pollution to speak of, the shadows looked a little blue. Maybe the town of Possibly felt lonely sometimes, too?

My phone was laid on my thigh, its screen dark. It had been almost three whole days and Mom hadn't bothered to text or call. Not even to see if I was okay and if Jack was fine with me staying with him. I would've been fine if she didn't want to tell me what she was doing—it probably wouldn't have been anything I hadn't seen her do a million times before—but she could have at least shown interest in what I was doing. Shown concern for my well-being.

Was that too much to ask?

Jack wasn't really much of a talker. I didn't have any friends to text. Mom could have at least helped make me feel a little less lonely by shooting off a *"How are you, Jordy?"* text. As I stared out at the blue glow of the moon on the rooftops of the buildings in Possibly, I realized that maybe I could create a friend.

My head rolled back to stare up at the moon, high in the sky, swollen with appropriated sunlight and the hopes cast off by dreamers all over the world who were fast asleep. The moon has no light or hope of its own, but it borrows some each day.

Maybe the moon could be my friend? I could tell it my thoughts. Who else did the moon have to talk to, anyway? The moon might be lonely. How many people give it the time of day? Ask it how it's doing? I could sit on the bed and tell the moon how I felt.

Just as I contemplated this ridiculous—and possibly insane—idea, the barn off in the distance, down by the creek, caught my eye. Lights were coming from it once again. Though, this time, it didn't appear as though lasers were coming from its roof. Instead, it looked like the soft glow put off by white Christmas lights.

How does it look like lasers and lights are coming out of the roof but I can't see the source of the lights?

I watched, mesmerized for several minutes, wondering what was going on at the barn. Finally, I pushed the middle dormer open again and listened to the breeze. Just like the first night, a song was riding the wind, but it was too faint for me to make out. And, just like that, the lights and the song were gone. Possibly was pitch black and my eyes were adjusting to the darkness once more.

I touched my phone screen.

Midnight.

The wind and I were each other's friends for a minute as I listened to the quiet and watched the darkness of the town. Finally, I shut the middle dormer once more, staring at the barn for a moment longer through the glass.

I slipped out of my shirt, threw it on the floor, and crawled under the covers.

THEY'RE AN ARTIST, NOT A GOVERNMENT AGENT

"So, I'm thinking it's a night club or something," I said as Jack inspected the channels he'd dug in the top of the table. "I mean, the first night I was here, there were, like, lasers coming out of the roof. Last night, it was Christmas lights. Kind of. And I heard music each night."

Jack focused on his work.

"What is it?" I asked.

Jack's eyes never left the table and his fingertip ran along a channel, inspecting it for depth and consistency as I blathered on at the other end of the table.

The two of us had risen early—as we had every day since I had arrived—and ate a breakfast of cereal. I didn't realize it when I'd had breakfast at Jack's the first morning, but he liked the same cereal I did. It didn't dawn on me until the morning after seeing the Christmas lights at the barn, but it struck me as incredibly lucky. I wouldn't have known how to approach food likes and dislikes with Jack. Not that I didn't feel like I couldn't talk to him about not liking the food he had on hand, but it would feel rude to tell him I didn't like the free food he provided each day.

So far, he was batting a thousand in the food department.

"Come on, Jack?" I pleaded. "If there's some cool place to go hang out at night, that'd be cool. There's nothing in this town! A club would be cool. I mean, if it's all ages and all. Not if it's only twenty-one and up. That would suck because then that would mean there is something cool here, but—"

Jack looked up at me and held a hand up.

Stop. He was saying. But he wasn't upset. He was amused.

After it was clear that I wasn't going to keep blathering on with questions and thoughts about the barn, Jack reached for his back pocket again. His notepad came into view and he flipped through to find a page to write upon. I tried to wait patiently, but my thoughts about the cool things that could be going on at the barn had me bouncing on the balls of my feet. When Jack had finally held the notepad out for me to read, my heart sank.

It's not a club. It read.

"Then what is it?" I asked desperately. "Like, I don't know, a missile silo or something? Are they doing strange government experiments or something?"

Jack rolled his eyes and began scribbling again. I waited, still bouncing on the balls of my feet as I waited for more written communication.

Auguste Anderson lives there.

My heart sank further. Jack held a finger up and started writing again.

Artist. But I don't know anything about the lights. I was in bed.

Jack showed me his last message, then shrugged at me.

"Well, shit." I kicked at the ground. "Uh, sorry."

Jack looked amused. He scratched out another message.

Sorry.

"It's okay," I said after looking at the message. "It's not your fault this town is boring. No offense."

Jack sat the notepad down and began running his finger along the grooves in the table again. What he was checking for so thoroughly, I wasn't sure. In fact, I didn't even know why he'd cut up the tabletop like he had. When I looked down at it, it looked like...*an ant farm?* Like those plastic ant farms you fill with chunky sand, then add ants, and you can view the way they dig their tunnels through the clear glass sides? That's what the top of the table looked like, but without the glass covering to keep anything inside.

"So," I kicked my toe at the ground again, "what's the school situation around here? I mean, I guess I've been kind of homeschooled by Mom. Is there even a high school here? Or are you going to break out a bigger notepad to teach me more about the three Rs or what?"

Jack looked up at me, a frown on his face. His hands started to move rapidly.

"Jack," I said, "sign language? I'm rusty. Remember?"

His head fell back and he would have groaned if he was able. Instead, he reached for his notepad and started to scrawl his indistinct block letters again.

Kids around here go to The Pueblo.

"What's that?" I asked immediately. "The high school or something? I haven't seen it downtown, so—"

Jack was scribbling again.

It's the building next to Starbuck's.

I had to think about the layout of Possibly for a moment before I realized what he was talking about at first.

"The...*mosque?*" It suddenly dawned on me. "That's...a school?"

Jack nodded and held his hand up to tilt back and forth.

"Uh, why's it called *The Pueblo?*"

Jack shrugged.

"Okay." I relented. "I mean, it's a mosque. But whatever. The kids around here go to school there?"

Jack nodded.

"I guess I should go check it out." I shrugged. "I'll be going there in a few months."

A thought that made my cheeks go red suddenly struck me.

"I mean," I said, "you know, if I'm still here and everything. I mean, yeah. I didn't mean to—"

Jack stopped me with a shrug and his own reddening cheeks.

I had asked Jack about the school in town, insinuated that I knew I would still be stuck living with him when the school year came around, and assumed he would be okay with that. I'd also made it clear that I was well aware that Mom wasn't coming back for me anytime soon. Of course, that was an assumption as well, but since she hadn't even sent a text in three days, it was likely I wouldn't hear from her at all for a long time. Unless I texted or called her first.

If I can get a signal in this town.

Maybe I'll have to walk back up to the highway?

The fact that I'd made all of my assumptions and insinuations was what had made Jack's cheeks rosy, too, I'm sure. Having me around, after being alone for a decade, and allowed his peace and quiet, was probably not ideal for him. To assume that he would want to continue on with our temporary arrangement, long term, after three days of staying with him was…*insane.*

Jack and I barely even knew each other. In fact, we were virtually strangers. My mom had married Jack when I was still a toddler. Then, when I was six-years-old, before I could really make any solid, long-lasting memories, she had swept me away to live on the road. I hadn't seen or talked to Jack in those ten years. My mom had dumped me off with a stranger, essentially. A stranger I was now assuming would be pleased as hell to have me hanging around all of the time. Or, at least, until I was old enough to go off and do my own thing, just like my mom had done.

"Um," I was kicking the toe of my shoe at the ground again and Jack was inspecting the tabletop awkwardly, "so, what are you doing here?"

Jack shrugged, avoiding my eyes.

"I can help," I offered. "If you want?"

Jack didn't respond.

"I don't really know anything about, uh, carpentry, but I'll fetch tools or whatever," I said. "You can teach me something?"

Jack shook his head, still looking down.

"Oh, okay."

Jack slumped, then reached for his notepad. My fingers played along the edge of the table as I waited for what he had to say.

I work better alone. I have a deadline. Maybe next time.

He wasn't looking at me as he held the notepad out for me to read.

"Okay."

Jack slid the pen into the wires of the notepad and stuffed the notepad into his back pocket, still avoiding my gaze. That was the final say in the matter. Jack had made it clear where we stood in regards to his feelings about my presence all day long.

"Got it," I said, slowly backing away from the table. "Yeah. I'll leave you to it, man. Maybe I'll go check out The Pueb— the coffee shop or something?"

Jack nodded, then started, looking as though he'd had a thought. He reached into his hip pocket and extracted a bill, then held it out to me. The same twenty bucks I'd returned to him when I had gotten back from getting his smokes at Grandy's. Tentatively, I stepped forward and took the bill from him, neither of us meeting each other's eyes. I stuffed the bill into my own hip pocket.

"Thanks," I said. "Um, I'll be back later?"

Jack nodded, his attention back on the table.

So, I turned and did my best to will away the redness I could still feel burning in my cheeks. When I rounded the house, out of sight of Jack, I slumped, my shoulders and head falling forward. At first, I thought I might go check out the barn— where the Andersons lived. But even that idea couldn't make me feel better. So instead, I decided that I really would go check out Starbuck's. If a guy in a green screen suit and a pirate ship couldn't make me forget things—especially with Wyatt roaming around firing his gun—nothing could.

Eventually, I'd find out what was up with the lights at the barn in the middle of the night. But my gut was too twisted up in knots to satisfy my curiosity that morning. If there's something that's good for a sour stomach, it's coffee. Right?

THE RAINBOW WALKWAY

D ue to the fact that the strange guy in the work boots, bib overalls, plaid shirt, and straw hat was taking his pickaxe to Liberty Lane outside of AMOR once again, I didn't make it directly to Starbuck's for a cup of coffee. Like the day before, a police officer was leaning up against the building next door to the radio station, watching the man work. *I Only Want to Be with You* by Dusty Springfield was the song du jour on AMOR, but I wasn't sure where I remembered the song from well enough to remember the name or artist. It was funny, standing there, watching the man take the pickaxe to the street with the song coming from all directions from speakers spread throughout town. Strange metallic "clangs" interspersed with the echoey sound of the song was distracting. It was probably just what I needed to take my mind off of my encounter with Jack and the humiliation I'd thrust upon myself.

For more than was probably a good idea, I stared at the man knocking out a hole in the concrete of one of the main streets of downtown Possibly. Then I'd watched the cop for a while, wondering why he just leaned against the building and smiled at the man doing his…*work?* Upon inspecting the man and his work for a bit longer than I had previously, I realized that I had been right. He was knocking out pieces of the concrete and replacing them with different colored bricks, all of them in a different color of the rainbow. His holes and placement were a bit erratic and scattered—he certainly hadn't kept up a pattern—but I could see what he was attempting to do.

A street made of rainbows.

It was kind of cool. Odd, but cool. The fact that the police officer—and apparently, everyone else in town—was fine with the man doing it was extraordinary. Everywhere else I'd ever been would have at least arrested a person for doing such a thing. At best, a huge fine would be doled out to the person caught doing what this man had been doing for what looked like some time. At worst, someone would get thrown into jail anywhere else in the country. For how long, who knows? Probably a lot longer than anyone would want to spend in jail.

The tram started to roll down Liberty Lane, towards the other end by the creek, as I stood there watching the man tear up the street. The conductor gave me a nod as he rolled by at a pace slower than a person strolls, and I nodded back. I forced myself to smile. If you're polite to the crazies, they tend to leave you alone. Or, at least, they don't act as crazy around you. That's what I've found everywhere I've ever been, anyway.

As I stood there watching the man tear up the street, I felt like everyone in town was watching me, even though I knew they weren't. I was familiar with the feeling. Embarrassing the hell out of yourself does that to a person.

Why'd I have to talk to Jack about school and stuff?
The guy probably didn't even want me around.
Why hasn't Mom texted or called me?

Thoughts swirled through my head and my heart couldn't decide which emotion to settle on as my eyes glazed over until I wasn't really watching the man tear up the street anymore. Sure, I was looking in his general direction, but I really wasn't seeing much. What had just happened at Jack's place kept replaying in my head. Why had I even mentioned my thoughts about school and the future? In fact, why did those things even pop into my head? It had only been a few days since Mom had dropped me off at the end of Two-Mile Trail.

As I'd walked down the dirt road, lugging my suitcases along, the thought of Mom eventually returning—probably before summer was over—and saving me from Possibly had been on my mind. Why had I suddenly shifted from thinking about Mom rescuing me at some point soon to thinking about where I would be going to school in a few months?

Then it hit me.

I'd been on the road with Mom for a decade. Since I was six years old. It was the only life I'd known for a long time. But it wasn't really a *good* life. Don't get me wrong, I love my mom and everything, but bouncing from city to city, motel to motel, having a different *uncle* every time—it wasn't great. In fact, I didn't really like it all that much. At least, not once I realized how lonely it was to be on the road with an underemployed actress.

So, when I realized that I had a chance to stay in one place for a while and maybe make a friend or…something…it had excited me.

But I'd gotten ahead of myself.

Without me realizing it, my feet had been spurred into action by my thoughts. I didn't want to stand around being ticked off and embarrassed. My feet had an idea of how to keep my mind occupied and distracted from the last few hours. A minute later, I found myself walking up to the big pirate ship in the center of downtown. A cup of coffee would make me feel better. Especially one loaded with chocolate, milk, and foam.

There was no longer a man in a green-screen suit waiting out front. Instead, it looked like Levi Lee had given up on being one with the hull of Starbuck's. Instead, he had decided that dressing in all silver from head to toe, plus applying silver make up to his exposed skin, and walking around like a robot was the thing to do. Levi Lee had on a silver tux—which I didn't figure they sold in Possibly—a silver top hat, silver shoes, silver socks, and his hands and face had been painted silver. He was doing a passable robot walk, but it wasn't perfect. When he saw me approach, he raised an arm jerkily and waved back and forth like a metronome.

"Hello, new guy!" he announced.

"Hello. New. Guy," I repeated in a robot voice.

"Right!" Levi Lee announced. "Hello. I. Am. Levi. Lee."

"Pretty good, man." I congratulated him on the voice. "Uh, give up on the green suit or something?"

Levi Lee nodded jerkily. He was definitely better at being a robot than he was being part of Starbuck's hull. I watched him for a minute as he moved his arms and legs as if they were on screws and pins, moving them robotically as he walked and waved—sometimes at nothing at all. His head turned back and forth smoothly, as though upon a well-oiled caster. Every movement was a little too smooth and quickly performed, though. Levi Lee had the basics down, but he wasn't fully convincing as a robot. However, I didn't have the heart to tell him that he should rehearse more. Of course, I didn't know why he wanted to be a robot—or part of the hull—so, I didn't know what he'd be rehearsing for, really.

No one stopped, aside from myself—to watch Levi Lee perform his strange robot routine outside of Starbuck's. In fact, while I stood there watching him, three different people entered the coffee shop and one left, and none of them even seemed to notice him. He definitely should have tried being a hull that day. He was more than invisible to everyone except me.

"You're doing pretty good, man." I only lied a little. "Pretty soon, people will think that robots are taking over Possibly."

"You really think so?" Levi Lee stopped his movements immediately and gasped with pleasure.

"Yeah." I shrugged. "Just stop breaking character, ya' know?"

Levi Lee kicked at the ground, realizing he had messed up his routine yet again.

"You'll get it," I said. "Just keep working."

Levi Lee went back into a robot pose and began moving his arms, legs, and head as he had been before, though he seemed to have lost a little confidence.

"Just don't get so mad at yourself when you mess up," I suggested. "That makes you nervous or something, I think."

"You're. Right," he responded robotically and his movements improved slightly.

"You're getting it, man!" I cheered him on.

Levi Lee let a small smile come to his lips but I could tell his concentration ratcheted up higher as he tried to make himself seem even more robotic. It suddenly dawned on me that Levi Lee just needed someone to believe in him and encourage him. He was a pretty friendly guy, and he was always willing to carry on a conversation, so maybe he would talk to me about the people in Possibly since Jack wouldn't.

"Hey, Robot Levi Lee?" I asked.

"Yes?" he responded perfectly as a robot.

"Would you mind being human Levi Lee for a minute?" I asked. "Just take a little break? Maybe you can help me with something."

Levi Lee immediately fell out of the robot routine, looking excited as a puppy dog at the opportunity to help out someone else. I was just glad he had on normal pants that weren't tight like the green-screen suit I'd seen him in the first few days I'd been in town.

"I'm at your service, my good man." Levi Lee bowed his head.

"Awesome." I tried not to wince at his weirdness. "Do you know anything about the barn? Ya' know? Further down the creek and just two streets over?"

"Well, sure." Levi Lee grinned. "You can't really miss a big red barn in Possibly, after all."

"Right," I said. "But I was wondering if you could tell me what goes on in there?"

"How do you mean?"

"Well, like, late at night I see lights coming from there," I explained. "Lasers one night and then something that looked like the glow of Christmas lights. I just wanted to know what that's all about?"

"Hmmmm." Levi Lee reached up to scratch his chin.

"Jack said that Auguste Anderson lives there, and—"

"They do," Levi Lee agreed.

"—I don't understand why there's a light show every night?" I continued. "Everywhere else in town is pitch black at night. Except the barn. Well, I think the lights always go off at midnight, but…well…what's going on there?"

Levi Lee thought about this for a few moments. A few more customers went in and out of Starbuck's. The smells coming out of the place each time the door opened were heavenly.

"They're an artist," Levi Lee explained. "So, maybe they have the lights on so they can see whatever they're creating?"

"Yeah," I said, "that sounds reasonable. But *lasers*?"

Levi Lee chuckled.

"I didn't see the lasers," he said. "That is odd."

"So…no idea?"

"Not really," he said. "I'm sure that if the lights are keeping you up at night that—"

"Oh! No!" I stopped him. "Nothing like that. I'm not complaining at all. Just curious about the barn and the lights."

Levi Lee just smiled, glad that there wasn't a problem.

"I guess I'm just nosy," I said.

"Well," he said, "if I see them, I'll let you know. Maybe you can meet them. Are you going to stick around and have a coffee? We have Nutella Lattes today."

He leaned in to wink at me when he said the coffee name, as though anything about Nutella or a latte was all that revolutionary. Putting coffee, milk, and chocolate together—no matter what type of chocolate, coffee, and milk it was—was not all that unique. I liked Nutella all right, and coffee was good, but putting the two together didn't make me squeal with joy.

"Do they have anything to eat in there?" I asked, glancing over at the door. "I'm kind of hungry, actually."

"Cookies, biscotti, scones, muffins—a sweet for every tooth, my good man," Levi Lee announced. "Just tell Starbuck you're hungry. He'll tell you what's good."

"Uh, Starbuck?"

"Starbuck." He nodded. "He's the owner. Of *Starbuck's*."

"You've gotta be kidding me." I snorted. "I thought maybe the owner kind of plagiarized the name or something."

"Of course not!" Levi Lee stood erect defiantly. "Starbuck was the first mate of the Pequod! Starbuck—*who owns this coffee shop*—was named after a great fictional character from American literature!"

"Oh," I said as I looked up at the pirate ship. "Um, but wasn't the Pequod a whaling ship from Moby Dick?"

This didn't seem to process well with Levi Lee as his head cocked to the side and he gave me a curious look, as though I had spontaneously grown a second head. Which was kind of funny, considering he was dressed and made up like a robot. After a few moments, I realized Levi Lee wasn't going to be able to come up with a response.

"So, Starbuck owns the place?" I asked.

"Owns and operates!" Levi Lee answered enthusiastically, his confusion suddenly gone. "He'll be behind the counter. Just let him know that Levi Lee sent you and he'll set you up, my good man!"

"All right," I said. "Thanks, man. Good luck with the robot thing."

Levi Lee gave me a strange, robotic salute, and then he was back to moving his arms, legs, and head as though he was once again a robot. I still had no idea whose benefit his act was for since not many people came or went from Starbuck's and no one except for me stopped to watch anyway. Instead of worrying about Levi Lee's performance art, I pulled the door in the hull open and stepped into the air-conditioned interior of Starbuck's.

Immediately, I realized that it wasn't just the exterior of the building that looked like a pirate ship. In fact, it seemed like Starbuck's really was a ship. It had just been hauled out to Possibly, the bottom stabilized, and the interior converted into a shop. Wood plank walls, wood masts and beams, and portholes were the main décor. Nets of varying sizes hung everywhere, as well as stuffed fish and other aquatic paraphernalia. A few circular wooden standing tables were in the center of the room. The coffee bar and check-out counter itself were to the left of the door—or towards the stern. That was the only part of Starbuck's that looked modern. Everything was wood, rope, and glass.

It was…a lot. But it was cool. I really felt like I was below deck in a pirate ship. If a fish swam past one of the porthole windows, I wouldn't have been all that shocked. The boat was *that* authentic—and we were in Possibly, Texas, after all. Anything odd seemed to be possible.

Huh. Maybe that's the reason they named it such an odd thing?

Behind the counter—which, of course, was all wood as well—I found a middle-aged man, dressed, unsurprisingly, like a pirate. Red and white striped, long-sleeved, billowy shirt, black vest, pirate hat, and eye patch showed over the counter. I assumed this was the namesake of the coffee shop. When he saw me approaching the counter, and especially since no other customers were present, the man smiled with pleasant surprise, one gold tooth showing. Because, why not?

"Ahoy, me matey!" he growled at me, raising one fist in the air triumphantly. "Are ye' here for a coffee?"

It'd be odd if I came to a coffee shop for a pizza. I had thought to myself.

"Yeah," I said cautiously. "Uh, Levi Lee—the robot guy outside—told me to say he sent me. I'm new to town and stuff. He said you had Nutella Lattes today?"

"Aye!" The man barked. "That we do, me matey! Wouldjer be likin' one?"

"I'll try it." I shrugged. "I'm also kind of hungry. What have you got?"

"Right over here," the man said, waving his arm at a display case to the left of the counter. "Ye' just see what ye' might be interested in while I make yer coffee!"

"Yeah," I said. "Okay."

I watched the pirate—Starbuck, I was still assuming—go about whipping up a Nutella Latte behind the counter while I checked out the treats in the case. The standard snacks were on display. Blueberry muffins. Vanilla iced scones, almond biscotti, a few croissants. Something that looked like banana bread or maybe even slices of carrot cake without icing. Starbuck was a master of his craft—coffee making, that is—because I had barely made my mind up on a giant blueberry muffin when he was handing me my coffee.

"Um," I said, "I'd like a blueberry muffin. They look really good."

"That they are," Starbuck growled jubilantly. "Ye' won't find a better muffin anywhere in town!"

Well, sir, I haven't seen any other place in town that sells muffins. I found myself thinking smart-alecky thoughts again.

Starbuck made a spectacle of pulling out a piece of parchment paper before reaching into the display cabinet with a flourish and grabbing a muffin. He extracted the muffin wrapped in paper and deposited it into a small paper bag he had produced from behind the display case. I took it from him gratefully as he held it over the counter to me. My stomach was positively rumbling. Then I moved down to the cash register—which was painted sea blue and had shells and gold coins glued to it.

"How much do I owe you?" I asked as I struggled to hold my coffee and paper bag with one hand and reach into my pocket with my other hand.

Starbuck inched down to peer at me over the counter with his one eye that wasn't covered with a patch.

"Ye' said you was new to town?" he asked. "An' Levi Lee sentcher here?"

I shrugged. "Yeah."

"First time is free, matey," Starbuck said with a wink of his good eye. "Keep your pieces of eight this time."

"Uh…okay?" I slid my hand that held Jack's twenty back into my pocket. "Thanks."

"Nothin' doin', matey!" Starbuck stood tall and pleased with himself behind the counter, then his good eye shifted when the door squeaked. "*Ahoy, mateys!*"

Starbuck's sudden greeting had me turning my head to see whom he was speaking to at the door. A couple of women were venturing in, their purses clutched at their sides as they talked excitedly to each other about whatever someone found exciting in such a small town. Them, and their purses, had gotten Starbuck's attention, so I felt dismissed. I was sad as I walked away from the counter towards the door since I hadn't had a chance to ask Starbuck about his name and the fact that the coffee shop should be a whaling ship instead. However, since I had gotten a free coffee and a muffin, I didn't let it bother me too much. I exited the pirate ship back out into the late morning warmth of a Texas summer.

Right next door was The Pueblo that Jack had mentioned and had caused me to embarrass myself, so I figured I couldn't do anything better than to check it out. I gave Levi Lee a nod of my head, which he returned, but in a more robotic way. It wasn't perfect, but he was doing much better as a robot than part of the hull.

I wandered over to The Pueblo, a mere six or seven yards away from Starbuck's, wondering how such an odd building popped up in Possibly of all places. As far as I could tell, there wasn't even a church in downtown Possibly. This made a mosque-like building even more unusual. Not that I cared one way or the other—religion wasn't my thing, and mom certainly didn't drag me to religious services while we were on the road.

However, in small town Texas, I would have assumed a Christian church would have dominated the corner of the street instead of a mosque. Possibly often presented the opposite of what I expected, which could be annoying. In this case, it was refreshing.

Way to be progressive, Possibly.

When I walked up to the entrance to The Pueblo, though, I immediately realized that the building was not for Muslim services or anything all that religious. In fact, the sign at the front proclaimed that the place was closed for the day. It also let me know that The Pueblo was actually an "artist studio and exhibition space." So…mosque, yes. Religious? No.

I plopped down on the steps into the building since no one was around and the place wasn't open. I wouldn't likely be in anybody's way if I used the steps to sit on while I drank my latte and ate my muffin. Besides, there was a trashcan right outside the front door that I could utilize when I was done. So, I ate my muffin and sipped my coffee—both of which were possibly the best I'd ever had in my entire life.

Not only was the muffin the fluffiest, lightest cake I'd ever eaten in my life, the sugary, cinnamon-y topping crackled as I chewed, the perfect crispy contrast to the cake. The brightest, freshest blueberries exploded with sweet juice, filling my mouth with the taste of summer. As a more than welcome surprise, a light, airy cream cheese icing filling tunneled down through the center of the cake. Even in all of the big cities I'd visited, I'd never had a muffin as exceptional.

That could be another reason for the name "Possibly." I thought to myself.

I was able to keep an eye on Levi Lee and watch him work on his robot routine. He was practicing opening the doors for patrons who came and went from Starbuck's. He was still not

94

quite robotic, but he was doing well enough. Wyatt's gun went off in the distance—somewhere back by the graveyard, I thought. Emily's name got screamed loudly for all to hear, then the splashing of water in the distance sounded. I ate my muffin and sipped my coffee and tried not to read too much into the crazy behavior of the strange people of Possibly. If I tried to analyze what was going on with everyone to make them so weird, I'd fry my brain.

Grandy was probably sitting outside of his gas station, wondering why birds fly south for the winter and don't send letters back home or something. Sofia was probably mooning over the letters to Shirlene that she had tacked up on the wall of the post office. Since I could hear the pickaxe on Liberty Lane, I assumed the road destroyer and the cop were up to their usual shenanigans.

And *I Only Want to Be with You* by Dusty Springfield sounded from almost every direction. That was the sound of Possibly, Texas:

Thwack!

Clang!

Bang!

Dusty Springfield.

Starbuck's door squeaking.

Emmmmmileeeeeee!

Sploosh!

Thwack!

Clang!

Dusty Springfield.

Starbuck's door squeaking.

The crinkle of my paper bag being wadded up and the slurping of my lips getting the last of the delicious latte out of the cup added to the music of the town. The downtown area was so small that almost anything anyone did that was above a normal speaking voice could be heard all over town. So, everyone in the downtown area contributed to the rhythm and sound of their hometown.

It dawned on me that the one thing I didn't hear—even though there were so many sounds—was chaos. The town did have a rhythm and a structure to its sound. It wasn't random or wild. It was almost like one note being played after another, just each note was slightly different than the previous. But if you sat still and listened carefully, you could pick up the rhythm in your head. Tap your foot along to it if you wanted to do so.

Shaking my head to get rid of such a weird thought, I tossed my wadded-up paper bag into the trash, then sent the paper coffee cup following after. Since I'd had a coffee and a treat from Starbuck's—as freaking delicious as they were—listened to Dusty Springfield, saw Liberty Lane's rainbow walkway, talked to Levi Lee, heard Wyatt's gunshots, and sat outside The Pueblo, I'd done just about everything I could do in downtown Possibly. It dawned on me that there were a few buildings I hadn't checked out—and then there was the strange woman in the tent across from The Pueblo—which was, luckily, opened on the side facing away from me. However, none of them really struck my interest.

Visiting the barn up the creek entered my mind again. However, since I knew that a person actually lived in it, I felt it might be weird to walk up, knock on the door, and ask about their personal business.

I'm sorry, sir and/or madam, but can you tell me what you're doing at midnight around here?

Anyone reasonable would slam the door in my face. After calling me a weirdo or something. The last thing I wanted was for someone to label me a weirdo in a town like Possibly. I couldn't think of anything more embarrassing. Unless, of course, you were labelled a weirdo because your pants *and* underwear fell down to your ankles while walking through town, or something.

Instead of making myself a nuisance to the family in the barn, my mind was pulled in another direction. When a small breeze kicked up in town, I heard the tinkling of the windchimes in the wooded down from Grandy's again. It was so faint up by The Pueblo that I almost missed it. However, the breeze carried the sound enough that my ears caught their tinkling noise.

I rose from the steps of The Pueblo and dusted off the seat of my pants, then cut down the road towards the trail that led into the woods. When I passed the weird miniature reddish-orange circus tent, I glanced over my shoulder at the open flaps. The same lady in the dress, shawl, with mass of hair, was sitting at the barely illuminated table within. When I looked over, my eyes landed on hers, and I realized she had been watching me. She gave me a gentle wave and a smile, as though she knew me already. Of course, she may have felt that since she'd seen me once before I was no longer a stranger?

I had to force myself to turn my head back around to watch where I was going so that I didn't walk into a tree on my way to the trail. Something in my gut fluttered at the thought of the lady in the tent, as though she seemed familiar but I couldn't figure out why. I pushed that thought out of my head as I strolled into the wooded area, my shoes kicking up dust on the path, just like they had on Two-Mile Trail the day I arrived in Possibly. The tinkling of all of the windchimes ahead in the clearing sang out to me as I walked the trail, beckoning me closer. Within a minute, I was coming to the end of the path that led out into the clearing.

Once again, I found myself startled and dashing behind a tree just inside the tree line of the clearing. The boy with the white diamond shape in his hair and on his forehead was looking at the windchimes again. Like the day before, he was dressed strangely. He was wearing black combat boots, laced up to mid shin, cargo shorts, a white tank top, and what looked like a black tutu. An honest to goodness ballerina tutu. Tulle and gauze, black and standing spritely out from his hips, the boy stood there, profile to me, as I watched him from behind the tree I was using as a hiding spot. He didn't seem to notice me; he appeared to be focused intently on the chimes. In fact, it almost looked as if he was talking to one of the chimes in particular.

In front of him, dangling pendulously from a tree, was a rather large windchime, made of old forks and spoons. The boy was mumbling something that I couldn't hear, smiling to himself as he looked up at the chime. I watched as he lifted the side of the tutu to reach into the pocket of his shorts. He pulled out a silver object, which I quickly realized was a fork, and he went about tying the extra fork to the already overburdened chime.

Once the task was complete, he took a step back and admired his work. He seemed to be muttering something else to the windchime, but I could only catch the cadence of his voice, not make out the actual words. Then he closed his eyes languidly and held his arms out and spun slowly in the clearing in front of the chime, a joyous smile on his face.

He is soooooo odd.

Just when I thought the boy might twirl himself until he was dizzy enough to fall, voices echoed down the dirt path towards downtown. At least a few people were walking down the trail towards the clearing in the woods. I glanced over at the boy in his tutu and he had stopped spinning; he was looking towards the opening of the path. For a split second, he seemed frozen in place, as though unsure of what to do. Then he was dodging chimes as he dashed into the woods, carving his own path through the trees towards town.

I stayed behind my tree just off of the trail, waiting to see who was coming towards the clearing full of windchimes. A few moments passed as the voices grew louder, and three teenage boys, probably the same age as me and the boy in the tutu, strolled into view. Obviously, the boy in the tutu had made a wise choice running through the trees towards town. The three boys seemed friendly, and they were laughing and being silly, but I imagined they wouldn't have been very kind if they found a boy in a tutu all by himself. They probably would have taunted him. Or pushed him. Called him names.

As the boys all entered the clearing, I slipped out from behind the tree and dashed back down the path towards Possibly. I didn't want to know why the trio of boys had come to the clearing. Usually, and I say this as a teenage boy myself, a pack of teenage boys is up to no good. Seeing how quickly the boy in the tutu had run from the clearing when he heard their voices was another indication that introducing myself to them was probably a bad idea. At least alone out in the woods. Maybe, I thought as I jogged down the path and back into town, if I saw them at Starbuck's or something, I'd introduce myself. But not when I was alone.

Back at Jack's place, I went to the backyard first, wondering if he had made any progress on his table project. Jack wasn't in the backyard with the table anymore, though. The table had been set upon a tarp and another was laid over it, both of them bound together with bungee cords to keep the table wrapped up. Curious about what was going on, I found my way into the house through the backdoor. Jack wasn't in the kitchen or the living room, and hollering out at him didn't produce any results. Not that he could have hollered back to me to let me know where he was in the house.

Climbing the first flight of stairs, I made my way down the second-floor hallway and knocked gently on Jack's door, wondering if maybe he had laid down for a nap. Or maybe he hadn't felt well. The house was deathly quiet, and the second-floor hallway was like a tomb. After a few moments, I finally heard Jack moving in his bedroom. I expected him to open the door to see what I wanted from him. Instead, after waiting for what seemed like an eternity, listening to him move around, he slid a piece of notebook paper under the door. I read the strange, block letters.

I'll see you tomorrow. Make sure you keep your windows closed tonight. It's going to rain.

That was all he had to say.

I spent the rest of the day hanging around in my room, all alone, with no signal on my phone, feeling like a desert tortoise. Dinner was a couple of sandwiches I made for myself with what Jack had in the fridge and cupboard.

Jack was right.

That night, it began to rain right after the sun went down. It was still raining well into the night as I sat on my bed and stared out of the dormers towards the barn down by the creek. Rivulets of rain water carved their way down the glass, the darkened town only visible when there was lightning in the sky. No lights appeared at the barn that night. But I slept like a baby as rain did its tap dance on the roof and window.

THE BOY FROM THE BARN

Jack refused to come out of his room the next morning as well. Still in my pajamas, my hair sticking up in a million different directions, I stood at his bedroom door and read another note he had slid under the door. Sunlight was dripping through the window at the end of the hall, golden honey that trapped the dust speckles that hung in the air like confetti.

Entertain yourself today. I'm going to stay in bed.

'Entertain myself?' That's what I'd been doing ever since I arrived in Possibly. Well, the first night, Jack and I had watched T.V. together. But it wasn't like he had come up with any other mildly entertaining activities since to keep our minds occupied. Mostly he had stuck to himself and worked on the table in the backyard, sanding, carving, sanding some more. Then covering it all with a tarp so that it wouldn't get wet when the rain came.

After a breakfast comprised of cereal—again—I found myself standing in the backyard, staring at the tarp-covered project Jack had been working on. The temptation to rip the tarp off and really inspect the grooves he had carved into the top was almost overwhelming. However, I could tell that Jack had put a lot of thought and dedication into the project. I didn't want it to get ruined somehow; especially by my hand. Having nothing better to do with my time made the compulsion stronger, though.

I had been staying with Jack for a little over half a week and I'd pretty much seen and done everything downtown Possibly had to offer. There were a few shops that I hadn't really paid much attention to that I could have checked out, but nothing I hadn't already seen looked all that interesting. Also, I had the lingering feeling that I didn't need to get too used to life in Possibly. It was obvious that Jack hadn't expected me to be hanging around at all, let alone long term. For all I knew, he had already texted my mom to let her know that she needed to come and get me as soon as possible.

Even though my stupid phone didn't get good reception in Possibly, Jack's most likely did. His was newer and fancier and was through the local cell service, whichever company that was. Because my phone was such a piece of crap, I couldn't even call my mom to defend myself against whatever Jack had to say about me. I mean, yeah, maybe I was a nuisance, but I hadn't really done anything wrong other than what my mom had made me do. After being dropped off on the highway, I'd walked to Jack's house and asked to stay with him. It hadn't been my choice, after all. So, thinking about Mom and Jack having a private discussion about what a burden I was really annoyed me.

And maybe it was just a little embarrassing to think about.

My cheeks felt hot as I stood and looked at the tarped-up table in the backyard. Mom didn't want me cramping her style on the road anymore, and it was obvious that Jack—though polite about it—didn't really want me around disturbing his peace.

And I wasn't so sure what I wanted.

Maybe I should just watch T.V.?

My toes kicked at the soggy earth, though I really wanted to kick the table. I just couldn't make myself be mad at Jack, though. He hadn't asked for me to come stay with him. He'd made sure I had food and a place to sleep, though. He'd even given me money to buy stuff, though money seemed to be useless in Possibly. Especially if you were the "new guy."

I found myself walking into downtown. Maybe if I walked around the smattering of buildings, I could find something to do that I hadn't seen or thought of before. At least I wouldn't be sitting around Jack's all feeling sorry for myself or mindlessly staring at the T.V. If I'd been a little braver, I would have introduced myself to the guys I'd seen in the windchime clearing. They were probably okay guys—and they would have at least known what was worth doing in such a small town. Maybe they knew of something further away from downtown that was worth doing?

I guess, maybe, Levi Lee will be my friend if I ask.

The thought of walking up to Levi Lee—in whatever costume he was wearing—and asking him to be my friend made me laugh out loud. Having already encountered him a few times, I knew his response would have been enthusiastic and to the affirmative. Levi Lee was definitely the human equivalent of a puppy dog. Eager to please, cheerful, enthusiastic, and good-natured. He'd agree to be my friend even if it wasn't something he expected. But I didn't really want to hang outside of Starbuck's all day and watch him perform, either.

When I passed by the graveyard, my eyes nervously flitted over to the shadows beneath the trees. It was sunny enough that I could quickly discern that no weirdos in black cloaks were hiding in the shadows, waiting to mourn at the headstones. Remembering the person sliding out of the darkness to mourn still sent shivers up my spine. Even if it was one of the regular types of weirdos who lived in Possibly, it had just been odd to see someone dressed like the Grim Reaper, hanging around a misty cemetery early in the morning.

I shook my head to clear that thought away and made my way down Liberty Lane. The guy with the pickaxe and rainbow bricks, the permissive cop, and the lazy tram conductor were up to their usual tricks. When I stopped to actually pay attention to the song du jour at AMOR, I realized Tiny Tim was on rotation yet again. However, this time, they were playing *Ever Since You Told Me You Loved Me (I'm A Nut)*. I didn't know what the DJ at the radio station found so interesting about Tiny Tim's music—but I also hadn't realized I knew so many Tiny Tim songs, either. So, who was I to judge?

Down the length of Liberty Lane I walked, checking out the buildings that weren't AMOR, and I quickly realized that the street also held a small grocery store, an art supply store, a lawyer's office—it could have been an accountant's office— and a "dry goods" store. Whatever the heck that meant. Something told me that it was also owned by the grocery store since they were side by side and a quick glance let me know they sold non-perishable groceries and toiletries and whatnot.

I cut down to the post office when I neared the creek and found that nothing unusual was going on at Sofia's place of work. When I walked by, she saw me through the window and waved, obviously remembering me, so I waved back. I raised my hands in question and she shook her head, letting me know there wasn't any mail for me to pick up for Jack. So, I waved again and cut to my right to head towards Starbuck's.

Levi Lee was outside, doing his robot routine again. He was getting better. When I smiled and waved at him, the corners of his mouth jerkily raised and he mechanically raised his arm, then waved it back and forth like a metronome. *Good for you, Levi Lee.*

I thought about stopping for another coffee since I still had the twenty bucks in my pocket that Jack had given me, but I knew that Levi Lee would talk to me. He was doing so well at his robot routine that I didn't want to ruin his vibe.

Further down the street, at The Pueblo, I saw a few people walking into the building out of the corner of my eye. Wyatt's gun went off in the distance and a cry of *"Emmmmmiiiiiiileeeee!"* sounded by the bridge as I turned to check out the mosque-like building. I smiled to myself as I thought about how I hadn't even twitched when Wyatt's gun went off. I was already getting used to his *poor timing*.

When my eyes settled on a person standing in the doorway of The Pueblo, my breath caught in my throat. At first, the person in the doorway didn't really register with my brain since I had been thinking about the gunshot and the screaming of the guy down at the bridge. However, it finally dawned on me that the person lingering in the doorway of The Pueblo was the kid I'd seen twice in the clearing in the woods. Of course, if it hadn't been for the fact that he had on jeans with a flowery scarf as a belt, flip-flops, and what I realized was his standard tank top, I might not have realized it was him. When he shifted slightly so that I could see the white triangle of hair and matching, mirror-image white triangle of skin on his forehead, I knew I wasn't mistaken.

Instinctively, I wanted to look away, for fear that he might turn and see me staring. I didn't want him to think I was staring for the wrong reason. Like, I didn't want him to think I was going to make fun of his clothes or the...*birthmark?*...on his head. My eyes refused to be averted, though. I stood there, a few yards away from The Pueblo, just staring at the kid as he loitered in the doorway, watching something intently inside of the building. After a few moments, I realized that he was too

105

focused on whatever he was watching to be aware of anyone watching him. So, I did. Watch him, I mean. I stood there, between Starbuck's and The Pueblo, and just stared at him.

The kid's level of concentration on whatever was going on inside of the building was mesmerizing. I'd never seen someone so self-possessed. The way he was dressed, the unusual marking on his forehead and in his hair—surely, he knew that people might be staring at him. However, he didn't seem to care about anything going on around him. He had simply found something that interested him and had shut out the outside world, unconcerned with what people might think of him and what he was doing.

Against my will, I found my feet shuffling towards The Pueblo, drawing me closer to the boy in the doorway. Moments later, I found myself standing behind the kid, close enough that I could reach out and tap him on the shoulder if I wanted. Either he hadn't noticed me move up behind him or he just hadn't cared. Or maybe he thought I was about go into The Pueblo and just hadn't paid me any mind because of it. Regardless, I stood there and stared at the back of him as he stared into the building. I hadn't even bothered to look inside the building to see what it was that had drawn his laser-like focus. Suddenly, it dawned on me that I had been calling everyone in Possibly a "weirdo" and I was being the weirdest of them all.

"Hey." I heard my voice but hadn't remembered willing myself to speak.

The boy jerked slightly at my sudden intrusion. Then, finally realizing that I was speaking to him, he turned his head to look over his shoulder at me.

"What are you doing?" I asked. "Uh, I mean, what are you looking at?"

The boy blinked slowly, as though he had to adjust his focus from what he had been looking at to this person who was nosily asking him about his business.

"What?" He shook his head as if clearing away thoughts. "Uh, what?"

His voice was melodic, yet deeper than I had expected. Maybe his outfits made me think his voice would be higher or child-like. But he had the voice of a grown man, regardless of his fashion sense.

"Uh," I said, "what are you looking at? In The Pueblo?"

Again, the boy was blinking at me, as though coming out of some stupor.

Oh, great. This guy is going to be the weirdest of everyone here. I thought. *Why should I have expected anything else? Look at the way he dresses.*

"Sorry." He sputtered. "I was—they're making anamorphic wire sculptures today. I—I was watching them. It's fascinating."

The two of us just stared at each other for a moment.

"I have no idea what that is," I finally said.

The boy's eyes lit up, and for a moment, I thought he was going to explain what exactly an anamorphic wire sculpture— or whatever—was, but a shadow crossed over his face and he stopped himself from looking so excited.

"Uh, just art stuff?" He shrugged.

"Oh."

"Yeah."

As we stood there, staring at each other again, I let my eyes wander up to the white diamond that looked like it had been stamped on the kid's forehead and hair. When my eyes wandered back to his, he was looking down at his feet. No longer self-possessed, he looked anxious. Obviously, he realized I was a stranger to Possibly, and he had no idea if I was going to be rude to him.

"I'm, uh, Jordan." I reached out with my hand. "Jordan Burke. I'm, uh, Jack Burke's stepson? I'm kind of staying with him. For now."

The kid wiped his hand on the thigh of his jeans, then reached out and gently took my hand. He shook it firmly, though I could tell he was still unsure about me.

"Auguste. Anderson," he answered shyly. "Nice to meet you."

"Yeah. Same." I nodded as our hands slid away.

Suddenly, the kid's last name clicked in my head.

"Anderson?" I asked. "Are you one of the Anderson's who lives in the big red barn down by the creek?"

The boy nervously met my eyes, as though unsure of whether or not he should tell a stranger in town where he actually lived.

"Um," his eyes flittered around, "yeah."

"Sorry," I said. "That was weird. It's just, I've seen your, uh, lights? My bedroom window is pointed in that direction. Jack, uh, told me Auguste Anderson lived there."

"Oh." That seemed to soothe the kid's nerves.

"Yeah."

Again, we were standing in silence, our eyes looking at anything but each other.

"So," I said, "uh, have you always lived here?"

"Yeah."

"That's cool." I nodded slowly. "I'm, uh, from everywhere, I guess?"

I chuckled lightly, hoping that the small joke might break the ice. I really wanted to ask the kid everything about himself—anything to have someone to talk to who seemed relatively normal—but I could tell that would just scare him off.

"Oh."

"Yeah."

We were getting nowhere fast. I was almost tempted to say *'well, nice meeting you,'* and then walk away, but I really had nothing else to do with my time. There were only two more streets in downtown possibly to check out and that would take less than ten minutes. I knew for a fact that those ten minutes would be uneventful. Unless Wyatt actually hit something with one of his bullets.

"Um," I forced myself to continue the conversation, "there's not really a lot to do here, huh? I've been here less than a week and I think I've seen everything in this town."

This brought a small smile to the kid's face, though his eyes still refused to look up at me.

"The coffee at Starbuck's is kind of good," I said. "I didn't know there was a Starbuck's that wasn't, like, part of the big chain of coffee shops."

The kid's smile grew and I could tell he was *this close* to looking up at me.

"Levi Lee is a nice guy," I added.

Those were the magic words. The kid looked up at me.

"A lot of people here are really nice," he agreed. "Have you met Grandy yet? He's the guy who runs the gas station?"

"Um, yeah," I said. "He seemed nice enough."

That was the politest way I felt I could respond. Grandy had, in fact, been nice when I had met him. He'd just been weird. But something told me that mentioning this to the kid—Auguste—was a bad idea. I certainly didn't want to tell him what I thought of Grandy's question about caterpillars and butterflies.

"Yeah," Auguste said with a grin, "he's a little odd. But he's super nice. Promise."

"Oh, yeah." I waved him off. "He was really nice to me. But, yeah. He's a little weird."

Auguste chuckled.

"Yeah." He nodded before looking down at his feet again.

Since he wasn't watching me any longer, I took a second to glance down at his outfit again. His jeans and tank top seemed normal, but the flowery scarf he'd chosen as a belt was obviously an item that he had found in his mother's closet or something. I'd seen plenty of people who experimented with clothes—shedding the idea of what is *boys' clothes and girls' clothes*—all over the country. I'd never seen a teenage guy in a small southern town do it, though.

"I, uh, like your belt," I said.

Compulsively, Auguste's hand grabbed the tail of the scarf and twiddled it with his fingers, though his eyes stayed down.

"Thanks."

That's all he had to say about the scarf.

"So, uh," I tried to think of a way to keep Auguste talking, "what exactly is this town's deal?"

"What?"

"Like," I said, trying to be careful with my words, "everything's…so different…than everywhere else I've been. Maybe, since you've lived here forever, you can tell me about everything? Um, show me around?"

"Uh, yeah, I mean, I guess." Auguste's eyes were suddenly fixed on something at the end of the street by the post office. "I mean, I'm kind of busy today, but tomorrow?"

"Sure." I smiled, relieved that Auguste hadn't scoffed at my suggestion. "I really have nothing to do, so if you—"

"Hey," he interjected, "I have to go. I'll come by Jack's tomorrow morning? We can walk around together?"

"Oh," I said. "Yeah. Sounds good. Auguste."

"Cool." Auguste was already in motion, ducking past me. "I'll see you tomorrow."

I turned to watch Auguste hurry away from The Pueblo and me. He walked down the side of the road towards the post office, his head down. A frown formed on my face as I considered how quickly he had dashed away. Even though he had agreed to show me around town and tell me a little bit about the place, it had seemed to make him nervous. Maybe he didn't intend to actually show up at Jack's the next day at all? Maybe he had just said that as a nice way to get out of talking to someone *he* thought was a weirdo?

My eyes trailed along the street, looking up towards the post office, and I finally spotted what had caught Auguste's attention when we had been standing together. The group of teenage boys from the clearing in the woods were walking down the street towards Auguste, laughing and joking. I started to cringe, wondering what would happen when they passed Auguste on the street. Would they shove him? Point at his scarf belt and laugh?

As the small group of boys drew closer to Auguste, he kept his head down, staring at the road beneath his feet. However, the boys had already taken notice of Auguste and were getting closer and closer to him. My whole body was tensing up, waiting to see what would happen. I've never really had to consider what I would do if I saw someone being bullied. Would I run for help? Jump in and help the bullied? Would I run and pretend I hadn't seen anything?

I didn't have to think about it for long. As he made his way by Starbuck's, Auguste started to pass the group of boys. My whole body was like a board as I waited for the inevitable. But something strange happened.

"Hey, Auggie!" One of the boys announced in the distance, raising his hand.

Auguste didn't look up from the road beneath his feet, but he raised his hand to give the other kid a high-five. The other two boys chimed in with *'heys'* as well, and the group of boys passed Auguste without any issue. I frowned to myself, not unhappy with what had happened, but confused by the nice display between the boys and Auguste.

Possibly was so weird.

But maybe that wasn't a bad thing.

When I got back to Jack's place, he was nowhere to be found, yet again. I checked the floor by his bedroom door. He hadn't left me a note. I could hear him moving around in his room, so I almost knocked to make sure that he was okay. That *we* were okay. Instead, I went up to my room and checked my phone.

No messages.

No calls.

No signal.

I climbed up and sat on my bed and stared out the window at Possibly.

MYSTIC MOLLY

Knocking, somewhere off in the distance, woke me up the following morning. Wrapped up like a burrito in the covers on my bed, it took a second for me to even realize where I was. I didn't even remember having gone to bed the night before. Time slowly came back to me as the knocking continued in the distance, muffled by walls and floor. The previous day's events filled my head, and I realized that I had spent most of the afternoon on my bed, watching Possibly through a glass filter. At one point, I had wandered downstairs for a sandwich and some chips—Jack had a pretty good selection of snack foods—and then ate on my bed while reading a book on my phone. I hadn't needed a signal to read any of the books I'd saved.

Sometime, probably around midnight, after checking out the greenish glow coming from the roof of Auguste's barn, I'd fallen back in bed. My instincts had obviously kicked in and my body had wrapped itself up in the covers. The room was stuffy, warm early morning Texas heat already making the temperature rise in my attic bedroom.

When the knocking continued and my ears adjusted enough to being awake that I realized it was coming from the front door, I tried to pry myself out of the covers. Thrashing and ripping—not unamused by the tangle I'd gotten myself in—I extracted my body from the bed. I yanked on some basketball shorts and a t-shirt and exited my room.

In bare feet, I padded down the first flight of stairs, hoping whoever was at the door wouldn't give up before I could answer their knocking. However, on the second-floor landing, I glanced over and noticed that Jack's bedroom door was open at the end of the hall. Golden sunlight was streaming through his window, bathing the room in the warm yellow of the early morning hours. As I stood there, I realized the knocking at the front door had stopped, and a voice had replaced the noise.

I skipped down the bottom flight of stairs, finding Jack at the open front door across the room from me. Sunlight framed him in a halo, so I couldn't really see who was at the door. I had to slink across the living room and glance around him to find out who had woken us both. Jack was fully dressed, though, so he might have been awake when the person came knocking. When I rounded Jack, I saw that the mysterious knocker was actually Auguste.

When he said he'd come to Jack's, he hadn't mentioned it would be so early. It was barely seven o'clock in the morning.

"—yeah," Auguste was speaking to Jack, obviously continuing a conversation I had walked in on, "Jordan asked me if I'd show him around town."

Though I couldn't see his hands, I saw Jack move, as though signing to Auguste.

Auguste laughed. "I guess it's nice of me, sure."

Again, Jack was moving like he was signing something.

"Oh," Auguste said, "if he's still asleep, I can come back later. I just thought since you're usually up by now that—"

I dashed the last few feet through the living room to stand beside Jack in the doorway.

"I'm awake!" I announced sprightly.

Jack jumped, his head whipping to the side to look at me. Auguste smiled.

"Sorry, Jack," I mumbled. "Uh, I was asleep, but I woke up when I heard you knocking."

Auguste winced.

"Sorry," he said. "Jack is always up at this time working, so I thought…well, anyway."

Jack signed something.

Auguste chuckled. "Yeah."

I had no idea what Jack had said to him.

"What?" I asked.

"He called you 'sleepy head.'" Auguste answered.

"Oh." I glanced over to see Jack smiling slightly.

The three of us stood there in awkward silence for a moment. I didn't know why Auguste knew sign language when I, Jack's stepson, was out of practice, but it wasn't a question I felt I should ask in front of Jack.

"So," I reached up to scratch my head, "still up for showing me around?"

"Sure," Auguste said. "Yeah. You ready, or…"

"Yeah." I glanced over at Jack. "Um, is it all right if I use that twenty bucks still?"

Jack nodded.

"Okay. Thanks."

Jack turned slightly so I could dash through the doorway and down the front steps. Auguste gave me a nod and smile as I stood there expectantly, then he turned to Jack.

"Finishing your table today?" he asked.

Jack nodded and then signed rapidly and excitedly to Auguste.

"Awesome!" Auguste responded, though he didn't tell me what Jack had said. "He'll be so happy."

Jack smiled, proud of whatever it was that they had shared. My head just turned back and forth between them, trying to figure out what had happened. Something was going on with Jack's table, but whatever it was apparently wasn't my business to know. Either that, or neither of them had considered that maybe I'd be interested in what they were talking about.

"Okay." Auguste turned to me. "Ready?"

"Uh, yeah," I said, glancing over at Jack. "Sure."

Jack raised his hand and waved to us both.

"Bye, Jack!" Auguste announced happily before skipping away. "See you later!"

Jack looked over at me.

"Uh, see you later." I gave him a quick wave, then dashed away after Auguste.

Auguste literally skipped down the road away from Jack's house, going in the direction of the graveyard. At first, I was embarrassed to be jogging alongside some boy who was *skipping*—especially since he was wearing bright orange clam diggers, flip-flops, and his ever-present tank top. The pearl necklace at his throat was another odd touch. However, I reminded myself that clothes should be experimented with, and Auguste wasn't self-conscious, so why should *I* be embarrassed?

When we got to the fork in the road at the edge of the graveyard, Auguste came to a sudden halt, and I nearly ran into him. He chuckled as I stumbled and grabbed onto his shoulder to keep from landing ass up in the road. He placed his hands on my shoulders and helped me stay upright until it was obvious that I wasn't going to topple over. When we were both safe and secure, standing there, he turned to look at the graveyard.

"Bend of the Road Graveyard," he said.

"Yeah?" I shrugged.

"It was here before the town was even founded." Auguste continued. "They say that when the founders of Possibly showed up to this land, there were these headstones and trees."

"Okay."

"They really liked this area by the creek, but there was this graveyard," he said. "But, instead of being jerks and relocating the dead—or just the headstones—or building over it completely, they just built around it."

"I mean," I began, "the town's not that big. Couldn't have been that big of a decision, right?"

Auguste laughed. Like his melodic, though deep, voice, his laugh also sounded like a song. It had a specific rhythm and cadence that was pleasant and inviting. He was a friendly, cheerful guy.

"They didn't know how big the town would get at the time, though, right?" he asked. "So, it was still nice of them to decide to build the roads around it. Just in case."

"Sure. I mean, that sounds fair."

"They say that it's possibly haunted," Auguste said, then realized his phrasing. "Hah. *Possibly*."

I chuckled.

"Um," I started, "I, uh, saw some—body—here the other morning. It was kind of weird."

"Yeah?" He asked.

"Yeah." I nodded. "Somebody in, like, a black robe with a hood. They just appeared out from under the tree, went and stood by that headstone there—"

I pointed at the headstone.

"—and then disappeared back under the tree. I mean, it was misty, or foggy, or whatever, that morning, but it seemed like they appeared and disappeared—"

"That's Malia," Auguste said.

117

"What?"

"She's a performance artist." Auguste explained. "At least three times a week, she comes to the graveyard and mourns at a different grave. She doesn't want any of the dead to feel like they've been forgotten. It's totally harmless."

I stared at him for a minute. *Harmless?* Sure. *Weird?* Absolutely.

"You know it's not really a *graveyard*, right?" I grinned. "I mean, it's not even connected to a church."

"Why does that matter?" Auguste winked. "Come on!"

Again, Auguste was skipping along the road, cutting to the right to take us into the main part of downtown Possibly. *Chuck E's in Love* by Rickie Lee Jones was the song of the day at AMOR. It grew louder as Auguste skipped and I jogged towards Liberty Lane. Even when more people came into view, and actually see the two of us, Auguste didn't stop skipping. Self-conscious he was not. So, I found myself wondering why he had been so reticent to look up at me or other people the day before. His head had been down a lot, his eyes on the ground as he had walked away from me at The Pueblo.

Once more, I found myself nearly crashing into Auguste when he stopped suddenly at the end of Liberty Lane. I didn't stumble like I had by the graveyard, but Auguste still chuckled at my surprise at the sudden stop. I just grinned shyly as he spread his arms out wide, as if presenting the street and all its majesty to me.

"Liberty Lane," he said. "It's not really, like, the main street of town or anything—"

"There's so many to choose from," I mumbled.

Auguste grinned at my snide remark. "—but everyone kinda considers it the main street. Probably because it has the tram alongside of it, and—"

"What is up with the tram, anyway?"

"Well—"

"I mean," I said, "who needs a tram that runs, like, forty yards? It doesn't even really go anywhere, ya' know?"

Auguste laughed. "Just let me do the tour here, sir."

"Okay."

Auguste's good-natured smile and his easy laugh put me at ease. Unlike Jack, who didn't want to tell me anything about town, Auguste was ready to explain everything. As long as I was patient with him about the details he planned to share.

"Sorry." I added.

"No problem," he said. "So—"

"Why does the radio station play the same song on repeat all day long?" I asked, forgetting my patience. "I mean, from six to six anyway. Which isn't *all day long*, by the way."

"Patience, Jordan!" Auguste demanded in a comedic voice.

"Sorry," I said. "Again."

Auguste watched me for a moment. I made a "zipping" motion over my lips, then pretended to put a key in my pocket.

"Okay." He looked away, then glanced at me again before continuing. "So, AMOR is over there. The radio station."

He pointed at the second building on the left, green and squat, but pleasant looking.

"Amos runs the radio station," Auguste said. "He's a really nice guy. But, well, I mean, he does play just one song a day for twelve hours. No one really knows why, I guess. We all suspect that it's his form of art, but we're not sure."

"Um, okay?"

Auguste shrugged with a smile, then nudged me and pointed down the street. My eyes darted over to check out what he was pointing at in the street.

"That's Earl Dean." He was pointing at the man with the pickaxe who was already awake and tearing up another spot in the street. "Liberty Lane is his project, I guess. He's making a rainbow in the street. He said that he hopes one day to have the entire street full of different colored bricks."

"I see that." I nodded as I pointed at the police officer stationed on the side of the street, leaning against one of the buildings. "But why? And why does the cop just let him?"

Auguste shrugged.

"What's he hurting, you know?"

"That's not an answer." I laughed. "He's tearing up city property."

"But replacing it with something prettier," Auguste said. "So, he's not tearing up city property—he's improving it. At his own expense and labor."

"That is a really weird way to look at it."

"What's wrong with weird?" Auguste mumbled.

"Nothing," I answered quickly. I didn't want to upset him like I had Jack with my 'weird' comments. "I'm just surprised that the city is okay with it."

"Well," Auguste started slowly, "it'll be really nice when he's done."

"How long has he been working on it?" I asked.

"Couple of years?" Auguste shrugged. "He can only do it on days that it's nice and dry, and some days he has to rest his arms and shoulders. It's hard work."

I just nodded. Auguste nudged me again and pointed at the tram at the other end of the track.

"That's Jasper," he said. "He's the tram conductor. He runs the tram up and down the street hourly."

"But why?" I groaned, though I wasn't unamused. "That doesn't make any sense at all."

"Why?" Auguste turned to me.

"Seriously?"

"Yeah. Seriously." He nudged me again with a smile.

I laughed.

"I mean," I began, "it's quicker to walk down the street on foot. You can get to the other end in seconds. The tram is slow. Also, it really doesn't take you anywhere, does it? Just up and down a street. And not all the time, either. *On the hour.* That just—it doesn't make sense."

Auguste stared at me for a long moment, then smiled.

"You're not a very whimsical person, are you?" he asked.

"What does *that* mean?"

He grinned. "Come on."

Auguste was dashing down the street before I could respond, so the only thing I could do was chase after him. We raced along Liberty Lane until we were almost to the creek, then hooked a right. The back of the post office building, tall, teal, and quaint, came into view. Auguste slammed on the brakes again, but I was ready for it.

"The post office," he said simply.

"Sofia Salazar is the postmaster," I added. "Yeah. We met."

"Did she tell you about the letters to Shirlene?"

"It might have been discussed."

"Well," Auguste said, "everyone goes crazy trying to figure out *that* mystery. Some people say that it's some guy who just has a wrong address. Or even some woman, I suppose. Other people say that Sofia is writing the letters herself. I mean, she doesn't have any envelopes or postmarks to show where they came from, right?"

"Right?"

"Other people say it's someone in town, writing letters to get over a lost love—or an unrequited love," he said. "Like, maybe there's not even a 'Shirlene' at all, you know? Maybe it's a pseudonym for someone else entirely."

"That's weird, too," I said, then realized what I'd said. "I mean, *how odd.*"

Auguste looked over at me and shook his head with a grin.

"We all hope that one day we'll find out who Shirlene is and why she's so important to get so many letters," he said.

"Okay."

Auguste didn't run away from the post office so much as power walk towards Starbuck's, and I fell in behind him. When the old pirate ship came into view, I could see that Levi Lee was outside the front door, doing his brand of performance art. He was standing on one leg, a silver platter balanced on his head and two platters held aloft by his hands. A look of stern concentration was on his face.

"That's Starbuck's," Auguste said, stopping a few yards away. "Coffee shop. Starbuck is a nice guy. Always dresses as a pirate. Hence the pirate theme, I guess? But is this a chicken or the egg scenario? Who knows?"

"Like," I asked, "does he dress like a pirate because his coffee shop is in a pirate ship, or did he get a pirate ship as a coffee shop because he likes eye patches?"

Auguste chuckled. "Exactly. No one knows. But he's a nice guy. Just eccentric."

"Okay."

"That's Levi Lee." Auguste pointed.

"I've talked to him a few times." I nodded along. "Nice guy."

"The nicest," Auguste agreed. "He's still trying to figure himself out. He's been doing his performance art for at least six months and he switches it up every few days. I guess he just hasn't figured out what he's trying to say yet."

"What?"

"Life is art." Auguste gestured grandly. "Our actions speak volumes about how we perceive the world."

"Uh…"

"So, why not make our actions art?" Auguste finished.

"I mean…what?"

Auguste laughed but offered no further explanation. He pointed down the street towards the mosque-like building.

"That's The Pueblo," he said. "It's an artists' studio and performance space. Church is held there on Sundays."

"Ah." I nodded. "I wondered where everyone…did church stuff."

"Yeah." He nodded. "Lilly is the groundskeeper for The Pueblo and also teaches the art classes. She's super nice, too. I'll have to introduce you sometime. All of the classes are free. If you ever want to take one, I mean."

"I'm not really an artist." I shrugged.

"Well," Auguste said as he turned to me, "what *are* you?"

I shrugged. Grinned goofily.

Auguste leaned in with a smile and tapped a finger against his temple.

"Life is art."

"You're weird," I said. "I mean, it's cool, though."

Auguste laughed loudly, then he was nudging me again.

"See the houses at the end of the street?" He pointed towards the other end of the road where four identical buildings sat perpendicular to the street we were on.

"Uh, yeah?"

"Second one from the right is Blooms," he said. "Have you met Agnes Broussard yet?"

"Who?"

"She's the lady with the broken leg in the wheelchair?"

"Oh." I frowned. "No. I haven't seen her."

Auguste slipped his phone out of his pocket just far enough to glance at the time, then he started glancing around, as though he was expecting someone.

"She should be heading into work at Blooms," he said, his head turning back and forth, looking around for someone. "Ah! There she is!"

Auguste pointed down the street towards the corner of The Pueblo. My eyes followed the direction of his finger, and seconds later, a woman in a wheelchair appeared on the street. Beehive hair, way too much makeup, a kitty cat sweater, leggings, a cast from her hip down to the middle of her shin, and tennis shoes. She was…something to look upon. The oddest thing about her wasn't her makeup, hair, or choice of clothing. The fact that she was using a crutch to push herself in her wheelchair—almost like an oar in a paddleboat—as her bad leg stuck out perilously in front of her, was the oddest thing. We both watched for a minute as Agnes Broussard swung the crutch to the right side of the wheelchair, dug it into the road, and pushed off. Then the left side. Right side. Left side. She kept *rowing* her way towards Blooms.

"What happened to her leg?" I asked.

"Well," Auguste turned to me to murmur, as though Agnes would hear us all the way at the other end of the street, "she was making dinner one night. Pimento cheese sandwiches? She got distracted by her cats and a sandwich fell off the counter. When she turned around, she stepped on the sandwich, slipped, and went ass end up. Broke her leg in two places."

"She…*slipped*…on a…*pimento cheese sandwich*…and broke her leg?" I didn't believe anything Auguste was telling me.

"Yeah." Auguste sighed and turned to look at Agnes with pity as she rowed her wheelchair up to the front of Blooms.

124

"Her doctor had been telling her to eat right for ages but she just wouldn't listen."

"Okay, okay." I laughed as I held up my hands. "I don't believe any of that. You're just pulling my leg or something, man."

"Hand to God." Auguste put a hand over his heart and the other he held aloft. "She stepped on a pimento cheese sandwich and…*weeeeeeeeeeeeee.*"

I laughed loudly.

"Okay, fine." I relented. "If you say so."

Auguste grinned and then he was pointing at a building across the street.

"Red-striped roofs?" he asked.

"Yeah?"

"One on the right is Samuel's Soda Spray," he said. "Samuel's a nice guy. Obsessed with all things bottles, bottle tops, road signs, Rorschach ink blots, and—"

"Wait." I stopped him. "What?"

"You'll see." Auguste waved me off. "We'll go get a soda sometime. He makes really good floats and milkshakes, too."

"All right?"

Auguste turned so he was looking towards the creek, so I followed his lead, turning so that the bridge that led into town came into view.

"Lovelorn Bridge Pass," he announced.

"Okay?"

"Legend has it," Auguste said, "that if you can't get over a lost love—or unrequited love—that if you climb up on the rail and shout the name of your beloved, then dive into the water, it will help you get over it."

"Ah." Things were making sense in a really whacky way. "I saw some guy do that. A couple of times. Does it work?"

Auguste shrugged. "Haven't had to find out yet. Grandy's is down there."

He pointed in the direction of the gas station off in the distance.

"Yeah," I said. "I met him. I had to pick up some cigarettes for Jack and I bought a soda. Took a soda. He didn't want to work that day."

"He's a philosopher."

"Who?"

"Grandy," Auguste said. "He's a horrible gas station attendant—most of the time he forgets to order gas when he runs out—but his real passion is philosophy."

The question Grandy had asked me about caterpillars and butterflies popped into my head.

"He spends most of his days sitting outside, enjoying the weather—when it's permissive—and thinking about life's deepest questions," Auguste continued. "He's super nice, too. He's just not super talkative most of the time."

I nodded along.

"And then," Auguste looked around, trying to figure out what he'd forgotten, "there's Mystic Molly."

He jabbed a thumb down the street towards the reddish-orange miniature circus tent. My eyes landed on the tent and I felt my stomach flutter. *Mystic Molly*.

"She tells fortunes, does Tarot readings, that kind of thing," Auguste said. "Wanna go have her read your palm or something? It's totally free the first time."

I stared down at the reddish-orange miniature circus tent. From having seen it on previous days, I knew that the flaps were probably open on the side facing away from us, so I wasn't able to look inside and see the oddly dressed woman beckoning us. A chill ran up my spine but I did my best to hide its effects from Auguste.

"I don't know, Auguste. I—"

"Auggie," he said.

"Huh?"

"Everyone really calls me 'Auggie' around here."

"Oh," I said, "I don't really believe in that stuff, Auggie."

"Why not?"

"Like...witchcraft and hoodoo and Voodoo and stuff?" I shrugged. "It just seems silly, right? Even if it's free."

Auggie chuckled.

"You really are kind of a stick in the mud, aren't you?" he asked.

"Hey." I nudged him, slightly annoyed, though I covered it with a smile.

"What's it hurt?" He shrugged. "Let Mystic Molly tell you what your future holds. Even if she's wrong, it costs you nothing. And you had a new experience."

"I guess," I mumbled. "It's just silly."

"There's nothing wrong with *silly*." Auggie nudged me and took off, skipping towards the circus tent at the end of the street.

My feet refused to move for several moments, but finally I was able to get them moving in the right direction, and I was following after the boy in the bright orange clam diggers and pearl necklace. I jogged alongside him as he skipped merrily towards the weird woman's tent, wondering why I was following along on such a weird excursion. It wasn't that I was scared or anything—or even superstitious—the woman was just...*weird*. Just like everyone else in town. Honestly, I also didn't really want to know what my future held.

What if it was bad?

Due to the size of downtown Possibly, I really didn't have to consider what visiting Mystic Molly could mean, or whether or not I was a nonbeliever or just scared. Within seconds we were skipping and jogging around the perimeter of Mystic Molly's tent, drawing closer to the opening on the other side. As we drew closer to the open flaps on the other side of the tent, my nose picked up on the smell of an unusual scent in the air. I'd never gotten close enough to the tent to know if the mystic in the tent was burning incense or anything, but it quickly became clear that she did enjoy incense—like most mystics.

When Auggie and I had reached the opening, my eyes immediately landed on the woman sitting behind the table in the dimly lit tent. Once again, she was wearing a heavy dress with long sleeves and a shawl was draped over her shoulders. Long, flowing dark hair cascaded down her shoulders and her eyes sparkled out at us as we crept up to the opening of her business. Auggie approached the open flaps with the confidence of someone without a fear in the world. I, on the other hand, felt overwhelmed by the sight of the woman in her dark tent and the unique smell emanating from within it.

At first, it was as though she only saw Auggie as he ducked into the opening of the tent, her smile just for him as he approached. But then her eyes landed on me, and a look of what seemed like concern clouded her face just long enough for me to catch it. A smile overtook her face, a correction once she realized that her expression was uninviting—and possibly telegraphing how this mystic reading was going to go.

Auggie seemed to be perfectly at ease in Mystic Molly's tent, as though maybe he had visited her plenty of times before. His friendly, cheerful manner and willingness to talk to anyone aside, it wasn't hard to imagine that this was the reason for his ease in approaching the woman. He'd lived in Possibly for his whole life. Obviously, he had encountered Mystic Molly at least once over the years, right? Even if we hadn't been formally introduced, I'd seen the woman twice in less than a week.

"Welcome, gentlemen." Mystic Molly gestured slowly towards the chairs across the table from her; her arms moved languidly, as though she had taken a muscle relaxer thirty minutes before we had arrived.

"Hello," Auggie replied and slid into the seat on the left. "How are you?"

Gingerly, I eased into the seat on the right, my eyes staying on the woman across the table from us.

"I'm well, Auggie," Molly replied. "How are you today?"

"I'm good." Auggie shifted happily in his seat. The kid was a bundle of energy, which, again, made me wonder about his mood the previous day. "This is Jordan."

Molly's eyes shifted over to me, and in the dim light, her dark eyes seemed almost black, though they seemed to sparkle at the same time. As though scanning everything around them, processing what they saw, extracting information to be used in her readings, her eyes were a bit creepy. Sure, she was smiling at me, and she'd been nothing but welcoming from the moment we walked into her tent, but she still creeped me out.

"Hello, Jordan," Molly said. "Nice to meet you."

She slid her hand across the table, pointy black tips for nails coming towards me, and I tentatively took it, giving it a quick shake. I'd always been told that handshakes should be firm and confident, but I couldn't bring myself to hold onto Molly's hand for long. A cursory shake was all that I could manage with the butterflies I felt in my stomach.

I couldn't help but wonder what was wrong with me. Molly seemed mostly normal. She didn't have a horn growing out of her head or anything; there weren't spirits floating around her head, waiting to be summoned for her reading.

Maybe I was more superstitious than I knew?

"Nice to meet you, too. Hello," I managed.

Mystic Molly seemed to size us both up for a moment, her eyes going back and forth, scanning the two of us, as though she was trying to read our intentions.

"What can I do for you two boys today?" she asked when her eyes landed back on Auggie.

"Oh," Auggie sighed, "just a general reading, I would think. Jordan's never had his fortune told before, so I thought it might be a nice way to welcome him to Possibly. He's new. He's staying with Jack Burke? Jack's his stepfather."

That was my life. All falling out of Auggie's mouth to some stranger before I could even decide if I wanted Mystic Molly to know it or not. The mystic nodded along, a small smile on her face as she listened to Auggie give her the gossip about the new guy.

"Just the usual for me." Auggie shrugged. "Nothing new going on in my world."

"I see," she said. "What are you trying to learn about yourself today, Jordan?"

The mystic's eyes were on me, practically boring into my soul, and I suddenly realized how happy I was that I'd already shaken her hand. My palms were sweating profusely. Discreetly, I wiped them on the thighs of my shorts.

"Um, I don't know…"

"Come on, Jordan," Auggie said. "It's so cool. Mystic Molly is one of the best."

"Now," Mystic Molly held a hand up, "don't pressure Jordan, Auggie. One must be ready to receive the spirit before it will speak."

"Of course." Auggie nodded, as though any of that made sense.

"If Jordan isn't ready, he isn't ready." Mystic Molly snuck a glance in my direction.

I didn't confirm or deny whether or not I wanted a *reading* or to *receive the spirit*, but my answer was obvious. Mystic Molly didn't have my permission to give me a reading, so she wasn't going to give me one. Instead, she focused her attention on Auggie, completely ignoring me as she shifted in her seat to face him directly. Auggie looked a little disappointed that I had chosen not to get involved in Mystic Molly's services, but he didn't say so aloud.

"Okay," Auggie said.

Mystic Molly's eyes flitted over to me, then she was focusing on Auggie again. She slid her hand, palm up, across the table to him, a welcoming smile blooming on her face. Auggie enthusiastically brought his arm up to the table and laid his hand in hers, palm down. The two of them looked at each other for a moment, as though they had acted out this ritual before. Auggie continued to stare at Mystic Molly as her eyes slowly slid shut. My eyes were laser-focused on the mystic as she sat there concentrating, holding Auggie's hand.

Again, I'm not a very superstitious person, but things suddenly seemed...*heavy*...inside Mystic Molly's tent. Though it provided respite from the hot Texas summer sun, thus it was much cooler inside than expected, the air seemed to be pushing down on us all of the sudden. The smell of the incense—which I still hadn't laid eyes upon—seemed to get stronger. Mystic Molly's eyes fluttered under her eyelids uncontrollably and a light breeze seemed to ruffle her hair.

One glance at Auggie and I saw that he was intensely focused on her, waiting for her to say or do whatever she was going to say or do. The air pushed down heavily upon us and the smell of the incense grew, everything seeming to come to a crescendo. Then, Mystic Molly's hair ruffled in the unfelt breeze a final time and her eyes fluttered open. For a second, she looked dazed, confused about where she was, and then a smile came to her face. She slid her hand from Auggie's and nodded at him.

"She still thinks about you," Mystic Molly said. "Every single day, Auggie. Every. Single. Day."

Auggie's face lit up and a happy gasp escaped his throat. Before I knew what was going on, Auggie had leapt out of his seat.

"Thanks, Molly!" He cheered.

Then he dashed out of the tent.

I was left sitting across from Mystic Molly, uncomfortable, anxious, and unsure of what to do. So, I rose from my chair jerkily and gave her a smile.

"Um, thanks," I said and headed for the tent opening.

"Jordan?" Molly's voice stopped me at the tent flaps.

"Uh, yeah?" I looked over my shoulder nervously.

Mystic Molly gave me a soft smile.

"I'm here whenever you're ready," she said before giving me a wink.

"Yeah," I said. "Okay. Yeah. Thanks."

Molly nodded and I dashed out of the tent opening, immediately jerking my head back and forth, looking for Auggie. I was just glad to be out of the dim light of the tent, the smell of whatever incense she had burning, the mysterious breeze, and the eerie gaze of the mystic. When my eyes finally landed on Auggie, he was across the street, lying in the grass, staring up at the sky. A huge smile was on his face.

I made my way across the street, kicking at the ground, then the pavement, then the grass on the other side of the street. When I came to stand next to Auggie's prone body in the grass, it was like he didn't even see me looming over him. He was staring up at the cloudless blue sky and smiling like an idiot. So, I plopped down next to him, folding my legs up into the lotus position.

"What was that all about?" I murmured.

"My grandma." Auggie answered immediately, his voice sounding dreamy. "She still thinks about me."

I stared at him.

"Every day, Jordan," Auggie said. "She still thinks about me every day."

A long sigh escaped his mouth and his smile turned beatific.

"Yeah," I said. "Okay. That's cool."

I didn't know what else to say to such an odd answer. So, Auggie's dead grandmother still thought about him in the afterlife or something? Did he really believe such nonsense?

Did he really think Mystic Molly had a direct hotline to the dead?

"I haven't seen her in…" Auggie trailed off.

I waited.

"Years," Auggie finally said. "But Mystic Molly assures me that she hasn't forgotten me. Every time I talk to Molly, it's always the same."

"I mean, that's great." I shrugged, trying to be kind. "It's always good to know the people we love never forget us. Right?"

"Right!" Auggie was suddenly sitting.

His legs still stayed stretched out before him, and he was propping himself up with his hands, but the movement was so quick it was startling. Kind of funny, too. Seeing Auggie so animated—even more so than he had been in the previous hour—was comical.

"So," I mumbled, "you really believe that hocus pocus stuff? I mean…that was just strange. We were barely there for a minute and Molly contacted your dead grandmother to find out if she had thought about you today?"

Auggie gave an amused chuckle.

"Oh," he said, "she's not dead."

He rose to his feet and brushed off the seat of his clam diggers with a fluttering of his hands.

"Huh?"

"The people we love never truly die." Auggie shrugged and looked down at me.

"Right."

That was all I could think of to say to such an odd statement. To such an odd morning.

"Look," Auggie said, "there's more to show you and tell you about. I mean, the tour isn't complete or anything. But I really want to go home and work on my art. Is that cool?"

"Sure." I nodded, though I was disappointed. Auggie and Mystic Molly had unnerved me, but his energy and the mystery of everything was intoxicating. I wanted more. "I'll, uh, go back home, and…do other stuff."

"Tomorrow!" Auggie jabbed a finger down at me excitedly. "We'll hang out again tomorrow. Cool?"

"Sure." I nodded.

Auggie smiled excitedly and started to skip away in the general direction of the creek. Apparently, he was going to follow its shore up to the big red barn in which he lived. When he was a few yards away, I realized there was one question about Possibly I'd had on my mind but hadn't asked him yet.

"Auggie?" I hollered.

He turned to me, the smile on his face still there.

"Yeah?"

"What's with the name?" I asked. "Possibly? Why do they call the town Possibly?"

Auggie grinned.

"Well," he said across those yards between us, "they say when the first settlers came here—like a really long time ago—that they weren't sure where they were. They didn't have GPS then, right? They didn't even really have reliable maps. They thought this might be Texas, but they weren't sure. So, one of them said it was 'possibly Texas' and it just kind of stuck. *Possibly, Texas.*"

I snort-laughed at that explanation.

"What was the other possibility?" I asked. "Oklahoma?"

Auggie gave me an odd smile.

"It was possibly not Texas," he said.

"Right." I drew the word out with a smirk.

"But it's quite possibly the best place to be." Auggie winked.

Then he was skipping away towards the creek once more, his flip-flops slapping at his feet and the hems of his clam diggers fluttering. I sat there, in the grass across the street from Mystic Molly's tent for quite a while, sweat slowly making a light sheen on my skin as the hours passed. Finally, when the heat was becoming overbearing and I was certain I'd had enough sun for the day, I got up and walked back to Jack's place. He was still in the backyard, working on his table project, though he seemed close to finishing it. I merely gave him a wave, letting him know I was home. I didn't go over and interrupt his private time working. There was no reason to make him regret my presence more.

Later that night, in bed, as I sat atop my covers and stared out at the hazy golden glow coming from the roof of the big red barn in the distance, I replayed that morning in my head. Things just got stranger and quirkier around Possibly. Even if I had Auggie to explain everyone and everything to me. The people, the places, the layout…it was all so alien to me. And I'd been just about everywhere in the country you could get to by car. Maybe I hadn't walked enough dirt roads?

After the lights at the barn disappeared, I crawled under the covers, and lowered my head to the pillow. Other than Wyatt's gunfire, I thought of how peaceful the town was. How everyone seemed to get along. One more thought entered my mind.

It possibly was the best place I'd ever lived.

Sometime, in the middle of the night, I thought I heard a door opening and closing.

But I wasn't sure if I was awake or dreaming.

A HOLE IN THE SKY

I t wasn't knocking that woke me up the following morning; it was the incessant buzzing of something just outside of my half-asleep consciousness. Everything sounded muffled, as though I was hearing things underwater, and I finally realized that I was asleep, slowly coming awake thanks to the sound emanating from…somewhere. I rolled over in bed, away from the dormers, and blearily searched for the source of the noise. My eyes landed on the blue glow of my phone on the bedside table, barely visible now that the sun was just starting to shine through the window.

I slapped a hand over my phone and dragged it across the smooth wood surface, dropping it onto the bed in my rush to answer it. When I brought the phone up so that I could see it through my hazy, half-asleep vision, I saw it wasn't a saved contact. But it wasn't a number I recognized, either. Well, I didn't think I recognized it. My eyes hadn't decided to work yet. I slid my finger across the screen and brought the phone to my ear a little too roughly, whacking myself in the side of the head in the process.

Man, I was sleeping good.

"Huh-hello?" I croaked.

I reached up to rub my eyes with my free hand.

"*Hey.*" A familiar voice replied. "*Jordan?*"

"Yeah?" I yawned.

"Hey. It's me. Auggie."

I felt very awake suddenly.

"Oh," I said," hey."

"Hey," he replied. *"I hope you don't mind—I got your number from Jack. He said you'd probably be awake. It doesn't sound like it, though."*

His expressive chuckle sounded on the other end. I chuckled back.

"Nearly," I said. "I was probably going to wake up any second."

I looked out the window. The sun was just coming over the horizon. I probably wasn't going to be awake any second.

"Good. Hey, I was wondering if you wanted to come over?" he asked. *"I wanted to show you the barn. Then maybe we could go to Starbuck's or something?"*

I looked around my room, wondering if I had clean clothes, then sniffed at myself, trying to decide if I needed a shower. The question wasn't whether or not I'd go to the big red barn—it was how quickly I could get there. I wasn't going to turn down a chance to see what was going on inside of the place after watching it through the window for so many nights.

"Definitely," I said, jolting upright in bed, suddenly wide awake. "I need to shower and stuff. Twenty minutes, okay?"

"Excellent," Auggie said.

Then the call ended.

He hadn't even said, "goodbye." You know, like a normal person.

I stared at the blank screen for a minute, yawned, scratched my head, then laid my phone back on my bedside table. My legs got flung over the side of the bed and I took a few moments to stretch and yawn, become fully awake. My feet hit the floorboards, which were just a little chilly on my bare soles, and I felt myself energized, ready to solve another Possibly mystery. I'd finally get to check out the inside of the big red barn.

Once out of bed, I proceeded to do what one of my "uncles" called "The Three S's" way back when I was a little kid: *shit, shower,* and *shave.* Well, except I didn't have to shave. For the last year I'd been able to grow precisely three hairs on my chin, and as far as I was concerned, they could all stay around for a while. If I shaved them off, who knew when I'd grow more? Probably not until I was closer to eighteen and that was still a year-and-a-half-away.

Out of the shower and with a towel tied around my waist, my hair matted wetly to my skull, I dug in my suitcase until I found a clean pair of underwear, a t-shirt, and a fresh pair of basketball shorts. It would be the perfect outfit to fight the summer sun. When I was dry and dressed, I ran the towel through my hair again and dragged my fingers through it. My hair wasn't nearly long enough to need a brushing after a shower, so my fingers worked just fine to get it into place. Two minutes later, my teeth had been brushed, my deodorant had been applied, and I had practically skied into a pair of flip-flops.

Downstairs, I jogged out of the back door to find Jack working on his table project again. I shouted a quick *'I'm going to Auggie's!'* at Jack without missing a step. I glanced over my shoulder to see him waving an arm lazily in the air to let me know he had heard. Jogging down the road that ran along the north side of Possibly, I passed the Bend of the Road Graveyard. Malia was decked out in her cloak, mourning at another headstone. The sight nearly made me trip over my own feet until I remembered what Auggie had told me about her "performance art."

Instead of stumbling, I waved at Malia as I passed, though she made no indication that she saw me running along the road. I shrugged to myself, unconcerned with Malia and her strange behavior, and continued along the road towards the barn. Within a minute, I was standing outside of the large green barn doors. They were cracked open just enough to display the giant gloomy room inside, but I didn't see Auggie waiting to let me in, so I knocked on the wooden frame, announcing my arrival.

Seconds later, the barn door swung open a few feet and Auggie appeared. He was smiling from ear to ear; stripes and flecks of black paint decorated his face. His appearance made me take a step back, confused by the fact that he looked like someone had used his face as a canvas. The rest of him looked normal—well, *normal for Auggie*. He had on khaki shorts, his tank top, and a black tutu cinched around his waist. Instead of his standard flip-flops, his feet were bare. *Space Oddity* by David Bowie was playing softly from inside the barn.

"One minute early!" Auggie announced.

"You were timing me?" I managed to ask, though I was still in shock at his appearance.

"Not really," he said. "I have no idea if you're on time or not. But it's nicer to pretend that you are, right?"

"I guess." I shrugged. "What's with the, uh, war paint?"

Auggie looked confused for a minute, his head leaning to the side as he considered what I had just asked him. So, I reached out and touched one of the black streaks on his cheek. I pulled my fingertip away, now blackened by paint, and held it for him to see.

"Oh!" Auggie laughed. "I was painting this morning."

"*This morning?*" I asked. "It's just past the butt crack of dawn and you've been…*painting?*"

"When inspiration strikes, it strikes," he said.

"Sure." I nodded. "That explains everything."

He laughed and turned to push the door wide. Sunlight flooded into the barn interior, golden and warm, spotlighting the flecks of dust that hung in the air like the world's tiniest and laziest insects. With the door having been nearly closed, I wondered how he had managed to paint anything without light to guide him. However, when I looked around the large open space, my eyes trailing upwards, I finally realized that the roof was open—an open skylight.

So, that's why I can see lights over here at night?

My eyes flitted about the room, expecting to see hay bales—or even paint easels—but what I found just didn't make sense. Large tubes of industrial air conditioning ducts were everywhere, tracing to and fro on the floor like a giant snake slithering around the room. They all seemed to wind and curl around a giant cylinder in the center of the room, which appeared to be open at the top, yet had no discernible entrance or exit.

Every inch of floor space in the barn seemed to be covered by the tubing, save the space directly in front of the door and the narrow spaces between the duct work. I'd been told by everyone—including Auggie—that he lived at the barn. Where were the beds? The couch? *The bathrooms and kitchen?* All I could see was what looked like an old barn that was filled with junk. There was no way that anyone could live amongst the piles of crap. Did they bathe in the creek or something?

What in the crap?

"Come in," Auggie said.

"Um, okay."

Auggie held the door wide for me and I inched inside, being careful so as to not bump into the duct work that lay just a few feet inside the doorway. Once I had cleared the opening, Auggie put his weight behind the door and slid it shut again. With the giant skylight above us, the door darkened the room enough that the dust motes in the air were no longer visible, but we could still see everything just fine. At least well enough to walk around without stumbling over the tubes.

"Welcome," Auggie said.

"Uh, thanks," I replied. "Um, what's all this?"

Auggie turned to me and smiled, his teeth even whiter in the now darker room.

"My art." He sighed happily.

"Art?"

"Well," Auggie explained as he moved away from the door, "*installation* art. I'm not much of a painter—I mean, look at my face—and I can't really draw. My sculpting is pretty good. But I'm really good at installation art. So, that's the kind of art I do."

He put his hands on his hips and surveyed the giant cylinder—*maybe it was an old, small grain silo?*—at the center of the room. I stared at the cylinder for a few moments with him, then turned to watch him as he looked up on his "creation" with pride.

"It's…impressive?"

Auggie laughed.

"You don't even know what it is," he cooed. "How can you call it '*impressive,*' huh?"

"You're right," I said. "I don't have a clue what is going on here."

We both laughed.

"Are you going to tell me?" I asked finally.

"No," Auggie said. "Not today. I just wanted you to see it."

"That's kind of a tease." I crossed my arms over my chest and glared at him.

He held his hands up defensively.

"It's not quite done yet," he explained. "When it's done—like a week or so?—you can come see how it works. You and I can be the guinea pigs."

"*Guinea*—what am I signing up for here?" I laughed nervously.

"It won't hurt you." Auggie rolled his eyes. "Stop being such a coward."

"I'm not a coward." I reached out and nudged his shoulder playfully and he stumbled back with a giggle. "I just don't want to be the idiot who agrees to something that might lead to losing a finger. Or leg."

"It won't do that," he said. "Promise. I just wanted you to see the barn since you were so curious about it and everything. Now you know it's nothing malevolent."

"Malevolent?"

"It means—"

"I know what *malevolent* means, jerk." I nudged him again. "I just never thought *that* about it is all. I just thought it was unusual that you lived here. And that there were strange lights coming from it at night. That's all."

"Mmmhm."

"Seriously."

"Okay." Auggie shrugged. "Well...now you know."

"But you're not going to tell me what all of this is?"

"Nope." He grinned.

"Ugh." I leaned my head back to groan at the skylight, though I wasn't unamused.

"Don't be a spoil sport." He nudged me like I'd nudged him. "In a week or so you can come see the finished product and you'll know what I've been doing in here."

"Okay," I said. "Okay. I've seen it. You'll show me the finished product soon. Got it. But…"

Auggie watched me.

"What?" he asked.

"Where—where do you live?" I looked around grandly. "I mean, I don't see beds and stuff. Or…anything?"

Auggie chuckled.

"I don't *live here,* live here," he explained. "The house is a little bit further up the creek, but on the same property as the barn. The barn is just my workspace."

"That's nice?" I frowned. "You have a whole barn to do your…art."

Auggie nodded. "Installation art."

"Installation art." I mocked him with another playful nudge.

Auggie stumbled back dramatically and the both of us laughed.

"Wise guy," I teased.

"Sometimes."

For a few moments, I looked around the gloomy barn interior, wondering what Auggie could possibly be doing that would be considered art. It didn't take long before I found myself giving up, realizing that whatever it was, I wouldn't figure it out before Auggie was ready to show it to me.

"So," I turned to him, "are we still going to get coffee, or what? I haven't had breakfast. Maybe Starbuck will have some of those muffins from the other day. It was really good."

"Blueberry?"

"Blueberry."

"Yeah," Auggie made a slurping noise, "he always has those. They're so good."

"Well?" I asked.

"Yeah," Auggie seemed to come out of some daydream. "Let me just turn my music off and we'll go. Meet you outside?"

"All right."

I headed towards the barn doors as Auggie ventured further into the barn, crawling over industrial duct work to wherever the music was coming from so he could turn it off. The barn door was considerably lighter than I had expected—or had just been hung exceptionally well—because I was able to swing it open with ease. Once the golden sunlight was flooding the barn interior once more, I turned to find Auggie had climbed over all of the duct work to a radio on the other side of the room from the doors. He switched it off and began his journey back over all of the duct work as I stood waiting for him.

Once he had made his way to the barn doors, Auggie ushered me out and then slid the massive green door shut behind us. Without another word to each other, we headed to the creek that the barn was settled beside and started to follow it further into town. Auggie and I, him with a light skip to his step and me slightly dragging my feet like always, didn't try to make conversation. We traveled down the creek in comfortable silence. We passed the row of buildings on Liberty Lane and then the end of the tram tracks without a word. I could just see the Jolly Roger high on the mast of Starbuck's, just over the tops of the trees, when we were nearing the back of the post office.

As we started to round the post office and hook a right towards Starbuck's, the sound of voices at the front of the teal clapboard building grabbed our attention. Auggie and I glanced over at each other as we walked and listened to the commotion. Finally, we gave each other a nod and turned to head towards the front of the post office so we could see what was going on.

When we rounded the corner of the building, the source of the voices came into view, though the reason for the loud discussion wasn't clear. Levi Lee, Starbuck, Sofia, and Wyatt were all out front, talking animatedly about something. I glanced at Auggie and he simply shrugged as we approached the small group of people.

Who's watching the counter at the coffee shop? I thought to myself.

"Well, it doesn't happen often," Sofia was announcing to the others as we approached. "It certainly does not."

"Arrrr, no it doesn't," Starbuck agreed.

"When did it arrive?" Levi Lee asked excitedly, prompting Auggie and me to exchange another glance as we came to stand beside the discussion group.

"Just this morning," Sofia announced.

The three men with her made "oooooh" and "awwwww" sounds. Then the four of them began speaking excitedly, making it impossible to tell what one person was saying from another. Auggie watched them all intently and my eyes flitted between him and the group of people in front of the post office. Finally, when it became apparent that Auggie wasn't nearly as nosy as I, and the people in outside of the post office weren't going to settle down long enough for me to figure out what was going on, I stepped up to address them.

"Hey!" I exclaimed, and all four of them suddenly stopped talking to look over at me. "Uh, what's going on?"

Sofia and Levi smiled at me. Luckily, Wyatt's gun was in its holster, so he didn't address me in his own special way.

"Well, hon," Sofia said, "we got another letter to Shirlene today."

"A Shirlene letter?" I asked.

"Yes." Levi Lee nodded. "Sofia said it was slipped into the mail slot sometime during the night. We're still trying to figure out who Shirlene is and who's in love with her. That's all."

Starbuck nodded along solemnly.

"Where is it?" I asked.

"Hung up on the wall with the others, of course." Sofia hooked a thumb over her shoulder.

I glanced over my shoulder at Auggie and he simply shrugged. The other four people began talking excitedly once more. So, I sidestepped their discussion group and pushed through the front door of the post office. Auggie was right on my heels.

It wasn't hard to find the letter in question, as Sofia had tacked it dead center in the middle of all of the others. Though, unlike the other letters, it wasn't nearly as long. My eyes scanned the script, reading it over and over.

Shirlene.
My hope is renewed and my love lives again.

That was all.

Jeez. I thought to myself. *These people will get excited about anything.*

AN INVITATION

J ack wasn't very talkative at dinner, but that was nothing new. He'd stopped working on his project in the backyard and even typed out on his cell phone that he had finished it, then made dinner for us. But he wasn't in the mood to talk much other than that single note before dinner. Well, that's not entirely true. Jack's culinary skills were definitely not those of a Michelin Star chef, so dinner had been boxed mac and cheese with chopped up hot dogs in it and canned green beans warmed up. Food's food to me, but Jack had pointed at his plate during dinner and made an "OK?" sign. I had let him know that it was fine and did the job of filling my belly.

Boxed mac and cheese with green beans definitely wasn't the worst meal I'd had in my entire life. Living in motels with mom for a decade meant that beef jerky or potato chips from a vending machine qualified as dinner at times. Maybe Jack only knew how to make things like chili, cucumber salad, and meals from a box—things with few ingredients and minimal creativity—but at least effort was put forth. I'd gladly eat Jack's simple meals over anything that came from a vending machine any day of the week.

After dinner, I offered to put up the leftovers—not that there were too many—and clean up. So, Jack sat in his chair and turned on some old T.V. show. *The Jeffersons*, I think. By the time I had cleaned up everything in the kitchen—which hadn't taken all that long—Jack was fast asleep in his chair.

He'd obviously had a hard day finishing up his table project in the backyard. Instead of waking him up to let him know he should move to his bed and avoid a crick in his neck when he woke up, I turned off all of the lights and went upstairs. I left the T.V. on so he wouldn't wake up in the dark.

The sun was barely setting when I stripped off my shorts and t-shirt and crawled on top of the covers, since my third-floor room was still a little stuffy. It made no difference to me that it wasn't quite bedtime. I was exhausted for some reason.

The excitement of the Shirlene letter. I thought to myself with a smile.

Staying up for hours to watch the lights at the barn wasn't even a thought in my head, I was so tired. Besides, since I'd seen the inside of the barn, the lights didn't fascinate me like they did the first few nights. Before my eyes shut and I could fall into dreamland, my phone lit up on my bedside table, casting its pale blue glow on the ceiling.

Wondering if maybe my mom had been able to get a text or call through—now that I knew a signal was *possible* in Possibly—*heh*—I snatched my phone from the table. I propped myself up on one elbow sleepily as I stared down at the screen.

Wanna go to church with me tomorrow? It's at The Pueblo.

It was from Auggie. I had programmed his number into my phone earlier in the day since I finally had it.

Did I want to go to church? Yikes.

Spending so much time on the road with my mom, we'd never really belonged to a church. I'm sure, back when Mom and I had lived in Possibly with Jack—back when I was too young to even form a lasting memory—we had probably gone to church once or twice. Maybe Mom had even taken me to church a few times during that first year on the road together. However, when I searched my brain, I couldn't form a picture in my head of what the inside of a church looked like—at least not one I'd ever visited for services.

In a few places in America—especially in the southwest—I'd ventured into a lot of old churches that had been around since the founding of the towns in which they were located. They were tourist-y things to do, though. I hadn't gone to, like, commune with God or anything. I mean, if I was looking for God—which I *wasn't*, thank you very much—the last place I would have looked was a church. The places were kind of creepy. Or sterile. Depending on how old they were.

A weird thought entered my head. If I wasn't looking for God, why was someone like *Auggie* looking for him? With his weird clothes and skipping…I mean, well, you'd think someone like Auggie would have been avoiding church and God as much as possible. I didn't want to make assumptions about my new friend, but guys like him usually avoided church-y people.

Then again, you are in Possibly. Things are different here. I had thought to myself.

Auggie was also so bright and cheerful that I couldn't imagine anyone giving him much grief over anything.

He also likes mystics.

The kid was so weird.

It made me smile.

Yeah. I had typed out. *I'd love to go to church.*

I did it without even thinking too hard about it. A few minutes later, Auggie responded.

150

Awesome! Meet in front of The Pueblo at 11?

I tapped out an affirmative, waited until Auggie said: "OK," and then I laid my phone back on the bedside table.

That night, I dreamt of caterpillars. But no butterflies.

GOD IS A WOMAN

"Come on, Jack." I rolled my eyes as he laid his pile of boards on the tarp in the yard. "Auggie invited me to church. You should come with us."

The table Jack had been working on had disappeared and he was setting out new lumber to start a new project. After falling asleep the night before, my caterpillar dreams lulled me into a deep sleep for the next ten and a half hours. By the time I woke up, I could already hear Jack outside, banging around, and I had wandered down in my pajamas to see what was up. I wouldn't say Jack looked entirely pleased to see me so early in the morning, and when he was trying to start a new project, but he hid his disappointment fairly well. Mentioning church, however, made it harder for him to keep a straight face.

"So?" I asked. "What do you say?"

Jack waved an arm at me without looking up.

"Jack. Man," I said, "come on. Church can be fun. Probably. Or, should I say, *possibly*?"

Buh-dum-tiss.

Jack did look up at me then. I could tell he was trying to keep the grin off of his face. It took a moment longer for him to wave me off.

"Fine." I sighed. "Don't come to church. I will apologize to God for you and everything."

Am I above basically calling someone a heathen? Not really. Of course, since I couldn't remember ever actually going to church, it was a bit hypocritical. I'd have to apologize to God for both of us, I supposed.

Jack waved me off again, but he looked amused, though he tried to hide it by lowering his head.

"Okay," I said. "Well, I guess I'll shower and stuff. Meet Auggie at The Pueblo."

Jack nodded, indicating that he was listening, then began searching his pockets.

"Um, I don't really do church," I admitted. "Do I need to, uh, wear nicer clothes or something? I think I have some khakis or something?"

Jack shook his head as he extracted his phone from his back pocket. I watched as he typed out a message and held the phone out to me.

It read: *Auggie's a good kid.*

I stared at the message for a moment, unsure of why Jack had fished his phone out simply to type out such an odd thought.

"Yeah." I looked up at him. "He's cool and all."

Jack nodded. Then he locked his phone and slid it into his back pocket once more.

"So," I said, clearing my throat, "I can go in regular clothes?"

Jack nodded once more.

"Okay," I said. "If you're wrong, and I get embarrassed, it's gonna be you and me, man."

He grinned and made a shoving motion.

Go on. Get out of here. I understood that one, though I wasn't certain it was official sign language.

153

"All right." I turned to head towards the house, though I stopped before I got to the back steps and glanced over my shoulder. "Hey."

Jack looked up at me.

"If you change your mind or anything," I shrugged. "You know."

Again, an arm was waved in my general direction and I took the hint. Jack was smiling, though, so he wasn't annoyed with my repeated requests that he join us at The Pueblo, so that was something. Upstairs, I washed the Texas dust and sleepy time sweat off in the shower, and then I dug through my suitcases to find my nicest pair of shorts and a polo to wear to The Pueblo. I wasn't certain that the clothes would be, like, completely appropriate for church, or whatever, but I didn't want to stick out. So, I didn't want to dress too nicely and I didn't want to wear basketball shorts and a t-shirt, either. Maybe nice shorts and a polo would be a good middle ground?

I sat on the edge of my bed, looking at the dirty clothes pile I had started since I'd arrived in Possibly and my still mostly full suitcases. Sitting in *my* room—even if it was in *Jack's* house—and having all of my things in a suitcase felt odd. Jack hadn't specifically made it clear that I was welcome to stay for as long as I wanted, but he hadn't said I had to leave as soon as possible, either. Having time to wait before I had to meet Auggie at The Pueblo, I found myself wondering what I should do—unpack, or be prepared to leave at a moment's notice.

Finally, I decided that repacking my suitcases wasn't that big of a hassle—and it was easier to get clothes out of a closet or dresser instead of rooting around in suitcases, so, I unpacked. I hung up shirts and pants and neatly folded and placed my shorts, underwear, and socks in dresser drawers. Then I stowed my empty suitcases on the floor of the closet. If Jack got tired of me and somehow got ahold of my mom to tell her to come get me, I could be packed in minutes. No sweat. At least, in the meantime, life would seem a little more normal. I'd have a few days in a normal—well, kind of normal—place where I wasn't living out of a bag.

By the time I had finished unpacking and stored my suitcases, it was getting close to eleven o'clock, so I made my way downstairs to let Jack know I was leaving. He actually looked up from his pile of lumber to give me a quick wave as I headed out on foot through the backyard. A few minutes later, I was approaching The Pueblo. That was the good thing about Possibly—nothing was more than a few minutes away on foot. Even if you strolled leisurely.

Auggie was outside, waiting to meet up as he promised. As I walked up, I watched him greet other Possibilians as they walked through the doors of the giant mosque-like building. He smiled and said "hello" to everyone, shook hands if offered, and was generally way too friendly for someone about to give up free time to go to church. It made me smile. When I finally reached the front doors, where Auggie was waiting, all of the other approaching church-goers had made their way through the door. With a goofy grin, Auggie held out his hand.

"Good morning," he said.

I looked down at his hand.

"You're kind of ridiculous," I replied.

"What's ridiculous about greeting your fellow man before celebrating the life God has given you?" His hand remained presented.

So, I slid my hand into his and shook it firmly.

"Didn't hurt, did it?" he asked.

"I guess not."

Auggie turned to glance through the doors of The Pueblo, so I took a second to check out his clothes. He had on jean shorts and a polo, clean tennis shoes. So, dressing up wasn't required, but he had forgone his usual quirky way of dressing. His hair was even styled and pushed back neatly. I wasn't so sure I liked that I liked the change. Then again, that wasn't my choice to make.

"So," Auggie turned just as my eyes wandered back up to his, saving me from him finding me checking out his clothes, "you ready for church?"

"I guess." I shrugged. "I mean, I never really go to church, so, how would I know?"

Auggie chuckled and grabbed my arm to pull me towards the open front doors.

"No one's ever ready for church at The Pueblo," he said cryptically. "But they almost always come back."

"That doesn't sound scary at all." I murmured as Auggie pulled me through the large wooden doors of The Pueblo. "Is this a cult or something?"

Auggie laughed uproariously.

"Because I don't want to be in a cult," I said, trying to whisper so only Auggie would hear. "This could totally be a cult. This town is weird, and—"

"There you go with that word." Auggie stopped and let go of my arm so he could turn to face me. "What's *weird*, Jordan? Tell me what's so weird about this town."

I looked around, making sure no one was nearby to overhear me insulting their town. The last thing I needed was an ass-whooping in a church. Well, a building where church was held.

The inside of The Pueblo looked somewhat look an open-air atrium one might find in ancient Rome. Large stone columns, stone floors, an open area at the center where grass and flowers were planted. High above, in the dome of the mosque-like building, a skylight allowed golden sunlight to pour down into the building, negating the need for lights during the day. Though, sconced lighting was on the circular walls around the building and on some of the pillars. I wondered, since Possibly seemed to go dark at night—why did they need lights in The Pueblo?

I'd never seen light pouring out of the roof of The Pueblo at night, and since they didn't have them on for church—which was during the day—why did they have lights at all? Possibly *was* a weird town. The people, the buildings, the...*everything*. But nothing seemed all that malevolent—as Auggie might have said. It was just quirky, maybe?

"I don't know," I finally said in a whisper. "It's just...different than anywhere else I've been. That's why I say it's weird."

I shrugged. Auggie watched me for a minute before a smile finally bloomed on his face.

"Weird's good," he said. "As long as it doesn't try to convert you or harm you. We should all experience some *weird* every now and then."

"I guess."

"This isn't a cult," he said. "We don't have a church in Possibly. The town, essentially, is against organized religion. It's, like, in the charter or something. But this is just a way for us all to get together and meet our spiritual needs in a non-denominational way. That's all."

"Okay."

"No one is going to ask you to eat a live chicken or sacrifice a goat or pledge your undying fealty to The Pueblo. Or some demon. Okay?"

"Okay," I said. "I'm sorry."

"Don't be sorry." He nudged my arm playfully. "Just, maybe, instead of calling something weird, just express what is confusing you. Ask questions."

"Okay."

"Are you going to say okay again?" He chuckled.

"No," I said. "Sorry. I just…yeah. This is a different, uh, new experience for me, man. I don't really know what to think about it."

"That was perfect."

"Huh?"

"Just saying this is new and different to you," Auggie said. "Admitting that it feels uncomfortable because you're not familiar with church or this town is cool. I can dig that."

"You can *dig that*?" I laughed, a little too loudly.

Auggie laughed with me.

"Okay," Auggie said. "*That* was weird."

"Completely."

He nudged me again and then his hand was grabbing at my arm once again. Without another word, he dragged me deeper into The Pueblo, pulling me to the center of the circular room towards the round patch of grass. As we approached, chuckling to each other, I noticed all of the other citizens of Possibly—at least the ones who had bothered to come for services—were standing around the circular patch of grass under the skylight. Auggie shoved me into place to stand on one of the floor tiles at the edge of the grassy area, then stepped into the spot next to me.

Wyatt, Sofia, Levi Lee, Starbuck, Grandy, and others I didn't quite recognize were lined up around the circle, standing on their own floor tiles. It had escaped my notice when Auggie had pushed me towards the circular meeting space—probably because I had been too busy giggling at his insistent demeanor—but there was a basket in the grass, right in front of each tile a Possibilian was standing on. Each basket seemed to contain old fruit—most of it looking to be a day from becoming completely rotten. I turned my nose up at the sight at my feet.

When I looked around the circle at the other Possibilians standing on their floor tiles in front of baskets of half-rotten fruit, I realized that none of them seemed confused or disgusted. Everyone stood in their place, waiting for…whatever…to happen. I glanced over at Auggie, surely, with concern etched all over my face, not to mention confusion, and he gestured for me to just wait. So, I waited. I stood in front of my basket of fruit as golden late-morning sunlight shined down into the grassy area of The Pueblo, and waited.

It wasn't long, the wait. After a few moments, footsteps on tiles sounded from one of the darkened corners of The Pueblo. My head whipped back and forth, looking for the source of the footsteps. None of the other people at the circle of grass looked around, they just stared towards the center of the patch of grass.

This has to be a cult. I thought to myself.

When a woman stepped out of the darkness behind the people on the edge of the circle across from me, dressed in a toga with a flower crown on her head, I thought about running for it. I'd seen enough horror movies to know that this was a sign that I was in danger. Even if Auggie didn't like my use of the word "weird," this was some weird crap. The woman, her bare feet making fleshy slaps on the tiles, walked towards the circle, her toga sweeping the floor behind her. When she reached the edge of the circle, stepping between Wyatt and

Sofia, it was like her eyes specifically sought me out. Our eyes connected and the corners of her mouth turned up warmly for the briefest of moments.

Then she was looking straight ahead and walking out into the center of the grassy area, the sunlight shining off her white toga, practically turning it into a beacon. The woman stood at the center of the grassy area for a moment, her eyes straight ahead, then she took a deep breath. Slowly, her arms raised from her sides to jut out straight from her body.

Here it comes. I had thought. *She's going to shoot out lasers and hypnotize us all, indoctrinating us all into her cult.*

Lasers didn't emanate from the woman in a toga. She didn't really do anything. What happened next didn't come from the woman at the center of The Pueblo. Everyone in the circle—including Auggie—started to boo and scream at the woman. Shocked, I jumped back slightly at the cacophony of rude noises coming from the town's citizens. When the first person—Sofia—reached into the basket at her feet, grabbed a rotten bunch of grapes and tossed them directly at the woman in the toga, I nearly screamed out.

The rest of the people in the circle followed Sofia's lead and started maniacally reaching into the baskets at their feet to retrieve rotten fruit to throw at the woman. Old grapes, tomatoes, even apples and oranges, were hurled at the woman as the boos, hisses, and screams continued. The screaming and throwing built and built, the fruit leaving a dark rainbow of stains on the woman's toga. But she did nothing. She stood there, her arms held out, as the citizens of Possibly violently chucked fruit at her. She didn't even look upset. A beatific smile adorned her face.

Of their own accord, my hands slapped over my ears, trying to block out the sound of the people screaming and booing. I

160

wanted to shut my eyes so that I didn't have to look at the woman being angrily pelted with fruit, but I found that I couldn't look away. The noise coming from my fellow church-goers swelled and fruit hit the woman quicker and quicker until I felt like I was in Willy Wonka's tunnel with him at the wheel of his boat. Just when I thought I would scream out, demand that everyone stop whatever the hell they were doing—though the woman in the toga seemed to welcome it—the noise suddenly ceased and the fruit stopped flying.

No longer did anyone hiss or boo or scream angrily at the woman. No more did fruit slap against her to leave gooey stains that oozed juice down her toga and skin. Everyone around the circular patch of grass stood there, their hands at their sides, the flesh and juice of rotten fruit dripping from their fingers to the tile at their feet. The woman in the toga let her eyes close lazily as she continued to smile and hold her arms out to her sides.

My hands slowly slid from my ears, shaking as they traveled down my body to rest at my hips once again. A hot tear trailed from the corner of my eye over the apple of my cheek as I watched the woman stand in the golden sunlight, unbothered by what had just happened to her. My bottom lip quivered as I stared at the no-longer white toga of the woman. Rotten, smashed fruit lay at her feet in fetid heaps as she stood there, basking in the rays of light that streamed through the skylight. Then, the group of people that circled around her at the edge of the clearing began to move.

Watching from the safety of my own tile, my hands shaking at my sides and tears slowly leaking from the corners of my eyes, I watched as the citizens of Possibly approached the woman quietly. I didn't know what to expect—were they going to slaughter her now? What other torment did they have in store for this poor woman who had endured their taunting and physical abuse?

How is this not a cult? I thought to myself. *This is messed up.*

Much to my shock, the woman's eyes opened, and she welcomed the people who had just pelted her with fruit and verbal abuse with open arms. What happened wasn't further violence or screaming, but a big, silent, group hug. The woman's arms found and patted as many backs and shoulders as she could as the citizens of Possibly hugged her warmly.

Sunlight continued to bathe the woman—and now the citizens of Possibly—in golden rays as they stood in the center of the circle of grass and hugged each other warmly. I slumped against the pillar at my side and let tears run down my cheeks. My hands were shaky, but I managed to reach up and wipe my cheeks dry with the backs of my wrists. Still, the people hugged quietly and bathed in the warmth of the sun at the center of The Pueblo.

What. The. Crap?

BLOOMING TAKES TIME

After walking around downtown no less than six times, my hands finally stopped shaking and my cheeks were dry, though my eyes were surely beet red. Auggie walked alongside me quietly the whole while, though I wasn't sure if he was silent out of fear of what I'd have to say, or respect for my need to process what had happened at The Pueblo. As we walked around and around, my eyes flicked and darted over to other Possibilians, wondering if they would randomly and violently throw something at me, too. Would they suddenly boo or hiss at me?

Auggie seemed to pick up on my uneasiness at what had happened during the *church service* and didn't offer to explain anything. He didn't defend it, either. He simply let me walk along, kicking at the dirt and pavement as I processed my own thoughts. Walking alongside me through town was his way of keeping me company without being intrusive. Every now and then, my eyes would dart over to him, and I saw that he wasn't staring at me, either. He was giving me as much space as he could without actually leaving me to be alone.

When I finally found myself walking by the backside of Mystic Molly's tent, I stopped on the side of the road. Then I flopped down in the grass, my legs jutting out directly in front of me as my hands came to rest in my lap. My eyes stared out at nothing as I tried to process my feelings about the woman, the violence, the screaming…my stomach was in knots and I suddenly realized that I hadn't had any breakfast that morning. It was probably a good thing because I might have upchucked all of it right there in the grass behind Mystic Molly's.

Auggie stood on the road for a while, watching me, obviously unsure if he was welcome to sit with me. However, he finally stepped onto the grass and sat down next to me. He pulled his legs underneath himself into the lotus position and hunched down, sitting comfortably next to me. I'm not sure how much time passed before my stomach stopped feeling like acrobats were performing in it, but I finally started to feel somewhat normal. I pulled my legs in and mirrored Auggie's position. My hands felt steadier and my eyes no longer felt like they might start flooding tears at the slightest thing. A soft, warm breeze blew through town, ruffling my hair and the hem of Molly's tent behind us.

"Why would you guys do that?" I muttered, my eyes on my lap.

Auggie didn't respond.

"What does it mean?" I asked the question in a new way.

My sitting partner kicked his legs out in front of himself in the grass and leaned back to prop himself up with the palms of his hands.

"What's it about?" I asked.

"What do you want it to be about?" Auggie finally asked.

I didn't have an answer for that. I would have preferred that nothing had happened at all. Then I wouldn't have felt sick to my stomach, wondering what was wrong with the people of Possibly.

"That's the church service they've been doing at The Pueblo as far back as I can remember," Auggie said. "We gather and throw fruit at her."

"Why?" I murmured, my eyes darting around nervously.

Auggie let that question hang on the warm summer breeze, flittering about our skulls for a few moments, then he shifted and sighed.

"The woman?" Auggie asked. "That's God."

I just stared.

"To me," Auggie continued, "it means that no matter how awful we are—humans—no matter how much destruction we cause. No matter how mean we are to each other. No matter how far we stray from God's goodness, she'll always welcome us back with open arms. She still loves us. It's never too late. To, uh, remember who you are. To be your best self."

Warm air ruffled my hair again and Molly's tent rustled in the breeze behind us. Wyatt's gun went off somewhere near Lovelorn Pass Bridge. I could hear the metallic "ding" of Earl Dean's pickaxe on pavement over on Liberty Lane. *Fill Your Heart* by Tiny Tim was AMOR's choice of song for the day. The grass tickled at the back of my knees and traced like tiny fingers along my bare calves. My nose picked up the scent of brewing coffee drifting over from Starbuck's. Possibly had gone back to what passed for normal in the space of minutes. All while I had been walking around in a stupor, wondering what the hell was wrong with everyone.

"It was unsettling the first time I went," Auggie said. "But I was kinda young then, too."

I reached up and picked at the salty tracks in the corners of my eyes.

"I probably shouldn't say this—"

"Go ahead," I said. "I'm already so weirded out."

"—but, it's kind of performance art," Auggie said. "Just like any other church. The Pueblo just gets to the point faster."

"*The point?*" I hissed, though I didn't mean to use such a harsh tone.

"All of us—humans—we're not all that great." Auggie turned to me with a smile. "But if we really try. If we'd just pause. We can be loving, caring, kind people. Take a second to consider how you're behaving—give yourself a moment to take a breath—and you'll realize you don't want to be the person you're being. That's all it is."

"Oh, yeah?" I scoffed.

"The woman in the grass in the toga?" Auggie ignored my tone. "No one forces her to be there. She's kind of like our preacher or pastor. She's also an artist. She enjoys representing God."

"So," I snorted, "God is a woman?"

"Why not?" Auggie shrugged. "God is all things. Some of those things are female. Why can't God be female? Also, we can't really expect God to come to The Pueblo each Sunday. They have better work to do."

"This town is—" I stopped myself.

Auggie didn't jump in to remind me that I shouldn't say what I was going to say.

"We're different," Auggie said. "No one is going to make you go back to church at The Pueblo. No one will think differently of you one way or the other. But *that is* our way of having church. We'll all still love you and accept you here even if you decide it's *too weird* for you."

"Why?" I muttered. "Don't want to lose a cult member?"

Auggie laughed. "You know we're not a cult."

"No." I sighed and plucked a piece of grass. "I just—it was—it bothered me."

"Why?"

"Really?" I snorted, though I still avoided his eyes. "Seeing somebody attacked like that? Screamed at? That's not right, Auggie, it's—"

My eyes finally connected with his. Auggie was just staring at me, waiting for me to finish the realization I'd come to on my own.

"—it's not what God would want."

He produced a gentle smile.

"And you never have to participate if you don't want to," he said.

"Why do you?" I demanded, though I tried to keep my voice calm.

"I don't," he said. "Not always. Actually, a lot of us don't throw the fruit at her on other days."

"Why today?"

"Today I—a lot of us—needed to be reminded what it feels like to be cruel," Auggie said. "So that we remember it for a very long time."

"Can't you just—crap, I don't know—remember without doing it?" I grumbled, prying more grass out of the ground.

"Sure." He shrugged. "I guess? But since it's safe to explore our feelings at The Pueblo—and no one really gets hurt— sometimes it helps to throw the fruit."

A deep sigh escaped my throat as I considered everything Auggie had told me. Did I feel differently about my friend now that I'd seen him scream and throw rotten fruit at a helpless woman who was supposed to be playing God? The snarl of his lip and the anger in his eyes as he stood next to me, grabbing fruit maniacally and throwing it at the woman in a toga flashed through my mind. But the aftermath—the sorrow in his eyes at what he'd done—the urgency with which he hugged her quickly after, washed away the first memory.

"I guess I get it," I relented. "I wish you had told me first."

"Well," Auggie answered, guilt riding his tone, "it doesn't have quite the same impact if people know about it first. If people know that it's going to happen and what it means to other people, they tend to not take it seriously. It doesn't make them think."

"Yeah. I guess I understand that, too," I said. "It just...it was violent and scary and...I felt a little betrayed. Like, why wouldn't you warn me?"

Auggie stared at me.

"I know we're not, like, *friends* yet." I shrugged, heat rising in my cheeks. "But it kind of hurt that you didn't warn me first."

"Another lesson, then."

My head turned to look at Auggie and our eyes connected.

"And you are my friend." He nudged me in the arm playfully. "And I'm sorry, too. I hope you'll forgive me eventually."

"I forgive you." I nudged him back, finally able to chuckle slightly. "Just...please warn me if we're ever going to attack someone with fruit again. Okay?"

Auggie laughed warmly. "That's the worst thing you'll see in Possibly. I promise. Everything else is pretty peaceful and kind."

"Okay."

"Wanna walk around some more?" he asked. "Shake off the rest of your sorrows?"

I laughed at such an odd question.

"Yeah."

So, the two of us rose from the grass and, without discussing it, walked west. It was then that I noticed I had chosen to fall down in the grass behind Mystic Molly's, which was right across the street from The Pueblo. Why had I chosen to discuss what had happened at The Pueblo so close to it? Normally, I would have gotten far away from something that had disturbed me so deeply before I sat down to have a calm discussion about it. Another warm summer breeze blew through town, chasing that thought from my mind.

Moments later, we were walking along the four buildings that lined up perpendicular to The Pueblo. When I glanced to my side, I caught sight of that lady who rowed herself in the wheelchair—*Agnes Broussard?*—through the plate glass window of her shop. I stopped on the sidewalk next to the building and turned to stare at her as she sat in her chair and worked at a little table inside. When I glanced up at the sign over our heads, I was reminded of the name of her shop, which Auggie had told me a few days prior.

Blooms.

Auggie came to stand beside me as I checked out the sign, then turned my attention back to the work Agnes was doing inside of her shop. After a few moments, she noticed me staring in at her. She stopped her work for a second, gave me a smile and a wave, then went back to whatever she was creating on the table in front of her wheelchair.

"What's she doing?" I asked.

"She takes old plastic bottles and straws," Auggie said, "cuts them up, uses a hot pad to soften and mold them, and turns them into flowers."

He motioned to a basket besides the shop's front door. I knelt to look at the contents of the basket as Auggie continued to stare in at Agnes. Inside the basket, as Auggie had said, were flowers created from recycled soda bottles and plastic straws. Agnes had cut oval pieces out of bottles and warped them with heat to make petals for the flowers. She had painted plastic straws green, and then she had delicately glued the petals in beautiful blooming arrangements around their tips.

Obviously, the flowers were artificial—no one would have mistaken them for real flowers, like they might with more realistic artificial flowers made of other materials—but there was a beautiful weirdness to them. They looked like they were flowers from some alien planet made of colored plastic. I dug through the basket lazily, checking out the uniqueness of each flower Agnes had created. A lily. A rose. A daffodil. Agnes was a peculiar—though extraordinary—artist.

"Those are free," Auggie said. "She always leaves a basket by the door of the flowers she doesn't think are her best so that people can help themselves to some beauty."

"If these aren't her best, I need to see the ones inside." I chuckled.

My eyes landed on a daisy Agnes had made and placed in the basket. The stem of the daisy found its way between my fingers, and I plucked it from the basket. I stood from my crouched position and turned to Auggie. He pulled his attention away from watching Agnes working on her latest creation, and turned to face me. My hand came up automatically and I held the daisy out to him. Auggie looked down at the flower, a blank expression on his face, before his eyes met mine again.

I shrugged. "For saying that we're friends."

The corner of Auggie's mouth turned up slightly and his cheeks seemed to flush, but he slowly raised his hand to gingerly take the plastic flower between his fingers.

"Thank you," he said. "Friend."

"You're welcome," I replied. "Friend."

Then we were staring into each other's eyes and it dawned on me that my fingers were still pinching the flower stem while

Auggie held onto the stem as well. I started to open my mouth to say something, though I wasn't sure what, but movement further down the sidewalk caught my eye. I tore my eyes away from Auggie's to glance over his shoulder at whatever had caught my eye. The group of boys I had seen with Auggie in the clearing in the woods, and also fist-bumping him on the street, were walking down the sidewalk towards us.

Immediately, my hand fell away from the flower and I stepped back from Auggie. A frown formed on his face, but he didn't lose his grip on the plastic daisy that seemed to catch the early afternoon sun perfectly. Auggie looked confused at my sudden movement away from him, but then the sound of the boys' laughter and talking caught his ears and a look of recognition washed over his face. Then his eyes and mouth went blank, and the Auggie I knew disappeared. Instead of fun, silly, joyful Auggie, I was looking at a blank slate.

"Um," I said before I could think too much about everything, "I should get back to Jack's place. It's probably about lunch time, right?"

"Right." Auggie's voice was hollow.

"Right." I parroted and stepped around him. "Thanks for, uh, taking me to church and stuff."

"You're welcome." Auggie's hollow voice followed me as I walked quickly down the sidewalk towards the boys.

They all gave me smiles as I passed, which I returned robotically before passing them. When they were behind me on the sidewalk, I broke into a jog. I didn't look back to see if they gave Auggie fist-bumps or high-fives—or if they even had any type of exchange. I just jogged the rest of the way to Jack's house. When I got to the yard, Jack gave me a small wave, but I ignored it. I continued at the same pace up the back steps, through the house, and upstairs to my room.

I fell backwards onto the bed and threw my arm over my eyes. My stomach churned and I felt hot as I laid there on the bed in the stuffy room.

Did I just throw rotten fruit at God?

RUE FOR YOU AND RUE FOR ME

phelia by The Lumineers assaulted my ears when I walked up to the barely cracked green doors on the big red barn the next morning. Auggie was blasting his stereo, much unlike the day before, when David Bowie had been playing softly. At first, I thought opening the door and presenting myself, with all of my guilt laid bare, would kill me. I mean, I knew I had hurt the guy's feelings, and I should apologize, but I didn't know if I could deal with the embarrassment that comes with admitting that you messed up so magnificently. Of course, it also crossed my mind that Auggie might scream at me and tell me to leave. Or worse, he'd act cold and distant, his voice hollow and his face blank like it had been the day before.

Honestly, I didn't know what had been going through my mind when I had given the flower to him outside of Blooms. It was a pretty flower and Auggie had been nice to me. He called me his friend. He'd taken me to church—even though I hadn't really enjoyed the experience. At least not while it was happening. Truth be told, *after* church, I realized that I had a lot to think about—philosophize over like I was Grandy sitting on cinderblocks. But getting to that point had been a bit traumatic, to say the least. However, Auggie was the reason that I realized there was so much about life, people, and, I guess, myself, that I'd never thought about before.

When I saw the daisy, and its shimmering iridescence in the sunlight, it made me think of him. So, I thought he should have it.

Was that it?

Or was I so overwhelmed at having a friend—*finally*—that I had to show him my appreciation for being my friend? Not that I'd never had, like, a friend, I guess. I'd met other kids while on the road with Mom. But they were friends for a few days while we were in the same town. Sometimes I'd find another kid to hang out with for longer if we hung around a place long enough, but it never lasted. And I always had to make the first move towards friendship. Though I'd had to introduce myself to Auggie first, he had jumped into the idea of hanging out with me with both feet, not once questioning anything.

Auggie was cool.

But when the other boys saw me giving him a flower...

A boy who wore clam diggers and skirts and pearl jewelry...

I just needed Auggie to understand what had happened. It had nothing to do with him because he was freaking cool. I still wanted to be his friend and everything. The last thing I wanted was for him to stop trying to hang out with me because he thought I was upset with him or something. Because I wasn't. We were still good in my mind.

So, I took a deep breath as *Ophelia* blared on Auggie's stereo, and I pushed the green barn door open, hoping that Auggie wasn't too busy with his art to talk to me. With the door swung wide and the sunlight pouring into the barn, I easily found Auggie in the usually gloomy room. As soon as the sunlight cast a streak across his face, he turned to see who had entered the barn, a smile on his face. When his eyes landed on me, it disappeared.

That was kind of a punch to the gut.

"Hey," I said.

I didn't step into the barn. I didn't know if my presence was allowed.

"Hey," he said back in that hollow voice I had feared.

He gave me a sharp nod and his expression went blank.

I screwed up so bad. I thought to myself.

"Um," I kicked at the ground, "can I come in, or…?"

Auggie stared at me for a moment before speaking.

"S'free country."

That wasn't exactly the invitation I had been hoping for, but it was better than nothing, so I stepped inside, leaving the door open behind me. Even though I didn't want to see Auggie's blank face, I still wanted to be able to see him while I apologized. So I could judge his reaction. Closing the door would have hindered that, even with the skylight.

"Uh," I said, "yesterday, with the flower—"

"I get it."

"Yeah." I shook my head, trying to clear my thoughts. "I mean, no. I wanted to say that I'm sorry. It probably seemed like—"

"I get it," Auggie said again, his tone firm.

"Look," I rolled my head back to look up at the ceiling, "I didn't mean to hurt your feelings, Auggie. It's just that—"

"I. Get. It."

Auggie's sharp tone made me look back over at him. It finally dawned on me that he was wearing dingy old sweatpants, old sneakers, and a band t-shirt. No skirt, clam diggers, or necklaces present. That made something in my chest ache.

175

He didn't look like himself.

"Whatcha, uh, doin'?" I asked.

I couldn't think of anything else to say.

"My art," he answered.

"Do you need help?" I asked, my toe kicking at the ground again. "We could hang out, or—"

"I don't need help."

"Auggie. Man, I—"

"What do you want, Jordan?" He crossed his arms over his chest. "I'm kind of busy with things, so…"

His voice trailed off and he shrugged, his whole body asking a question. All I could do for several moments was stare. I'd never had to navigate this kind of thing before. I'd never had to be a real friend.

"I was embarrassed," I said.

When all else fails, tell the truth. Even if it's embarrassing.

Auggie just stood there.

"Giving a flower to a guy," I shrugged, "even a plastic one, is kind of…I didn't want to be made fun of. That's all."

"Those guys wouldn't have cared," Auggie said.

"I didn't know that."

"Did you think about giving them the benefit of the doubt?"

"No."

"I need to do my art." He waved me off.

"Please let me help," I took a few steps further into the barn. "I'm really sorry, Auggie. I really am your friend—and I'd take it back if I could."

"The flower?" He snorted and turned towards the table to shut off the music. "You wouldn't have to. I threw it back in the basket."

I was grateful for him turning off the music because carrying on a conversation over blaring music was beginning to give me a headache. My chest felt other things about the discarded flower.

"No," I said, then adjusted my volume to the now silent room, "No. I'd take back being a jerk. I'd take back hurting your feelings."

"Fine."

"Fine, what?" I asked. "Are you going to forgive me?"

"You hurt my feelings, Jordan."

He slumped against the table, bracing himself with his forearms.

"It was kind of a shitty thing to do, you know?" he added.

"I know."

"Friends don't do shitty things to each other."

"I should have known that, too," I said.

Auggie stayed there, leaning against the table, his eyes not meeting mine, so I moved further into the barn, stepping over some of the ductwork. I didn't get too close because I thought that might make him scream at me. Until he had forgiven me, I wanted to give him his space.

"Where are your," I tried to think of the right words, "usual clothes?"

"This is how I wanted to dress today."

"It doesn't really suit you."

"How would you know what suits me?"

I ignored the jab.

"You're a cheerful guy." I shrugged. "Those aren't very cheerful clothes. I like it when you're cheerful."

The corner of his mouth turned up, though he tried to hide it from me. Auggie turned his head to the side, looking away from me, so I was left to look at the back of his head. It kind of bothered me that I couldn't see the white diamond on his forehead and in his hair.

"What's the, uh, white thing?" I decided to ask. "On your forehead and in your hair?"

Auggie didn't look back over at me. Hopefully, he was still trying to hide a smile from me.

"It's kind of cool," I said. "Like a superhero mark or something."

"Oh, come on," He was suddenly looking at me, grinning ear to ear. "You're just trying to get on my good side to make up for being a jerk."

"Nah, man." I laughed. "It's kind of cool. I mean, I've never seen someone with that before, but, it's cool."

Auggie pushed off from the table and crossed his arms over his chest again, but the smile didn't leave his face.

"It's poliosis," he said. "A few things can cause it, but I have an inherited defect in melanisation."

My eyes grew wide and I ran a hand over my head as I made a "whoosh" sound.

Auggie laughed.

"Melanin? The stuff that determines the shade of skin and hair? I have a genetic defect where the melanin there is kind of…I guess, absent? It's not contagious. It doesn't hurt or anything. It's just—"

I waited.

"—weird." He laughed.

I smiled at him.

"I've had it forever," he said with a shrug. "As long as I can remember. I used to be embarrassed by it. I'm not embarrassed by much anymore."

His words were like knives, though I knew he didn't mean to be spiteful.

"I'll try really hard to learn that skill," I said.

Auggie nodded at me and his hands slipped down to his sides, no longer aggressively protecting himself from me.

"Okay," he said.

"Can I help you with your art, then?" I asked.

Auggie sighed. "I really do like working alone. I'm not still upset or anything. It's just...it's kind of a personal thing for me, you know? It's meditative and gives me time to just be with myself and my thoughts. It's not that I don't want you to help, but—"

"No." I stopped him. "I get it. I really do. I think. No hurt feelings. But can we maybe hang out later? Or tomorrow?"

Auggie was smiling again. "I'd like that. Later would be cool. After lunch?"

Then I was smiling as widely as him. "Hells yeah."

"Cool," he said. "I'll text you?"

"Yeah, man." I nodded as I started to turn towards the door. "I'll be waiting. Or just come by, okay?"

"Sure."

"Maybe we can even find something—some project—that can be our thing, ya' know?" I suggested too eagerly as I made my way to the door, but I tried not to be embarrassed by my obvious excitement. "You know. If you want."

"Hey." Auggie's voice stopped me when I reached the door, so I turned to look at him.

"Yeah?"

"I can teach you American Sign Language," he said.

I grinned. "That'd be perfect."

He nodded towards the door. "Then get. I'll see you in a few hours."

"Deal."

"Leave the door open, huh?" he asked. "I kind of want to see the sun."

That made me happy, but I didn't respond. I left the door open when I made my way out. And I walked back to Jack's with a smile on my face.

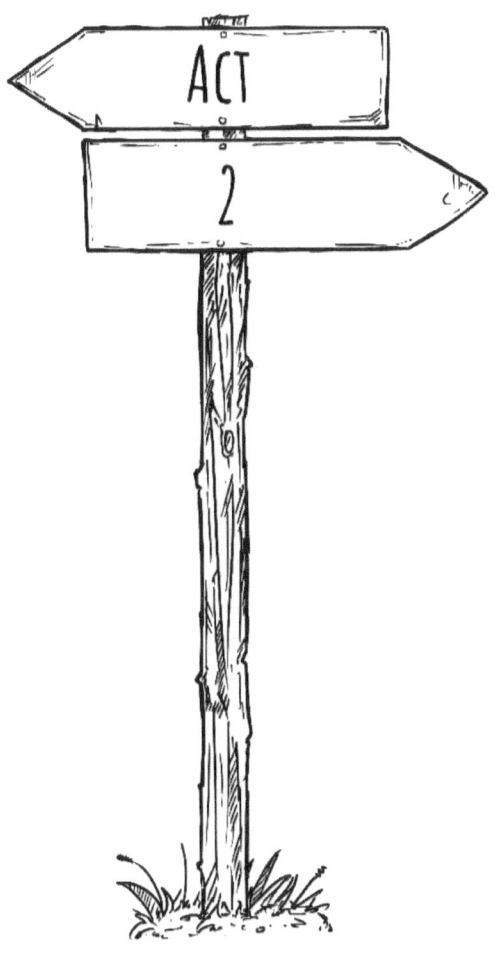

BUILDING A BRIDGE

"**Y**ou're totally not paying attention to me," Auggie said. "If you'd just focus instead of getting distracted by everything going on—"

"*Everything?*" I turned my head back to him. "Yeah. Possibly has so much going on, Auggie. Watch out New York City— *Possibly is where it's all happening!*"

I was met with a blank stare from my friend, but I could tell that he was doing his best not to grin at my silliness. We were sitting on the ground under one of the trees outside of Starbuck's, our to-go cups of café mochas nestled in the grass beside us. A few weeks had gone by—and true to his word— Auggie was slowly beginning to teach me American Sign Language. Each morning, after I showered off my sleep, we met at the barn and walked into town together. Not that it was that long of a trip for either of us. We said "hello" to Earl Dean and Jasper on Liberty Lane, even nodded at the police officer—whose name I learned was Officer Hanning—and stopped in to say "hello" to Sofia and check to see if a new letter from Shirlene had arrived.

After that, we would wave at Wyatt—who rarely returned the gesture—then we'd make sure to wave at Grandy and Mystic Molly. We'd greet Agnes Broussard through the front window of Blooms and nod at Samuel as he opened his soda spray each day. Lilly would get a gesture of greeting from us, too, before we headed over to Starbuck's. Levi Lee was always excited to see us approaching and would quickly revert from robot to human—*he was still into that art*—so he could give us a proper greeting in return. Then Auggie and I would venture inside for muffins and coffees, shoot the breeze with Starbuck for a bit, then we'd make our way outside for a lesson.

For hours each morning, we'd pick at our muffins and sip our coffees as Auggie did his best to teach an unteachable person. Formal schooling and structure weren't really my thing, but I did my best to follow along and let Auggie lead the lessons. Mostly, I'd steal blueberries from Auggie's muffin when he wasn't looking, plucking them out deftly with the tips of my fingers before popping them into my mouth. The sticky, sweet, chewy berries that seemed to explode into juicy bits between my teeth just tasted like summer.

Which was coming along nicely.

The end of June had slammed into the beginning of July and the sun told the tale each morning as it climbed higher and higher into the sky. Most amazingly, the weather hadn't gotten hotter. Sure, it was summer in Texas, but the warmth was bearable. A decent pair of shorts, a t-shirt, and some flip-flops, and the weather was actually pleasant. The grass in Possibly hadn't turned brown and crinkly like it did in a lot of the southern towns I'd lived in during the warmer months of the year. Green and lush, almost like shag carpet, Possibly looked like God had done the lawn work himself. Of course, I'd seen the way people took care of their homes and businesses in town. It really wasn't the type of town where grass went un-watered or untended to in other ways.

Under a tree, sitting in the grass outside of the coffee shop, it was easy to let a morning slip away from us—especially with a treat and a drink from Starbuck's. Wyatt still shot randomly into the air all morning long, Earl Dean still "thwacked" his pickaxe into Liberty Lane in the distance, Levi Lee still did his crazy little performance art, and people opened and closed doors in the businesses downtown. AMOR still played its one song a day for twelve hours a day. And summer was pleasant. Especially sitting on the grass under the tree near Susurrus Creek with Auggie, who was willing to teach me the same thing over and over again until I got it.

We'd heard *Back in the Saddle Again* by Gene Autry dozens of times, thanks to Amos over at AMOR, before Auggie addressed the fact that I was running thin on attention. It had been the same thing every day for a week. Well, Amos played a different song each day, but my mind always seemed to drift once lunchtime started to come around. I wasn't sure if it was just a natural inclination of mine to get bored with lessons after a few hours or my stomach was trying to tell me it was time to eat. Something about my gut makes it impossible for it not to warn me when another meal time is approaching.

"You know what I mean." Auggie nudged me in the shin with the toes of his right foot. "You're supposed to be paying attention to what I'm teaching you. Not anything else."

"I'm sorry." I groaned. "We've been sitting here for hours. Just like we do every day. I don't think I'm ever going to remember all of this."

"Have you been practicing?"

I picked at the grass with my fingers, avoiding Auggie's gaze.

"Well?" he asked.

"No." I pretended to be annoyed. "No. Okay? I haven't. Does that make you happy?"

"Not really."

"Jack's just," I shrugged and finally looked at Auggie, "he's not an easy guy to get to know. You know? I mean, yeah, you guys seem to get along and all, but you've had more time. I haven't seen him in…forever. What if I sign the wrong thing and upset him or something? I suck at this."

Auggie smiled warmly.

"You don't suck at this," he said. "And Jack will be, like, super stoked that you even bothered learning more signs. I promise. Even if the conversation is a little awkward at first."

"I guess." I picked at the grass some more.

Jeez. The grass was so soft.

Auggie chuckled as he kicked his legs out in front of himself and leaned back, propping himself up with his hands in the grass behind him. His head laid back on his shoulders and his eyes closed placidly as his face turned up towards the canopy of tree limbs above us.

"You know," he said, "you don't actually have to be able to make the signs yourself, right?"

"Huh?"

"Well, Jack isn't deaf, for crying out loud," Auggie chuckled, his eyes still closed and his head still leaned back. "He can't speak. As long as you can read the signs, that's all that matters."

"Oh. I hadn't thought of that."

"People rarely think of the challenges of people who are different from themselves."

"Ouch."

"I'm not chastising you," Auggie said as his head tilted to the side and his eyes opened to take me in. "It's just fact. Regardless, you only have to be able to tell what he is signing. That way, when you say something to him, he can sign back. He won't have to get his phone or his notepad. That will mean everything to him."

"Really?"

"Promise."

"Okay, yeah. I get that. That makes sense. But I kind of want to be able to use it, too. At least a little bit so that he knows I understand sign language now."

"Then you're going to have to pay attention during lessons."

I nodded to myself as Auggie turned his face back to the canopy of trees and his eyes languidly shut once more. A soft breeze blew through downtown Possibly, ruffling mine and Auggie's hair. I couldn't help but smile at the refreshing coolness and the smell the breeze carried with it. Something…wild and sweet. *Honeysuckle?* Something was growing in the woods on the other side of Susurrus Creek—or the creek itself—that was picked up by the wind.

My eyes drifted to look at the creek and Lovelorn Pass Bridge. It took everything I had to not roll my eyes cynically as Brandon—the boy I'd seen the day I arrived in Possibly—climbing up the railing on the bridge. Auggie was still relaxing in the shade as Brandon stood perilously upon the narrow railing, threw his arms out wide, and screamed: *EMMMMMMMMMMILLLLEEEEE!* When he fell to the creek below, I sighed. The sound of his body splashing into the water below rode that sweet breeze. The guy obviously had an enduring case of the fuzzies for Emily.

Emily, apparently, had not felt the same way about Brandon.

With no one else to stare at on the bridge, my eyes drifted to Two-Mile Trail and the sign announcing one's arrival into town. I frowned as I took in the growth just beyond the sign, beginning to partially block the way in and out of town. Weeds grew here and there on the dirt trail, a few tree limbs had fallen, and several brambles were beginning to encroach on the trail.

"I've been here, what?" I asked Auggie. "Two weeks? Three?"

"Three weeks, two days, I think," he sighed.

"No one has kept the trail clean," I said. "It's getting all grown over."

Auggie's eyes opened and he turned his head to look beyond the bridge.

"That happens," he said.

"Who takes care of the brush and clean up?"

"It tends to work itself out," Auggie said. "Everyone chips in one way or another around here."

"What if someone tries to come to town?" I asked. "By the end of summer, it's going to be completely overgrown. It was bad enough on foot. I can't imagine what will happen if someone tries to drive down Two-Mile Trail."

Auggie laughed. "No one has driven down Two-Mile Trail in…I don't even know. One look and anybody would turn their car around."

"Well, how will people get to town?" I asked. "How would anyone drive out?"

"If anyone actually leaves town, they usually take the highway." He jerked his head in the direction of Jack's place. "You're the first person I've seen actually come to town on Two-Mile Trail in a long time. And I didn't actually see you arrive, so you could be lying about that."

I laughed. "I did. Promise."

"Did you meet anybody else on the trail?"

"What? No?"

"See?" He shrugged. "It's not much to worry about."

I gave up. Obviously, the other long-term residents of Possibly were unconcerned with what lay just beyond Lovelorn Bridge Pass. Who was I to make a mountain out of a molehill? Then again, I couldn't help but wonder why the radio on the pole was placed at the end of Two-Mile Trail that led into Possibly proper. I'd found all of the other radios in town during my walks with Auggie each day—at the corner of the post office, alongside The Pueblo, behind Blooms, affixed to the outside wall of Samuel's Soda Spray, down by Grandy's Auto, and staked in the grass by Bend of the Road Graveyard. But why have one at the end of the trail that led into town if no one was expected to use the trail?

Possibly was just odd.

However, it was still the best place I'd ever lived.

"So," I asked, "why the radio?"

"Hm?"

"On the other side of the bridge?" I explained. "Just at the end of the trail by the town sign?"

"I told you," Auggie said cryptically, "these things sort themselves out. Eventually, the trail will get cleared and someone will come walking into town again. It just happens."

"Fine," I rolled my eyes, though I couldn't help but smile. "Be all *I'm a Possibilian and we're all weird and set in our ways and you'll figure it all out one day.*"

Auggie brayed with laughter and sat up to look at me. I smiled mischievously at him.

"You'll officially be a Possibilian one day, too," he said, then seemed to have a thought. "I guess right now, you're just a *Possibility.*"

"Oh, yeah?" I asked. "What's the initiation like? Do I have to chuck corn cobs at the town sow that's painted to look like a spaghetti monster who lives amongst the stars or something?"

Auggie was laughing so hard he was rolling in the grass, holding his stomach.

"Or jump off the bridge and scream someone's name while knitting a scarf using yarn made of human hair?"

"Stop! Stop!"

I laughed, and even contemplated teasing him further, but Auggie looked as though his sides might actually split, so I swallowed any further comments.

"You're ridiculous," Auggie gasped for air as he sat up, holding his sides. "Absolutely ridiculous."

"Okay," I said. "Those ideas are ridiculous. How do I become a Possibilian, then? Officially?"

Auggie wiped his eyes and shrugged dismissively.

"Everyone knows when the time has come to accept that Possibly is their home," he said. "One day, you'll just know that this is where you want to stay."

"Is this where you try to convince me to stay?" I asked, my cheeks warm.

Auggie was no longer laughing. He wasn't even smiling.

"No one in Possibly will try to convince you to stay," he said. "If you want to stay here, that's a choice you have to make. It's a choice everyone makes."

"I didn't mean…anything by that. I was just teasing you. Promise."

It took a moment, but Auggie finally produced a small smile.

"I think the first step," he said tentatively, "is that you learn sign language. Because if you choose to stay, Jack will appreciate it. It'll make you a more well-rounded person, too."

"You think?"

"I know."

"Okay. How long do you think it will take me to learn enough?"

Auggie considered me for a moment.

"I think if you set your mind to it, you'll be talking to Jack and reading his signs by the end of summer," he said. "But only if you focus."

"Really?"

"Well, you won't be fluent," Auggie admitted, "but you can have some pretty good conversations without a cellphone or notepad. I've taught everyone around here at least a little bit. In case Jack ever becomes social."

I grinned.

"Okay. Then let's do it. I'm going to be a great student. Promise."

Auggie smiled. "Good. Now, face me, block out everything else, and we'll get serious."

I spun on my butt in the grass to face Auggie, crossed my legs, and gave him my full attention. That's how it began. Under the tree outside of Starbuck's, I decided to be a good student.

That was how June had melted away under the tree outside of Starbuck's each morning. Auggie and I would meet—either at the barn or at Jack's place—and we'd walk through town. We'd say "hello" to everyone, check for any new letters from Shirlene, get a coffee and breakfast from Starbuck's, then spend the early morning hours under the shade of the tree outside. Sometimes we'd venture into Samuel's Soda Spray for a float or a soda, maybe even an ice cream cone, but we always ended up in the same spot.

Our tree.

NOWHERE ELSE ON EARTH

The radio was typically on in the kitchen when I went downstairs for breakfast. So, when I ventured downstairs for breakfast on the first of July, and I was met with silence, I was confused. Had Jack slept in, or had he simply turned the radio off when he went outside to begin his work in the backyard? Since he wasn't in the kitchen finishing breakfast, those were the only other options. I ran a hand through my mussed hair, scratching at my scalp as I yawned and tiptoed across the kitchen tile to the back of the house.

The sounds of Jack reached my ears before I actually laid eyes on him. Once I'd pushed open the backdoor, I found Jack in the yard, as was usual on bright, sunny mornings, working on another project. I padded down the backsteps in my bare feet, letting the door shut behind me. Dewy grass slithered between my toes, tickling me as I strolled across the back lawn sleepily.

When I approached the table Jack was working on, he looked up, and gave me a small smile. Since I had his attention, I touched the tips of the fingers of my right hand to my chin, lowered it to my other waiting hand, moved my right hand to the crook of my left elbow, and raised my left open hand. Just a simple sign.

Good morning.

Jack stared at me.

So…I repeated the sign.

Good morning.

Time ticked by as Jack stared at me across the length of the table, his expression betraying nothing of his thoughts. I was about to repeat the sign when Jack gave me a curt nod, then lowered his head and went back to work.

"Good morning," I said.

Jack looked up just long enough to repeat the sharp nod, then he was looking back at his project once again. I wanted to try again with the ASL, but Jack's snippy response to my first attempt led me to believe that I'd signed wrong. Obviously, I hadn't signed "good morning" so poorly that he hadn't understood it, but it had upset him enough. So, instead of asking him how the table was going with ASL—which I might have butchered even worse, considering how nervous his response to my first attempt had made me—I just asked him out loud.

"How's the table coming?"

Jack looked up briefly, nodded his head side-to-side as to indicate his thoughts on the project, then went right back to looking at the table. He hadn't even stopped working to respond.

"Do you need any help?"

Jack shook his head curtly, but didn't bother raising his head again.

I didn't want his obvious rebuff of my attempt to communicate with ASL hurt my feelings, but it did. Auggie and I had spent a few weeks working together—not enough to be fluent or all that impressive—but I had tried. Auggie had given up time to teach me, I'd given up free time to learn, and Jack didn't seem to care. In fact, he almost seemed bothered by my attempt to say "good morning."

A parade wasn't what I'd been searching for when I signed "good morning" to my stepfather, nor did I want a trophy. Something like a smile wouldn't have been bad, though. Jack smiling and signing back would have been amazing. I was just trying to connect with the guy since I hadn't seen him in…I couldn't remember how long, honestly. Jack was a nice guy—nice enough to let me stay with him without so much as a heads up from Mom—so I wanted to be friendly, if nothing else, with him.

I kind of wanted him to act like a stepfather.

As I stood there, watching him from the other end of the table, I realized what I desperately wanted that from Jack.

A father figure.

Maybe that made my attempts at ASL less altruistic, but it was what it was. I wanted to be able to communicate with Jack in a way that was easiest for him, and for him to treat me like his stepson.

I felt equally disgusted with my desperation and Jack's dismissal of my attempt. It was Auggie all over again. Kind of. I desperately wanted to be accepted while putting my foot in my mouth in my attempts to become friendly. Well, in Jack's case, it was my hands, not my foot.

"So," I said finally, "you seem like you're going to busy with this for a while."

Jack nodded without looking up.

"I'm going to go have breakfast, I guess," I said. "Um, then maybe I'll shower and, I don't know, find something to do?"

Jack didn't even nod, let alone look up.

"All right," I said.

Without another word—and especially without another attempt at signing—I slogged back through the dewy grass and up the back steps into the house. Since I had nothing else to do, I found a box of cereal—Lucky Charms, my favorite—in the pantry, and made a bowl of cereal. I contemplated turning AMOR on while I ate at the kitchen table, but I found that I couldn't stand listening to the same song on repeat, even if it only took a few minutes to eat a bowl of cereal. So, I ate in silence and washed my bowl up and put it in the draining rack when I was done.

After my pitiful, yet delicious, breakfast, I trudged back upstairs. Once in my room again it occurred to me that, while lonely, though not as lonely as living in motels, Jack's house afforded me a luxury I had never experienced. I had privacy. I'd always shared motel rooms with Mom. Most of them were only one room—unless the bathroom counted.

Before my shower, I climbed back under the covers on my bed—just in case Jack got a hair up his ass and came to check on me—and did what teenage boys do best. And as often as possible. On the road with Mom, once I realized jerking off was a thing, shower time was the only sure opportunity I had to explore my body as a teenager. There, in my own room, on the third floor of Jack's house, as dust motes hung in the sunlight that streamed through the window over the bed into my darkened room, I felt explosions I'd never felt before.

Sure, I had to cover myself, just as an extra precaution, but I had privacy. And time. I could do something that is so natural for…almost everyone. Not having to hurry or stress during the experience was glorious. So great in fact, that I contemplated taking a nap right after the stars and motes stopped dancing in my eyes.

I forced myself back out of bed and into the shower instead. Once out of the hot shower, I was even sleepier than I'd been after my fun under the covers.

After putting on some fresh boxers and a t-shirt, I crawled back up on my bed, my room still unlit, though the sunbeam from the window provided enough light. I folded my legs under me and sat next to the window and stared out at Possibly.

Did Auggie masturbate?

What about those guys I'd seen on the street who gave him high-fives and fist bumps?

Was it weird to be curious about that?

Did…Jack masturbate?

Looking out over Possibly proper from my window, I found that I had been calling everyone in town weird since my arrival. Now I was wondering if I was weird just for being curious if I was normal.

I'd never had another guy—neither a father figure nor a guy my age—to talk about those things with when I thought of them. I didn't even know if that's something guys talked about with each other. My only experience was TV shows I'd watched in motel rooms, and if there was one thing I'd learned on the road—show business was one big lie.

Was I weird for wanting some other guy I could ask about those things?

Did I desire answers, or was I…*curious*?

Shaking my head clear of thoughts, mostly so I wouldn't think of masturbation and get myself excited again, I pulled my knees up to my chin and rested it upon them. Days drifted by slowly in Possibly, it seemed. Time seemed to mean nothing. The sun didn't rise and set. It strolled. Leisurely cutting a path across the sky, it tiptoed east to west, lending its warmth and illumination to the town unobtrusively.

Through my window, I could see AMOR and Liberty Lane. Bend of the Road Graveyard, the top of The Pueblo and

Starbuck's. I could catch glimpses of the teal siding of the post office. If I squinted hard enough, I could see the orange fabric of Mystic Molly's tent. Of course, Auggie's barn was down by the creek, a fiery beacon in the hot summer sun.

I almost grabbed a book to read in the sun by the window, but found I preferred watching life—what little I could see from my window—go by in Possibly.

It was peaceful. Possibly, that is. I could see people come and go here and there on the streets, though they were often blotted out by trees and the shops at times. Even getting into July, the grass was lush like shag carpet and the trees' emerald gems tinkled in the soft breeze that seemed omnipresent. People came and went, did their jobs, performed their art, and acted as weirdly as they wished without judgment.

It was the strangest town I'd ever found.

And I found that I was becoming enamored with it.

I couldn't imagine being anywhere else. I couldn't even imagine my life on the road with Mom before she left me in Possibly.

Jack's curt nods and silence aside, Possibly was easy. Weird, certainly, but it seemed that as long as you didn't bother others, freedom, choice, and acceptance were the mottos around Possibly. It made me think of Auggie's comments about art.

Did my thoughts prove I was an artist since I could see the beauty in the tiny town tucked away at the end of a trail that was becoming slowly overgrown?

If I was an artist, what was my art? I'd never drawn anything in my life that didn't look like a blob.

I found myself sitting there, wondering how I would capture the scene from my window artistically if I were to make an attempt. Everyone in town—aside from Levi Lee—seemed to understand the artistic part of their soul.

Did Levi Lee masturbate?

I shook my head again as my cheeks grew hot.

As things were, my only choice, that I could see, was to visit The Pueblo. It was one of the few places in Possibly proper I hadn't let Auggie drag me to visit. Maybe Lilly—or one of the other artists there—would inspire me. Give me some insight into my thoughts and abilities.

I wasn't sure how the day passed and I never left the window, but the sun finally put itself to rest hours later. I'd had no contact with anyone except Jack all day. I'd only eaten cereal at breakfast. And I found that I was okay with all of it.

When I stripped my shirt off and tossed it to the floor, I checked my phone for old time's sake.

I miss you, Jordy. One day, we'll be back together. Promise.

Mom finally remembered me. I didn't know whether to smile or tap out a response about how angry I was with her. Without strong feelings pushing me either way, I simply locked my phone and slid it back onto my bedside table. Maybe I'd feel like responding the next day. Or the day after that. She had taken her time in texting me; she could wait for my response.

Before climbing into bed, I sat up on my knees in front of the window as the moon cast the town in blues and blacks. My eyes automatically went to the Auggie's barn. Without a second thought, I pushed my dormer window open and leaned forward, listening carefully as I stared at the dark roof down by the creek. Seconds later, the Possibilian breeze—it was a citizen, too—carried an indiscernible song to my ears. When the lights appeared through the skylight in the roof, I smiled.

A vision of Auggie zipped through my brain. A flash of a white diamond.

I left the window open when I slid under the covers so that the breeze could carry Auggie's berceuse to me. However, if I was honest, it sounded like a dirge. Though I couldn't make out the tune or lyrics, it made me think of the windchimes in the clearing in the woods.

Hopefully, Auggie would be at The Pueblo the next day.

As I drifted off to sleep, I could have sworn I heard a door open and close.

That night, I dreamt of a car crash. My mom screaming at me. But it didn't disturb my sleep.

THE PUEBLO

Lilly, a sturdy woman in a white tank top and bib overalls, was enthusiastic to see me walk into The Pueblo the following day. Of course, other than Wyatt, almost everyone in Possibly had a welcoming attitude towards everyone else. Wyatt was the only one with a revolver and carte blanche to use it, apparently, so that explained that if you thought about it.

By "sturdy," I don't mean to say that Lilly was exceptionally large, though she was definitely not a slender woman. Lilly simply looked as though she could sling a bag—or an unruly teenage boy—over her shoulder and throw it or him around. She didn't take guff. I could see it in her eyes. However, her eyes also told the tale that if you treated her right, she'd treat you better than well.

She didn't look for trouble, but she wasn't taking any, either.

"What kind of art do you like?" she asked when I was brought to her attention by one of her students who had set up an easel and canvas in the atrium.

All I could respond with was a shrug of my shoulders and a guttural noise from my throat.

Lilly cackled and slapped at her knee at my response. I liked her immediately. Just like everywhere else in Possibly, AMOR was playing inside The Pueblo during Lilly's art classes, though at a much lower volume. Probably so it didn't disturb the students.

Make Someone Happy by Jimmy Durante was the song du jour. It made me smile. Just like Lilly's reaction to my response.

"I take it you ain't never done much art?" she asked.

"No ma'am," I said. "I just…maybe it's something I need to try?"

She pointed a finger in my face. "You're a good kid. I like you…?"

"Jordan."

"I like you, Jordan," she said.

Lilly and I had seen each other around town, but we'd never been properly introduced. She spent most of her days in The Pueblo and I spent most of my days learning with Auggie. The opportunity had never presented itself. Even with all of the waves and "hellos" we'd shared over the previous weeks, we'd never had an actual conversation.

She reached around and put a hand on my shoulder blade, guiding me away from the student she had been watching when I approached them. With no reason not to, I allowed myself to be guided to the other side of the patch of grass in the middle of the atrium. That golden Possibly sun shone down on us, somehow not turning the room of stone into an oven. The Pueblo was pleasantly cool, full of natural light, perfect for an artist's work. I imagined.

"Well," Lilly spoke, "you see, we got our painters, our sculptors—"

I looked around as she gestured, taking in the students as she pointed them out.

"—some people who like to sketch. Got some folks who like to work with clay, others with stone or metal. Oils, acrylics, charcoal…the medium finds the artist more often than not."

"What does that mean?"

"You won't really know what works for you until you work," she said. "Since you've never really done much art before, maybe we start you out with some acrylic paints and see what happens? Maybe we can figure out what type of art you're best suited for?"

I shrugged again. "Yeah. That sounds cool."

"Great!" Lilly slapped my back jovially, nearly taking my breath away.

Sturdy.

"I'll be right back," she said.

Sturdy or not, Lilly dashed around The Pueblo as if made of feathers. She practically floated as she zipped around, grabbing a free easel, canvas, paints, and brushes. I did my best to help her set up my station on the edge of the round of grass, but I mostly let her take charge. Who was I to tell an artist how to set up an artist's work station?

Before I knew it, the canvas was clamped onto the easel, Lilly had placed a mason jar of clear water to the side for me, and handed me a palette and brush. I stood before the easel, staring at the vast whiteness, wondering what I would be instructed to do. I'd never even attempted to paint something, but with a teacher, I couldn't be too terrible. Right?

"Okay," I said. "Now what?"

"Well, paint, of course."

"I'm sorry?"

"Paint something."

"Uh...paint what?"

"What you see," Lilly slapped my back, nearly sending me flying into the easel, as a cackle erupted from her throat. "Specifically, paint how you see. Don't paint this room the way it looks, paint it the way you see it. Otherwise, it's not the best art."

"But how?" I coughed.

"How doesn't matter. We're just trying to figure out what you take to," she said. "Just start painting. See what happens. Maybe you'll find you take to it like a duck to water."

"Not likely," I mumbled.

"We got a few rules around here," Lilly crossed her arms over her broad chest. "Not being grumpier than me is one of 'em."

"Sorry."

Lilly softened. "Don't worry about the process for now, Jordan. Just paint what you see. I need to know what you can do before I can start to figure out what might be best for you."

"It's gonna be bad." I cringed. "Like, really bad."

"Art's never bad." Lilly grabbed me firmly by the chin and turned my head to look at her.

Typically, anyone putting their hands on me forcefully in an attempt to make me comply annoyed me. Lilly just had a way about her. I wanted desperately to ask her if she had kids. Or grandkids. She had one of those timeless faces that, although it was obvious she had experience, looked as if she could have been not old enough or old enough to have grandkids.

"Art is art because it's a reflection of how the artist sees the world around them."

I murmured, "Is not making fun of new students one of your rules?"

Lilly's eyes softened considerably and she pinched my chin between her fingers.

"I'll give you helpful critique, but I will never laugh at you." She let go of my chin and ran her finger across her chest. "Cross my heart."

I breathed out. "Okay. I'll do my best."

"That's all you gotta do, sugar." Lilly squeezed my shoulder.

What I had expected was for Lilly to step back, give me a little room, and just observe while I started painting. Maybe give a tip here or there. Or, I don't know, give me some idea of how to start. Instead, she turned on her heels and walked back to the student she had been helping when I approached her. Her leaving didn't make me more or less nervous because I wasn't sure how to feel. I'd just been given the means to paint and no instruction.

For a moment, I considered quietly setting down the provided painting supplies and sneaking out of The Pueblo. That would probably get the message across about how confident I was in my ability to just make art on the fly. And I knew how to run like hell. What was Lilly going to do? Chase me down and drag me back to my easel until I produced art?

You make art now!

After watching Lilly out of the corner of my eye for a moment, I realized that chasing me down was exactly what she'd do. Possibly wasn't Memphis or New Orleans, either. Even if I could outrun Lilly—which was fairly likely—she'd still find me. Sooner or later, she'd show up on Jack's doorstep with her arms crossed over her chest.

Jack would hand me over, too. If just for the shits and grins.

So, with a deep sigh, I looked around the room. I was supposed to paint what I saw. Or, rather, *how* I saw it. I realized I had to figure out what I saw and how I saw it. Though every part of my brain was telling me that I was wasting my time— *you're not even an artist*—I forced myself to take in the atrium around me.

Brown walls. No. Rusty, sandy brown walls. Made of...bricks? Stones? Possibly hand-carved blocks of some kind? Maybe it was clay that was hand-packed and molded? I didn't know how old The Pueblo was, so I could only guess the technology available when it was built.

Stone columns, slightly less brown than the walls—*definitely sandy brown*—rose from the stone floor to hold the dome above us aloft. The dome, brownish-red—*burnt sienna, maybe?*—from the outside, was sparkling white on the inside.

The skylight above, only visible from inside The Pueblo or if you were high enough above the building to see it, let in that golden Possibilian sunlight. Was the inside of the dome sparkling white, or was it off white, or tan, or light brown, but the sunlight that nourished Possibly bleached it white? The sun didn't hit every corner on the inside of the dome due to the skylight's positioning and shape. If the sun was responsible for the blindingly white color, it would have happened in stages. Parts of the dome would be less white than others. Then again, I had no idea when Possibly was founded—it hadn't been on the town sign—so I didn't know how long the sun had been working on the dome.

Below the dome, in a perfect circle, edged by stone, was the lush green grass that seemed to cover every inch of Possibly that wasn't paved or worn down into a trail. The sunlight made it sparkle like thinly sliced blades of emerald, nearly giving it a cartoonish look. It just never seemed real. If I hadn't spent so many afternoons lounging in the grass around Possibly with Auggie, I would have thought it was Astroturf or some other synthetic grass.

The other students around me, under Lilly's watch, were creating their art. Some sculpted or molded, others painted and drew. Some seemed perfectly content to stand by their work and think. Maybe they were trying to figure out how they saw things, too. Everyone was smiling, or, at the least, not unhappy. They were content. Lilly would laugh with a student she'd stop to check on from time to time, but always quietly so as to not disturb anyone more than necessary.

Breathing deeply through my nose, I let my eyes fall shut. And I listened to the sounds of The Pueblo.

Murmurs of students exchanging pleasantries or questions. Lilly talking softly to someone when they had a question or observation. The *swish swish swish tap tap tap clink clink clink* of brushes being rinsed in jars and tapped dry. Soles of shoes scraping against well-worn stone.

A smile came to my face as a breeze whistled down from the skylight in the dome, carrying the sound of birdsong with it. If I really concentrated, I could almost hear the gurgling of Susurrus Creek. Even though The Pueblo was a good one hundred yards from the creek, the breeze still managed to help it deliver its message.

Next door, Starbuck had made blueberry muffins. Along with the sounds of the birds and the creek, the breeze carried the scent of Possibly. Soft and cakey, light, yet dense and filling where it mattered, gooey and sticky from all of the berries. Crunchy and crumbly on top from the sugar and cinnamon crumble topping. Down, through the center of the softball sized muffins, was that sweet cream cheese icing filling. Almost like cheesecake, but softer. *Crunchy, gooey, cakey.* My mouth watered thinking of the muffins.

It dawned on me why Possibilians would enjoy having The Pueblo as their "church." It had all the sights, sounds, and smells of their happy, quirky, little town. It was an oasis. It was safe. Going to high school in The Pueblo didn't seem like such a bad idea. To do my studies while listening to the sounds of Possibly, while smelling Starbuck's creations each day, would be heaven.

I opened my eyes.

The room wasn't brown.

Copper.

Bronze.

Dark amber.

It wasn't *brown.*

It was the color of a golden park statue, well-worn, dulled, and smoothed by fingers that had loved it over its lifetime. Because it had seen life. It had life.

The circle of emerald shavings at the center of the room proved it.

I didn't know how to make those colors with the dozen or so different colors of acrylic Lilly had squirted onto my palette, but I'd have fun figuring it out. I gripped my brush. Maybe, even if I couldn't paint the room in a way that would be representative of the room itself, I could at least express how I saw the room. Just as Lilly had instructed. I'd do that.

Hours ticked by and the coppers and bronzes and dark ambers took on new dimension. I did my best. Other students finished their work and left in a daze of contentment. Or they moved on to other art projects. Lilly continued moving about the room, checking in on this student here, checking in on that student there.

She mostly gave me a wide berth, but a few times she stopped by to check my progress, saying nothing as she did so. I took that to mean that whatever I was doing was okay by her, even if it wasn't what she would have done.

I only knew when afternoon arrived from the way the sun shone down into the atrium. Lilly had a group of students come in and start working on molding wires into sculptures. It hadn't gotten my attention when Auggie showed up at The Pueblo for class, until I happened to catch him out of the corner of my eye, standing a few feet away, watching me work.

He was looking at me blankly, as if he didn't know me. I didn't stop painting.

After a while, he joined the students working on the wire sculptures, and I continued painting. Another hour or two ticked by, though I wasn't certain, and my painting was only half done. But I was zapped for the day. My wrist ached, my eyes were nearly crossed from staring at the canvas all day, and my hands and forearms were speckled with every shade of the rainbow.

I had barely finished rinsing my brush out in the murky mason jar, and was tapping it dry, when Auggie approached me again. Through hazy eyes, I looked up at him, then glanced over to see that his class was dispersing as well. He smiled at me and held his hand out to me. A small wire figure, maybe four inches tall, laid upon his palm.

"For you," he said. "I, uh, made it for you."

"Thanks," I said.

I reached out and took the small figure from him with a smile and examined it.

It was a caterpillar.

Made of what looked like copper wire. Then again, I doubted Lilly had copper wire on hand for students to use to create their art.

"It's amaz—"

Auggie was gone.

I frowned to myself and looked back down at the caterpillar sculpture in my hand. Weird spikes and antennae came out of its head, back, and sides. It was an odd-looking caterpillar, like an undiscovered species hiding deep in the Amazonian rainforest. As though perching on its belly with its head raised grandly, its tail mirroring its head, it was cute. It gleamed in the beam of Possibilian sun as I turned it in my fingers. I continued turning it every which way, admiring its gleam and intricacy until I turned it just so and froze.

It was a caterpillar.

Unless you turned it to look from the side at just the right angle.

Then it was a butterfly.

Wings and all.

MORE THAN ONE TRUTH

"*Anamorphic*," Auggie said again as he leaned against his worktable, facing away from me. "When a sculpture or piece of art looks like one thing—or nothing at all—from one angle, and something completely different from another angle."

"Anamorphic," I repeated.

"Right." He chuckled.

Faith by George Michael was playing on his radio. I wanted to ask him why he always played his own music while working instead of just listening to AMOR like everyone else, but thought it was pointless. If I had the choice, I'd listen to more than one song on repeat all day, too. AMOR usually picked a decent song each day, but twelve hours straight of any one song was just too much.

"Sometimes, when you look at things from a different angle, it looks different," he said. "That's life, I guess. That's art."

I didn't know what to say.

"Things change when we change our view," he continued. "Sometimes what we thought was true is different when we gather all the facts. Or, maybe, we expand our understanding of the truth."

"I get that," I said. "I really like it. Thank you."

"You're welcome," he said, grabbing a tool from his table and banging away softly at a piece of metal.

I stood there, watching him, holding the *anamorphic* wire sculpture delicately in my hand. I'd carried it like a precious stone all the way from The Pueblo to the barn. Just to thank Auggie. And to ask about it.

"I liked your painting."

I reached up to rub the back of my neck with my free hand.

"It…it's just my first try. I've never painted before," I said.

"Don't do that." Auggie stopped working to turn and look at me.

"Do what?"

"Diminish a compliment with an excuse."

I smiled. "Thank you. I had fun painting it."

He smiled back. "You're really good with colors."

"Honestly, though," I asked, "if you weren't there when I painted it, would you know what I had painted?"

"No," he said.

I sighed.

"But I would be able to tell how you felt," he said. "It was…inspiring."

I looked down at my feet so my rosy cheeks were hidden in the shadows.

For what felt like an eternity of seconds, we stood in the barn, me by the door, Auggie by his worktable across the room.

"Have you seen the fliers?" he asked.

"Huh?"

"The fliers? Around town? I think they have one at the post office, Starbuck's—there might have even been one up at The Pueblo today?"

I shook my head.

"They've been up for a while," he teased.

209

"Tell me about the fliers," I said with a laugh.

"It's the annual Fourth of July BBQ the day after tomorrow."

"Makes sense. That is the fourth."

He laughed. "There's lots of good food. Music. Amos usually adds at least one extra song to the line-up at AMOR. There's dancing and stuff. Mingling. Fireworks once it gets dark. That kind of thing. It's all free."

"Sounds fun."

"Do you…wanna go? With me?" he asked. "Like a buddy thing?"

I smiled.

"We could eat until we puke and watch fireworks and stuff. It's usually…it's fun. Yeah."

"I'll go," I said. "On one condition."

Auggie squinted at me.

"You have to tell me what this is."

"Huh?" he asked.

"Your art…installation?" I gestured vaguely around the room. "Tell me what it is."

More duct work—big enough for two men to fit inside snaked around the room, twisting and turning, over and under. The large metal cylinder—maybe a section of an old silo—still sat at the center of the room under the skylight. I desperately wanted to know what Auggie was creating. I would have gone to the Fourth of July BBQ with him, even if he refused to tell me, but I had an opportunity to learn about his work, so I took it.

"It's an observatory," he said. "Kind of."

"What?"

"Well, see," Auggie stepped away from his worktable towards the giant metal cylinder in the center of the room, "all of the tubes can be crawled through. But you have to find the exact path to get to the two that open into the room in the center. In the silo."

It was part of a silo.

"It's pitch black inside the silo," he said, "so, when you're inside, and you're looking up at the stars through the skylight, it's like an observatory. The silo blocks out all of the light and helps your eyes adjust to the dark better and quicker. So you see the stars more clearly. You see more of the stars, actually. There's not much light pollution in Possibly, so that helps."

I stared at him.

"The gag is," he continued, "you hit a switch. Here."

He pointed at a level by his worktable.

"Lights come on. The lights and the skylight are on a timer. As soon as you hit the lever, you dash into the ductwork and try to find your way to the middle. If you get to the silo before the timer runs out, there's another lever you can pull to stop the timer."

"What happens if you don't get there in time?"

"The skylight closes and the lights stay on."

"If you pull the other lever?"

"The lights go out, but the skylight stays open," he said. "Then you can stare up at the stars all you want. You can watch all the universe your eyes can see for as long as you want. Until dawn if you like."

I smiled.

"Do you want to see it work?"

"Uh, yeah," I said, grinning widely.

"Tonight," Auggie said. "Eleven-thirty?"

"Okay."

He nodded.

"I—I don't know if this is weird," I said, suddenly wanting to tell Auggie a truth. "But I saw you a few times before I actually introduced myself to you at The Pueblo that one day."

"Yeah?"

"Um, yeah. In the woods?" I rolled my shoulders. "What's with the windchimes? Did you put all of those windchimes out there? Sometimes I hear them in town if the breeze is just right."

"No. I didn't put them all out there."

"Who did?"

He made a goofy face at me.

"No one knows," he said.

"Right."

"Seriously," he said. "No one knows. Or no one will say if they do. They've been there forever. Sometimes, like, people will add something to one of the windchimes—I have—but I don't know how they got there originally."

"Oh. Okay," I said. "But, like, what's up with them?"

"It's kind of a silly Possibly thing."

"Tell me. I won't laugh."

He sighed. "Well, there's an old wives' tale that windchimes ring when the dead are around—it's a way of letting the living know that the ones they loved that have passed are nearby and thinking of them. So, the people around here say that if they ring when you're there, someone is thinking of you. And, if you want them to know you're thinking of them as well, you can ring the chimes yourself."

"That's cool."

"Yeah. Sometimes people add things to them. Makes it more personal. When they ring for you or you ring them for someone else. That's why some are full of keys or bottle caps or…whatever."

"Is it okay to just go whenever you want?" I asked, kicking at the ground. "Like, if you wanted to see if they rang for you? Or to ring them for someone else?"

Auggie smiled softly.

"It's public property," he said. "It's open to everyone. Just don't remove anything except trash on the ground. And *never* take something off one of the chimes. They're important to people here."

"Okay."

Again, we found ourselves standing there in silence, not really staring at each other, but not exactly not staring at each other.

"So, eleven-thirty?" he asked.

I nodded. "Eleven-thirty. Let's see the stars."

"Hope you're quick," he said with a grin. "And good at mazes."

WRONG PLACE, WRONG TIME

J ack still wouldn't converse with me when I tiptoed out of the house that evening. He had been up watching television in the living room when I crept downstairs. At first, I thought maybe he would wave me down and ask me where I thought I was going. Or he would give me a reproachful look that would send me scurrying back up the stairs to my room. Instead, he glanced over from the T.V. at the sound of my footsteps in the kitchen, considered me for a moment, then turned his sleepy eyes back to the television.

"Auggie's going to show me his art installation at the barn," I said.

Jack turned to give me a nod to acknowledge he had heard me, but then went right back to watching T.V. Apparently, my whereabouts in the middle of the night were of no concern to him. Of course, we were in Possibly, Texas. What kind of actual trouble could I get into in the middle of nowhere in Texas? Then again, it reminded me of being on the road with my mom. She had shows to chase, Jack had T.V. to watch.

There wasn't enough concern left over for me.

"All right," I said. "I'll see you later."

Jack waved at me over his shoulder.

That was it then. Jack wasn't concerned that I was about to walk out the front door into the dark night of Possibly, Texas and stroll over to Auggie's barn. It wasn't far, and we were in a safe town, but it wasn't like Possibly was known for its street lights. The only light I'd have for my walk across town was whatever light the full moon provided. Maybe my cellphone flashlight since it wasn't good for much else out in the middle of nowhere. Reception remained spotty at best.

"Thank God I'm not on my way to school," I said with my hand on the doorknob. "Most child abductions happen on the way to school."

Jack's head turned slowly to shoot me a look that conveyed everything he thought of my mental health.

"But I'll be fine, I'm sure. No reason to worry."

Jack rolled his eyes and smiled, then waved me off again.

Okay. So, maybe he cared a little, but apparently, he still didn't think there was anything to be concerned about when it came to me walking to Auggie's in the middle of the night.

"See you at breakfast, I guess," I said.

Then I was out the door and jogging down the steps.

Possibly was warm during the day, as one would expect of Texas in summer, but at night it was pleasant. Maybe even a little cool. I had to believe that Susurrus Creek, and whatever body of water it was fed by, carried the breeze into town. Since the creek never seemed to drop by even an inch, and it was summertime, it had to be fed by a larger body of water. Probably somewhere further south since the water flowed north.

Just as expected, and as I'd observed from my dormer window for dozens of nights, Possibly was pitch black in the middle of the night. All of the businesses downtown shut off all of their lights once the business day was over and their doors were locked. Not that their lights would have illuminated the area by Jack's place much. I would have had to walk in near darkness at least until I got further away from Jack's place anyway.

On the road with Mom over the years, I'd walked in a million different towns at night. Even all alone. Mom wasn't exactly a helicopter parent, to say the least. Some of the places were relatively small—not *Possibly small*—but small. Other places, like Nashville, Memphis, and New Orleans were enormous compared to Possibly. Even though those places were usually well lit and had dense foot traffic well into the night, they weren't safer than Possibly.

Walking in New Orleans at night alone was much more dangerous than laying in the middle of the road in Possibly at night.

But nighttime in Possibly, unless I was in my room, staring out of the dormer window, gave me the chills. It wasn't that I expected Wyatt to jump out from behind a headstone in the graveyard and demand my money—of which I had none. It was just that I'd never been in a town that seemed to be as alive as Possibly at night. It had...*a feeling*. Once its residents turned in for the night, the town itself was allowed to breathe. And breathe it did.

Headstones. Graveyard.

As I approached Bend of the Road Graveyard on my way to the barn, my heart seemed to start its own little stroll within my chest. I eyed the small cemetery warily as I walked down the center of the road. Even though the day had not been exceptionally hot or humid, and the night was simply cool, not cold, a mist or fog seemed to cling to the grounds and gather around the headstones.

There's always something about gravestones and fog.

Continuing to walk along the road, though at a much more cautious pace, I psyched myself out. A vision of the lady in her hooded black cloak stepping out from under a tree sent a chill up my spine. Before I could talk myself out of being ridiculous, I cut to the right and dashed for Liberty Lane.

I wanted to put AMOR, and the other businesses that lined the road, between the graveyard and me. Once I got close to the creek, I'd cut back north towards Auggie's barn.

Sure, taking a longer route, especially at night in the dark, was a stupid idea. However, if I had seen the lady in her cloak—*Malia?*—I would've dashed right back to Jack's house. Texting Auggie to say I was too frightened to take a two-minute walk to his barn at night would have killed me. Not just that it would have been embarrassing, but because I desperately wanted to see his art.

Bend of the Road Graveyard would not keep me from seeing Auggie's homemade observatory.

Luckily, on Liberty Lane, I didn't encounter Wyatt and his gun, Malia in her cloak, or any other Possibilians who were more than a little weird. Levi Lee in his green-screen suit or Agnes Boudreaux in her wheelchair would have been fine. A little weird is okay. "Slightly off" is not the same as creepy.

Fortunately, by the time I reached the end of Liberty Lane, with the creek straight ahead, I was still alone. I cut a left and made my way north along the edge of the creek. The breeze blew along the creek, rustling my hair. Somewhere, further south, a low whistle, almost like a moan caught the breeze and drifted towards me. I didn't turn around.

The last few yards to Auggie's barn were quick. Because I ran. The low moan-like whistle—like someone blowing into the mouth of a jug—followed me the entire way. By the time I was throwing open the green doors of Auggie's barn, my heart was thundering. However, when I entered the barn and Auggie looked up expectantly from his worktable to grin at me, all was forgotten. My heart decided it didn't need to win a marathon anymore.

I smiled back at Auggie.

"I'm here," I said stupidly.

"I see that."

"Am I late?"

Auggie glanced up at the skylight—not a clock or a cellphone—and then looked back at me.

"You're here at the perfect time," he said. "You ready to see some stars?"

I don't know why, but when Auggie said that, it sent a shiver up my spine. Not like the shivers and gooseflesh that ravaged my body on the way over from Jack's place. It was something different.

"Uh, explain how this works again?" I asked. "There's a timer?"

Auggie's eyes lit up and he excitedly skipped over to the silo. Knowing that was a cue, I closed the barn doors and shuffled over to join him. I watched as Auggie fiddled around gleefully, tweaking this, moving that—none of the levers and buttons he was pushing looked like they actually did anything. But I always felt that if a light didn't come on or some machine didn't start doing something when a button was pushed, it had no actual function. What did I know?

"Okay," he said, obviously satisfied with what he'd done, "this lever here is what starts the whole thing."

Auggie grabbed the lever jutting out of the slot in the side of the silo.

"Okay?"

"When I pull it, we have ten minutes to make our way through the ducts to the center of the silo, and—"

"Seems easy enough."

Auggie grinned wickedly.

"You'd think, yeah. But some lead to dead ends. Some twist back around on themselves. Some crisscross…only one path, the right combination of turns, will get you to the center and into the silo."

"Um—"

"And there's a lever inside you have to pull," he continued. "Once you pull it, the timer is shut off, the lights go out, and the skylight won't close. Then you can lay back and enjoy the stars. If you get there too late, the timer is rigged to shut the skylight and the lights stay on, and…you're shit out of luck, my friend. No stars for you."

"No stars for me," I said, sad at the thought.

"But don't worry. There's a hatch on the side of the silo if you do get to the center. You don't have to find your way back out through the maze," he said. "And if you get well and truly lost in the maze, I have no problem cutting you out."

Auggie bounced around excitedly.

"Have you tested it?" I asked.

"Dozens of times."

"Have you learned the right path and beat the timer yet?"

He sighed. "Not yet."

"Then I'm screwed," I said with a laugh. "This is your creation."

He shrugged. "Who knows? You not knowing anything about it might be to your advantage."

"True," I said. "So, whoever gets to the middle first pulls the lever and waits for the other?"

"Hm." He was frowning. "I think whoever gets there first should wait. It's more satisfying, getting to see the stars, if we both get there in under ten minutes."

I swallowed. "Yeah. That seems fair."

"Sweet!" Auggie jammed a fist in the air triumphantly.

"You'll wait for me?" I asked. "I mean, you'll probably get through the ducts first. If I don't get there in time, you won't pull the lever?"

"Nope."

"That kind of ruins it for you, though."

"Well," his right shoulder rose and fell lazily, "the victory won't be as sweet if I don't have my friend to share it with. Stars burn brighter when more eyes are on them."

I smiled.

"And you'll wait for me?" he asked. "If you get there first?"

"Of course."

Again, he was beaming at me.

"So," he shook his head, "there are two entrances to the duct work. One, uh, over there by the worktable, and one over there."

Auggie pointed across the considerable length of the barn to where a jumble of ductwork led. I'd never really paid much attention to the barn. My focus was usually on small parts of Auggie's installation art. Or on Auggie himself. But the barn was massive. When I'd first considered Auggie's observatory maze, I thought it'd be a piece of cake. Taking in the massive interior of the barn around me, and all of the ductwork, knowing that there were twists and turns and dead ends—and that I'd have to *crawl* through it—I wasn't so confident.

The cavernous wooden room, though I wasn't great with measurements by sight, was seventy-five to one-hundred feet wide and long. The ceiling seemed to reach to the heavens, but was probably only twenty or twenty-five feet above us. Any hayloft that had once been in place had obviously been removed so Auggie had all the space to work on his installation art. The silo was massive, so a loft would have gotten in the way.

I couldn't even estimate how much ductwork roped around the room—or where Auggie could have gotten all of it—but it trailed everywhere that wasn't directly around his worktable. Just from eyeballing it, I knew that if Auggie and I met in the same section, we would barely be able to squeeze past each other. Auggie was a smaller guy, and I was average. If we could run through tunnels to our destination, ten minutes would probably have been plenty of time to figure out the maze. On our hands and knees, it had to be impossible.

My heart thumped a little harder, thinking about crawling into the narrow space and finding my way in the dark. Also, having been laid out in a barn for who knew how long, there could potentially be rats or bugs—maybe even an overly friendly raccoon or possum. I couldn't believe that Auggie had hosed down and scrubbed all of the ductwork, so there could also be rust and grime. Maybe sharp edges that I could snag my shirt on or cut myself on.

"Are the ducts…are they clean?" I asked.

"Yeah," Auggie nodded slowly. "I mean, they're dusty from being in the barn for so long, but there's nothing gross."

"What about animals?"

He laughed.

"I de-skunked them myself."

"So, no spiders or anything?"

He winced. "I can't guarantee that, but I've been crawling through them almost every night, so I don't think any animals have found them to be a suitable home. Most things that like to live in dark, small spaces don't like to be disturbed all of the time."

Every night. Auggie had been testing the installation art almost every night. When he pulled the lever, lights came on and the skylight was open. If he didn't make it to the lever inside the silo in time, the skylight closed. He always practiced around midnight. And he hadn't figured out his maze yet. That's why I'd see the lights at night and their sudden disappearance at midnight.

I smiled to myself. Another Possibly mystery solved.

"So?" Auggie perked up. "Are you still up for it? It's nearly eleven-fifty."

Ten-minute timer. He starts his maze at eleven-fifty.

Yup. Mystery solved. The barn wasn't a dance club or a hideout for secret government agents, or a docking port for space aliens. Auggie's art installation had been the culprit all along.

"Um, yeah," I said. "Ready as I'll ever be."

"Do you want to go in by my workbench or at the other side of the room?" he asked.

"Which do you usually use?"

"Workbench entrance."

"I'll take the other one." I gestured vaguely to the other side of the barn. "I haven't been in either and I don't want you going in blind when you're maybe starting to learn the other one's twists and turns."

He scoffed. "Yeah. Not likely. It's pretty twisty and turn-y."

We both laughed, then Auggie nodded his head towards the other side of the barn.

"Get ready," he said. "Take your position, sir."

Suddenly, filled with excitement and no longer with concern and dread, I jogged across the barn, the shadows enveloping me. It took me a second in the low lighting at the other side of the barn to find the opening to the ductwork. But once I found it, I stood next to it and waved across the room at Auggie.

"Find it?" he hollered.

"Got it!" I answered.

"Okay," he said as he walked over to the lever on the outside of the silo and gripped it in his hand, "once I pull down, the timer starts. Go right away. Don't waste time. We've got this!"

I held a thumb up.

"Got it!"

"Ready?"

"Ready!"

I watched Auggie smile at me from his spot next to the silo, hoping that I wouldn't let him down. If he got to the silo's interior and I didn't, I'd feel awful for ruining his success—especially after he had been trying for so long. Regardless, I was going to do my best. If I messed up, Auggie would forgive me. And we could try again. And again. Night after night. Until we finally laid under the stars together. The thought made me smile.

A mechanical grinding sound emanated from the silo as Auggie's hand pulled down on the lever. The interior of the barn flooded with lights and I blinked at the sudden blindness it caused. I barely had time to look up at the ceiling to see what looked like millions of twinkling Christmas lights shining down on us from the ceiling yards over our heads. I could only tell the skylight had opened thanks to a dark rectangle in the middle of all of the brightness.

"*Go!*" Auggie screamed gleefully.

I jerked at his command, grinning stupidly. Then I raced to the opening in the ductwork on my side of the barn, fell to my hands and knees, and crawled inside.

Absolute darkness overwhelmed me as I slid into the metal tunnel; I froze. What would happen if I couldn't find my way into the silo? What would happen if I couldn't retrace my route and back out of the tunnels? Would I have to scream for help and have Auggie locate me so that he could cut me out of the ductwork with some tool?

My heart began to thunder in my chest again and I twitched as imaginary spiders crawled along my arms. Panting, barely inside the dark ductwork, I considered crawling the few feet back out of the tunnel and hollering at Auggie to do the maze without me.

After a few seconds, the darkness seemed to soften, most likely from the light that was peeking in from behind me through the ductwork's opening. I convinced myself to ignore the phantom creepy-crawly feeling in my arms, and took slow, deep breaths. It dawned on me that the bright lights that came on when the lever was pulled was probably to make it harder to adjust to the darkness of the ductwork. It was probably part of the experience of Auggie's art installation. That made me give a small smile.

Jerk.

As my pupils dilated and adjusted to the inky blackness, I realized that being able to see well would make the maze less of a challenge. What was the point of a maze and the reward at the end if I didn't have to work for it? Time was ticking by, and though I had no concept of how many seconds had passed as I simply waited near the entrance to the ductwork, I knew our time was finite.

If I didn't move as quickly as possible, if I didn't make good guesses about where to turn, I would never make it through to the silo in time. The worst that could happen was that I would run out of time and fail the maze. If that happened, and I couldn't find my way out, Auggie would have a plan to save me. He traversed the maze on his own dozens of times and had gotten himself out. What did I actually have to worry about? Bumping my head?

With a grin, I urged myself forward, crawling on my hands and knees through the dark metal tunnel. As I made myself move from the entrance into the ductwork, I moved cautiously, unsure of what was ahead and unable to see it. However, after a few moments of nothing but empty space around me, and only brushing up against the side of the ductwork once or twice, I found my courage. I picked up my pace and began crawling like a baby after the distracted family cat.

When I plowed face first into a dead end, I cursed under my breath, rattled by the sudden stop.

I wanted to get mad at myself for letting my guard down, but a grin came to my face instead. The bump hadn't hurt anything but my pride. The ductwork wasn't solid steel or anything—and how fast can one go on their hands and knees anyway? I reached out to my left and found another barrier. When I reached to my right, I found empty space, and waved my hand around to make sure I wouldn't turn and hit my head again. Becoming fairly confident that turning right would lead down another clear path, I shifted and pushed forward.

It seemed like I crawled for even longer after my turn...before I hit my head again. Another smile, and more groping in the dark, and I found my next turn. After a few minutes of twists and turns, I saw light up ahead and growled with frustration. Was I doubling back to the entrance? How much time had passed? Was the light ahead the inside of the silo? Did I need to keep following my path or look for another turn along the way?

I was becoming frustrated, but in an amused way. Auggie had done so much work to make an actual maze of the ductwork. He hadn't made anything simple, which he easily could have done. Auggie could have taken the easy way out, but he wanted to make a real art installation—he put in the work. I paused again and took a deep breath. Listening carefully, I thought I could hear banging around in ductwork somewhere in the barn. Auggie was still finding his way to the silo.

Without a second thought, I began groping along the walls as I crawled, switching arms back and forth as I moved forward. When I found another turn on my left side, I took it without hesitation. Going forward had seemed like the wrong idea. Back into the darkness I went. Scurrying like my life depended on it, or there was a million dollars waiting in the silo for me, I made my way through the ducts. I didn't pause again to listen for Auggie. I groped and crawled, took turns on instinct.

After what felt like forever—*surely, the timer had run out?*—I saw a faint light up ahead again. Frustrated, figuring I'd made my way back to the entrance once more, I wanted to give up. Something inside of me told me that the light wasn't the entrance, however. So, I plowed ahead, scurrying faster as I crawled through the ductwork maze. Seconds later, I was popping out of the metal tube. I was coming out into a circular metal room, and I immediately knew I had figured out the maze.

Grinning triumphantly, I came to my feet and spun around happily, looking for Auggie. All I found was metal walls and another dark opening to the maze across the silo from me.

Auggie was still trying to find his way through the maze.

Immediately, I looked up, wondering how late we both were, but the skylight was still open and the lights were still on. I grinned widely, ecstatic that we were going to beat Auggie's art installation and see the stars together. Once again, I spun on my heels, looking for the second lever. Once I located it nestled in a slot in the wall halfway between Auggie's tunnel and mine, I raced over and grabbed it tightly. My eyes fixed on the opening to Auggie's tunnel. As soon as he popped out, I'd yank the lever, and victory would be ours.

Seconds, maybe even minutes, ticked by as my fingers tightened on the lever and I waited for Auggie to appear. I could hear him moving in the ductwork somewhat—a hollow noise muffled by all the metal around me, but he didn't seem to be getting closer. In fact, it seemed like he was moving away. I bounced on my heels and whined to myself, praying Auggie would find his way quickly and I could stop the timer by pulling the lever.

The metal room made up of the inside of the silo wasn't as large as it had seemed from outside in the interior of the barn. About ten feet wide, it seemed almost claustrophobic. I wasn't sure what the standard size for silos was—or what all sizes they came in—but this one was no bigger inside than an average teenager's room in a typical house in America. Just big enough for a few people to lay on the ground and stare up at the stars. If they beat the timer.

I got so lost in my thoughts, I'd nearly forgotten about Auggie. So, when I heard metal clanging getting closer to the opening of Auggie's tunnel, I jumped. Grinning widely, I stared at the opening, just waiting to see Auggie's head pop out so I could finally pull the lever.

Just as the sounds of Auggie crawling along were so close I knew he'd pop out any second, a whirring sounded overhead.

My head snapped back to find the skylight gliding shut, blocking out the sky inch by inch. Did Auggie have until the skylight was fully closed to get into the silo? Or was our time already up?

Had we failed?

Desperately, I looked back at the opening of Auggie's tunnel, but still saw no sign of him. My fingers tightened on the lever. Should I pull it? Would Auggie want me to pull the lever since I had made my way through the maze, or would he want me to wait for him as we had agreed? Another glance up at the skylight, and it was inches from being completely shut.

I wanted to watch the stars with Auggie.

But we had made a deal. I wouldn't break our deal. Even if it meant we wouldn't get to look at the stars together.

With that, the skylight snapped shut. A loud "thump" sounded through the barn.

And Auggie popped out of his tunnel, panting and laughing.

"I got so turned around!" he exclaimed after a quick glance up at the closed skylight. "I'm so sorry."

With a smile and a sigh, I loosened my fingers and let my hand fall from the lever.

It would be okay.

"Hey," I said as I held up my right hand, the index finger and thumb pinched together, "we tried. You were *this close.*"

"But look at you," he grunted as he stood and stretched his back, "you made it on your first try!"

"Luck." I shrugged.

Both of us smiled and leaned back to look up at the now closed skylight. Our opportunity had passed. There would be no stars for us.

"You could have pulled the lever," Auggie said, still looking up at the ceiling.

"What's the point of stars if you don't have someone to gaze at them with?"

"True," he said. "I guess we were just in the wrong place at the wrong time. It was a full moon anyway. The stars wouldn't have seemed as bright. Maybe this was good?"

"Maybe. The moon would have been awesome, though. So? Next time?"

"Oh, we're kicking this thing's ass next time!"

We both whooped and hollered, determined that our next adventure with the art installation would be victorious.

The stars would still be there for it.

FOURTH OF JULY

A MOR was playing *Gimme a Pig Foot and a Bottle of Beer* by Bessie Smith. It was the perfect theme song for strolling through downtown Possibly on a hot July day while sipping Mountain Dew from an actual glass bottle. On Independence Day, as Auggie and I had planned, we went to Possibly's Fourth of July BBQ. Around ten-thirty, the two of us met at Bend of the Road Graveyard—which wasn't nearly as creepy with the sun out—and walked to Liberty Lane together.

Off of the street, just past the tram tracks, dozens of smokers and grills had been set up by the tiny hamlet's residents. Sticky, pungent puffs of smoke belched from them in gusts, scenting downtown Possibly with the aroma of liquid smoke, meat, and mesquite. The taste of brown sugar and molasses seemed to waft through the air and stick at the back of my throat, but was quickly washed away by another sip of soda.

Though I'd had breakfast, I had caught the smell of the BBQ back at the graveyard, and my stomach groaned with pleasure. I wasn't sure what all was being prepared in the plethora of grills and smokers on Liberty Lane, but my stomach wanted to taste it all. Of course, lunch wasn't to be served until noon—apparently, some of the cooks had been setting up before sunrise to make sure everything was ready—so I had to swallow my hunger.

Not one to be run off by a community activity, Earl Dean and his pickaxe were doing their work on the asphalt of Liberty Lane. No one paid him much mind other than Officer Hanning. He wasn't hurting anyone. So, Possibilians left him to his work as they zigzagged to and fro, greeting their friends and family, peeking in the front window of AMOR, talking to the cooks at the grills and smokers, and saying "hello" to Jasper as he lounged lazily in his tram car.

Even on the Fourth of July, and with so many people on the street, Jasper was sticking to his up and down the tracks on the hour schedule.

Wyatt, though he seemed to be helping out at grills and smokers along Liberty Lane, didn't forget to fire his gun periodically.

Schedules—or maybe, habits—were important in Possibly, apparently.

Auggie and I said our hellos on Liberty Lane when we first arrived, but our first order of business was to procure the aforementioned Mountain Dews in glass bottles. That task was completed by visiting Samuel's Soda Spray. While he planned to close at noon for the BBQ and the rest of the day's activities, he had chosen to open during the morning. Though there were plenty of coolers full of drinks lining the sidewalk outside of AMOR on Liberty Lane, nothing inside of them could compare to Samuel's offerings.

After leaving half of the town's residents behind at Liberty Lane, we found what seemed like the other half in a line outside of Samuel's. The line stretched nearly from the corner of The Pueblo, around Mystic Molly's tent, and down the street into Samuel's. The line moved quickly, all things considered, because Samuel was a wiz behind the counter. Chocolate malt? Minute or less. A fountain drink? Five seconds, tops. A sundae? Give him thirty seconds and you'd have the most delicious sundae you've ever had.

With Levi Lee behind the register—one of his part-time jobs aside from being an "all-around handyman"—the two had the line moving rapidly.

However, under the summer sun, as nice as it usually seemed to be in Possibly, the line couldn't move quickly enough. As Auggie and I moved with the line, the moments we were standing under the shade of trees or store awnings were the best.

The Possibilian breeze still blew through town, carrying the sounds of Susurrus Creek, but it was warmer than usual. Downtown Possibly felt like an oven. An oven on its lowest setting, obviously, but the warm summery days made pleasant by the cool breeze seemed to have abandoned the town for its Fourth of July BBQ.

As Auggie and I were standing in line for Samuel's, just outside Mystic Molly's tent, I felt a drop of sweat trickle its way between my shoulder blades, down my back, and into my shorts.

Swamp Ass.

I didn't want that. Glancing around, I noticed that Mystic Molly was seated at her table in her darkened tent. She was watching the crowd shuffle by, but her eyes didn't focus on anyone in particular for long. Outside of her tent, propped up against the right flap, she had a sandwich board which proclaimed that she was doing Tarot card readings for free. Though mysticism and the occult didn't appeal to me—maybe even creeped me out a bit—the interior of the tent was shaded.

Its darkness beckoned to me as I stood in the sun and sweated into my ass crack.

"Auggie," I said, "let's get a Tarot reading."

Auggie glanced out of the side of his eye at Molly's.

"I don't really care for the Tarot," he said and went back to look down the line towards Samuel's.

"Come on." I gripped his forearm and pulled him towards the tent. "It won't take too long. And it's free!"

Auggie sputtered as I dragged him out of the line and the people behind us moved up to take our place. Outside the opening to Molly's tent, Auggie pulled his arm out of my grasp with a laugh.

"We lost our place, Jordan! We'll have to go to the back of the line, and—"

"Come on," I said, pleading, not wanting to explain that my buttcrack was becoming Florida in August. "Just one reading. We weren't waiting that long anyway."

He rolled his eyes playfully.

"Fine," he said. "Hopefully, Molly tells us we are going to win a million dollars or something."

With a laugh, I nodded with my head towards Molly's, though my stomach was already clenching up from the thought of a reading from the mystic. As we stepped out of the sun and into the tent, I immediately felt cooler. Molly's tent seemed to be at least ten degrees cooler than outside.

It didn't make sense, how the inside of a tent could be so cool since it was baking under the sun like everything else in town. However, Mystic Molly's was downright pleasant. Even though a Tarot card reading was not something I really wanted, at least it was a free way to cool off.

Molly's eyes sparkled as we approached. Her lamp was lit, flickering golden fire in her eyes. Molly was still dressed like an old-fashioned fortune teller at a carnival, her long-sleeved dress of black, and her cobweb of a shawl draped around her shoulders. Silver hoops hung at her ears and a slash of red lipstick streaked across her mouth.

"Happy Independence Day," Molly said in greeting.

"Hi, Molly," Auggie chirped and plopped into one of the chairs opposite the table from her. "Happy Fourth."

"Happy Independence Day," I mumbled as I slid into the chair next to Auggie.

Molly's eyes were only for me, though she had acknowledged Auggie's greeting. It was if she knew I was the one who wanted a reading. Well, maybe I didn't want a reading, but she knew I was the reason for our visit. My desire to get out of the heat had brought us to her table. Of course, no one had to be a mystic to figure that out. We hadn't been that far away from the opening of her tent when I told Auggie we should get a Tarot reading. Molly had probably just overheard our conversation, so she knew I was her customer.

"Do you fancy the cards?" she asked.

"Uh," I shrugged, "I guess? It's free, right?"

"Jordan," Auggie mumbled.

Mystic Molly laughed jovially.

She reached to the deck of oversized cards at the center of the table—which I had not noticed when we sat down—but her eyes never left mine.

"What would you like to know, Jordan?" she asked. "And yes, it's free."

I gave her an apologetic smile and found myself shrugging again.

"I guess whatever the cards tell you? I don't really know what I want to know."

Auggie chuckled and Molly grinned wickedly at me.

"A man not afraid to know his own fate," Molly said. "Interesting."

For some reason, Molly's playful comment made my breath become a hard rock in my throat.

My fate?

Before I could object, or insist to Auggie that I'd made a poor decision, Molly was shuffling the cards. Within seconds, she had set the deck back on the table, cut it ten different ways with the speed of a ferret, and produced three cards from the top of the deck. One by one, she laid them out before us. Auggie leaned in excitedly, practically hanging his face over the cards as Molly examined them. I did everything I could to not look at the table.

I was afraid I'd see some guy getting his throat slit depicted on one of the cards.

There was no reason for me to believe that's what I'd see, but I couldn't force myself to look.

For what seemed like ages, Auggie stared down at the cards and Molly examined them. When she finally looked up at me to speak, Auggie sat back so he could watch her as she laid my fate out for me. I wasn't sure I was breathing.

"When you take a step back, you will see the spirits," she said cryptically. "Among the stars, you will make a choice that will have you meet your fate in a body of water."

"W-what?" I stammered.

"It's a free reading, kid," the corner of Molly's mouth turned up. "You get what you get."

Auggie laughed uproariously. I frowned at Molly, though I wasn't unamused.

"Is this where you tell me to slide you five bucks for two more minutes?" I asked.

Molly grinned.

"I will gladly accept your money," she said, drawing the three cards back into the deck, "but there is nothing else to tell you."

My frown deepened.

"You don't really understand business, do you?" I quipped.

Though I was mostly joking, I made sure to add enough sass so Molly knew I was displeased. She didn't care. Both her and Auggie chuckled at my comment. Auggie rose from his chair, obviously better at taking hints than I, and grabbed my arm.

"Come on, Jordan," he said. "You got your reading."

Molly and I stared at each other as I rose from my seat. As Auggie skipped from the table and across the tent, out into the sun once more, Molly and I kept our eyes on each other. I backed away from her table, trying to read into her soul through her eyes, to decipher what her small grin and those sparkling, lamp-lit eyes were telling me.

Maybe I believed in mystics a little.

When I felt the sun on my back, I looked away from Molly and started to turn towards the opening between the tent flaps.

"Jordan?" Molly called softly.

"Yeah?" I turned back to look at her.

"Pay attention to the stones."

"Uh…"

"They'll help you understand."

Well, that wasn't cryptic at all.

"Uh, yeah," I said. "Okay."

With that, Molly flicked a hand, dismissing me with another smile. So, I turned, breaking eye contact, and stepped out into the summer sun once again.

The Possibilian breeze was back, blowing through downtown pleasantly. Although it was still warmer outside than it had been inside Molly's tent, the coolness of the breeze brought a smile to my face. I'd been inside Molly's long enough to staunch the flow of sweat on my back. Glancing around, looking for Auggie, I found him standing at the front door of Samuel's, waving me over ecstatically.

"Well, come on!" He waved me over. "The line's empty now!"

I grinned proudly.

"Told you I have the best ideas," I said as I sauntered over arrogantly, swaggering, my arms swinging at my sides comically.

"You, my friend," Auggie said, magnanimously as I approached, "had the best idea."

"Thank you, my good sir," I said with a bow of my head.

Auggie laughed and held the door for me as I ducked into Samuel's.

Only one person was left in line when we approached the gleaming white and stainless-steel counter. The crowd had died off enough that Levi Lee was no longer at the register, leaving Samuel to make his concoctions and cash out customers. It took Samuel seconds to provide a fountain drink to the customer ahead of us, then a few seconds longer to produce the two ice-cold Mountain Dews in glass bottles for Auggie and me.

Auggie and I spent a few minutes examining the Rorschach ink blots that decorated the wall opposite the counter in Samuel's. My interpretation of a particular print that caught our eye was a ghost, and Auggie agreed. Whenever we found an inkblot the two of us could agree on in Samuel's, we stopped looking. Why find something to argue over when you can leave a place in agreement over something?

We made our way back outside, ready to continue our Fourth of July BBQ adventure in downtown Possibly. Between sips of the refreshing Mountain Dew and the breeze blowing in off the creek, the Fourth of July was turning out to be a pleasant day in town.

Instead of immediately making our way back to Liberty Lane, we hung a left at the corner of Samuel's marching through the grass towards Starbuck's. Levi Lee was already next to the door of the pirate ship, his green-screen suit on, bunching up rudely in certain places, pretending to be a robot. I wasn't sure why he had brought the green-screen suit back *and* continued his robot schtick, but it wasn't for me to show concern. Levi Lee would figure his art out on his own, just as I would.

Auggie and I stood across the street from Starbuck's sipping our sodas and watching Levi, trying not to distract him as we considered his new pursuit of art.

"An invisible robot?" Auggie suggested.

I shrugged and we both chuckled.

When movement down the street caught my attention out of the corner of my eye, I turned my head to see what was going on by the post office. Sofia was standing outside, doing something to the door. It being a holiday, I had to wonder why she was within so much as a hundred yards of her work. Then again, it was hard to be a hundred yards away from anything in downtown Possibly, such was its size.

I gave Auggie a nudge with my elbow and he turned to look where I was focused. We exchanged a glance, shrugged, and began to stroll down the street towards the post office. When we approached the post office, crossing the street to get a better look, it became clear that Sofia was taping a piece of paper to the front door. When she caught sight of us, she turned her head to give us a wide grin.

"There's no way I'm opening on a holiday, but I just couldn't wait until Monday to share it!" she exclaimed.

Auggie and I gave each other another look, and the same realization hit us. We both grinned and dashed to the front door to stand on either side of the postmaster. She took a step back to stand between us, admiring her handiwork.

On the front door of the post office, she'd taped up the latest letter to Shirlene.

"Got it day before yesterday, I reckon," she said. "Been out for two days due to the holiday. But there it is. Another romantic proclamation. Makes the heart sing, doesn't it?"

Auggie grinned mischievously at me behind Shirlene's back and I had to stifle a chuckle.

As Sofia looked on proudly, her eyes swimming with stars, Auggie and I turned our heads to the front door. Together, we read the latest anonymous letter to the mysterious *Shirlene.*

I cry into the darkness: "Shirlene. Shirlene. Shirlene. Shirlene! I love you, Shirlene!" My heart will not know peace until I have you, Shirlene.

Reading the letter over and over, I had to smile, though I was becoming increasingly frustrated by the letters. I'd only been in Possibly for just under a month and I was already captivated by the mysterious notes that arrived at random, slipped into the slot at the post office. Who was sending them? Who was Shirlene? What was so special about Shirlene to garner such admiration and desire? Why were the letters so...*PG?* Did the sender not know how to spice things up from time to time?

Auggie sighed next to me.

"This person definitely loves Shirlene," he said. "Maybe they'll find her soon?"

I had nothing to add. The love was obvious. If a bit too chaste for my taste.

WHO TURNS DOWN BBQ?

"A new letter arrived for Shirlene today," I said to Jack. "It was pretty saucy, but, like, in a Christian Romance book kind of way."

Jack glanced up from the table in the backyard to grin at me, then he was right back to work. I couldn't understand why the man was in the backyard working on the table when he could be downtown getting free food and drinks.

"Sofia taped it up on the front door of the post office," I continued. "If you want to go check it out, I mean."

Jack shook his head without looking up, but I could see his smile under the shadow of his bent head. There wasn't anyone in town who wasn't at least mildly amused or interested in the letters to Shirlene. When I'd first seen them, on my second day in town, I wanted to be annoyed by such an open display of yearning. The letters had grown on me due to everyone's enthusiasm. I was certain that when I met up with Auggie again downtown, I'd see a crowd outside the post office.

We'd both gone home to use the bathroom.

I'd offered to let Auggie use my bathroom at Jack's house, but he declined. He murmured something about wanting to change shirts.

I didn't say anything, but I saw the pit stains. I had a pair of my own.

"Yeah," I mumbled, "it's kind of silly. But...honestly...*who sends those letters, you know?*"

Since my first few days in Possibly, I'd developed theory after theory about the letters that were slipped into the post office slot at night and tacked up on the wall. It was possible Sofia was writing the letters. Maybe she wanted to add a little excitement to her job and give the town something to enjoy? Wyatt was always running around, shooting his gun. People had gotten used to him and mostly ignored him, even when he was firing off a round. He could easily slip by the post office and slide a letter into the slot. No one would pay him any mind.

Grandy—there was a guy no one talked about much. He sat off on his own down at the gas station and philosophized to himself all day. Maybe at night he was sneaking letters into the post office slot? The writing certainly fit that of a guy who waxed poetic about love.

Starbuck's was just next door. He could have easily slid the notes through the slot on his way home at night after the post office was closed. Mystic Molly was sneaky and mysterious. It could have been her. The guy always jumping off the bridge and screaming to forget Emily could have been the culprit. Changing the name on the letters so that people didn't know it was him was feasible.

Malia lurked around the graveyard. Maybe she used her hooded black-cloak to sneak by the post office at night. Samuel didn't seem the type, nor did Earl Dean, Jasper, or Officer Hanning, but they seemed to have the time and opportunity as well. Auggie very well could have been the mysterious letter sender...but I had a feeling he would have chosen a different name for his intended.

The only person I hadn't considered a suspect was Agnes Boudreaux. The sound of her rowing her wheelchair around

242

downtown drew attention to her immediately. Sneaking by the post office at night would have been difficult for her. *Unless she didn't really break her leg and it was all a ruse.*

Levi Lee even came to mind a time or two. Maybe he yanked on his green-screen suit—that filled out obscenely in places—and declared himself invisible so he could sneak by the post office. It was entirely possible it was him testing out new performance art.

Then again, it seemed to be that the letters had been arriving longer than Levi Lee had been trying to figure out his art.

Unless I wanted to spend a night hiding near Lovelorn Pass Bridge to watch for the letter sender, the mystery was hopeless. Then again, I wasn't sure I wanted to know the identity of the letter writer. Wasn't life more fun with a little mystery?

"Are you going to come have barbecue?" I asked Jack. "They're going to be serving anytime now. Free drinks are all over the place."

Jack paused, which surprised me, and looked up at me. He seemed to be considering something. Then, almost so quickly I didn't catch it, he brought his hand up and made a pinching motion with his index finger and middle finger against his thumb.

No.

It wasn't the answer I wanted, but its delivery took my breath away. I found myself with two choices. There was the option to act like an excited puppy that Jack had actually communicated to me with sign language, or I could play it cool and act normal. Normal was what I tried.

"You sure?" I asked.

Jack looked uncertain again, then raised his fist and tipped it back and forth.

Yes.

"All right," I said. "It all smells and looks really good, though. You'll be missing out."

Jack started to go back to the table, ignoring me.

"I could even bring you a plate if you want?" I suggested quickly.

I didn't want to lose Jack's interest in actually conversing with me using sign language. Also, I was already planning in my head to tell Auggie about the development. The more Jack and I conversed, the more I had to tell Auggie.

Jack looked at me again as though he wasn't sure about my suggestion, but after a moment, he made the "OK" sign. Then he pointed at his chest, then made a "C" with his hand and moved it down his throat towards his stomach.

I didn't know that sign yet, but I could figure it out.

"You're hungry?"

He gave me a small smile and signed "yes" again.

"Give me two minutes, man." I grinned. "I'll be right back!"

Without waiting to see how Jack would deal with my excitement, I spun on my heels and dashed away. I jogged around the house and across the front yard, down towards Bend of the Road Graveyard. When I approached the first headstone at the western end of the graveyard, I cut to the right and was jogging onto Liberty Lane within seconds.

Lines were forming along the street, so I knew my timing couldn't have been more perfect. Smokers and grills were being opened, ready to serve those with plates who shuffled along Liberty Lane, ravenous and happy to be fed. Before the lines could get any longer, I grabbed a paper plate and a set of plasticware wrapped up in a paper towel from the table set up at the northwest corner of Liberty Lane, and sprang into action.

One trip down the south side of the street got a serving of brisket and ribs added to the plate I was preparing for Jack. Another trip down the north side and coleslaw, potato salad, and corn on the corn was added. Stopping by one of the coolers, I grabbed a Coke for Jack to wash it all down with later. I couldn't run back to the house as quickly as I had run to downtown, but a minute later, and I was holding the plate out to Jack by the table he was working on.

Jack's eyes lit up with hunger when I shoved the plate under his nose. He started to reach out to take the plate, then stopped himself. He lifted an open hand to his mouth, palm inwards, then brought it down.

Thank you.

"Anytime," I said, grinning.

Jack produced his cautious smile and accepted the plate. I didn't want to hover over the guy or make myself a nuisance after the progress we'd made, so I began backing up.

"So," I said, trying to sound nonchalant, "fireworks later. All the food and drinks you could want if you're still hungry later. You should come downtown."

Jack didn't sign exactly, but he shrugged, and I knew what he meant.

Maybe.

That was good enough for me. At least he was considering joining the festivities.

"Well, okay," I said, still backing away. "I'm going to meet back up with Auggie. Uh, feed my face too, I guess."

Jack gave me a nod, but he was already unrolling his plasticware and tucking into his plate. I wanted to wait around to make sure Jack liked what I had put on his plate for him. But that would have been creepy and possibly undone some of our progress, so I spun around and began jogging back towards downtown. Watching Jack would have only made me hungrier anyway.

FIREWORKS

hy didn't you tell me that I was going to die?" I groaned as I rolled around in the grass.

"I had no idea you have no control over yourself," Auggie said.

We were in our spot outside Starbuck's, under the shade of the tree, laid out on the lush green grass. I was tempted to pull off my shirt so that I could feel the emerald carpet against the skin of my shoulders. It was cool against the backs of my legs, so it had to feel heavenly against my back.

The afternoon sun had strolled across the sky and was slinking away to the horizon as the breeze ruffled my hair and cooled my skin. The hand-size leaves of the tree cooled our spot further, making it feel more like spring than summer. But I was in misery.

After taking Jack his plate of food from the barbecue, I had run back to the downtown area, only to find Auggie waiting by the table full of plates and utensils, ready to feast. One quick trip down each side of the street, and we were seated beyond the tram tracks on Liberty Lane at one of the picnic tables that had been set up in the morning. Along with Sofia, Jasper—forgoing his tram duties to eat—and Levi Lee, we ate until we could barely move.

Brisket, ribs, smoked sausage, even a hamburger apiece, along with macaroni salad, potato salad, corn on the cob, coleslaw, baked beans, and biscuits, were stuffed down our gullets. Since it was all too much, we even partook in a slice of cake and ice cream that was available. Two sodas apiece washed it all down. Over an afternoon, we ate enough calories to get a growing teenager through a week.

"I'm dying," I groaned comically.

Auggie laughed at me and patted his extended stomach.

Even though most of the town's residents were still on Liberty Lane, mingling and telling stories, watching the kids play with sparklers, Auggie and I had chosen to rest under the tree. Red, green, and blue sparks flew up and down the street and children giggled, carefree and excited. We were far enough away to feel separate from everyone else, but close enough to hear the talking and laughter drifting on the breeze. My stomach may have been trying to split open, but the obvious joy exuded by the town's residents made me grin.

Possibly was…alive. I'd never been to a place where the town's residents all got along. Where food was shared freely, and in such abundance, and no one fought or argued. I'd never been to a town where the kids ran up and down the streets with fireworks and giggled in such a carefree manner. No adults were yelling for the kids to "be careful." Everyone had autonomy and the trust of others. Even the kids.

Jaded as I was by my time out in the world—well, the U.S., at least—I wanted to feel skeptical about everything. But Possibly was quite possibly the best place to be.

Sleepy and seemingly mundane, it had an energy that made me feel as if I was me…but also part of something bigger. A community, maybe? I could be me, but I could also belong. Everyone in Possibly had their own thing—their art, their business, their friends—but they also had each other. Acceptance and passivity seemed to be two more mottos of my new hometown.

It wasn't just a motto. It was a practice.

Possibilians bothered no one and expected the same in return. And, for that luxury, they rewarded each other ten-fold. Levi Lee could wear his green-screen suit that didn't hide everything well enough, but he was welcome to eat five helpings of ribs at the Fourth of July BBQ. Wyatt could walk around town, firing bullets into the air, but his help was warmly accepted at the grills. Harm none and be unharmed in return. Be yourself but part of the community.

Maybe it was too simple, too reductive, but it was a good motto. It was a great practice.

Along with the sounds of the people celebrating on Liberty Lane, a new sound was delivered by the cool breeze.

Luckenbach, Texas by Waylon Jennings was playing on AMOR.

"What?" I sat up abruptly, propping myself up with my hands in the grass.

"Huh?" Auggie's face screwed up.

"Amos changed the song!"

Auggie shrugged. The sun was setting in the west behind him, casting his face in darkness, unreadable, since the remaining sliver of sun blinded me.

"I told you he does that sometimes," Auggie said. "Well, on special occasions. Tomorrow he'll be back on his routine. He'll probably get crazy again on Labor Day, Halloween, Thanksgiving, Christmas—"

"Why does he do that?" I interjected. "It's...weird, right?"

Auggie smiled. He'd gotten used to forgiving my use of the word.

"I don't know," he said. "I think maybe it's just easy? Or maybe he wakes up and feels a song is the 'mood of the day' and runs with it? It's just the way he's always been. And it's not like anyone pays him to run the radio station, so who would any of us be to complain? We don't have to listen."

"Really?" I laughed. "There are speakers everywhere. You can't escape it if you're downtown."

"They could be unplugged. Smashed," Auggie said. "Someone could ask Amos to quit."

"Well, sure."

"But it's kind of nice," Auggie said. "He sets the mood for the town for the day. He wants us all to have theme music for the day."

I thought about that.

"Yeah," I said, finally. "It is."

Auggie nodded along to the music, rubbing his stomach with a free hand.

Listening to *Luckenbach, Texas*, in Possibly, Texas, was perfection I didn't know my life had been without until that moment. I'd never really paid much attention to the song, nor did I ever consider it a "patriotic" song. Even as I listened to it as I sat outside of Starbuck's with Auggie, I still didn't see it that way. However, it captured the day and the town perfectly. It was the perfect mood music. Amos had certainly perfected his own art.

"Hey," I turned my head to Auggie again, blinking as the last sliver of sun stung my eyes.

When I reopened my eyes, the horizon was deeply red, the sun gone for the day.

"Yeah?" Auggie sighed happily.

"Do you think I actually have some talent?" I asked quickly. "Like, with art, I mean?"

"Of course. Everyone does. Why would you question that?"

I shrugged as the sky began darkening.

"Nothing seems to really take," I said. "Okay. So, I've only tried painting so far, but it wasn't great, and—"

"Life is art."

"Huh?"

"You'll figure it out," Auggie said with finality. "I promise."

I sighed, mildly frustrated, mostly amused, and fell back in the grass again.

"I'll just choose to trust you."

"You're a wise man," Auggie chuckled.

"When do the fireworks start?" I asked. "I might die from massive barbecue belly before if they don't hurry."

Auggie laughed uproariously.

"As soon as it gets dark enough," he said. "So, soon, I think?"

"Do we need to go find a good seat to watch them?"

"Wyatt and Grandy shoot them off near Lovelorn Pass Bridge," Auggie said. "We actually have the perfect spot. Unless you want to sit with everyone else."

I darted my eyes to the side to look at Auggie. He was looking off towards the bridge expectantly.

"I like it here," I said, letting my eyes close happily.

Staying under the tree in the lush grass was appealing for two reasons. One, I wouldn't have to move around and further upset my stomach. Two, I didn't want to share my friendship with Auggie with everyone else during the fireworks. It felt odd to me. Made my stomach feel odd in a different way than all of the food I'd consumed. I didn't question it.

So, we stayed under the tree. I lounged in the carpet of emeralds and Auggie sat back, propping himself up with his hands, contentedly sighing from time to time. The light slowly disappeared, deepening the shadows, and I was finally able to turn my head and stare at the first real friend I'd ever had.

Auggie didn't exactly ignore me, but he didn't seem to notice my staring, even when he opened his eyes to check the light.

Vaguely aware of the voices of people moving closer to the creek in preparation for the fireworks display, I couldn't focus on anything but Auggie. Even as the shadows grew and enveloped us under our tree and the buildings around us turned navy blue and the stars began to peek out of the velvet above, I only had eyes for Auggie. He stared off towards the creek, grinning joyfully as people shouted excitedly for the fireworks to begin.

When the first boom erupted and sparks flew through the sky, erupting in a shower of red, white, and blue, Auggie's face was lit up by the burst of light. His grin widened until all of his teeth showed as he stared up at the sky in awe. I couldn't help but smile at the appearance of the fireworks, though I wasn't looking at the sky. I was looking at the diamond I found so fascinating.

Each firework that burst in the sky cast its hue on the white diamond on Auggie's head. Yellow, green, red, blue, even purple, my friend was a kaleidoscope of color. He cheered and hollered along with the people down by the creek, and I found myself sitting up to see him better. Inch by inch, I felt myself scooting closer to him, wanting to be closer to his face.

Auggie turned to me and grinned widely. I was so focused on that diamond that his words were soundless. He said something excitedly, then turned his head back to stare up at the shower of colors in the sky.

For a moment, I nearly reached out to grab his face and turn it to look at me. To pull him close and do something I'd never considered doing to another human being in my life.

Instead, I shook my head to clear my thoughts, the sounds all around me rushing in like my ears had been drained of water. Then I turned my head to the sky and joined Auggie in smiling up at the ballet of sparks.

SUSURRUS CREEK

The bank of Susurrus Creek was like a cliff, both on the Possibly side and on the Two-Mile Trail side. A person could sit at its edge and dangle their feet over the side without touching the water. That's what Auggie and I did after the crowd disbursed once the fireworks were over. The lights in the town behind us were blinking out as we sat near Lovelorn Pass Bridge on the Possibly side, lazily swinging our feet over the water.

Even in the near dark, I could tell that the opening to Two-Mile Trail was becoming more overgrown as the days ticked by. It produced an odd feeling in my gut I couldn't quite understand. Auggie had said it would sort itself out, so I did my best to ignore the odd feeling.

Susurrus Creek never flowed like roaring rapids, but sometimes it drifted by peacefully like a lazy river, and at other times, it whisked by like a hummingbird in flight. I theorized that the breeze and weather, along with how full the body of water that fed it was, had a lot to do with it. After the fireworks, it was in lazy river mode. Creeping by lethargically a few yards below the soles of our shoes, Susurrus Creek whispered softly as we stared up at the pinpricked velvet above us.

"Wyatt and Grandy put on a better display every year," Auggie said, breaking the silence we'd sat in for half an hour. "I time them every year. Well, kind of. Just in my head. I don't have a stopwatch or anything, but this year they went five minutes longer."

"Not to sound rude, but I'm just glad they didn't hurt themselves," I said with a chuckle. "They seem like they...would do that."

Auggie chuckled.

"There's a big difference between who we are and what we do," he said. "What we've done and what we're capable of doing."

"You're so cryptic." I smiled and looked down at my feet.

I didn't want to look at Auggie. Seeing that diamond shining bright in the dark was a bad idea.

"I'm not," he said. "You just don't listen."

He nudged me in the side with his elbow playfully.

"So," Auggie continued, "I have a theory."

I forced myself to look at him, but made sure to focus on his eyes.

"Yeah?"

"The letters to Shirlene actually arrive in an envelope, addressed to Shirlene. With an address and everything. But maybe it's, like, some crazy address that doesn't exist," Auggie said. "So, since she knows they're undeliverable, Sofia opens them and posts them on the wall. May as well get some excitement out of it, right?"

"Sure, yeah," I shrugged, suddenly not so distracted by Auggie's poliosis mark, "that's a solid theory."

"You got a better one?"

"I'm leaning towards Sofia, too," I said. "But I think she's actually writing them. If not her, my next guess is Grandy. They're kind of poetic, right? He's a philosophy guy. That might check out."

Auggie reached up to rub his chin.

"That might be," he said. "Both seem possible."

"It'd be really wild if it was like, Wyatt or Agnes, though. They'd be my least likely suspects."

"What about Jack?"

"Jack?" I gasped. "I would never suspect him."

"No, I mean, wouldn't he be one of the least likely and that's why it would be shocking?"

"Oh, yeah," I said. "It's not Jack's style. I don't think. He's not really clear with his feelings. Then again, that probably means he's less likely to write love letters to some mysterious woman."

"Agreed."

"Even if he did, I don't think he'd show anyone," I added.

"Concur once again," Auggie said with a chuckle.

The two of us swung our legs lazily over the creek and looked down at our shoes, having no further theories to share about the Shirlene letters. I thought to ask Auggie about when we'd try his installation art maze again, but something told me he'd invite me when he was ready. Pushing for an invitation would not be unwelcome, but maybe not polite.

Susurrus Creek drifted by as the Possibilian breeze whispered along the back of my neck, tickling the hairs there with its cool breath. Even with the nearly full moon—waning as it was—shining down above us, the town was cast in blue and black shadows. With Auggie by my side, I didn't feel as nervous as I had when I'd walked to his barn alone. Companionship makes darkness more tolerable.

Though we had nowhere to be and Jack wouldn't be worried about me, I knew that we'd both eventually have to go home. I didn't know what to say to Auggie, but I didn't want the night to end. It had been a perfect day. Auggie's parents would probably worry about him if he stayed out too late. Then again, I'd never laid eyes on Auggie's parents. I had no idea how they'd feel.

Why had I never met Auggie's parents?

Just as the thought entered my head, the breeze shifted direction violently, sending a gust down Susurrus Creek, causing my hair to fall into my eyes. A chill ran up my spine as I reached up to swipe my forehead clear. As I cleared my eyes of my hair, a low, hollow whistling sound echoed down Susurrus Creek from the north. Another chill ran up my spine. Without willing it, I reached over and grabbed Auggie's forearm.

He didn't even flinch. Instead, he chuckled at my surprise.

"You know," Auggie said calmly as the whistling sound tapered off as if being sucked back up river, "Susurrus Creek has always been incredibly haunted."

Though having Auggie with me while by the creek at night, him saying such a thing still unnerved me.

"Wh-what?"

"The whole town, really," Auggie patted my hand that was still on his forearm reassuringly. "They say that anyway. The whole town is crazy haunted."

"Who says?" I gulped.

He shrugged. "Everyone? I guess?"

"Stop it," I said, managing a nervous chuckle.

"I'm serious," Auggie playfully nudged me again. "Like, the spirits of miners and settlers and maybe indigenous people or something? They all haunt the town."

I wanted to ask Auggie why he wasn't scared, too, but that would force me to admit that my shivering wasn't from the breeze but from what he was saying.

"You sure it's not Malia doing performance art?" I teased, though my spine still felt like icy fingers were trailing up its length.

Auggie laughed. "Don't believe me. It doesn't matter. But this town is haunted. So they say."

"Bullshit," I squeaked.

My statement was meant to sound confident. I had sounded petulant.

"Why wouldn't it be?" Auggie asked, turning and propping one knee up on the bank to smile at me. "With its history, there's no way it couldn't be haunted."

"Bullshit," I repeated, managing a sing-song voice this time.

Auggie laughed loudly.

I smiled, pleased I had amused him.

"I'll prove it to you," he said.

"How will...how will you do that?"

Nervously, I chewed at the inside of my cheek, my eyes darting around to see if Auggie was going to summon a spirit out of thin air. It was a ridiculous thought, but Possibly, though wonderful, was a ridiculous town.

"Well," Auggie said, leaning in conspiratorially, "there's an old legend around here."

"I'm listening."

"They say that if you walk around the perimeter of downtown Possibly thirteen times—*backwards*—then visit Bend of the Road Graveyard at midnight, you'll see at least one of the spirits," he whispered wickedly. "You never know which ghost will appear to you, but they'll appear. Then you know for certain that Possibly is haunted."

I stared at him.

"You're making that up. Right now. You pulled that out of your ass."

Again, Auggie was laughing. "On my life."

"Fine," I nudged him. "Have you done it before?"

He shrugged. "No. I never had a reason."

"Right," I said. "Because you know it's a lie you just made up."

"If I was lying about that, why would I say I haven't done it?" he asked. "I would have said I'd done it and saw a ghost to make the lie more plausible."

I thought about that.

"I wouldn't have believed that either."

"Because you don't believe in anything."

The gooseflesh on my neck proved that somewhere, deep down, I believed in…*something*. I didn't tell Auggie that.

"Okay, ye of little faith," Auggie stated haughtily. "Let's do it."

"Do what?"

He rolled his eyes playfully.

"Tomorrow," he said. "After your sign language lesson. You. Me. We're going to walk backwards around Possibly thirteen times. At midnight, we'll go to the graveyard and watch."

"Then what?"

"Either a ghost will show up and you can eat your words, or nothing will happen and I will have to concede that maybe it's not true."

"It's a lie, you mean."

"It may be a lie, but not mine," Auggie said. "I'm just repeating what I've heard. So, if it's a lie, it's not my fault. I'm just a gossip, not a liar."

I managed to laugh, forgetting, for a second, that we were considering looking for ghosts.

"Um…"

The thought of spending more time with Auggie after my sign language lesson was a pleasing thought. Doing something that might prove Possibly was an incredibly haunted town was not. What would I do if we proved the town was haunted now that I had mentally conceded that it was my new hometown? I couldn't just run back out of town on Two-Mile Trail. What would I do then? Mom wouldn't be waiting to whisk me away from the oogey-boogeys.

"Are you scared?" Auggie wiggled his eyebrows at me.

"Yes."

Why I had chosen to tell the truth, I had no idea. It had simply slipped out.

"Oh," Auggie winced and looked down. "Sorry, Jordan. I didn't—"

"We'll do it," I said, stopping him. "I'm scared. But I'll do it."

Auggie looked up hesitantly, a small smile on his lips.

"You sure?"

"Yes," I said. "And then we'll see you are a gossip. And you will owe me two milkshakes from Samuel's."

"Two milkshakes?" Auggie gasped dramatically.

"Yep," I said. "To make up for being a gossip. It's your penance."

"What do I get if we see ghosts?"

"Um," my eyes darted around, "what do you want?"

Auggie grinned wickedly, which made my stomach do flip-flops.

"You have to work harder to find your art," he said.

It wasn't what I'd expected to come out of his mouth, but it wasn't unfair.

"Deal," I said.

Auggie held out his hand and I hesitantly took it, giving it a firm shake.

Ten minutes later, I was walking up the steps of Jack's place. Though I was embarrassed by it, Auggie had walked me all the way to Jack's from the creek. He hadn't asked if I wanted him to, he had just taken it upon himself. Once I was in the yard and headed to the front door, he'd said his "goodbye" and headed off towards the barn. I was embarrassed to admit it, but Auggie walking me home had made me feel safe.

Inside, Jack was on the sofa, laid back, his eyes nearly shut. The T.V. was playing some old western film on low volume. When I opened the door, his eyes shot open and he sat up to look at me. I closed the door and stood there looking at him. After a moment, he signed "fun?"

"Yeah," I said. "I had fun."

Jack gave me the slightest of grins, then reached for the remote and shut off the T.V. He stood and stretched, then indicated he was going to bed. Then he signed "goodnight," touching the tips of his fingers on his right hand to his chin, then held up his left arm across his chest and dipped the fingertips on his right hand over it like the sun setting.

"Goodnight," I said.

I watched as Jack made his way through the living room and up the stairs, disappearing into the shadows of the dark second floor. When he was gone, I smiled. He didn't say, and he never would have—just as I never would have asked—but I sensed he had been waiting up for me. Just to make sure I got home safely. Mom didn't even do that. Jack waiting up had felt like...home.

After I'd stripped down to my boxers and was crawling into bed, I stole a glance out the window towards Auggie's barn. Lights were shining from the skylight. When I glanced at my cell phone screen, the hazy blue light casting my bed in a bubble of light, I saw that Auggie had one minute. I put my phone on my bedside table and knelt there at the window, the moonlight making my chest look pale blue. A minute later, I saw the lights slowly blink out.

They hadn't shut off suddenly as though Auggie had stopped the timer in the center of the maze. The skylight had closed as though he had failed.

I didn't want to be glad that he didn't solve the maze without me, but nevertheless, I was. When Auggie finally beat the maze and got to use his observatory, I hoped I was with him.

THIRTEEN
CIRCLES

"So," Levi Lee's first word was punctuated by a gunshot down by Grandy's, but we both ignored it, "I'm a mime magician, but I'm really bad at magic."

Levi Lee was stationed in front of Starbuck's, as was usual, but his green-screen suit was gone, replaced by a tuxedo with tails. A top hat rested upon his head. I wasn't sure if I missed the green-screen suit or not, which confused me, so I chose to push that to the back of my mind. Golden curls peeked out from underneath Levi Lee's top hat and beads of sweat dotted his forehead, which was painted white—like the rest of his face. But he smiled. It wasn't an exceptionally warm summer day, but the tuxedo, top hat, and face paint had to be oppressive. However, even the heat couldn't dampen Levi Lee's spirit.

"Like, you're bad at magic usually? As yourself? You can't do it?"

Jeepers Creepers by Louis Armstrong was playing on all of AMOR's speakers around town.

"Well, no," he said. "But, like, my magician character is bad at magic. It doesn't matter if I am."

"Ohhhhhh. I get it."

I didn't get it.

Levi Lee smiled at my statement, so it didn't matter if I got it. He obviously understood what he was going for—I thought—his art hurt no one, and he was happy. Did anything else really matter?

"But aren't mimes supposed to not talk?" I asked.

He cringed.

"Yeah," he said with a full-body sigh. "That will be the hard part. Being a hull was a nightmare, man! Being a mime is going to be so much worse. A hull isn't a person, so at least I could tell myself—*'Levi Lee, you're not a person. You can't talk.'* But mimes are people, so they could talk if they wanted to, right?"

"Right."

"I've got my work cut out for me, my good man!" Levi Lee crowed.

In the next few moments Levi Lee straightened his bowtie, fixed his tails, tipped his top hat just so, and proceeded to pull a string of tulle scarves out of his pocket, but they kept falling apart. With mock surprise and horror, Levi Lee tried scooping up the scarves as they drifted to the ground, dropping some, sending some flying off in different directions—generally making a mess of his "magic."

Watching Levi Lee try another form of art made me wonder if it would take me forever to figure out what my form of art was as well. From what I'd gathered, he'd been working a long time trying to understand what fit him best. Obviously, performance art was going to be his art, but how that presented was the question.

"What did you do before this?" I asked Levi Lee. "I mean, before you tried your hand at art?"

He took a second to finish his routine with the errant scarves, then stood up before stuffing them haphazardly in his pocket, smiling proudly at me.

"All-around handyman, my man," he said.

Considering Levi Lee, his young face, his golden curls, and naïve ways, I had to wonder how much experience he could have as a handyman. He didn't look much older than me—maybe early twenties?

"Around here?" I asked.

He shrugged and smiled. "Lots of places."

"You're not from Possibly?"

"Is anyone from Possibly?" Levi Lee leaned in and winked at me.

"Uh…"

He looked as though he was about to say something else, maybe explain his cryptic smiles and statement, but the words never left his mouth. An exuberant shout from behind me interrupted us.

"Jordan!" Auggie's voice assaulted my ears.

Levi Lee was already working on another "magic trick" before I had turned all the way around to greet my approaching friend. Auggie jogged up to us, his white diamond practically glittering in the sunlight, swinging a metal bottle from each hand. He wasn't even out of breath when he skidded to a stop in front of me outside of Starbuck's. Of course, nowhere in Possibly was far to run, so that probably explained everything.

"Hey," I said.

Auggie held one of the metal bottles out to me. "Water. I filled them up at Samuel's."

"Oh."

"I was going to get a cone for each of us, but he was super busy. He let me fill up the bottles, though."

"Uh…"

"We're going to be walking in the sun," Auggie said. "Water is good."

I chuckled. "Oh. Okay."

"I've been out and about on the town," he continued excitedly. "Getting water, checking the post office for a new letter to Shirlene, and—"

"Was there a new letter?" I asked with equal enthusiasm.

"No," Auggie frowned, "but I'm sure it won't be long. Whoever is sending them is too in loooooooooove to stop."

Auggie's assessment of the situation made me laugh.

"Auggie!" Levi Lee exclaimed. "Check it out, man. Inept magician!"

I turned to look at Levi Lee as Auggie assessed him. He was standing there in his top and tails, displaying his arms widely and proudly with a smile.

"Sweet!" Auggie crowed from behind me. "You're going to make a mess of magic tricks?"

Levi Lee beamed.

"Exactly!"

"That'll be awesome," Auggie said. "We're going to go ghost hunting—well, the first step—but I'll come by and see your act soon."

Levi Lee smiled and nodded, as if everything Auggie had just said wasn't totally batshit crazy, as if it was the most normal thing he'd heard all day.

"Great! That'll give me time to practice."

Auggie and Levi Lee exchanged a quick, but enthusiastic, fist bump, and then Auggie was racing away, leaving me to chase after him. Him racing away from Starbuck's confused me since the two of us were supposed to meet there to start our backwards walk around downtown. As he raced between the pirate ship and The Pueblo towards Liberty Lane, I had to wonder if he had changed his mind. When he continued across the tram tracks and then across Liberty Lane, waving at Jasper, Earl Dean, and Officer Hanning on the way, I mimicked his actions and continued my chase. When we ran alongside AMOR and popped out across the street from Bend of the Road Graveyard, things started to fall into place.

Apparently, we were going to start where we'd end up. Or, at least, that's what I assumed.

"You ready?" Auggie asked as he slid to a stop.

I stopped abruptly, nearly tumbling over from the grass and into the road.

"What?"

"We have to walk backwards around town thirteen times," Auggie said with a frown. "Remember?"

"Of course, I remember." I nudged him. "You just confused me the way you took off from Starbuck's. That's all."

"Oh. Okay," Auggie said. "So?"

"Yeah," I said. "Why else would I have met you?"

"My dazzling personality, obviously," Auggie took his turn nudging me.

I stole a glance at that white diamond.

"It was definitely for the ghosts."

Auggie cackled, which made me smile and my gut flutter. I liked making Auggie laugh.

"So?" I asked. "What do we…"

Auggie nodded, switching to the business at hand.

"Easy enough," he said. "Or, from what I've been told, of course. I'm just a gossip."

I rolled my eyes.

"But we just turn around," Auggie turned with a flourish as he spoke, and I followed his lead, "and then we walk. Backwards. Around downtown thirteen times. Starting here and ending here."

I stood there, thinking about the backwards trip around downtown Possibly, and I couldn't help but wonder if I was coordinated enough for the task. Thirteen times, walking backwards, around Possibly was a bit of a walk. It wasn't far but it was at least a couple miles. Walking backwards wasn't all that difficult, of course, but doing it for so long increased the odds I'd stumble. Not that I was particularly clumsy—I was good at running like hell—but I'd never tried to be coordinated backwards.

"I'm going to fall," I said. "But whatever."

Auggie chuckled. "Stop being so negative."

"Okay."

"Let's go," Auggie said with another nudge to my ribs. "We want to see ghosts, after all."

Lurching to keep up as Auggie suddenly took off at a fairly rapid pace backwards, I managed to stay on my feet as we headed west.

"Actually," I said, looking down at my feet, "I'd rather we didn't see ghosts."

"Oh, yeah?" Auggie asked. "Scared?"

He was teasing, but he wasn't wrong.

"Well, yeah," I said. "But if we don't see ghosts, you owe me two milkshakes. Remember?"

He chuckled. "And *when I'm right*, you have to work harder on finding your art."

"Yeah, yeah."

Auggie and I fell into a rhythm as we marched backwards down the street along the graveyard. We managed to turn to the left towards Liberty Lane without a hitch. By the time we had reached The Pueblo, and neither of us had so much as stumbled, we fell into an easy banter. Both of us wanted to discuss Amos' selection of music for the day. *Jeepers Creepers* was a little too on the nose as background music for our mission, which we both agreed on. I quipped that Auggie had probably slipped a request to Amos that morning, but Auggie denied all responsibility.

Not wanting to risk ruining our fun day, I let the topic die.

As we walked, Auggie gave me more backstory on the businesses and citizens of Possibly proper. As we walked towards The Pueblo, Auggie explained that the three buildings in a row with Blooms were empty. They were still waiting for some Possibilian to come up with a business plan and utilize their sweet location downtown.

We walked backwards past Mystic Molly's tent where her sign proclaimed: *"Bottle Caps Today!"* Auggie had to explain that Molly could read the future in practically anything. Bottle caps. Dice. Toenail trimmings.

I didn't ask any questions.

When we walked to the south end of town and made our way around Grandy's, Auggie waved to the town philosopher as he sat on his cinderblocks and pondered...God knows what...but Grandy just stared off into space. Auggie wasn't fazed by the rebuff.

"He's obviously onto something now," Auggie said excitedly.

Lovelorn Bridge Pass was empty—no lovesick teenager screaming a girl's name and leaping into Susurrus Creek. Sofia was outside of the post office, apparently getting fresh air, when we passed by. She gave us a wave and a smile.

"Ghost hunting?" she asked loudly.

"Ghost hunting!" Auggie crowed back happily.

I just smiled, embarrassed that I was participating in such an odd Possibly legend.

We crossed Liberty Lane and walked behind the row of businesses that lined the street, waving again to Officer Hanning, Earl Dean, and Jasper once more. Within moments, we were back at Bend of the Road Graveyard. The whole first lap took three or four minutes, even going backwards.

Auggie lifted his water bottle, unscrewed the cap, and took a healthy drink, never once breaking stride. So, I mimicked his actions and took a drink of my water, too.

"Do you think," I said as we walked and recapped our bottles, "that we could stop at Samuel's and get a soda or something? Water will get boring."

"Once you start the thirteen circles, you can't stop," Auggie warned me gravely, though his eyes twinkled mischievously. "If you stop, you have to start all over."

"Wish I'd been told before we started," I mumbled.

"Huh?" Auggie grinned.

"At least this won't take long," I said. "Pick up the pace."

Auggie laughed at me and began walking backwards faster, so I matched his speed. Within moments, the two of us were laughing and practically running backwards. Zipping past the graveyard, The Pueblo, Blooms, Grandy's—everywhere in downtown Possibly without paying mind to anyone we encountered. Our focus was solely on each other, our laughter, and making sure we didn't run into anything. We made two more laps around Possibly—all without stumbling—before we slowed to a rigorous walk once more.

On our next lap, walking at our previous pace, Auggie explained that no one was certain where Starbuck's pirate ship came from before it was converted into a coffee shop. It was just in downtown Possibly from the get-go. People assumed that maybe Susurrus Creek was once a raging river and the pirate ship had somehow been shipwrecked, but it was only a theory. No one could explain why a pirate ship would be sailing on a river in the middle of Texas so that it could even get shipwrecked there.

Grandy's, Auggie explained on our fifth circle, was a similar story. No one who lived in town presently really knew the history of the gas station.

On the sixth and seventh circle, Auggie tried to explain Lovelorn Bridge Pass and where its legend originated. With a bit of defeat on his face, Auggie simply said that some legends around Possibly appear out of nowhere and people "just go with them." I grinned at him and he told me to "be quiet."

It was likely that someone once jumped off the bridge out of anguish or a broken heart following a romantic entanglement. After that, everyone just started mimicking that behavior and a legend was born. It was also just as likely that someone made up the legend and everyone simply believed it, but he couldn't give me a solid answer for it.

Auggie could remember Lovelorn Bridge Pass's legend for as long as he'd been in Possibly, so it was likely pretty old. The fact that people still observed it and participated in jumping off of it into Susurrus Creek from time to time spoke to its hold on the community. Then again, there wasn't much to Possibly apart from its legends, so Possibilians tended to stick by them.

On our eighth and ninth circles, Auggie explained that Sofia Salazar had opened the post office and declared herself postmaster when she first came to town when she was a young woman. There had been no local service, so she saw a need and had the desire. She claimed the teal clapboard building down by the bridge and the creek and declared it a post office.

Everyone went along with it. It hurt no one. No one got much mail in Possibly anyway. Unless your name was Shirlene and you didn't exist.

Circle ten was used to give me the history of Earl Dean, Officer Hanning, and Liberty Lane. It was a short story, so one circle was all that was required. Earl Dean decided one day that

Liberty Lane needed to have rainbow bricks instead of boring asphalt. He got his pickaxe, went to Liberty Lane, and began hacking away at it. Officer Hanning—the only policeman in town—showed up, asked Earl Dean what he thought was doing, tearing up town property.

Earl Dean hadn't even stopped hacking at the street as he said: *"I'm making it prettier."* At a loss, Officer Hanning asked Amos and Jasper what they thought he should do about Earl Dean. Both men said: *"If people don't like it, they can go around. He ain't hurtin' nothin'."* So, Officer Hanning spent his days watching Earl Dean *make Liberty Lane prettier*, unless there was something more important going on downtown that he had to attend to each day.

No one in Possibly cared that Earl Dean wanted to make art out of Liberty Lane—in fact, many of them thought it would be beautiful once it was done—so Earl Dean was left to his art.

The eleventh and twelfth circles were devoted to Amos, AMOR, and his habit of playing one song "all day long" from "6am to 6pm." Auggie mostly laughed about Amos since no one really had an excuse for the way he went about his life, either. Lots of theories floated about town—Amos was playing songs for someone he was in love with, he was setting mood music for the day, or he got obsessed with one song and played it all day to get it out of his head. Whatever the reason was, speakers had popped up around Possibly seemingly overnight many years ago and...people just went with it. Some people even listened to AMOR on their own radios at home.

I didn't have a chance to ask Auggie why he didn't listen to AMOR on his radio in the barn. As we started our thirteenth lap around Possibly, he began to ramble about his barn and how lucky he was to have such an amazing space for his art installation. By the time he had stopped talking about the barn, I hadn't even had a chance to ask him about his parents. *Where are they? Why haven't I met them? Can I see your actual house?*

As the last word left his mouth, we were stopping across the street from Bend of the Road Graveyard once again. Auggie stopped, his forehead sparsely beaded with sweat, and started to unscrew the cap of his water bottle. I followed along, taking a long drink from the cool metal canteen. I reached up and wiped my sweat away and the sudden compulsion to wipe Auggie's forehead for him fluttered through my mind.

I pushed it away.

"Well," Auggie was staring across the road at the graveyard, "I guess that's that. Tonight, we'll find out if I'm a gossip or a truth-teller."

I chuckled nervously. Now that we'd completed our thirteen circles around Possibly, there was no turning back. I had to see things through. Didn't I?

"Where are people buried now?" I asked, though I hadn't been aware it was on my mind. "Like, now? If someone dies now?"

Auggie didn't respond.

"The graveyard would fill up quickly, right?" I asked.

"They don't bury anyone here anymore," Auggie said. "They say some of the people here have old, old, old, old relatives buried in Bend of the Road Graveyard. It's probably true. Some names look familiar. I guess, maybe, once people die, they bury them out in the newer town division. I mostly stick to Possibly."

"What have they done with dead bodies since you got here?" I asked.

Surely, Auggie knew where the funerals were held.

"No one has died since I got to Possibly," Auggie said with a shrug.

Then he was turning to me with a wide grin.

"Come on," he said.

Before I had a chance to ask what was up, Auggie took off at a spring in a south-westerly direction, his bottle swinging at his side. Frustrated, but also amused, I took off after my friend, gripping my bottle at my side as well.

The two of us raced away from the graveyard, past Liberty Lane, The Pueblo, Blooms, and Mystic Molly's tent. I was barely able to keep up with Auggie's lithe body, zipping here and there, heading off towards the woods, but I didn't lose him. When he headed down the trail that led to the clearing with the windchimes, I started to become nervous. However, I kept pace with Auggie, following him along the tree-lined path until we were skidding to a stop in the middle of the clearing in the woods.

Auggie turned to me, his hair getting ruffled briefly by the breeze.

"Windchime Hollow," Auggie said simply. "That's what it's called."

I didn't turn to him, but instead, looked around the clearing at all of the windchimes hung at the periphery. Windchimes of all shapes and sizes—just as I remembered—hung from nearly every tree along the edges of the clearing. Some tinkled in the breeze, some clanged, some were too heavy for the current breeze to move them.

Colored glass glinted in the sunlight and bottle caps that hadn't rusted yet shone. Leaves of green, as jewel-like as the Possibilian grass, swayed lazily in the hollow. One would think that so many windchimes would create a cacophony, but it was peaceful in the hollow. Maybe during windstorms it was deafening, but there with Auggie on a mild summer day, it was nice.

"People really think that…they can communicate with the dead here?" I asked the only logical question.

Auggie shrugged.

"It makes people feel better," he said. "So…why not? You know?"

I just nodded along, unsure of what to feel or say.

"It's not just the dead, though," Auggie continued. "I guess people come here and add to the chimes or ring them anytime they're thinking about anyone. Maybe it's stupid or—"

"It's not."

"—okay, but it's therapeutic. It makes people feel better. So, why not?"

I finally turned and smiled at him.

"Yeah," I said. "It's nice, I guess."

We stood there for a few moments, our eyes locked, before Auggie gave a sigh and stepped back. The breeze whispered through Windchime Hollow once more, ruffling our hair and causing the smaller chimes to make their tinkling noises.

"I'll come get you tonight? About eleven-thirty?" Auggie asked. "To go see our ghosts?"

"Sure," I nodded.

"I'll go now," Auggie said. "In case you need some time."

I didn't know what Auggie meant at first, but he cocked his head towards the windchimes across from us and smiled. I understood then. Without another word, Auggie turned and headed back down the trail that led into and out of Windchime Hollow. He didn't race away, sprinting like he had when we arrived at the Hollow. Auggie strolled away at a leisurely pace, pointedly not looking back. To give me privacy? I wasn't sure.

After he had disappeared down the trail and the shadows of the trees that lined the path claimed him, I turned my attention back to the windchimes. The wind was picking up, cool and fragrant, carrying the smell of summer grass and the woody scent of the trees.

As I sauntered across the clearing, my eyes fixed on a windchime strung with old metal keys, hung from a large pine tree, I wasn't sure what to think. Was Windchime Hollow really harmless? Was it healthy for people to place their comfort in what was essentially an art installation? The fact that no one really knew who had begun the tradition of hanging the chimes and adding to them made me more unsure of it.

With cell phones and letters and emails and other forms of communication, why would one ring a windchime for someone? Even if they were dead, why wouldn't someone just go visit their grave instead? Or say a prayer at night? If someone was dead—and you believed they could be communicated with—couldn't you talk to them…*anywhere?*

Was it ridiculous to ring one of the chimes and believe Auggie's story? To buy into yet another Possibilian legend?

The decision was made for me. When I came to a stop in front of the chime made of keys, a gust blew through Windchime Hollow, and the keys fluttered as if they were nothing, clanging together.

People in Possibly say that if someone is thinking of you—alive or dead—that the chimes will make their music.

So, when the chime settled, I reached out, grabbed one of the heaviest keys, and swung it. The windchime clanged again, keys tapping into keys, filling Windchime Hollow with the sound of metal clanging against metal. It should have sounded harsh, like someone working in a factory. Instead, it sounded like a song.

Like a song I had in my head but could never remember the tune.

THE FUTURE DISCUSSED

Jack was turned away from me, his hand resting on the handle of the fridge door as he examined its contents, when I got back to his place. When I left Windchime Hollow, the tinkling of the chimes following me down the trail, I realized that my lower back had turned into a swamp. Possibly wasn't experiencing the hottest day, but after walking around town thirteen times, then racing to Windchime Hollow, it was understandable that I'd gotten overheated. On the way back to Jack's, I'd paced myself, finishing off the bottle of water Auggie had given me on the way.

As I walked into the house, I made a beeline for the sink and unscrewed the cap of the water bottle. I filled it up from the tap halfway, then poured it all down my throat, swallowing the cool water greedily. Gasping for breath and partly satiated, I held the mouth of the bottle under the tap again. I let the bottle fill all of the way to the top before turning off the tap and taking another healthy swig from the slick metal bottle.

When I turned away from the sink, Jack had closed the refrigerator and was staring at me, an amused smile on his face. Obviously, slurping down water like a maniac was kind of funny.

"What?" I smiled.

Jack started to sign, but most of the signs I didn't understand.

"Sorry, man," I said with a wince, "I'm not following you."

Jack stopped mid-sign, frowned thoughtfully, then his eyes lit up. He took his right hand and touched his thumb to his four other fingers and brought it to his mouth.

Eat.

Then he brought that arm down and used his left hand to touch his forearm.

Breakfast.

"I already had breakfast," I said.

Jack smiled and held up a finger.

"Okay," I said.

Jack held up four fingers, then he made the sign for "eat" again, then brought his hand down to touch the back of his left hand.

Dinner.

Jack looked at me questioningly.

"Breakfast for dinner?" I asked. "Do you want to do breakfast for dinner?"

Jack nodded as he held his fist up in front of his chest facing me and rocked it back and forth.

Yes.

"I love breakfast for dinner," I shrugged. "It's probably my favorite thing."

Jack held his right hand up and curled all of his fingers in, except he left his thumb pointing towards his chest and his pinky pointing towards me. Then he moved his hand back and forth between us, his pinky aimed at me and his thumb jabbed at him.

Me too.

Our progression from hardly interacting, to communicating with notes and cell phones, to actually using sign language made me want to grin so wide my face would split. Somehow,

I knew that if I made a big deal about the sign language, it would set Jack and me back. He wanted to communicate with me in the way he knew how to best, but he didn't want to make a production of it. I could respect that.

"So," I asked, "like eggs and sausage? Maybe biscuits? Gravy if you're a really awesome guy?"

Jack grinned and made the sign for "yes" again.

"I'm in," I said. "Sounds good."

He tapped his left wrist with his right index finger, then held his right hand up with the three middle fingers extended and his pinky and thumb touching.

"Six works for me," I said. "That gives me time for a nap."

Jack grinned and started to head towards the living room.

"Auggie and I did that thirteen trips around Possibly backwards thing," I said as Jack sunk into the sofa. "You know about that?"

Jack rolled his eyes and nodded, obviously amused.

"We're going to go to the graveyard at midnight," I said. "To see the ghosts?"

He shook his head but he was grinning the whole time. He gave me the "ok" sign.

"Yeah. It's kind of dumb I guess."

Jack shrugged, then held his hand back and tipped it back and forth. I didn't know the sign—or if it actually was sign language—but I got the gist. Jack thought it was dumb, but it was also harmless. *Go have fun. What will it hurt?*

I laughed and started to turn towards the stairs. Going upstairs, stripping down to my boxers and airing myself out while I napped was the plan. However, a thought entered my head, something I wanted to ask Jack. While he was in a good mood and we were getting along was the best time to do it. I didn't want to miss the opportunity.

"Jack?" I asked.

He was flicking through channels on the T.V. but looked up at me.

"So," I said, "the kids around here go to school at The Pueblo?"

Jack eyed me for a moment, emotionless, then he gave me a nod.

"Does Auggie go to The Pueblo?"

A slight grin teased the corner of Jack's mouth. He nodded.

"Maybe," I said carefully, "I can go there? If it's cool that I...stick around that long. Ya' know? If that's a thing that happens. Just a thought. The Pueblo is kind of cool. Lilly is cool."

For the longest of moments, Jack stared at me. I wasn't certain if he wanted to tell me to get lost and not even think about sticking around that long, or if he was uncertain if I was serious.

Finally, he lifted his right index finger to his lips, then moved it forward quickly.

Sure.

"Cool," I said, not wanting to make a big deal of anything again. "It'll be cool to know one of my classmates, right?"

Jack nodded then spelled out Auggie's name before tapping the fingers of his right hand to his lips and then bringing it to his left hand. Then he took his right hand with only his index finger and pinky sticking out, held his index finger under his nose, and rotated his wrist a few times, bringing his pinky up and down.

Auggie's a good kid.

"Yeah," I said. "He's all right. For someone who believes in ghosts."

Jack held his belly and his mouth went wide, though no noise came forth. However, he was laughing. Just as I loved making Auggie laugh, I loved making Jack laugh. If not for the same reason.

When I made my way upstairs finally, leaving Jack to his T.V. shows, I stripped down and stared out the dormer window at the barn. In the early afternoon sun, its red paint blazed like a beacon by Susurrus Creek. I wondered what Auggie was doing as he waited for eleven-thirty to come. Was he as excited—and nervous—as I was?

I didn't slide under the covers. I was still too warm to need them. But I napped peacefully for hours.

GHOST IN THE SHEET

Taaaaap. Tap. Tap.
   Tap.
   Tap. Taaaaap.
Taaaap. Tap. Tap.
Something was tapping inside my head.

After dinner with Jack, followed by T.V. time watching silly comedies, I had gone up to my room and laid down on my bed to stare out at Possibly. I must have drifted off into a heavy slumber because when I heard the tapping, I was startled to the point that I nearly fell out of bed.

What was inside my head?

Taaaaap. Tap. Tap.

Tap.

Tap. Taaaaap.

Taaaap. Tap. Tap.

Roused from my sleep, I sat up in bed and shook my head to chase away the tapping noise coming from inside my skull. When the tapping continued even after I had shaken off my sleep, I jerked my head around, looking for the source of incessant clatter. Nearly coming out of my skin, I jumped when my eyes landed on the dormer windows and the shadowy figure just beyond, perched on the roof outside of my bedroom.

Then my eyes locked with the figure's and I smiled.

Auggie.

Auggie was crouched on the roof outside of my window, smiling in at me.

Thank God I hadn't stripped down to my boxers for my second nap.

"Hey," I said.

Mindlessly, I hadn't thought that he might not be able to hear me through the closed window, so I leaned over my bed and raised the window.

"Hey," I repeated.

"Is baby boy sleepyheaded?" he asked with a grin.

"Shut up," I said. "What are you doing on the roof?"

"It's time to go ghost hunting, friend!" He crowed up at the night sky.

I looked up at the starlit sky through the window, that velvety, speckled sheet blanketing the sky above us.

"That doesn't explain why you're on the roof and peeking through my window."

Auggie seemed to blush, but without light, I wasn't certain.

"You have to leave through the window," Auggie said, glancing away for a moment. "You can't go out through the front door."

"Sure," I nodded, "that makes sense."

"It'll jinx seeing the ghosts," he said as if it was the most obvious thing in the world. "If you leave through the front door, you bring the living energy with you. Because only living people exit through doors. Obviously."

"Obviously," I gave him an overly enthusiastic nod.

"Come on," he said. "Don't make me yank you through the window."

I laughed and sat up on my knees.

"Should I tell Jack that—"

"He's already in bed," Auggie waved me off. "I've already been by his window."

"Oh."

Auggie jerked his head. "Come on."

Before I could respond, Auggie had scooted to the side of the roof, swung his legs over, and disappeared over the edge. I gasped, wondering how he was making his way to the ground. I was on the third floor. He couldn't have just dropped to the yard below; the fall would have broken his ankles in a best-case scenario.

Quickly, more to check on how Auggie was, I scurried out the window and slid to the edge of the roof. I breathed a sigh of relief when I saw that he was skittering down the old rose trellis under my window like a monkey. Auggie was a peculiar fellow. He favored tutus and pearl necklaces and fingernail polish at times, but he could climb and run and get dirty as well as anyone else.

Of course, it was stupid of me to equate or not equate one thing with the other.

One was his fashion sense; one was athletic ability. They were not mutually exclusive traits.

As soon as Auggie hopped from the trellis and landed safely in the yard below, he looked up at me with a wide grin as I hung over the side of the roof.

"Come on," he stage-whispered up to me.

"Hold your horses," I said, mostly to myself.

Carefully, and with less prowess than Auggie, I swung my legs over the edge of the roof and wiggled them around until they found purchase on the trellis. Inch by inch, I slipped off of the roof and lowered myself down to the trellis. Slowly at first, then quickly picking up speed once I realized the trellis was sturdy, I made my way down to Auggie. Moments later, I was leaping from the bottom of the trellis and landing next to Auggie in the yard.

He grinned at me.

"We're officially in *ghost world* now," he said.

"Yeah. That makes total sense, too."

He nudged me. "Come on. We want to get to the graveyard and get a good spot before midnight."

"Okay."

"We don't want to miss them, do we?"

"That would ruin this entire day, I suppose."

Auggie started to step away, then turned back to me.

"You starting to believe yet?" he asked.

"No," I said with a wide grin.

Auggie laughed lowly.

He said nothing more but punched me in the arm lightly before he turned away once again and sauntered from the side of Jack's house. I watched him for a moment, decked out in cargo pants, a black, flowy skirt worn over them, Chucks, and a tank top completing his outfit. The moon seemed to find his pale skin in the night and make him glow as he walked through the darkness. He had almost gotten to the edge of the yard before I realized I hadn't taken a single step. Finally, I urged my feet into motion and chased after him.

Silently, Auggie and I left the yard and stepped out onto the road, turning left towards Bend of the Road Graveyard. Like every other night, Possibly was utterly dark. Only the moon and stars provided any light by which to see, though they seemed brighter than anywhere else in the world. The light pollution in Possibly was basically nonexistent, so any bit of moonlight made traveling through downtown Possibly a piece of cake.

Auggie and I walked side by side, our arms brushing against each other lightly here and there as we made our way down the road. Pebbles were kicked by the toes of our shoes, sometimes playfully at each other as we traveled. The graveyard was only twenty yards or so away from Jack's place, so there wasn't much time to fill with talk. Before I knew it, we were standing at the junction in the road where we could turn right to go into downtown Possibly, or take the roads that went up and around or down and around the graveyard.

No decision was left up to me. I was just along for the experience of ghost hunting in Possibly. Auggie had a plan in mind. He motioned for me to follow him as he dashed off to the copse that was in the center of the "O" junction between Jack's place and the graveyard. Together, we scampered behind the tree closest to the road and knelt down, facing the graveyard.

Looking across the road, I was surprised at how visible the headstones were under the moon. I'd never really noticed on other nightly walks or when staring out my window at Possibly during the dark hours. However, they were like beacons there on the north side of town. More than likely, the type of stone the markers had been carved from was the reason for their brilliance in the dark. However, squatting there, in the dark, waiting to see ghosts, it was eerie more than fascinating.

"Shhhhh," Auggie whispered.

"Are we going to scare the ghosts?" It was mostly a joke, but my voice cracked, which I hoped Auggie didn't notice.

"Maybe they're as scared of us as we are of them?" Auggie turned his head to give me a quick wink. "We don't want to scare the dead."

"Right."

"You never know."

"What do we do now?" I whispered.

Auggie shrugged. "We wait. See if they show up."

"Why do they show up *here*?" I asked. "What if they decide they want to show up at Molly's? Or Windchime Hollow? Or—"

"We started our thirteen circles here and ended them here," Auggie stopped me. "They'll show up here."

"If they show up."

Auggie turned to me, an expression between a frustrated frown and an amused grin plastered across his face.

"You really have to find something to believe in."

"You keep saying that," I said with a roll of my eyes.

Auggie jabbed a finger at the ground.

"Park it. Shush. We're going to see ghosts."

Grumbling, though not unamused, I dropped to my rear in the grass under the shadow of the tree and did as I was told. I shushed. And I waited. Auggie turned his attention back to the graveyard, ignoring me completely. With wide eyes and his whole body tense with anticipation, Auggie moved so that he was no longer crouching, but sitting on his knees and waiting. With no idea how long we'd be waiting, comfort was paramount, I supposed.

Bringing my knees up to my chest, I wrapped my arms around them and rested my chin atop them. Though I wanted to ask a million questions of Auggie, I forced myself to keep my eyes on the graveyard, watching for any sign of movement. For a bit, as minutes ticked by, my whole body felt tense, as though a spring was compressed, ready to pop and send me into the branches above. As time passed, I felt less and less concerned with the fact that we were actually waiting to see if ghosts showed up in a graveyard.

My eyes were becoming more accustomed to the low-level light of the moon and the shadows became less ominous around us. Auggie stayed kneeling in the grass, half of his body hidden by the trunk of the tree. The Possibilian breeze whistled through town softly, ruffling our hair with its cool breath, but nothing else stirred. No other citizen of town came walking down the road on their way to…wherever one might go in the middle of the night.

Birds weren't chirping, critters weren't scurrying, and Auggie and I stayed stock still as we waited to see if our ghost hunting experiment had been worth the effort put forth. Though nothing stirred but the breeze, downtown Possibly wasn't completely silent. I could hear Susurrus Creek in the distance—water slapping against the shore as the creek slipped through town on its way to wherever creeks go.

I hadn't thought to grab my phone before I climbed out of my bedroom window and onto the roof to follow Auggie, so time meant nothing. Whether two minutes or two hours passed was impossible to know, but as Possibly tucked into the dead hours of night, I could tell it was getting colder. A shiver ran up my spine as I hugged my knees more tightly to my chest for warmth. Auggie seemed unaffected, not so much as twitching at the cold.

Before I knew it, a light mist was rolling in from the east— from the direction of Susurrus Creek, crawling westerly through town. Another shiver ran through my body as the mist inched along the road towards us, slowly but surely blanketing the grounds of the graveyard. My eyes were fixed on the glowing headstones as the mist created a miasma around us.

I'd never been a superstitious person, nor was I decided on whether or not ghosts existed, but the sudden appearance of the mist gave me the heebie-jeebies. Though I'd watched

Possibly through the dormer window of my third-story bedroom many nights—even at midnight—I'd never seen a mist roll into town from the creek. After having walked thirteen circles around town, beginning and ending at the graveyard, in order to summon ghosts, and then having the mist appear suddenly, I was beginning to feel on edge.

Suddenly, it struck me. There were no ghosts in Possibly. Nothing was haunted. I didn't know how I knew, but something told me it was an undeniable fact that Possibly was not haunted. Auggie and I had talked about ghosts after the Fourth of July festivities. He was having a bit of fun with me, waiting to see how long I would last by the graveyard before I ran home scared.

The thought brought a grin to my face.

The thirteen trips around town, Windchime Hollow, meeting me on the roof of Jack's place—all of it—was just a ruse. He was toying with me but also inventing fun and creative ways for us to spend time together. That's…that's what friends did.

Right?

Full of newfound bravery, I grinned and turned my head to Auggie.

"Hey," I said to the back of his head, "what time is—"

"*There!*" Auggie gasped, his eyes suddenly wide as he jabbed a finger at the graveyard.

"What?"

I whipped my head back around to look at the misty graveyard across the road from us, my eyes darting around to find what Auggie had spotted.

At first, I saw nothing but the miasma created by warm air and cold air meeting over a body of water and then being blown lazily by a breeze. Nothing was in the graveyard; of that

I was certain. Just a few trees, the headstones, and the mist. However, when I started to turn my head back to Auggie to ask him what he was going on about, my eyes finally landed on what had caught his attention.

A figure.

A white figure was walking up the road from the direction of Susurrus Creek.

Shaking my head in disbelief, wondering if a Possibilian was on a midnight stroll, I tried adjusting my eyes to the dark and the mist that lay between us and the figure. Seconds crept by slowly as I stared at the figure off in the distance that was partially cast in shadow. As it drew closer, gliding along the road towards the graveyard, I realized I was not looking at a person. Details started to become clear as I watched it move along the road lazily.

The figure wasn't just someone who looked white in the light of the moon, but it was actually…just…*white*. Because the figure was covered in a sheet. My first instinct was to laugh, seeing someone walking up the road in a white sheet like an old-timey ghost, but a shiver ran up my back instead.

There were no eye holes cut in the sheet for a person to see through. The sheet hung so low that it fluttered along the road around the figure. To make matters worse, a rope was tied around the neck of the figure, securing the sheet in place. Not like a noose, no, but just a single knot cinched impossibly tight around its throat. Knotted at the figure's throat and draped to hang over its shoulder, it dragged along the road behind the figure as it glided towards the graveyard.

"*What the*—" I gasped, then slapped a hand over my mouth.

Auggie didn't react. He stared at the figure.

The mist seemed to part for the figure as it moved along the road, creating a path for the ghost to make its way to the graveyard. Shivers ran through my body, making me jerk and convulse as I kept my hand clenched over my mouth so as to not make noise. The figure didn't seem to notice us—though, how could we tell since it had no eyes—but continued along the road drawing closer and closer to the graveyard, dipping in and out of the moon's light and the shadows.

Just when I thought I would scream out in terror, movement in the corner of my eye caught my attention. I whipped my head around, terrified to take my eyes off of the…*ghost*…but needing to know what was moving in the distance.

Coming down the road, gliding just like the other ghost, came another figure in a white sheet with a knotted rope around its neck. It was walking towards the graveyard as though it had come from Jack's place. My fingernails dug into my cheek as I clenched my hand more firmly over my mouth. I knew my eyes had to be like saucers as I watched the second figure gliding along the road, its sheet and rope dragging along behind it.

Following the second figure with my eyes, I watched as it drew closer to the graveyard. When it had traveled far enough, I was able to fix my gaze where I could see both figures traveling along the road towards each other. Auggie hadn't moved, he was simply watching as the ghosts made their way to each other. Finally, the two figures stepped off of the road and into the graveyard, the mist continuing to create a path for them.

The ghosts walked through the graveyard as though, even without eyes, they were watching each other. Finally, the two met at the largest headstone at the westernmost point of the graveyard. Only the tree we were behind and the expanse of the road separated us from the ghosts, and I felt that I would come out of my skin. I'd hop up, run away in terror, cackling like a loon.

At the large headstone, the two ghosts stopped, a mere foot of space between them. Even without eyes, I could tell they were staring into each other's souls as the mist reorganized around them, surrounding them in the miasma as they stood there staring at each other.

My hand was clenched so tightly over my mouth, my lips and cheeks were starting to ache. I began to shake as I stared at the ghosts with eyes that refused to blink from sheer terror.

We had summoned ghosts.

There were ghosts in the graveyard.

Auggie hadn't been lying to me.

Possibly was…haunted.

No. That wasn't possible. Even in Possibly.

There was no such thing as ghosts or summoning them or any of it. We couldn't be watching two actual ghosts in sheets standing in a graveyard having a midnight mass of some sort.

Malia.

Malia came to Bend of the Road Graveyard and did her "performance art" from time to time. One of the figures in the sheets had to be Malia. She had gotten someone to help her put on another show—maybe at Auggie's suggestion? That had to be it.

Though I was terrified, I felt my spine straighten as I leapt up from my spot behind the tree. I had barely stepped past Auggie as he knelt by the tree before he was leaping from the grass as well. I felt him grabbing at the back of my shirt, trying to stop me as I tried to duck out from under the shadow of the trees to expose myself to the ghosts. I wanted whoever was in the sheets to know that we were there and I didn't believe any of this. I needed to prove that I wasn't scared.

"*Jordan. No!*" Auggie hissed.

Ignoring him, I tried to pull away, to wrench my shirt from his grasp. As usual, Auggie was full of surprises, and his grip proved to be powerful. Angrily, though mostly desperately, I turned away from the ghosts and swiped at Auggie's arms.

"*Stop it!*" I commanded him. "*I'm going to see who these people are!*"

Auggie's hands fell away with surprise at my tone. As soon as I was free of his grasp, I whipped back around, prepared to dash across the street to confront the ghosts. However, once I was turned back to the graveyard, the ghosts were gone.

So was the mist.

It had simply…disappeared.

Jerkily, in complete disbelief, I stumbled out from under the tree and into the road. Step by step, I clambered across the road towards the headstone where the ghosts had held court. I could hear Auggie shuffling along quickly behind me, following me across the road to the graveyard. Though I was moving slowly, I was gasping for breath when I stopped in front of the headstone, my head whipping around, looking for where the figures could have hidden.

They were…gone.

There had been nowhere for them to hide so quickly. No trees to duck behind, no headstones large enough to crouch behind. Nothing. They had disappeared.

"Holy shit," Auggie said quietly.

"What the…Auggie…what…where'd they go?" I gasped, my head still whipping around.

With no other option, I glanced down at the tombstone, wondering if there was any significance.

Burke.

That was the name on the gravestone.

Quickly, I spun around to face Auggie.

"Where'd they go?" I demanded, though I wasn't angry.

I was spooked. Unnerved.

Auggie started to speak, stopped, started again, then gave up. He shrugged. His eyes were still the size of saucers.

"Burke!" I jabbed a finger around my back at the headstone, though my eyes didn't leave Auggie's. "That's Jack's last name."

"And yours." Auggie nodded.

"Is that Jack's family? Does that mean something?"

Auggie shrugged again. "Some families have been around here for forever. I don't know."

Nothing could have prepared me for my reaction. I found myself leaning back and laughing loudly up at the velvety sky. Auggie stood a few feet away, watching me quizzically as I laughed until I was holding my stomach, nearly doubled over with amusement.

"What is it?" he finally asked.

"Oh, come on," I said, finally realizing what an idiot I had been. "You told me Possibly is haunted. Then we walk those circles? We come out here at night and two *ghosts* show up and decide to meet in front of a headstone that belongs to some old relative of Jack's? You're pulling my leg, man. I was so freaking scared!"

I laughed long and hard, bending over to brace my hands against my knees.

Auggie simply watched me as I laughed until I couldn't laugh anymore, filling downtown Possibly with the sounds of my nearly insane amusement. Surely, people who lived above or near their businesses downtown were disturbed by the sound in the middle of the night. But no lights came on, no doors opened, and no sound but my laughter could be heard.

When I finally settled down, certain that I had figured out Auggie's game, I stood up straight to look at him. Wiping my eyes, I shook my head back and forth in amusement. I wanted to be mad at Auggie. To tell him that he was a jerk for working me up and getting me so scared. I wanted to demand the names of his cohorts. One could have easily been Jack—the one that had come from the direction of his place. But Auggie was frowning at me.

"What?" I finally asked.

"Where'd the mist go, Jordan?" he asked.

"What?" I frowned. "The mist?"

The mist.

I could explain the ghosts' disappearance. They had just been quicker than I thought. They had dashed away before I had turned to catch them. The headstone was an old relative of Jack's. But…how did a mist blow in and disappear so quickly?

I froze.

Auggie stared at me, his frown fixed to his face, for the longest of moments.

"Come on," he said with a sigh, jerking his head towards Jack's place.

"What?"

"It's time to go home," he said. "The ghosts are gone. Apparently."

Auggie turned and began walking slowly towards Jack place down the road. For some reason, I felt guilty. It felt as though I had ruined Auggie's evening. I started to holler out to him to wait, to let me talk to him or explain, or…anything. Instead, I gave up and chased after him.

In silence, the two of us walked down the street, as though we had sheets over our heads, not uttering a word as we made our way back to Jack's place. Even as we crossed from the street into Jack's yard and made our way to the front steps, we said nothing to each other. It wasn't until we were standing near the steps to the front door that Auggie turned to me. He was no longer frowning, but he still managed to look disappointed.

"You can go in through the door," he said softly. "The ghosts are gone now. You don't have to worry about them following you."

"I wasn't...okay."

Auggie gave me a sharp nod, then turned, as though to head back to his barn. At the last second, just within the perimeter of Jack's lawn, he turned to me again.

"You really have to find something to believe in, Jordan," he said, simply.

I didn't respond. I just looked down at my feet. In my peripheral vision, I could see Auggie turn and continue on his way down the road. Obviously, he was going back to his barn. He had nothing else to say to me.

I had ruined everything.

For the longest time, I stood at the base of the steps and watched Auggie make his way down the road. When he was finally swallowed up by shadows, I sighed and turned to the steps.

A minute later, upstairs in my room, I was stripping my shirt and pants off. I climbed up onto the bed and closed the dormer window since we hadn't thought to close it when we had snuck out to the graveyard. I planned to slide under the covers and pray to fall into a quick slumber so I wouldn't have to hate myself for any longer that night.

For some reason, before I retired to bed, I reached over to the bedside table and tapped the screen of my phone. The eerie blue electric light filled the room. I had one missed text.

From my mom.

Urgently, I swiped to open my phone and brought up the text app. My thumb was shaking as I tapped on the screen to open her message.

You're in a better place, Jordy. Maybe it's best that you're there. We'll be together again one day. Until then, I love you and miss you.

Before I slid under the covers, my phone got thrown across the room. I hadn't thrown it hard enough to break it, but the resounding "thunk" made me feel a little better.

Sleep took its time arriving, but once it did, I fell into a deep, restless sleep filled with dreams of ghosts in sheets, headstones that said "Burke," and friends who thought I sucked.

A FIGHT

appy by The Rolling Stones was the song du jour on AMOR the following morning. I found out when I wandered down to the kitchen in my boxers. Decidedly, it was not a song that matched my mood. It did, however, seem to match Jack's morning disposition. He was bopping around the kitchen, making a hot breakfast at the stove as the radio played on the counter. I'd never seen Jack look so happy and carefree in the time I'd been in Possibly.

Had he been dressed as one of the ghosts the night before?

Was he gloating about how scared I'd been?

His mood made me even more annoyed, but I knew that was my problem and not Jack's. So, I slid into a seat at the table, waiting to see what he was whipping up for breakfast. Bacon and eggs perfumed the air and I could smell the toaster having its way with bread. Everything smelled heavenly, and my gut was begging with me to fill it. Jack's mood on top of that should have turned my frown upside down, but I couldn't make myself feel happy.

Like the mist that had rolled in from Susurrus Creek the night before, my mood hung around me like a miasma. It was if a veil of brattiness had been draped over me while I slept and I had been unable to extract myself from it when I awoke.

Jack turned to me, smiling widely, a spatula in his hand, and signed: "Good morning."

I didn't manage a smile, but I responded with the same sign. That was enough to appease Jack because he smiled wider and

299

turned back around to tend to the steaming skillet on the stovetop. The toaster clicked and toast sprang up. Leaving the stovetop, Jack stepped over and extracted the slices of toast to slather them with butter while they were fresh and hot. Watching the butter melt into the toast made my stomach groan with appreciation again.

"Smells good," I said, managing to find something nice to say, though my tone didn't match my words.

Jack shot a pleased look over his shoulder at me, then he was back to work.

I hated that he was so happy and I was so…dour. Not that I was jealous of Jack's mood, or annoyed by it, I just hated that I couldn't find it in me to match the tone he was trying to set for the day. Jack wasn't the problem, so he didn't deserve my mood.

But what was the problem?

Ghosts.

Ghosts were the problem.

And Possibly.

The entire town was the problem.

Since arriving in Possibly, though I'd done my best to find something wrong with it, I'd found nothing but goodness. The people were nice. They were kind to each other. They minded their own business and went about their lives while allowing each other the same privilege. I'd never been fed so well since arriving in town. I had a warm bed that was in the same place night after night. I had security and safety.

The best coffee I'd ever drank and the best treats I'd ever ate could be found a short walk from Jack's place. I could take art classes for free from a woman who wanted nothing more than to see me find myself and what I was good at creating. I'd made a friend who enjoyed art and music and teaching me sign language, who found new and exciting things for us to do any day of the week in a town as small as Possibly, Texas.

Other teenage boys in town that we encountered on the street didn't care if I hung out with Auggie. They wouldn't bat an eye if I gave him a plastic flower to show my appreciation for his friendship. No one teased or taunted other people for being different or doing things that were not necessarily typical.

Grandy philosophized down at his gas station and Levi Lee did all kinds of weird performance art right out in the open by Starbuck's. Mystic Molly sat in her tent all day, waiting to tell people's fortunes. Agnes Broussard used old plastic bottles to make flowers and Sofia Salazar hung up misdirected love letters for the entire town to swoon over.

Wyatt walked through town like Yosemite Sam and fired his gun randomly into the air whenever the mood struck him. Earl Dean took a pickaxe to Liberty Lane nearly every day, and Officer Hanning simply stood by and watched. Jasper took an hourly trip up and down Liberty Lane on the tram for no apparent reason, and Amos played the same song all day long on AMOR.

And no one cared.

Everyone was so...*accepting.*

It was becoming annoying because there was nothing annoying about it. There was no fault to find in Possibly or how Possibilians lived their lives and let others live their lives.

Possibly was...perfect?

I'd never lived anywhere that was perfect. That never had strife or arguments or tragedy. There was no drama or news to speak of in the tiny, sleepy little town on the bank of the perpetually full Susurrus Creek. Nothing happened, yet everything was new and exciting. There was always something new to discover about Possibly—even if a lot of it was due to the behind-the-scenes machinations of people in sheets who walked down the road at midnight to thrill the new guy.

Possibly was perfect.

Impossibly small and outdated, a town steeped in Americana and art and friendship and acceptance, Possibly was quite possibly the best place to be.

So…why was I so angry?

It wasn't out of the question to assume that a boring life was an adjustment for a guy who'd spent his life on the road with his free-spirited mother. I didn't have to run like hell from cops after busking on a street corner. If I busked in Possibly, Officer Hanning would just watch along with everyone else. I didn't have to worry where my next meal would come from when meal times came around. There was no concern over finding friends—friends found you in Possibly.

Mom's text.

In my heart of hearts, though I'd never admitted it to myself, I had expected Mom to get bored on the road without me. To miss me as a mother is supposed to miss her child. By the end of summer, I expected to be sitting under the tree outside of Starbuck's with Auggie, doing our daily sign language lesson, and I'd look up. Mom's car would be rolling carefully…*oh, so carefully*…across Lovelorn Pass Bridge. She'd come retrieve me.

She'd sweep me into her arms and tell me how big of a mistake it was to dump me on the side of the road on Two-Mile Trail.

That wasn't going to happen.

Maybe it's best that you're there.

That's what her text had said. After weeks without me, Mom had realized that having me around all the time was cramping her style. That having me around made her life less enjoyable.

I had been unwanted for…how long? For how many days, weeks, months, or even years, had Mom been thinking about ditching me with Jack? How much had she been itching to push me out of her life so she could be free of me?

Jack set a plate in front of me, startling me from my thoughts. I jerked in my chair and looked down at the table in front of me.

Bacon, eggs, and buttery toast. One of my favorite breakfasts in the whole world.

I looked up at Jack and he made a drinking motion.

"Water, please," I said.

Jack gave me a smile and a nod as he set his own plate on the table, then went to the sink to fill a glass for me. I was picking up my fork and contemplating stuffing my face when he sat down at the table across from me. He slid the glass of water across the table to me and set a coffee cup alongside his plate.

"Thanks," I muttered.

Jack swooped his open hand from in front of his face down to his chest.

You're welcome.

Immediately, Jack snatched up his fork gleefully and dug into his scrambled eggs. As he scooped a healthy bite into his mouth, I poked at my eggs with the tines of my fork, suddenly not very hungry. The eggs and bacon were still steaming. The butter he had cooked the eggs in glistened on them and the bacon still spattered lightly from the hot fat rendered out in the cast iron skillet. The butter on the toast had been applied so liberally that it pooled in the divots in the bread.

I should have wanted to shove my face into the plate and inhale, but I just couldn't.

Even food could not change my sour mood.

Jack waved a hand at me, and when I looked up at him, he brought all of his fingers in his right hand together in a point and brought them to his mouth. Like a bird pecking at his lips, his hand moved back and forth.

Eat.

He smiled at me.

I continued to pick at my food.

"Mom texted me last night," I said. "Finally."

Jack had been turning his attention back to his plate, but at the mention of my mother, he looked back up at me sharply.

"Yeah," I nodded. "Finally."

He didn't necessarily use sign language, but Jack indicated with a waving of his hand that I should continue. I should spill the details of the text.

"She said it was better that I was here. That it was *best* that I was here," I grumbled. "But it's okay. Because she misses me and everything. So, that's cool."

I dropped my fork on my plate and it clattered on the edge before tumbling to the table. Jack looked down at my fork as it rolled from my plate to the table. For a few moments, he stared at my fork as it lay there, unused next to my uneaten plate of food. Finally, he looked up at me again.

"She's not coming back for me," I said, looking up to meet his eyes. "I'm just...I was...just a burden, man. She doesn't give a shit about me anymore. If she ever did. She dumped me on the side of the road outside of Possibly and went on about her life."

Jack frowned at me, his brow furrowing deeply.

"She couldn't wait to dump me, man," I continued. "See ya' later, kid. Good luck with life. We'll meet again one day. Probably. *Possibly.*"

Jack started to sign, but I only caught every third sign.

"I'm not that advanced yet, Jack," I mumbled and looked down at my plate. "Auggie hasn't gotten to those lessons yet."

Immediately, he stopped signing and reached for the breast pocket of his shirt. A second later, he had his small notepad out and was flipping through it for a blank piece of paper. I waited, picking at the side of my plate with my fingernail where a chip had been made in it during washing or being put away in the cabinet after use. Jack wrote furiously on the notepad, not looking up until he had written the last word.

Finally, he held the notepad across the table where I could look at his strange block-style letters.

Did you really expect Margie to come back? You know your mother. Better than anyone.

"Yeah," I nodded angrily at him. "I kind of did expect my freaking mother to not abandon me in the buttcrack of Texas for the rest of my life, Jack. That's exactly what I expected."

His frown deepened and he began jotting on the pad again. Seconds later, he was shoving the notepad in my face again.

Why'd you ask about school? The Pueblo? If you weren't planning to stay?

I rolled my eyes.

"What else was I supposed to do? What else could I do, man? Planning the next day is all anyone can do around here," I grumbled. "Not like there's much else."

Jack's mouth turned up in a snarl and he started to retract the notepad to write more. Angrily, I reached out, snatched the pad and tossed it towards the living room. Jack's eyes grew wide in shock as I snarled across the table at him.

"It doesn't freaking matter what you have to say, Jack!" I growled. "What can you say to explain why my own mother was happy to ditch my ass here? To leave me with someone I barely know in a town I can't even really remember? She didn't even ask you if you were okay with it! Does that not bother you, man? She didn't give a shit what either one of us wanted. She just did what Mom always does! She's—Mom's a—I hate this place! I want to…I want to go home!"

Jack stared at me angrily for the longest of moments as I glared back across the table at him, my eyes threatening to spill over. Finally, his expression softened and he lifted his hand, shaking a finger at me as if admonishing me. But then he pulled his fingers together in his right hand and touched them to the corner of his mouth and then his cheek like a bird pecking.

Where's home?

He glowered at me and repeated the signs.

Then a third time. A fourth.

"*I don't know, Jack!*" I screamed, throwing my hands up in the air. "*I've never had a home! But any place is better than this damn town! Stop freaking asking me!*"

Punctuating my sentence, I banged a fist on the tabletop, making our plates and silverware clatter. Jack, aggravated by my display, snatched his plate off of the table, and chucked it across the kitchen. With an ear-splitting clatter, it shattered against the cabinet below the sink. I jumped in my seat, my spine stiffening at the sudden display of violence from Jack.

He never lost his cool like that.

Before the shards could even settle, Jack was out of his seat and marching through the kitchen to the stairs. I sat stock still, waiting as Jack stomped through the room and then up the stairs, his feet like clubs against each step.

Jack climbed the stairs angrily and I sat and listened as he entered the second-floor hallway. His angry footsteps marched down the hallway just as fierce as they had sounded on the stairs. Then the sound of his bedroom door slamming echoed through the house.

Happy by The Rolling Stones continued to play on the radio.

ANOTHER FIGHT

"Feeling any better?" Auggie smiled at me from his worktable when I slipped through the barn doors.

After cleaning up Jack's plate and food from the kitchen floor and wiping the cabinet clean, I'd thrown all of the breakfast food and the shards of the plate away. I'd washed up the skillet and cups and put everything away. Angrily, I had turned off the radio so I didn't have to hear The Rolling Stones anymore. It was apparent that Jack, like he often did when he was upset, had decided to retire to his bedroom for the rest of the day.

My options were limited.

Staying at Jack's place and hiding in my own room on the top floor was the easiest of all of my choices. Walking around downtown Possibly to blow off steam was the second-best option. However, walking around downtown would guarantee that I would run into someone and my attitude was not conducive to friendly banter with anyone. Since I didn't want to risk seeing Jack so soon after our fight, and I didn't want to be rude to any other people in town, I had walked from Jack's, past the graveyard, and down to Auggie's barn.

The double doors had been thrown wide open so that the sun could get inside. Auggie was hammering away at something on his worktable, a smile on his face. *Down with the Sickness*, the Richard Cheese version, was playing loudly on his radio. It was a nice change after hearing *Happy* play during my walk across Possibly. As funny as the version of the song was, and the fact that it was a welcome change, it did nothing to fix my mood.

I was still angry.

I was pissed at my mom.

I felt abandoned and unloved.

Burden.

Mom had made me feel like I'd always been a burden to her. And Jack had blown a gasket when I simply tried to explain my feelings.

No. I wasn't *feeling any better.*

Auggie stared at me, the hammer in his hand frozen in place above whatever he had been pounding on when I entered the barn.

"Jordan?"

"What?" I responded a little too sharply.

Auggie frowned and slowly lowered the hammer to the worktable, letting it come to rest upon the wooden surface as he stared at me blankly.

"Are you feeling any better?" Auggie asked after a few moments, his voice controlled and even.

"Better about what?" I grumbled, leaning against the doorframe.

"Um," he said with a sigh, "everything? Last night? Life?"

I kicked at the dusty floor with the toe of my shoe, avoiding his eyes.

"Jordan?"

"What, Auggie?" I spat as I looked up. "What do you want?"

"Wow. Okay." Auggie stepped away from his bench and crossed his arms over his chest to stare at me quizzically.

"What is it?" I snapped. "What am I supposed to be feeling better about?"

"I—"

"The fact that my mom doesn't give a crap about me? That she'd rather I stay here and rot with the rest of the people in this town than go out and live life?" I growled. "That I don't even know why anyone would want to live in this freaking town?"

Auggie's eyes grew larger the longer I talked and his arms slowly slid from his chest to hang limply at his sides.

"That my *friend* lies to me and makes up weird stories and sets up some weird performance art to mess with me? That he finds ways to make sure we spend time together because he doesn't have any other friends? That I'm just serving a purpose for everyone? Or that some people have no use for me at all?"

"What?" Auggie's mouth was agape.

"Don't pull my leg anymore, man," I waved him off angrily as I pushed away from the doorframe. "What were you doing before I showed up in Possibly? Sneaking around and watching people make art at The Pueblo? Observing? Not participating? Hiding away in your barn? Hiding from the other guys in town? Making your...*crap art*? I'm not your friend. I'm a convenience!"

Auggie, his mouth still agape, blinked at me in disbelief as I glowered at him from across the barn.

"I hate this freaking town!" I bellowed finally. "It's the most boring, backwoods, ridiculous place I've ever been to in my life! And I've been to tons of towns in Florida!"

Like a child, I stomped my foot and clenched my fists at my side as I glared at Auggie across the expanse of the barn. For the longest of moments, he continued to stare at me like a fish gasping for water. When I thought I couldn't take the silence any longer, and my fists were shaking, Auggie finally closed his mouth. His eyes changed. It was like he was looking through

310

me instead of at me. His arms went lax at his side and he sighed.

I thought he'd speak, his mouth opened slightly as if he might, but at the last second, he closed his mouth and began to walk towards me. As angry as I was, the closer Auggie got, the more terrified I was that he was going to deck me. Lay me out with a single punch—that's how calm he was, to the point that violence might be on his mind.

However, when he approached, he started to step past me, as if to leave the barn. At the last second, he stopped, facing out of the barn as I continued to stare inside of it.

"No one is making you stay here, Jordan," he said softly. "You're welcome to leave anytime you want. You have a choice."

I lowered my eyes to the ground.

"And you don't have to be my friend," he mumbled. "In fact, it's probably best if you weren't."

Then he continued walking, stepping out into the bright sunlight of summertime in Possibly. My instinct was to spin around. To begin apologizing profusely for taking my anger and hurt out on the only real friend I'd had in…forever. But I couldn't force myself to do it.

How long I stood in the open doorway of the barn, I wasn't sure, but Auggie was long gone when I turned around and left. *Down with the Sickness* drifted off in the distance as the barn receded behind me and The Rolling Stones replaced it.

Happy?

No. I wasn't.

I was stuck in Possibly. That was obvious.

And I always would be.

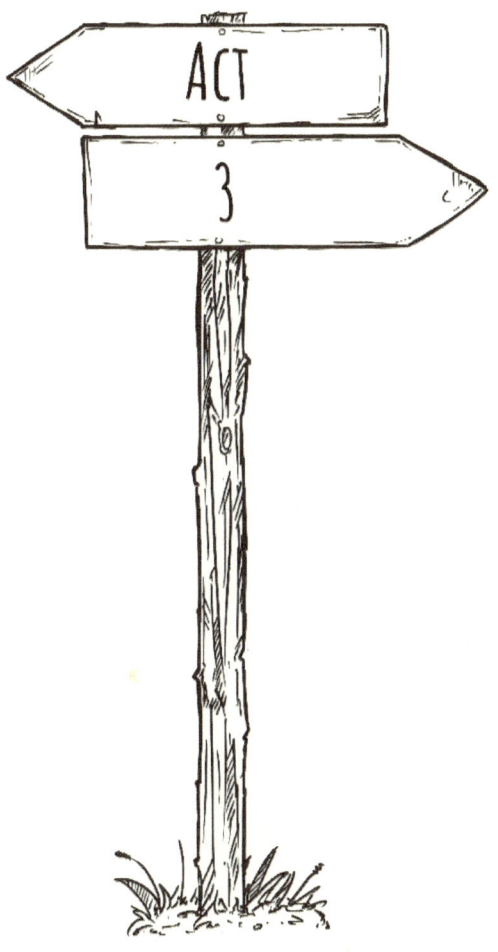

ACT

3

ONE IS A LONELY NUMBER

"**D**on' forget to swab the decks, matey!" Starbuck boomed from the check-out counter. "I likes ter keep a tight ship!"

Looking up from my place at the back of the pirate ship-slash-coffee shop, I gripped the mop handle tightly as I gave Starbuck a smile and a nod.

"That's what I'm doing, captain," I said, chuckling with amusement.

"Aye. That yer are. Carry on, matey!"

Starbuck turned away too quickly to catch the small salute I gave him. Since my employer decided to get back to cleaning the coffee creation station—his name for it, not mine—I went back to *swabbing the decks*. The mop glided effortlessly over the planks of Starbuck's coffee shop. He'd kept the place so clean that Starbuck had practically made linoleum out of the wooden plank flooring. In fact, I would have gone so far as to say that someone could eat directly off of the floor. Not that I would ever recommend it to a customer. Rules are in place for a reason, and I didn't want to sweep up any mess a customer left anyway.

Besides, why sit on the hard floor when there were plenty of tables and chairs waiting to be utilized? If nothing else, customers could go outside and enjoy their coffee and treats in the Possibilian summertime sun; feel the breeze from Susurrus

Creek. Then again, summer had officially settled in for a stay in Possibly, so the tables and chairs inside were probably the best bet.

July had slithered away like a humid fog, pulling August, arid and fiery, along to replace it. I'd lived in and visited many places where August was completely intolerable. Places so hot and humid that walking outside would take a person's breath away. Possibly wasn't that bad, mostly because the perpetual breeze that came off of the creek seemed to keep things a few degrees cooler than would be typical of a tiny little town in Texas. However, out of all of the summer months, August was proving to be an absolute sizzler compared to June and July.

Luckily, I spent most of my days inside with air conditioning, so Possibly hadn't managed to defeat me all summer long. Swamp butt was unavoidable when I walked to Starbuck's each day to start my shift, but it wasn't too bad. It only took a few minutes to get from Jack's place to work, so the damage was minimal.

"Arrr, I'm gon' whip up a frappe, matey!" Starbuck's barked. "Wouldjer like one fer yer walk home?"

"Sounds great, captain," I said. "Thanks."

Halfway through July, after finding out that help—in the form of my mom and her car—was not coming, and finding that I didn't have a friend in the world, I had gone looking for a job in town. The first place I stopped was Starbuck's because a teenage kid wanting to earn cash and a coffee shop just seemed to go hand in hand. Though he usually managed to run the shop just fine on his own, Starbuck said he'd be glad to have help during the morning hours. So, he hired me on the spot.

Each week day morning, I'd walk over to Starbuck's and start my shift at eight o'clock. Until noon I'd sweep and mop, wipe down surfaces, take out trash, or do any chore Starbuck needed me to complete. It wasn't the most thrilling work, but it put some spending money in my pocket.

Not that there was a lot to spend money on in Possibly. Without the use of a car, I couldn't really go anywhere else to spend money, either. Jack, I had found out, didn't even have a car. Most people in Possibly didn't—because they didn't go anywhere. They thought of their little town as an island. Anything they needed could be found within walking distance.

Groceries could be delivered from the store out on the highway leading out of the north end of town or purchased in the small grocery and dry goods stores on Liberty Lane. Coffee and treats could be found at Starbuck's. Samuel's Soda Spray had drinks and ice cream and the occasional hot dog and hamburger day. Grandy's Auto picked up the slack. It was an odd concept to me, being perfectly happy living within the same square mile, day in and day out, but Possibilians were some of the most content people I'd ever met.

After my fights with Jack and Auggie, I still hadn't had a reckoning about my new hometown. Frustration and annoyance seemed to be how I dealt with my feelings about the tiny little berg, but I was beginning to slough those feelings off as time went by. It was probably the heat. It's hard to be angry when it's hot outside. A guy has to reserve his energy for more important things—like getting everywhere on foot in August.

"Comin' righ' up!" Starbuck announced, his statement punctuated by the sound of the blender kicking to life.

Quickly, I finished *swabbing the decks* and plopped the mop into the wheely bucket. By the time I had pushed it into the backroom, dumped out the old water, rinsed the mop in the industrial sink, and washed my hands, Starbuck had my frappe waiting for me at the check-out counter. He gave me a toothy grin and a wink from the eye not covered by a patch as I slid it from the counter into my hand. I grabbed a straw from the cup on the counter and saluted my boss again.

"Thanks, captain," I said.

"Aye," he growled happily. "See ya' t'morrow?"

"Like always," I replied.

Starbuck propped himself up on the counter to enjoy his drink as I made my way out. By the time I was pushing through the front door and out into the sizzling summer heat, I had stuffed my straw in my cup and slid the paper into my pocket. I'd toss it in the trash at home.

Levi Lee was outside of Starbuck's, as was usual, but he was back to the green-screen suit. He still hadn't added a pair of shorts to his getup, so I struggled to avert my eyes. He was pressed up against the hull of the pirate ship to the side of the front door, pretending to be part of the ship once again. Apparently, an inept magician mime just didn't work out like he had thought.

"Hey, Levi Lee," I said, trying to make my tone chipper.

He didn't respond.

"Good job, man!" I congratulated him.

"Hey! Thanks!" His voice came from within the suit.

I winced.

"*Shit,*" he mumbled.

"Sorry," I muttered before dashing away.

Once out of range of Levi Lee, I leisurely made my way down the street towards The Pueblo. It was hot, but I didn't want to rush back to Jack's place. Not just because Jack and I still had a strained relationship, but because I wanted to enjoy my frappe. Of course, the fact that Jack had barely signed anything to me or written a note to me that wasn't absolutely necessary in weeks was a big part of it.

Around the house, the two of us took a few days after our fight to come to a silent agreement. We would coexist. We ate meals separately, though Jack typically prepared all of them, we didn't talk after meals when we watched T.V. unless it was necessary, and we didn't even wish each other "goodnight" and "good morning." We were essentially strangers who were roommates.

I'd tried a few times to engage with Jack. I'd gone so far as to go outside and watch him work, asking questions about what he was up to or if he needed help. He'd always brusquely brush me off, making it clear that my help was neither needed nor wanted. So, after a few days of that, I'd given up and fallen into our silently agreed upon routine.

Even though I wanted to say that I didn't give a single turd that Jack was no longer interested in speaking with me, I found that it hurt my feelings more than I would have expected. Having him pretend that I wasn't even in the house half of the time was painful. It was awkward. And the worst part was, I had no idea how long it would last. Without any promise that Mom would ever come and take me away from Possibly, life with Jack would be…my life. Surely, once I was eighteen, and had enough money in my pocket, I could take off and start my own life wherever I wanted. But that was two years away, and I wasn't going to delude myself into thinking that Mom would rescue me before that time was up.

For the foreseeable future, my life would be silence at home, a few hours at Starbuck's five days a week, somehow complete high school, and then…who knew? I had no idea what the future held for me and I found that I didn't care.

There wasn't much in my life—or around Possibly—to get all that excited about.

As I passed The Pueblo, my chest actually ached. I'd returned to Lilly's classes a few times since my falling out with Jack and Auggie, but my art never improved. I'd painted and sculpted and even took a turn on the pottery wheel. Everything I tried to make turned out looking worse than when I had started. So, I had stopped going. It wasn't just that art didn't seem to be my thing, it was also that Auggie would sometimes be in classes while I was at The Pueblo. Avoiding him and pretending he wasn't there so we didn't have to talk was even more awkward than being in the house with Jack.

Not going to classes seemed to be the best solution.

From time to time, as I'd walk to Starbuck's each morning, or back to Jack's place at noon, I'd see Auggie walking through town. Usually on his way to Windchime Hollow or Mystic Molly's. Sometimes he'd be on his way to Samuel's or Grandy's for a treat. He never came into Starbuck's while I was working. It pained me to see him and avoid him, but I didn't know what to say to my former friend. I had no idea how to apologize for the things I'd said to him—and I wasn't sure that I wanted to apologize anyway.

Hadn't I believed what I'd said to him?

Why apologize if you meant what you said?

Strangely enough, the thing I missed most was my daily sign language lessons with Auggie. With us no longer talking, my education to help me learn to communicate with Jack better completely stopped. I began to realize that without Auggie's help, I'd never become proficient at signing. Finally, on a whim, and since I couldn't get adequate cell service to check YouTube, I'd asked Sofia if she knew where I could get a book to help me learn more. The next day, she had a stack of different books to help further my lessons.

The books had become a refuge from everything in Possibly that drove me crazy. Most afternoons, after my shift at Starbuck's, I'd hang out in my room with the books. I'd sit by the dormer window on my bed and teach myself new signs. It wasn't as easy going as when Auggie taught me, but it was better than nothing. Of course, Jack refused to sign or communicate with me in any other way, so I wasn't certain there was a point to all of it.

But it helped keep me sane. It kept my mind off of everything else.

One thing the books couldn't do was provide companionship.

Since arriving in Possibly, I'd become friendly with most of the people in town, though I wasn't sure if I would have called most of them "friends." However, Jack and Auggie were two people I talked to every day. They were the people I counted on for routine and comfort. Since both of them had stopped talking to me, I didn't really have anyone to call a friend.

I was a desert tortoise once more.

People around town were still friendly and warm enough. I could find someone to have a decent conversation with if I wanted—*as long as I wasn't interrupting their time being a ship's hull or something*—but it wasn't the same.

Ultimately, as one does at some point in life, I came to find that one is a lonely number.

Loneliness creates an ache that is too far down to soothe.

Yet another reason to hate Possibly.

As if I didn't have plenty.

When I got back to Jack's place from Starbuck's, he was in the yard working on one of his carpentry projects. His hammering echoed around the property. I didn't wander around to the back of the house and try to talk to him. Instead, I went up the front steps and into the house. Dumping my now empty frappe cup into the trash, as well as the straw paper from my pocket, I headed upstairs.

Once I was stripped down to my boxers and had crawled up to sit by the dormer window, I pulled out the sign language books.

Sometimes, though implausible, books can be friends. At the very least, they can take one's mind off of the loneliness.

MENDING BRIDGES

Jack was out in the backyard the following day. Like always, he was pounding and shaving away at a woodworking project, ignoring the world—but especially me. A dewy fog blanketed the yard since the sun hadn't risen enough to burn it away. When I stepped off the back steps, the fog seemed to swallow my bare foot, chilling me to the bones and causing droplets of condensation to collect on my skin. I hadn't bothered to do more than put on basketball shorts since no one was going to come to Jack's and see me half-clothed.

Across the yard I traipsed, the wet grass tickling and pulling at my feet as I made my way from the house and over to Jack. As I approached him, he didn't even look up to signal that he knew I was there. It wasn't that he didn't know, obviously, but it was the routine we had fallen into over the last few weeks. Jack ignored me, I let myself be ignored.

I was done with it.

"I'm going to help you," I said.

Jack faltered in his hammering for a second, but then went right back to his project.

"Did you hear me, Jack?" I asked more loudly than was necessary. "I'm going to help you with your project."

Still no response from him.

Anger boiled up in me and I slammed a hand down on the wooden tabletop he was sanding.

"I'm going to help you, you stubborn bastard!"

Jack's movements stopped, his hand holding the sandpaper frozen against the wood. He didn't look up, though.

"Let me help you," I said, my voice cracking. "Please."

For a moment, I thought Jack would look up at me, maybe frown with consternation, but relent to my request. Instead, he started sanding again, his hand moving slowly at first, then picking up speed, aggressively sanding away at the wood, smoothing out some imperfection only he could see.

Resigned, I walked away from Jack and his project and slogged back through the yard to the back steps. Turning around, I plopped down on the steps, trying to ignore the wetness from the morning dew, and stared at Jack.

"I'm going to sit right here," I said loudly enough that he could hear me across the yard. "When you need help, I'll be waiting. I'm not leaving."

Jack continued on about his business.

The morning sun sauntered across the sky and hours ticked by, the fog burning off incrementally until lunchtime arrived. By the noon hour, the grass was baking in the August sun and the steps felt more like sauna stones against my backside. Sweat was trickling down between my shoulders blades and running towards the waistband of my shorts.

I didn't move.

Even when Jack stopped working and brushed past me on the steps up into the house, I sat and waited like I said I would. When Jack came back outside, just a few minutes later, he had a plate containing a sandwich and chips. A soda was in his other hand. He went back across the yard, laid the plate on the table, and went back to work. In between working on the table, he'd take a bite of his sandwich or chips, or take a sip of his soda, but he ignored me.

I continued to sit and watch.

Jack continued to ignore me.

He only came near me to go up the steps to return his plate to the kitchen, to get a drink, or use the bathroom.

Even as the afternoon grew orange and hazy, and the sun began its descent towards the horizon, I didn't move. By dusk, Jack seemed to be done sanding the table—I couldn't imagine spending a whole day manually sanding a table so thoroughly—and he covered it with his tarp. Then he headed back inside, brushing past me as he went up the steps for the last time that day.

I stayed on the steps. My skin felt cracked from sitting in the summer sun all day, and my lips were chapped. My throat felt like a desert. But I stayed outside until the sun had disappeared from the sky and the first stars were starting to twinkle.

Back inside, Jack had a bowl of leftover spaghetti from the night before. He wasn't sitting at the table, waiting to have a family dinner. Instead, he was in front of the T.V., watching some innocuous comedy as he ate.

All I could do was make a plate of spaghetti and set it in the microwave to heat up. As I waited, I drank three glasses of water, directly from the tap, then filled a fourth to go with my dinner. Then I sat at the table and ate my pasta and drank my water. Alone. Jack didn't even come into the kitchen once he was done with his bowl.

So, I cleaned my plate and glass, put them in the draining rack, and made my way to the stairs. When I had reached the second floor, I could hear Jack rustling around in the kitchen, cleaning up his dinner plate. Up on the third floor, I stripped my shorts and boxers off in my room and then ducked into the shower. Minutes later, even though it was barely evening, I was climbing under the covers of my bed. I hadn't even bothered to put on pajamas.

The sun exposure from the day made me feel sick, as though I had the chills. I shivered and shook under the covers in bed, wishing I had an extra blanket, but I was too proud to ask Jack for anything. Sometime, probably around nine o'clock, I fell into a deep sleep.

A door opened and closed somewhere as I drifted off.

Was Jack leaving?

In my imagination, awake and daydreaming, I am the desert tortoise. Alone and wandering my arid ecosystem, fulfilling the duties bestowed upon me by whatever power decides what we will be when we are given life.

When I dreamed that night, I was a caterpillar. But not quite. I was in a chrysalis, waiting to see what life would bring. Wet and warm, packed in tightly, I had nothing to do but wonder what would happen when my shell split and I climbed out into the waiting sun.

As that happened, as the pod split and light poured in and fluid seeped out, and my eyes adjusted to the new world around me, what would come of me?

Would I become a butterfly? Would I forget that I was once a caterpillar?

Would anyone care that the caterpillar they'd known was missing?

I awoke the following morning, my shoulders raw and angry against the crisp sheets of my bed. Gingerly, I made my way to the bathroom and examined myself in the mirror.

I wasn't a tortoise. I was a lobster.

Another shower was had, though this time I wasn't shivering. I felt as though the world was a brick oven and I was a pizza being burnt to a crisp. I adjusted the shower knobs so that the water was just warm enough to clean with, but cool enough that it didn't feel as though it was stripping my flesh from my bones.

After my shower, and the delicate use of my towel to dry off, I couldn't find anything in my medicine cabinet to soothe my sunburn. So, I slipped on a pair of light sweatpants and a lightweight long-sleeve shirt. In the bathroom mirror, a red-faced demon peeked out at me, cackling hysterically at my hubris.

Downstairs, I scarfed down a bowl of sugary cereal—my favorite—and made my way outside. Jack had already eaten and was working on the table in the yard. On the second step was a bottle of aloe vera gel and a bottle of sunscreen. I glanced over at Jack, but he was still in "ignore the kid mode," so I snatched up the bottles and bolted back into the house.

I didn't get far. Once inside the house and in the kitchen, I stripped off my shirt and sweatpants carefully and slathered my body with the aloe vera.

Immediate relief.

It didn't fix my sunburn, but it soothed my dry, red skin. Made me feel a little closer to human. Before I set the bottle on the kitchen table, I squirted a healthy glob into my hands and rubbed it into my face slowly. A moan of relief escaped my throat as the skin of my face slowly began to feel less and less like sandpaper.

After using the ointment that Jack had set out for me, I slathered any skin that would be exposed to the sun in the sunscreen. Then, shamefully, I made my way back outside. Just as I had the day before, I sat down on the steps—though more carefully this time since my skin felt like it would split open at any sudden movement.

"I'm going to be here," I said to Jack. "I'll help you when you're ready."

Jack didn't respond. He didn't pause his work or acknowledge me.

So, I sat and watched Jack as the morning sun slipped by overhead.

When the sun was directly overhead and sweat was darkening the pits and back of my shirt, Jack suddenly stopped working. He stood by the table for the longest of moments, as though contemplating something deathly important. Finally, when I decided that maybe I should go inside to reapply sunscreen, he looked over at me.

Though he was incapable of making the sound, his whole body moved as though he sighed. He looked at me, waving to make sure he had my attention, and I sat up rigidly. Jack signed "lunch" to me.

"You want me to make lunch?" I asked, a little more enthusiastically than I had intended.

He signed "yes."

"Okay," I said, trying to control my voice as I rose from the steps. "Anything okay?"

Jack didn't sign, but he nodded.

I turned to march up the steps, grimacing at the ass-shaped wet spot I'd left on the steps. I'd actually sweated through my sweatpants, which loaned credence to their moniker.

Inside of the house, in the blissful AC, I threw together two sandwiches and chips on a couple of plates and grabbed two sodas. Lingering to enjoy the AC and dry out a little bit, I spent too much time making sure the sandwiches were stacked perfectly and sliced in two with precision. Before I was ready to face the heat once more—both literally and figuratively—I made my way back outside.

Jack was picking away at a piece of the table with his thumbnail, examining some minor imperfection when I made my way out to stand beside him. At my approach, he glanced over at me, then went back to picking. I couldn't tell what it was that had him concerned with his work, but I set the plate gently down on the table in front of him.

"Sandwiches and chips?"

Jack gave a quick nod. I set the soda down.

"And a soda," I said.

Jack snatched it off the table and I froze; afraid I'd offended him. He set it on a hip-high block of wood to his side. He brought both hands up in front of his chest as if cupping the air, not quite facing me, then lowered both hands marginally while bringing his fingers together.

Wet.

"The table is wet?"

Jack jabbed his thumb at the can.

"Oh," I said, "yeah. Sorry. I didn't think about that. Sorry."

He waved me off. I stood there watching him, holding my plate, my soda can tucked under my arm as he concentrated on the table. Jack frowned, his eyebrows knitted together, then turned to face me, though he avoided eye contact. He brought both hands up to mid-chest and tapped the tips of his fingers of one hand against the other like two birds pecking at each other.

I looked down at the table for several moments.

"Yeah," I said. "It looks even to me."

Jack's frown softened a bit and he lifted his index finger of his right hand to sign again. Like Danny from *The Shining*, he flicked his index finger up and down as if "Tony" was talking.

"Yeah," I chuckled. "I'm sure. It looks even to me, anyway."

Jack made the "okay" sign. He was still avoiding looking at me, so I took that as my cue that while he was conversing with me again, my closeness wasn't exactly appreciated. So, I went back across the lawn to the back steps and sat down. I placed the soda can on the step next to me and laid the plate on my lap. I'd give Jack room to stare at the evenness of his table while he ate his lunch.

Before I could tuck into my own sandwich and chips, I popped the tab of the soda and took a healthy swig. Finally, when I set it on the step beside me again, I looked over at Jack.

"I'm sorry, man," I said. "I'm sorry."

Jack stood there for a moment, and I was certain he was going to ignore me, but he finally made an okay sign, still not quite facing me. Then he made a sign with his hand like bullhorns, and used his thumb to jab at his chest a few times.

Me too.

I smiled. "Okay."

Jack was a man of few words. Literally and figuratively. I didn't force him to say anything else or acknowledge our gradual march towards forgiveness.

I could be okay with "me too."

He had been okay with "I'm sorry."

What else was needed?

WHY CAN'T WE BE FRIENDS?

Shirlene.
The days are long and the nights unbearable without you.
My fear is that my love burns brighter than yours.
But you will forever have my heart.

"I'm telling you," Sofia spoke over my shoulder, "that man—or woman—has it something bad for Shirlene. If these letters keep coming, I'm going to hunt the sender down myself. If Shirlene don't want 'em, I'll take 'em."

I snorted with laughter.

A stop at the post office had been on my itinerary after work so I could pick up Jack's mail for him. It turned out he only had a couple of envelopes. Before I left the post office, like every other Possibilian—*was I a Possibilian?*—I had to stop by the Wall of Shirlene Letters. Mostly because Sofia had mentioned that a new one had arrived. I ended up reading it with her rushing around the counter to read along over my shoulder.

Surely, Sofia had read the letter at least a dozen times since its arrival, but she seemed to never tire of the mystery of Shirlene. Nor did she get bored with reading the love letters over and over. Even though she had access to all of them all day long, they inspired an excitement in her that was enviable.

328

I couldn't remember the last time I'd felt that excited about anything.

"It might turn out to be someone you hate," I said over my shoulder. "Or someone who doesn't really...match up...to your, uh, needs?"

It was Sofia's turn to laugh.

"Well," she said, finally, "it'd be worth the effort. There's obviously a good one out there just wanting to be loved. I got some love."

"I don't know, Sofia," I said, turning to face her in the icy interior of the post office. Floorboards creaked underfoot in a way that felt homey and lived in, not as though they were in disrepair.

She took a step back to give me space.

"It could be a stalker," I continued. "This person does seem pretty obsessed. Especially for someone who doesn't have Shirlene's real address, you know?"

Sofia contemplated this for a moment, hemming and hawing over the idea.

"Nah," she said, finally. "I disagree, Jordan. This person obviously has it bad and just got their wires crossed with the address."

"Fair enough."

I thought about it for a moment, unsure if I should solicit Sofia's opinions or theories, but finally decided it couldn't hurt.

"Who do you think it is?" I mumbled.

"Hm?"

"Who do you think is really sending the letters to Shirlene?" I asked after clearing my throat. "Like, do you think it's someone in town? In Possibly? Do you think there's a real Shirlene? Is that her real name? Is it some type of performance art? It's just so odd that there has to be something going on with these letters, right?"

I punctuated my sentence with a jab of my thumb over my shoulder at the wall.

Sofia looked amused.

"You know," she said, crossing her arms over her chest, "we've been talking about that since the day the first one arrived."

"Really?"

She nodded slowly. "All-a-us in town. Is it one of us? Is one of us in love with another one of us and just doesn't know how to say it? Is one of us pulling the whole town's leg? Who is the most likely suspect if it is one of us? You know?"

"And?"

"We don't have the foggiest idea," she said, then started cackling and slapping at her knee. "We've all been the suspect at one point or another."

"Well, crap."

She gave an exaggerated shrug. "Sorry. You're fairly new to town or you'd know that we've been theorizing over the letter writer's identity forever. And who Shirlene really is. Does she exist? Is that a fake name or a metaphor? No one knows. And if they do, they ain't talkin'."

With a sigh, I threw my hands up lazily.

Sofia mimicked me and we both laughed.

"Well," I held the two pieces of mail up, "thanks. I'll make sure Jack gets these."

I headed to the door.

"Anytime," Sofia said. "Tell him I said to not be a stranger. He could make his way downtown every now and then instead of hiding out over there. It's not a far walk."

I grinned at her over my shoulder and she gave me a wink, then I was stepping out into the August heat. The teal clapboard siding of the post office shone like a precious gem in the bright midday sun. Sofia kept the post office so cold that the summer heat was even more oppressive than on a typical day. Even a few minutes inside the post office would make a person forget how hot summer in Texas could be. Then, once they got outside, it would nearly knock a person over.

The sun was committing assault against the world.

A quick flick of my eyes, and I spotted Levi Lee slumped beside the door of Starbuck's. At first, my instinct was to rush over and make sure he was okay. Especially since his green-screen suit was in a wadded pile on the ground next to him. Seeing Levi Lee sitting there in his boxer briefs against the hull of the ship was a reason for concern.

However, after a second, Levi Lee's head turned lazily and he spotted me. His arm rose languidly and he waved at me, a small smile turning up the corners of his mouth.

"*Someone turned the thermostat to Hell!*" He waved at me.

I chuckled.

"*Yeah!*" I responded. "*You might want to come visit Sofia and cool off, man!*"

Levi Lee nodded and slowly pulled himself up off the ground. When he was standing beside the door of Starbuck's, clad only in his underwear, I looked away quickly. He had sweated through his underwear and they were clinging to him salaciously.

"*Put on some pants first, Levi Lee!*" I suggested.

I was met with silence for a moment.

"*Oh! Good advice!*"

I just imagined the guy looking down to find what I'd seen before realizing that, even nude, he couldn't have been more

331

indecent. How a man could…*be like Levi Lee*…and so unaware of how he was…built…was beyond me. Obviously, no one had ever told the guy that he should keep baggy loose-fitting pants on at all times. Then again, everyone's tolerance and acceptance of such things was different. In fact, it wasn't that it necessarily bothered me.

Levi Lee's physique, I mean.

In fact, I didn't mind at all.

Surely someone did though, right?

Then again, was I assuming offense for everyone else in town, when in reality, no one gave a damn if Levi Lee decided to march through town naked in all of his glory?

That was how Possibly operated after all—you do you and I'll do me. Don't bother me and I won't bother you. If walking through town in a green-screen suit that showed off his assets far too well was what made Levi Lee happy—though I didn't feel that was his reason for doing so—then everyone was going to allow it. In fact, Levi Lee seemed to be oblivious to his assets. To him, it was just natural to go about his business the way he did. He was always covered up, after all, so why should he assume that anyone would be bothered?

Why did I assume that?

Was I assuming people would be offended, or was I trying to avoid a distraction? Was I avoiding my own hidden thoughts Levi Lee made me think?

I shook my head to clear that train of thought from my head. When I'd ventured over to Sofia's from Starbuck's—when Levi Lee was still pressed up against its hull—I had two errands in mind. I'd completed one of them, so it was time to move onto the next. Levi Lee was a grown man who had lived in Possibly much longer than I. He could figure out the best way to present himself to the rest of the town without my help.

As I made my way from the post office, I decided to walk along the bank of Susurrus Creek. It might have been totally in my head, but walking along the creek seemed cooler than walking through town. The breeze seemed to glide over and rise up off the water a few degrees cooler. The sounds of the rushing water had a placebo effect as well. It *sounded* cool, so it made me *feel* cool.

That was dumb, I knew, but if something works, you don't really question it. Walking along the bank of Susurrus Creek made the August sun more bearable, so I was going to go with it.

D'yer Mak'er by Led Zepplin was playing on the radio speakers around town and matched the warm, lazy mood of Possibly. Everyone who was out and about was shuffling slowly, doing all they could to avoid overexertion. Or they were strolling with long, happy—yet slow—steps to their destination, letting summer know it hadn't gotten the best of them.

Jasper was sitting in the tram car at the end of the tracks on Liberty Lane by the edge of Susurrus Creek. Instead of reading his book, he was fanning himself with a magazine, appearing as if he wanted to melt and slide out of the tram to a puddle on the ground.

"Ain't been this hot in a witch's share of summers," he said to me as I walked by and smiled at him.

"It's bad, yeah," I said with a chuckle.

What seemed like it was becoming an ever-present feature, a trickle of sweat was snaking its way between my shoulder blades, moving south quickly, under my shirt.

"No month can last longer than thirty-one days," Jasper said. "August will leave when it has worn out its welcome."

How to respond to that eluded me, so I simply nodded and chuckled in agreement. Jasper went back to slumping in his seat and fanning himself, and I continued on my way north along the creek. As I strolled across Liberty Lane, I spotted Earl Dean and Officer Hanning. They had changed their routine.

Instead of Officer Hanning leaning against the side of AMOR, watching Earl Dean pickaxe the street, they were both sitting outside of AMOR, their backs propped up along the wall. Their legs were stretched out before them lazily, effectively blocking the sidewalk. Each of them held a bottle of soda, taking leisurely sips, engaged in an easy conversation about God knew what. I'd never really seen Earl Dean speak to anyone, other to greet them in passing, but it made sense that if he would have a conversation with anyone in town, it would be Officer Hanning.

They spent most of their days together, after all.

And it's sensible to make an easy friendship with the man who refuses to arrest you for an arrestable offense.

I gave them both a jovial, but reserved, wave, and they returned the gesture. They were in the shade of the building, so they managed to be a bit more enthusiastic with their actions. I didn't change course to approach them and see what they were talking about in the shade. The red barn further up the creek was the only destination for me.

As I passed the row of buildings that lined the north side of Liberty Lane, *D'yer Mak'er* faded away and the sounds of a different song tickled at my ears. I couldn't quite make out what song Auggie had playing inside the barn, even though the doors were open, inviting the sunshine inside. As I made my way across the grassy area behind the buildings on Liberty Lane, and then up the last patch of road to the barn's entrance,

I could make out the song. It was *Pale Blue Eyes* by Velvet Underground.

Auggie's hammering added percussion to the song, permeating the air just outside the barn with a melancholy medley. When I first recognized the song, and the unenthusiastic hammering, I almost decided to hook a left and book it to Jack's place. Giving him the mail and then hiding away in my room, clad only in boxers and reading my sign language books, was a preferable alternative. However, I had told myself I would complete my two tasks before the day was over.

I was outside of the barn. I could see Auggie at his worktable at the back of the barn. His head was down and he was focusing on whatever he had on the table before him, oblivious to my long shadow creeping into the barn. If I ran away, it would only be harder to come back later. So, I steeled my spine and stepped up to the door. Unsure if I should announce my presence verbally, and startle him, I reached up tentatively and knocked on the doorframe.

Auggie faltered, hammered twice more, then put the hammer down on the table. He turned towards the barn doors with a smile on his face. When the sunlight caught the lower half of the diamond on his forehead, it seemed to glitter. It made me want to smile, but I knew that a smile might not be welcome. It might be too assumptive.

When our eyes met, Auggie's smile disappeared. It didn't slide from his face with disappointment or trepidation, it simply vanished. His face was a blank mask, and he was staring through me with unseeing eyes. That pained me more than if he had scowled or turned up his nose. Auggie looked, simply, indifferent.

"Hey," I said.

He didn't respond right away; he continued to stare through me.

"What?" he asked robotically.

"I came to apologize," I said with a shrug. "I wanted to tell you that I'm sorry."

"Okay. Good."

"And I hoped that we could get over our fight," I said.

Auggie's uncaring eyes didn't change.

"You've apologized. I don't have anything to say," Auggie said, his voice flat, his eyes just as empty as when he first spotted me.

"Seriously, man?" I sighed.

Auggie turned back to his worktable, ignoring me, and picked up his hammer. Once he had slung the hammer down against whatever he was working on, but before he could repeat the action, anger rushed through me, and I found myself barreling into the barn. Auggie continued his hammering as I stormed across the barn, aimed for the worktable. When I marched up to his side, anger rolling off of me, Auggie didn't even seem to notice. He just went about his business as though a pissed off guy wasn't bearing down on him.

"You know what?" I growled; my fists clenched at my sides. "You are really unforgiving for someone who didn't mind taking me to that weird shit at the church—The Pueblo!"

Auggie continued to hammer.

"You asked me to go to The Pueblo and didn't even warn me that it was going to be wild, but I didn't stop talking to you. I didn't give you the cold shoulder. I talked to you about it. And I forgave you. I may not be perfect, Auggie, and yeah, I said some mean stuff to you, but I'm trying to be the bigger person here. I came to apologize for being a jerk to you and you won't even look at me."

More hammering reached my ears.

Anger continued to boil up inside me as Auggie refused to acknowledge my presence, instead preferring to focus his energy on the roll of metal on the table. My fuse was lit. I wasn't lying to Auggie. I'd had reasons before to be mad at him, but I'd given him a chance to explain himself. I hadn't just brushed him off and pretended he wasn't even a person. I'd tried to be understanding. I tried to comprehend that Possibly was a different place and the customs might be different.

Auggie hadn't even considered that the change to my life—moving to Possibly—might have jolted my system. It hadn't been an easy adjustment for me. I was still going through it.

But he didn't care.

"You know what?" I asked, throwing my hands up angrily. "Starbuck was the name of the first mate on the Pequod in *Moby Dick*. It's not the name of the ship."

Auggie hammered harder.

"And it was a whaling boat—not a pirate ship."

His hammering got louder.

"Do you know what a pueblo actually looks like, Auggie?" I seethed. "Did you know The Pueblo doesn't look like a freaking pueblo?"

The hammer came down faster and more violently against the table and metal.

"Did you know radio stations all over this country play a variety of songs by a variety of artists?" I asked. "They don't just play one song all day long for twelve hours until the town's residents start to go batshit crazy?"

Auggie's hammer was so loud against the table I was having to scream over it to be heard.

"Any other place in America?" I asked, chuckling angrily. "Wyatt would be in a home. He'd be locked away. So would

Grandy. So would half of this damn town because everyone is batshit crazy. Everyone here is psychotic. No one anywhere in America acts like the people of this town—and if they do, they're locked up."

The hammering stopped and Auggie threw it against the wall of the barn behind the table, spinning to face me. Red was creeping up his neck into his face and his hands were rolling up into fists at his side.

"Yeah!" I screamed. "This town is stupid! The people are stupid! You! You're...you're..."

I couldn't say it.

"What am I Jordan?" Auggie demanded, his eyes no longer empty, but fiery with rage. "Tell me what I am, Jordan!"

We stared into each other's eyes, anger rolling off of both of us as *Pale Blue Eyes* played softly in the background. I twitched, wondering if I was going to throw a swing at Auggie. However, when I considered the thought, I felt my stomach sink. I didn't want to hit Auggie. I wanted to grab him by his shoulders, pull him into me violently, and put my mouth on his. The redness of his face. His anger. Everything about his body language. The fact that I had stirred up such passion in him made me want to press my mouth to his.

My hands immediately unclenched and I felt every ounce of blood drain from my face. Subconsciously, I stepped back.

Reality punched me in the chest.

What was it that I had been adjusting to—what I was trying to understand—that had frustrated me so much over the last two months?

Was it Possibly? A change in scenery? Or...was it something else?

I'd had to adjust to a million different places over the course of my life on the road with my mom.

Why was Possibly so different?

"*TELL ME, JORDAN!*" Auggie rushed forward, his arms out in front of him.

His hands connected with my pecs and he pushed me back. The guy weighed so little compared to me, and if I knew anything, it was that he wasn't trying his hardest to push me. I still took a step back out of habit.

"*SAY IT, JORDAN!*" Auggie pushed me again, his eyes suddenly misty. "*SAY IT! WHAT AM I?*"

Once more, Auggie rushed at me, his hands braced out in front of him, ready to slam into my chest and shove me backwards. I reached up, my stomach doing flip-flops, and caught Auggie's wrists, stopping him. His forward momentum nearly caused him to plow into me, but he stopped himself at the last second. The two of us stood there, only his hands on my chest separating us, Auggie's fiery eyes boring into mine.

The anger had been completely flushed from me, replaced by confusion. And desperation. And longing. And fear.

My hands trembled as my fingers clutched at his wrists, gripping them just tightly enough to keep his hands against my chest. Auggie snarled at me, glaring into my face as I held his hands against my chest and prayed for my stomach to settle. A whirlwind of thoughts swirled through my head as I stared down into the fiery eyes of my…*friend?*

As we stood there, unspeaking, staring into each other's eyes, Auggie's expression softened bit by bit. His breath was warm on my face and his hands felt like fire against my chest. I didn't want either to be taken away. Auggie's eyes didn't return to their former blank, uncaring state, but the anger was flushed from them, replaced by an emotion that was…unreadable. Maybe disappointment? Gently, though with intention, he pulled his hands from my grip.

When he stepped back, taking his hands from my chest, I nearly moaned with displeasure.

Auggie stared at me a moment longer, the space between us like a widening chasm, then he was looking anywhere but at me.

Finally, he spoke: "Go home, Jordan."

"I—"

"Get out," he said softly, but with resolve. "Leave."

"I—"

"Please. Now, please."

With no idea what it was I wanted to say to Auggie, or what I had intended to say, I let my eyes linger on him for only a moment longer. Then I turned on my heels and shuffled back to the barn doors. I intended to honor Auggie's request to just leave, but when I crossed over the threshold and stepped out into the sun, I found myself turning to get one last look at Auggie.

"You're not stupid, Auggie," I said just loudly enough to be heard by him. "You're brilliant."

Auggie didn't look up, but he kicked the toe of his shoe against the ground.

"I think you're brilliant," I said.

Then I left.

THE DAY THE WORLD WENT DARK

Wrathful, black storm clouds descended on Possibly, Texas the following day. Bloated with unshed rain, and torpid in their movements overhead, thunderless lightning etched through them sporadically, like illuminated veins practically electrifying the air in town. The Possibilian breeze ceased and the town grew quiet and still. When I rose from bed and my bedroom was still dark as night, I had looked through the dormer windows to see if maybe I had been woken in the middle of the night by something. When I saw the angry clouds hanging bulbously in the sky over Possibly, my gut sank.

Something was coming.

Though I'd lived—even if briefly—on the Gulf Coast during hurricane season, and in Tornado Alley during the spring and early summer, I'd never seen such angry clouds.

They weren't carrying in a hurricane—Possibly was landlocked far from the Texas coast. A tornado was possible, but the clouds didn't remind me of how the sky had looked before other tornados I'd seen. As I knelt there on my bed, staring out at the black clouds through my window, I had a thought that even the craziest of Possibilian would scoff at if they heard it.

The clouds weren't just bringing weather…they were bringing scorn.

Anger.

Angry was what the sky was.

Over what or whom, I wasn't sure, but I knew, somewhere deep inside me, that the black clouds above were out for vengeance.

Down in Possibly, I could see that the streets were mostly clear. Anyone walking in town hurriedly made their way into whatever building was their destination. No one lingered on the corners catching up with each other. Earl Dean was nowhere to be seen on Liberty Lane. Levi Lee wasn't outside of Starbuck's, pretending to be part of the hull. Obviously, he was inside helping out or at home—wherever that might be.

Though Starbuck would have understood if I hadn't shown up for work on such a day—especially since my job wasn't integral to the operation of his business—I clambered out of bed and made my way to the shower.

As I was stepping out onto the bath mat and reaching for my towel, the house vibrated with the arrival of thunder. Overhead, the bathroom light flickered as the sound of the thunder shook the house, then shone brightly once the thunder ceased. I wrapped the towel around me, as though scandalized, covering myself as I watched the light overhead, waiting to see if we would lose power.

Rain pounding against the windows and side of the house was what I had expected to hear after that first belch of thunder, but the world grew quiet once again. With the towel clasped tightly around my waist, I tiptoed across the third-floor hall to look out of the window into the backyard. Jack was nowhere in sight, but his table project in the backyard was encased in the blue tarps, which were strapped down securely with bungee cords.

Apparently, he had woken with the same thoughts. Something was coming; it was going to be bad. Today was not going to be a day where woodworking in the backyard would be possible.

After drying off in my room, fixing my hair, and dressing for work, I jogged downstairs to find that Jack was at the kitchen table, eating breakfast. He looked up when I arrived and signed that he had made breakfast for us. Even with the nervous energy zig-zagging throughout my body, that brought a smile to my face. Having Jack acknowledge me—and be pleasant—was a relief.

Following my encounter with Auggie the previous day, every little kindness felt like a stitch to the wound in my heart.

"What did you make?" I asked.

Jack signed that he'd made bacon, eggs, and toast.

"Yum," I said. "I think I'll slap some eggs and bacon between some toast. I'll eat on my way to Starbuck's."

Jack nodded along slowly.

"I want to beat the rain."

He started to sign, then seemed to realize that maybe it was too advanced, and produced his notepad from his breast pocket. I waited until he had finished writing his block letters, then read what he had to say over his shoulder.

Do you think you should go to work today? Starbuck will do fine without you.

"Yeah," I said. "I thought of that. But I think it'll be okay. It's just a storm. Right?"

Jack gave me a crooked grin and shrugged.

It wasn't as if Jack and I had known each other long. I'd only been living with him for a few months—and I could barely remember him from my early years—but he seemed nervous. The storm was unsettling to him as well. That didn't ease my worry.

"It'll be fine."

He gave me a firm nod, but the serious look in his eyes let me know that he was concerned.

"I'll hurry to Starbuck's. I swear."

Jack signed.

It's cold outside.

"It…cold?" I frowned; certain I had misunderstood.

He nodded slowly, giving me a look that let me know he knew that was ridiculous, too.

"Like…*cold*…or unseasonably cold?"

Jack thought on that then lifted his hand and tilted it back and forth while tilting his head back and forth.

"Gotcha. You guys probably don't get many cool days here in August, huh? Seems like the end of times?"

I smiled and Jack grinned widely, his mouth opening as though he was laughing, though no sound came out. Through his fit of laughter—or his version of it—he jotted another note quickly on the notepad and held it up to me.

Up to you. Be careful.

"I will. Promise."

Jack went back to his breakfast as I scooped eggs onto a slice of toast and topped them with bacon, though he watched me out of the corner of his eye. Typically, such a thing would annoy me, being watched over without need, but, for some reason, having Jack showing care for me again helped melt away some of my anxiety over the impending storm. I'd do my best to make sure he didn't have a reason to stop caring about me again. Or, at least, acting as though he didn't care.

I slid another slice of toast atop the pile of eggs and bacon and pressed it down with the palm of my hand.

"Breakfast panini," I proclaimed, holding the sandwich up as I spun to look at Jack. "Kind of."

Jack grinned at my ridiculousness, just as the sky belched out another roll of thunder. The two of us froze as the house rumbled along with the thunder. When things were still and quiet again, Jack started to sign.

"I promise I'll be careful," I stopped him. "It will literally take me forty-five seconds to get to Starbuck's."

Jack's whole body straightened and fell, as though he sighed. Then he waved me off with a tight smile.

Up to you. Be careful. He hadn't written it down again or showed it to me again, but I knew what he had meant by the movement.

"Thanks for the breakfast, man," I said. "I'll see you in a few hours."

Jack signed "goodbye" to me and I responded verbally, then I jogged out the front door. As I hustled across the front yard, taking a giant bite from my sandwich—and losing a few of my scrambled eggs in the process—it dawned on me that Jack hadn't been playing the radio as he normally did in the mornings. The reason that it occurred to me so suddenly was that in the distance, from the speaker mounted on the pole alongside the road down the street from Jack's had Amos' voice pouring from it. I had walked outside just as he was announcing the song of the day. Probably for the twentieth time that morning.

"You've been listening to AMOR, the most popular radio station in Possibly, Texas. All day long from 6am to 6pm. That was Tiptoe Thru' the Tulips with Me *by Tiny Tim. Next up—*Tiptoe Thru' the Tulips with Me *by Tiny Tim!"*

When the opening ukulele sounds poured from the speaker as I jogged along the road and Tiny Tim's falsetto began, a shiver ran up my spine. Veins of lightning zig-zagged through the heavy, inky clouds overhead, and thunder clapped in the distance. Growing closer and closer, coming from the east past Susurrus Creek, the thunder rolled through town as the clouds produced their light spectacle. The pavement underfoot shook angrily. I picked up my pace and my jog turned into a run. I stuffed the rest of the sandwich down my gullet, choking it down like a python as I raced to work.

The rain was going to come any moment. I just knew it. When it came, it wasn't going to drop sprinkles and droplets in a delicate dance. The clouds would open up and begin dumping every last bit of rain they held, punishing the land below. I would be soaked within seconds. Buckets would pour down and I'd have no other choice but to either show up to Starbuck's soaking wet or run back to Jack's and not show up for work.

Once the rain started, I had no idea how long it would last, but the clouds overhead practically screamed that their fury would not burn out quickly.

Jogging along the road, I'd barely made it past Bend of the Road Graveyard and was just approaching Liberty Lane when thunder crackled overhead. It wasn't a rumble or a boom, but more like someone had lit a trail of gunpowder. Stopping at the end of Liberty Lane, my head crooked back to look up at the darkness overhead. Lightning crackled through the sky like a Tesla coil and another shiver ran up my spine as the thunder popped and hissed.

Even the lightning wasn't enough to fully illuminate the sky overhead. It turned patches of the black clouds into dark and light gray, but their intensity wasn't diminished by the flashing.

The Possibilian breeze returned, blowing in off Susurrus Creek as I stared at the sky. First, like a whisper, then as a howl that blew my hair back on my head, ruffling it as the lightning crackled on.

There was no way that lightning could last for as long as the storm managed, but like most things in Possibly, it defied logic. Lightning continued to shoot veins through the clouds overhead as another crackle of thunder hissed across the sky.

Where was the rain?

A thundering boom emanated from the sky, making me jerk and duck down, as though I could hide from the menace above me. The sudden boom nearly knocked me from my feet from the surprise. Tiny Tim's falsetto and ukulele struggled to be heard over the threatening storm.

Just as the thunder tapered off, and the howling wind whipped itself up into a fury, my hair dancing on my head like a whirlwind, the back door of The Pueblo burst open. My head whipped around to see what had caused the sudden movement on the otherwise still street. Had the wind blown the door off of its hinges?

Lilly marched out the backdoor of The Pueblo, a look of fury on her red face. Clad in her ever-present bib overalls and long-sleeved shirt, her boots stomping at the ground, she marched from the backdoor of The Pueblo and across the grassy patch behind it. She stomped across the tram tracks and into the center of Liberty Lane, her hands balled into fists at her side. Lightning lit the street like a dance club as Lilly hollered with fury.

"*AMOS!*"

I shivered again as I stood at the end of the street, watching her glare at the front of AMOR and scream for its proprietor. Students who had been at The Pueblo—including Auggie—

347

were gathering at the backdoor, huddling in a group, anxiously watching Lilly stand in the middle of Liberty Lane and scream. Glancing to my right, Agnes was wheeling herself out of the front of Blooms to try and see what was going.

When would her damn leg heal?

Lilly had screamed so loud even Agnes had heard her. Starbuck and Levi Lee had stepped out the coffee shop and had rounded the building to watch the scene. Even Molly and Sofia were sneaking over from their respective places of work to find out what all the fuss was about. Lilly had the lungs to draw a crowd, and a crowd had heeded the call.

Another crack of thunder and prickle of lightning and the front door of AMOR opened. Amos stepped out onto the sidewalk; a mile-wide smile plastered on his face. Lilly's arms shook at her sides, and before Amos could cross the width of the sidewalk to step out into the street, another holler ripped through town.

"STOP PLAYING THOSE DAMN SONGS!" Lilly demanded, fury pouring off of her. The wind howled down the street, people's hair rustling and the fabric of their shirts and pants whipping around like flags. *"I'M A LESBIAN AMOS! I AIN'T NEVER GONNA LOVE YOU LIKE THAT!"*

A murmur—that wasn't the breeze for once—rippled through town and my mouth turned into an "O" as I stared at the scene unfolding before me.

"Stop all your damn nonsense and give it up, man!" Lilly hollered with finality.

When I whipped my head to the side to look at Amos, he was crestfallen, his chin nearly on his chest as he looked down at the sidewalk. Lilly had begun marching back towards The Pueblo when I looked back in her direction. She stomped over the tram tracks, across the grassy patch behind The Pueblo, and barreled through her students, back inside. When I looked back over at AMOR, Amos was nowhere to be seen, but the front door of the radio station was closed once more.

Exchanging a few glances with the art students—even Auggie—and the other Possibilians who had come out to observe the show, I was unsure of what to do. Auggie had even frowned at me and raised his shoulders, confused as I was as to what was happening.

But we had all finally figured out why Amos operated the radio station in the way that he did.

Collectively, all of us remaining observers remembered the storm brewing overhead. Agnes wheeled herself back into Blooms quickly. Molly and Sofia jogged for cover, Starbuck and Levi Lee were headed back around the pirate ship, and Lilly's students were shuffling back inside, closing the backdoor to The Pueblo behind him.

My heart went out to Amos as though I had been rejected right along with him. To have someone you're enamored with so deeply that you start a radio station to play songs dedicated to them every day reject you—so absolutely—had to tear a person apart. As an observer it was painful enough. I couldn't even imagine how Amos felt.

Was Lilly Shirlene?

Had Amos been the anonymous letter sender?

If the letters stopped…would that be my answer?

Was everyone else in town thinking the same thing?

Without another thought, I took off in a run towards Starbuck's as another crackle of thunder sounded and a streak of lightning shot through the sky. Off in the distance, down by Grandy's, Wyatt's gun sounded. Tiny Tim's falsetto and ukulele disappeared as every speaker in town went quiet.

The rain didn't come; the clouds didn't disperse. For the first two hours of my shift at Starbuck's, I swept and mopped the floors. I scrubbed the tables and chairs and wiped down the walls and countertops. Thunder continued to rumble overhead, shaking the ship's walls as Levi Lee and Starbuck did their best to keep busy, though customers were nonexistent. Every few minutes, lightning lit up the porthole windows like demonic eyes before letting them go dark once again. The wind howled angrily against the walls of the ship.

As we sauntered into our third, silent hour at Starbuck's, the three of us ended up sitting at one of the unused tables, not speaking. Starbuck was switching his eyepatch back and forth, trying to decide which eye it felt best on. To my amusement, though not shock, it occurred to me that Starbuck's eyepatch was for aesthetics and not utility. Another Possibilian oddity.

Levi Lee sat quietly in thought, obviously contemplating his next artistic endeavor.

I found myself wondering if I shouldn't have brought a book to work for once. At least it would have given me something to do. I contemplated asking Starbuck if he wanted me to go home for the day to save on my pay, but figured he was the boss and would have thought of that already. If he wanted me to go home, he'd say so.

Within minutes of sitting in quiet contemplation with the two men, I thought I'd go insane. Between our communal silence and the ominous thunder and lightning and howling wind that refused to produce any rain, I was coiling up tightly like a spring. As Possibly was prone to, we weren't left to our boredom for long. Another scream ripped through town. So loudly that we could hear it inside Starbuck's, the three of us jerked in our seats at the sudden noise which was not thunder.

Exchanging glances, it was obvious that none of us had actually caught what the person outside was screaming—nor did any of us have a clue why someone would be screaming. As a group, we rose from our seats and headed to the front door. I led the way through the glass door out onto the patch of grass in front of the pirate ship. Levi Lee came up to stand beside me and Starbuck flanked my other side. Thunder boomed and lightning flashed once again as the wind screamed through town.

"*LILLLLLLLLLLLLLLLLLLLLLLY!*"

The three of us whipped our head towards the source of the noise by Susurrus Creek.

Immediately, my eyes landed on Lovelorn Pass Bridge.

Wyatt's gun sounded off in the direction of The Pueblo. I didn't bother to look—I only had eyes for one person.

Though several people were gathering in clusters in the area of Possibly around the creek by Lovelorn Pass Bridge, my eyes stayed on Amos. Not just because he was standing alone, but because he had climbed up onto the railing of the bridge. His arms were held out wide and he was wailing Lilly's name up to the heavens. Thunder competed with his screams and lightning flashed like a strobe as he screamed pitifully.

Don't jump. I felt tears at the corners of my eyes.

It wasn't just that I felt horrible for what Amos had just been made to endure publicly, but also it was that jumping into Susurrus Creek during a lightning storm had to be one of the most dangerous things one could do in town. What if Amos jumped into the water, simply to get over his obsession, and then lightning struck the creek? A simple, yet heartbreaking, rejection could easily turn into utter tragedy in a split second.

Whipping my head around to search the crowd, I quickly determined that Lilly was not amongst the crowd watching

Amos' display. She had probably stayed at The Pueblo, resolute in her decision to reject Amos so callously.

Not that I could blame her; she was obviously a lesbian.

Amos just wasn't ever going to make her happy.

Her methods had been the issue.

Then again, what madness might someone be drawn to if they are subjected to another's obsession for so long? Amos had been on his mission to win Lilly's heart for…years? Auggie had said that AMOR had been playing the same song all day long for twelve hours for as long as he could remember. Lilly had obviously snapped.

The howling wind, rumbling thunder, and flashes of lightning led me to believe that if there was ever a day to snap, Lilly had chosen wisely.

"*LILLLLLLLLLLLLLLLLLLLLLLLY?*"

I looked back over to Amos, perched precariously upon the bridge's railing, as he howled a final time. The thunder stopped. The sky darkened. The wind drew in a breath. And everything went silent. It seemed as if the town was taking a collective breath, holding it in anticipation as we watched Amos teeter on the rail of Lovelorn Pass Bridge.

Then he jumped.

Dropping like a stone, Amos went over the rail like a spike, his body turning to send him plunging head first into the water below in Susurrus Creek. Levi Lee took off in a sprint as the sky roared again and a flash of lightning turned the town a blinding white. I started to take off after Levi Lee, intending to help him fish Amos out of the creek, but Starbuck grabbed my arm, holding me back, just as the sky let loose.

Rain dropped in buckets from above, stinging my eyes and obscuring my vision as Starbuck kept me from running to the creek. I jerked my arm in his grasp, but he grabbed ahold of my other arm with his free hand and turned me gently to face him.

"*Go home, matey!*" he declared loudly, fighting against the sound of the storm. "*I'll help 'im out!*"

Then he let go of me and raced towards the creek. I watched him disappear into the sheets of rain. At first, I thought I should chase after him. Ignore his command. However, how many men would it take to fish Amos out of the creek? I would only be a hindrance to their efforts. Levi Lee alone could probably get the job done without anyone else's help. Other than art, he had proved perfectly capable at any task set out before him.

I don't know how long I stood there, the rain soaking me to my bones, looking off towards the creek, which I could barely see through the rain. Finally, however, I spun around and raced away, running as fast as my feet would take me towards home. Water splashed up, over, and into my shoes as I dashed along the streets, my hair like a drape over my forehead that I had to push out of my eyes with the back of my hand.

The street was flooding by Bend of the Road Graveyard when I approached, and I wondered if that would create a problem for the bodies buried there. Shaking away the thought, I continued on my way, racing through the deluge, the water sucking and pulling at my sneakers as I came out the other side. The last fifty yards to home were miserable, my legs wanting to give out from underneath me as I tried to spot the house through the torrent of rain. Luckily, the rust-red roof stood out like a beacon, so I knew I was nearly free.

The front yard at home was already becoming a swamp as I sloshed and stomped through it, racing for the steps, but I didn't let it deter me. I raced through the yard and up the front steps, reaching for the door handle. I whipped the front screen, then the door open, and ducked inside, quickly turning to close the screen and door tightly behind me. For some reason, I flipped the lock, as though trapping the storm—and everything else—outside.

Jack was sitting at the kitchen table, working on a crossword. When I entered the house like a whirlwind, his head snapped up to look at me. I stood just inside, dripping on the floor, looking like a rat that had lost a fight with a washing machine. For a few silent moments, he looked me over, obviously wondering why I had been caught in the rain. Finally, he signed:

Dry clothes. I'll make soup.

"All right," I said.

Trudging across the kitchen, defeated, tired, cold, feeling hopeless, and bothered by the interaction between Amos and Lilly for reasons I couldn't understand, I made my way to the stairs. When I passed by Jack, he stood from his chair and nudged my arm. I turned to look at him and he gave me a small smile, then reached up and tapped his hand against my cheek softly.

I didn't know what that meant to him. Or if it meant anything in sign language, but I got the gist.

Before I knew it was how I'd react, I felt myself slump against Jack and my arms went around his middle. I was so…empty.

He didn't react right away, frozen by the suddenness of my strange reaction, but finally, I felt Jack's arms go around me. As he held me to him, patting my back to soothe me, it was possible that tears fell from my eyes onto his shoulder. It could have been rain. Jack was getting wet either way. But I knew that rain wasn't what made my vision blurry.

A LIGHT IN THE DARK

"Jack!" I gasped as I raced down the stairs into the kitchen. "Something's going on downtown!"

Downtown Possibly had been a black void outside of my window that night. Sitting cross-legged on my bed in my boxers at bedtime, I was staring out at town. No one moved on the streets—though people rarely did at night—and not a single light shone from the windows of the buildings in town. I had opened the window so I could at least feel the Possibilian breeze, but even it had tucked itself away for the evening.

After I had gotten home—and collapsed against Jack in a pitiful display of indecipherable emotion, the rain pelted the house for hours. Buckets dumped from the sky and the wind howled, the lights flickered and the power threatened to go out numerous times. I'd gotten a shower, regardless of the storm, and joined Jack back at the kitchen table.

A pot of steaming hot chicken noodle soup—heavy on the noodles and chicken, light on the veggies, just as I liked it—was waiting on the table. It couldn't have been from scratch since Jack hadn't had enough time to whip something up while I was in the shower, but I didn't care. It tasted better than canned, so it didn't matter either way. The two of us ate our lunch in amiable silence with hunks of crusty bread that were slathered in butter, which melted into the bread and the soup as soon as the heat touched it. Both of us devoured our soup in great spoonfuls, butter running down our fingers and making our lips glisten, as we savored the meal.

After dinner, Jack had asked—via his notepad—if I wanted to learn to play Cribbage. I'd never even heard of the game, so the next three hours were spent learning and playing. I'm a teenager. Playing an old people card game with my stepfather wasn't supposed to be an exciting evening activity, but I actually had fun. I never won a single game against Jack, but it was nice to spend time with him that was comfortable, even in its silence. After cards, we watched some stupid sitcom on T.V. before I decided bedtime had come. Jack indicated that he was going to stay up to watch a little more T.V., so I'd left him to it.

I found myself sitting in my boxers on my bed, staring out at downtown Possibly and Auggie's barn like I did almost every night. Unlike every other night, there was nothing to be seen or heard. No lasers or lights show from Auggie's barn. No music drifting on the breeze. No sounds of Susurrus Creek whispering across town. For a while, I stared at that black void and thought about Amos' predicament with Lilly.

A person had to be entirely heartless not to feel for the guy. The public humiliation. Finding out the person you loved would *never* love you back in the same way had to be the worst. To have the whole town find out you had no idea that you were chasing after the wrong person—and in kind of an obsessive way—had to be devastating.

Then again, I felt for Lilly, too.

To have someone obsess over you—though, I had no idea of the history between Amos and Lilly, or how she even knew about his obsession—had to be annoying. Day after day of dealing with unwanted advances—whether the person knew it or not—had to drive a person mad. I desperately wanted to know how Lilly knew that Amos was playing his daily song for her. Had he flirted with her or mentioned that he was interested? Had someone else tipped her off?

There was so much about Possibly and its citizens that I wanted to know.

But people in Possibly didn't talk about each other or gossip. Auggie probably would have told me about Lilly and Amos if I was in a position to ask him. He'd told me the history of a lot of the Possibilians in town. Then again, everyone, including Auggie, had seemed shocked by the interaction between Lilly and Amos on Liberty Lane.

Maybe nobody had known?

Which made Amos' humiliation even more painful.

I couldn't blame the guy for leaping off of Lovelorn Pass Bridge to get over Lilly so quickly. A wound like that couldn't be fixed with a bandage.

Regardless, the town had shut down after Amos' display. The rain could have been blamed for sure. A tempest such as the one the black clouds had brewed would shut down any town, no matter how big or small. However, Amos' heartbreak seemed to be more impactful on the town. Wyatt's gunshots couldn't be heard for the rest of the day. No one raced from building to building in the deluge, and the lights went out everywhere—except Jack's place—before night even fell. It was if Amos' predicament had taken all of the air out of Possibly.

Just when I thought I'd fall asleep, and dream up theories about Possibilians and all of their secrets, I saw the lights. It was faint at first, the glow that was coming from Liberty Lane, but in all of the darkness, it was if someone had lit a beacon. Tiny, firefly-like lights were popping up and down the street, glowing in brilliance until I could almost make out Earl Dean's rainbow bricks from my third-floor window. Frozen in wonder for a moment, I simply stared at the lights and how they shone against the still damp pavement.

Once I was able to shake off my stupor, I'd leapt from bed and pulled on fresh jeans and a t-shirt, then slid my feet into my sneakers without bothering to put socks on first. My shoes were still a bit damp from getting caught in the storm earlier, but I paid the clammy feeling no mind. Instead, I'd raced down the stairs and announced excitedly to Jack that something was going on downtown.

Jack crooked his head to look at me over his shoulder, his brows knitted together.

"I don't know, man," I said. "There are some kind of lights all over the place on Liberty Lane. Like, I don't know, fireflies or something."

He didn't react at first, but I could see from the cycle of expressions on his face that he was contemplating what could have caused lights to appear on Liberty Lane.

"Let's go check it out!" I bounced in place, suddenly imbued with curiosity. "I want to know what it is!"

Jack dramatically looked up at the clock on the wall hanging over the T.V.

"Yeah, I know," I said with a laugh. "Who cares? What else do you have going on?"

That made Jack grin. His chest rose and fell, as though a giant sigh of acquiescence rolled through him, and he pried himself up out of his chair. I bounced giddily like a kid whose parent had just promised to take them to get ice cream as Jack slipped on his work shoes by the door. As soon as he was ready for the walk, I ripped the front door open and dashed down the front steps. Glancing over my shoulder, I made sure that Jack was following.

Down in the yard, water squished under my sneakers, but the yard wasn't as swamp-like as it had been earlier in the day. The Possibilian breeze had picked up just enough to whisper through my hair as Jack met me on the lawn. He grimaced at the sound of his feet meeting the soggy lawn, but didn't hesitate in following me quickly to the road.

It took some urging and show of excitement, but I got Jack to pick up his pace as we walked towards downtown. When he saw the lights glowing from Liberty Lane in the distance, it took less encouraging on my part to get him to hustle. Without asking him, I knew he saw the same thing I did on Liberty Lane. The lights couldn't have been from one of the shop's owners turning on their lights. It couldn't have been a flashlight or even a spotlight. It was too soft, too warm, yet the light still illuminated the street well.

When we reached Bend of the Road Graveyard, the two of us took off in a jog simultaneously without consulting each other first. Jack had a grin of pure curiosity and wonder on his face, and I knew my expression matched his as the two of us raced to the street. Jack and I slapped and pushed at each other, as though racing and trying to throw the other off their game. I laughed and swatted at him and he grinned and made his version of a laugh as we approached the corner of Liberty Lane.

I don't know what I had expected to find on Liberty Lane; I had no idea what Jack had thought about the lights. What we found was equally confusing and mundane.

Someone had taken fairy lights and strung them up and down along the buildings on the street. Twinkling slowly, the golden-yellow light illuminated the road as though a street fair was about to be set up. Lights were wrapped around Jasper's tram car, parked at the west end of the tracks. The trees that lined the south side of the street were covered in the lights as well. Yet no one was in sight. It was just Jack and me.

The two of us exchanged cautious smiles as we turned around slowly, taking in what had to be thousands of twinkling lights all around the street. A silence that only the calm after a storm can bring surrounded us, enveloped us, and if it wasn't for us, and the breeze, everything on Liberty Lane would have been deathly still. Except for the twinkling lights.

I stared in wonder, curious as to what it meant. Obviously, someone had hung the lights...but why? What did it mean? Why would someone come out so late at night after the storm to do such a thing?

Is this art?

When every speaker in town suddenly crackled to life, Jack and I both jumped in surprise.

You Can't Always Get What You Want by The Rolling Stones started to pour from the AMOR speakers all over town as the lights twinkled like fireflies around us.

Jack and I turned to each other, grins on our faces.

What is going on? Jack signed.

"No idea," I said. "I—"

"Y'all do this?" Both of us jumped at the sound of Sofia's voice.

We spun to find her appearing between the trees behind the post office. Possibly's postmaster was in rubber boots and her nightgown, her hair up in a scarf. I wanted to laugh at her appearance—not because she looked bad, but because it was...appropriate. Had she been woken by the lights and the sound of AMOR suddenly coming to life in the middle of the night?

Jack tossed his hands up defensively as I responded.

"I saw the lights from my window," I hollered down the street. "The music started when we got here."

"Well, I'll be," Sofia said. "I was in bed reading and looked out the window and saw the lights."

Jack and I shrugged in unison. We didn't have any information that would be helpful to her.

"It's pretty," she said as she strolled down the street towards us, her boots squishing against the pavement. "If nothing else."

"Who do you think—"

I didn't have time to finish my question. Starbuck and Levi Lee came tromping across the tram tracks from the grassy patch to the south that led to the pirate ship. Starbuck was in old-timey pajamas—something Lucy and Ricky would wear on *I Love Lucy*. Levi Lee was clad only in basketball shorts that barely reached his knees. Levi Lee was looking around with starry eyes, as though he had never seen fairy lights before, and Starbuck was massaging his chin as though in deep thought.

"What be this?" Starbuck bellowed, though he seemed more amused than annoyed.

"Dunno," Sofia answered for us as the men joined us on the street. "Jack and Jordan got here right before I did. Said they ain't seen no one."

"I saw the lights from my window," I said, repeating my story as though it mattered.

"Arrr," Starbuck growled, "we saw it from the sleeping quarters in our hammocks."

So, that's where Levi Lee lived. In the sleeping quarters of the ship with Starbuck.

Were they…related?

"I thought Liberty Lane was on fire," Levi Lee nodded along. "I was half-asleep."

He'd barely had time to finish his thought when Wyatt shuffled onto the street from the direction of The Pueblo. Agnes was rowing herself, huffing and puffing, down from the south end of the road. Then, like the storm that fell from the black clouds earlier in the afternoon, all of Possibly seemed to be flooding the street. Jasper, Earl Dean, Officer Hanning, Mystic Molly, the teen boys that traveled in a pack around town, Samuel, Grandy, and even Auggie crept out of the shadows to join us to stare up at the lights and listen to The Rolling Stones.

For the longest of moments, all of us just stared in wonder, murmuring questions and theories to each other as we listened to the song. No one had any idea what was going on or why Liberty Lane was suddenly lit up like a carnival in the middle of the night. We all agreed on one thing though—we didn't mind in the slightest.

"What's going on down here?"

We all jumped as Amos came barreling out of the front door of AMOR, still in his night clothes, his slippers slapping against the sidewalk. His hair was sticking up in all directions and he looked as though he had literally rolled out of bed. Possibly hit the floor on his way out.

Poor guy, I thought to myself.

Everyone froze, unsure of what to say to the man who had, unfortunately, been Possibly's main character of the day. Well, everyone except Sofia, of course.

"Why don't you know?" she said, placing her hands on her hips playfully. "That's your radio station playin', ain't it?"

Amos jerked, his head whipping around sleepily as he tried to shake his mid-slumber stupor from his brain. Everyone laughed. But we weren't laughing at Amos. We were laughing with him. Because all of us were as clueless as him. For a second, Amos bucked up, his spine straightening as his mouth turned downward unpleasantly. Once Sofia clomped across the street, her rubber boots slapping against the wet pavement, so that she could slap him on the back jovially, he realized that no one was teasing him.

He reached up to scratch this head, suddenly realizing what his hair looked like, and blushed.

"I guess I should get in there and shut this off," he said with a jab of his thumb at the speaker outside the door. "Don't know how that happened. Sorry, folks."

Everyone spoke up simultaneously to either tell Amos it was "okay" and "let it play!" The roar from the Possibilians shocked Amos at first, but a grin slowly bloomed on his face as Sofia clung to his arm and smiled up at him. Seeing Amos happy after the day we'd all had was worth having us all dragged out of our homes in the middle of the night.

Who would begrudge a neighbor a little lost sleep if it helped them get over heartbreak?

It became apparent that everyone hadn't planned to get out of the house in the middle of the night for nothing. When Levi Lee grabbed Sofia and spun her away from Amos, leaving our radio broadcaster standing by the open front door of his business, everyone laughed. Sofia and Levi Lee strolled out to the middle of the street, her rubber boots squishing on the pavement, and they began to dance uninhibitedly around to The Rolling Stones.

Everyone seemed to partner up, or dance in groups, dancing merrily around the street under the twinkling lights— as though this was a totally normal thing to do. Even I—who never danced in public before in my life—joined in, dancing in the middle of the group on the street. I didn't have a partner, but I danced along with everyone else. My eyes discreetly found Auggie a few times—he was dancing a few yards away—but I didn't approach him.

At some point, though I hadn't noticed him leave and return, Samuel went to his store and got a cooler full of sodas and began passing them out. So, everyone grabbed a drink, popped their tops, and went back to dancing. Much to my surprise, Mystic Molly approached me and invited me to dance with her. Though nervous to dance with another actual, living, breathing human being, I accepted her offer with warm cheeks, and spun around the street with her.

Laughing, sipping our sodas, and exchanging comments with other Possibilians as we passed them, we danced under the twinkling lights until Earl Dean asked for a chance to dance with her.

With no dance partner to speak of, I stood off to the side by the tram tracks, sipping my soda, grinning widely at my fellow citizens of Possibly. Grins were plastered on faces, drinks were being enjoyed, and it was all ridiculous. What town is overjoyed at being disturbed in the middle of the night by phantom lights and loud music? What town deals with such an invasion by dancing and drinking in the middle of the street?

How is this normal?

Why couldn't *this be normal?*

Standing there, overjoyed, watching my fellow Possibilians go with the flow, I had a realization.

What is normal?

What's typical?

Why did I have to make sense of something to simply enjoy it? Did a person have to understand something to lean into it? Wasn't the feeling of joy at participating in something harmless enough to inform a person that they were doing the right thing?

Why did it matter that Possibly—and all of its citizens, including me—were weird?

Were we happy?

Who was being harmed?

Possibly, though I'd never understand it, nor would I understand how the citizens seemed to have a hive-mind and simply go along with the ridiculous things other citizens did, was heaven. No one was causing trouble or making anyone feel weird. The situation was weird, but we were all just people who chose to lean into it instead. We were choosing joy.

What's wrong with that?

I smiled to myself, sipping my soda under one of the trees bundled with lights, and stared out at the happy faces dancing in the streets. Laughter rolled through Liberty Lane and the Possibilian breeze felt like God's breath on my skin as it whispered through town. It may have been a warm August night following a torrential storm, but it was pleasant. In fact, it felt more like spring than summer. It was glorious. And that, more than the music, lights, dancing, and drinks, had shaped everyone's mood.

Across the street, by the front door of AMOR, Lilly had finally shown her face. Amos and her were shaking hands amiably and smiling. It wasn't not awkward, their exchange, but it was easy enough that I knew things would be okay.

The storm had passed.

Further down the street, by the south end, my eyes found Jack dancing with Sofia. They were grinning and she was laughing as Jack expertly spun her around. The way he looked down at her as he held her in his arms, his eyes twinkling as he grinned, I had to wonder, *was Sofia our mysterious Shirlene?*

Was Jack the mysterious letter writer?

I finished my soda and thought to myself: *Who gives a shit?*

One day, maybe I'd find out who was sending the letters, but that night was not the night to worry about it. Another night would come and maybe the mystery would be solved. I'd just have to go with the flow until then.

Watching everyone paired up, or in groups, dancing around, I couldn't keep my eyes from searching the crowd. When I found Auggie, dancing around with Agnes as she spun her wheelchair as best she could, my smile faltered. I didn't let myself lose my smile—I was too happy to let it go—but my heart felt heavy.

Auggie was happy and laughing. So, I didn't approach him.

It was Amos' day to make up with Lilly. Possibly didn't need two soap operas in one day. Besides, like Amos' former obsession with Lilly, my fight with Auggie wasn't widely known. I wanted to keep it that way. Given time, Auggie and I could eventually talk—and I wouldn't be a jerk. Maybe we wouldn't be the kind of friends we'd tried to become, but we'd be friendly. I'd have to be okay with that. Just like Amos had to accept that Lilly was never going to love him back the way he wanted.

Just when I was certain that it was time to walk back home so that I wouldn't be a wet blanket for the impromptu celebration, Levi Lee danced up to me, a fresh soda in his hand. He took my empty bottle and shoved the fresh one in my hand. Then, with a wink, as though he understood everything— though there was no possible way he could—he grabbed my free hand and tugged me back into the street. I let go of my gloom and joined him in dancing with the other Possibilians.

So, Levi Lee and I danced with everyone, and I did my best to forget my worries. The night was too joyous to get bogged down with worries anyway.

As we spun around the street, laughing and talking with others, my eyes still wandered, though I tried to keep them from lingering on Auggie when I spotted him. I tried to focus on everything else going on around me. All the happiness.

When my eyes landed on the pathway between AMOR and the building to its right, a curious thing caught my attention. Someone, in a black hooded robe, was standing in the shadows, just beyond the glow cast by the fairy lights.

Malia?

My feet slowed, though I continued dancing, as I looked at the person staring out at the crowd. No, not at the crowd. At me. I swallowed hard as I danced in slow motion and stared into the depths of the hood. *A black void.* My heart was beginning to race when the hooded figure gave me a single nod, and for some reason, I understood something.

As the hooded figure slipped back between the buildings, swallowed by the darkness between the buildings, I braved a smile. And I continued dancing.

LET'S TRY AGAIN

Walking to work the next day—a little later than usual, thanks to the late-night dance party on Liberty Lane—to *Bad Bad Leroy Brown* by Jim Croce was an experience. I'd never had theme music to follow me through life before, but something about the song, the timing, and my good mood made me feel Amos was playing it just for me. Jack was nowhere to be found after I'd taken my morning shower following breakfast, though he'd cleaned up the kitchen before absconding. So, I left the house and swaggered down the steps and across the lawn.

As I made my way into downtown Possibly, I whistled along to the song, pumping my arms to the beat, unable to keep the smile off of my face. Not that things were perfect—I still had to resolve things with Auggie—but life was good. The previous night's activities had made something inside of me shift. Shed a light on something I'd been ignoring ever since settling in at Jack's place.

Possibly was weird.

And weird was okay.

Weird was perfect.

Especially when everyone was allowed to be weird without judgment. Possibly didn't have to be perfect. It didn't have to make sense. I didn't have to understand the town or every

Possibilian to simply sit back and go with the flow. Life should be easy; Possibly was easy.

What more could a guy want?

Levi Lee was outside of Starbuck's when I got to work, dry as a bone, thanks to the temperate day the storm had delivered to us. He was in ballet tights, a t-shirt, and sneakers, performing ballet. Poorly. Just like his green-screen suit, the tights proved to be overly obscene on Levi Lee.

It was a complete shock when I realized that maybe I should—*and possibly wanted to*—enjoy the view instead of worrying about whether or not it was obscene. No one else in Possibly gave a damn that Levi Lee made such a display of…*himself*…so who was I to be offended for them? And…I found that I did enjoy the view. Though, I wasn't sure I wanted to figure out everything that meant.

But, just like Possibly, I didn't have to understand it. I could just enjoy it.

So, I did.

"What do you think?" Levi Lee asked, half out of breath as he came to a stop mid-spin as I approached Starbuck's. "Ballet? Maybe it's my art?"

I chuckled. "You know what?"

"What?" He beamed at me.

"Who's going to stop you, man?"

He thought about this for a minute, then his grin widened.

"Yeah!" He thrust a fist in the air. "Who's going to stop me?"

Levi Lee reached up to push a tangle of golden curls off of his forehead, and though I wasn't concerned about enjoying his display, I made sure to keep my eyes on his face. There is a thin line between appreciation and creepiness.

"Hey," he asked, "can I ask you something?"

"Sure," I said, stopping short of reaching for the door handle of the coffee shop. "Ask away."

"Do you think I'm any good at performance art?" he asked. "Honestly? Maybe it's not my thing, you know? I'm a great handyman, but maybe I'm just not meant for art? What do you think? You're pretty honest."

I smiled at him, unsure exactly how to word what I wanted to say. Finally, I realized exactly what needed to be said.

"Do you want to do art?" I asked.

"Well...yeah," he said with a goofy grin as though it was the oddest question ever. "It's what we do here."

"Are you doing art you enjoy?"

"Yeah."

"Then you're creating art. You're living your life on your terms. That's art."

Levi Lee stared at me for the longest of moments, his smiling growing exponentially on his face.

"Life is art," he said, finally.

"It is," I said. "I think I'm finally getting that through my thick skull."

He laughed and I joined in as I reached for the door handle.

"Hey," he said.

"Yeah?" I asked, my fingers wrapping around the steel bar.

"Weird question..."

"Surely not in Possibly," I said. "Everything's so normal here."

Levi Lee chuckled. "Do you want to get a coffee?"

"Come on inside," I shrugged. "I definitely need a pick-me-up. And I'm sure Starbuck won't care."

"With...me," Levi Lee asked, looking down at his sneakers for a second before meeting my eyes again. "Together. A coffee."

It took a second for what he'd proposed to register with me. When it finally struck me, I was both panicked and proud.

What Levi Lee was implying—and could possibly be true—made my heart do a few jumping jacks. The fact that Levi Lee—out of all people in Possibly—had *asked me to have coffee* took the sting out of the scare, though.

Honestly, even in Possibly, where everyone did whatever came naturally to them, it was taking me forever to figure out who I was. Had Levi Lee figured it out before me? Did I want to "have coffee" with him?

I knew of one person that I wanted to have coffee with, but I wasn't certain it was all that sudden of a realization.

"How old are you, Levi Lee?" I chuckled nervously.

"Nineteen last time I checked," he said with a proud smile.

Another mystery solved. Levi Lee was nineteen. To me, that was age appropriate. At least we were both teenagers. However, I'd mostly asked his age because I was curious, and an opportunity arose where I could ask without simply being nosy. There was no breaking of the unofficial Possibilian Code. I sighed and smiled at Levi Lee.

"I don't think I do, man," I said. "I'm sorry."

Levi Lee smiled and shrugged.

"Life is art," he said.

"What does that mean?" I chuckled, hoping I hadn't hurt his feelings and he was simply brushing off the pain.

"Sometimes you think you're throwing clay and it ends up you're painting a landscape," he said, cryptically.

Or maybe not.

"Yeah," I nodded with a smile. "Sometimes it doesn't quite work out the way you think."

"Still friends?" he asked.

Friends? I hadn't thought of Levi Lee as having been a friend. Or anyone in Possibly. Besides Auggie. I liked the way the word sounded coming from my fellow Possibilian.

"Always," I said.

Levi Lee beamed and took a few steps back.

"If you want to bring me a frappe later—as friends—I wouldn't say 'no,'" he said before doing another twirl.

"Sure thing, man," I said with a laugh and headed into Starbuck's to start my day.

Over the course of the next two hours, *Two Doors Down* by Dolly Parton and *Midnight Train to Georgia* by Gladys Knight & the Pips played from the radio behind the counter in the shop. Amos had broken his pattern. Of course, he still played all three songs back-to-back all day long, but he was no longer stuck on one song all day long.

It was possible that Lovelorn Pass Bridge did more than cure lovesickness, I thought to myself.

All morning long, the sounds and smells of Possibly returned. Customers came in and out of Starbuck's for sugary treats and even sugary coffee. Wyatt's pistol could be heard nearly every fifteen minutes. AMOR played its three songs of the day. Levi Lee practiced his new art. When Agnes wheeled herself into the shop for a coffee two hours into my shift, she told Starbuck—with great surprise—that Grandy was thinking of stocking new items in his store.

Things were normal. As normal as they could be in Possibly.

It seemed that sometimes all a place needs is a good storm to set things right.

I took my break around the time Agnes came in for her coffee, delivering a frappe to Levi Lee as promised. He was grateful for the drink, choosing to sit and talk with me and cool down as I took my fifteen minutes away from cleaning. Mostly, he rambled on about his art and how he was going to discover what he did best sooner or later. I mostly nodded along and encouraged him.

It didn't escape my attention, halfway through my break, when Jack and Sofia appeared outside of the post office. Apparently, he had come into town to get the mail himself. Apparently, he'd decided to stick around and…visit. They stepped out of the door together, smiling, with Sofia talking his ear off and swatting at his arm playfully. I wasn't sure the conversation was one-sided or not, but when Jack signed to her and she responded, I had my answer.

The Mystery of Shirlene was answered. Even if I was the only one who knew it.

It was obvious, not just from their body language as they canoodled at the front stoop of the post office, that Jack had a thing for the postmaster. From what I could tell, she was not averse to the attention from my stepfather, either.

Jack said his "goodbyes" to Sofia, both of them grinning ear to ear, before he walked away, a distinct lilt to his walk. When he passed by Starbuck's on his way down the road back to his place, he caught my eye. Levi Lee was still talking my ear off, oblivious to anything else around us, so I just gave Jack a wink. His cheeks grew rosy and he tried to avoid my eyes, but he finally winked back before hurrying on his way.

That made me smile.

Even Jack could be embarrassed.

After my break, I headed back in to continue "swabbing the decks," as Starbuck would have put it. Not before I reassured Levi Lee that we were friends and he hadn't done anything to change that fact. Levi Lee made me smile. He came off as what a lot of people might have referred to as "naïve," but he was a nice guy. He made me laugh. He didn't care that he wasn't great at his art. Being friends with Levi Lee—even if we never got a coffee together in the way he'd suggested—would make my time in Possibly better.

For however long that was.

And, I suddenly realized, I didn't mind if that was a long time.

That realization hit me like a ton of bricks as I was doing my final duty of the day—mopping the entire café. I had spent the last few weeks wondering why I had to be in Possibly. Why my mom hadn't come to rescue me. In my heart of hearts, I'd truly felt as though Possibly was the worst place in the world to find myself. But as I mopped the floor, I realized that I didn't hate Possibly and it wasn't the worst place in the world.

It was different than everything else I'd ever known.

That had made me want to reject it, to declare it mundane and backwoods. However, it was the easiest life I'd ever known, living in Possibly. There was no hustle and bustle, no running like hell from the cops. No wondering where my next meal would come from and if it would have enough nutritional value to keep me from feeling like crap for days. It wasn't exciting, but it wasn't stressful.

Maybe I missed the excitement of the road—something Possibly could never match—but I didn't miss everything else. Once I got used to the easy going way of living of Possibly, and the way the people of Possibly lived simply and peacefully, I found that I didn't miss the excitement either. What's the point of excitement if it comes with conditions and consequences?

Near the end of my shift, after I'd put away my cleaning supplies and cleaned up in the backroom, I walked back out into the café to an empty dining area. At the counter, Starbuck was passing a freshly made frappe to the only customer in the place.

Auggie.

I froze as he thanked Starbuck and turned away from the counter, clutching his drink. When our eyes met, he didn't quite smile, but he didn't scowl at me, either. I wasn't sure if I should say anything to him, but I didn't have to wonder for long.

"Hey," he said, shuffling cautiously away from the counter towards me.

"Hey back," I said, hoping it wasn't the wrong thing to say.

Auggie's eyes flitted around for a moment as he chewed at his lip, obviously trying to figure out what to say to me. I was glad that he was doing the thinking because my mind was drawing a blank. I desperately wanted to say something to him, but I didn't know what to say.

Actually, that wasn't entirely true. I knew exactly what to say to Auggie, but I didn't know if I had the courage to say it.

I'm a jerk and I was wrong.

Do you want to get coffee sometime?

After what had happened between Lilly and Amos, did everything that Auggie and I had said to each other really matter? Did we really want to have a years-long storm brewing between us before one of us blew up in front of the whole town? Why not just skip to the handshake and forgiveness part of it all?

"Yesterday was crazy, huh?" he asked, looking over at me to smile, finally. "In a good way, I mean. Kind of. At least last night was. That was fun."

I nodded. "I've never danced before. In public, I mean. With other people."

He braved a smile.

So, I decided to be brave, too. At least a little bit. I leaned in conspiratorially as I spoke.

"Who do you think strung up all the lights and played the song?" I asked.

Auggie chuckled.

"Right?" he asked and took a sip of his frappe. "Another Possibly mystery to solve."

I laughed. "Yeah. That seems to be a thing here. You guys—*we*—like our mysteries."

Auggie cocked his head to the side, a queer smile playing along his lips.

"We?"

I shrugged. "We."

His smile turned into a grin.

"Speaking of which," I leaned in to whisper, "I solved the Shirlene mystery."

"Oh?"

"I think the letters are going to stop. I could tell you all about it sometime," I said, averting my eyes from his. "If you want?"

Auggie took a while to think about what I'd offered, and I was beginning to worry that he might tell me to go jump off a pier. Or a certain bridge. Finally, he spoke.

"It's a full moon tomorrow night," he said. "I was going to give the silo one more chance. It won't be great for star watching, but the moon should be amazing. And maybe the stars will look good, too. Do you...do you want to try again?"

I grinned down at the floor before raising my head to look at him.

"I'd love to try again," I said.

"Eleven-thirty?" he asked. "Just like always? Or the once?"

I laughed. "I'll be there."

Auggie and I left Starbuck's together, but went in separate directions after exiting the shop. He headed off to his barn, and I headed to Jack's place. Home. My first real home in so long that I couldn't even remember.

Later that night, as had become habit, I stripped down to my boxers and crawled into bed. I knelt by the dormer window and pushed it open. The Possibilian breeze whispered into my room, delivering the sounds and smells of town, cool enough to summon gooseflesh to my chest and arms, as grasshoppers chirped in the distance and fireflies danced along the bank of Susurrus Creek.

It had only been dark for an hour, but I could hear indecipherable music on the wind, coming from the direction of Auggie's barn. Where lights were already coming from the skylight.

I couldn't wait to try again.

If life was art, and art wasn't easy, sometimes you just had to keep trying.

Because art doesn't come naturally to all of us, after all.

As I drifted off to sleep, it felt as if I was drifting away into a black void. Then the light came, burning away the void, and a scene unfolded of an evergreen valley where cool breezes whispered through tree leaves and made the grass perpetually dance. Dew drops shone like gemstones on blades of grass and flower petals and tree leaves. Where chrysalides, stuck to hearty plant stems split open, saturating the earth with their nutrients and butterflies emerged, shaking off their wings, heavy with moisture.

The butterflies, unsure of what the purpose of their transformation was, flapped their wings lazily, drying them as the sun warmed and woke them from their weeks-long slumber. With nothing else to do, they took flight. Because that's what butterflies do. Not because there was nothing else to do, but because they could. It didn't have to make sense, but flight was how they announced their new way of being.

It was how they announced that, though changed, they were still there.

Just different.

Somewhere, in my dream, I heard a door open and close.

LIFE IS ART

"So," I said coyly, "you and Sofia?"

Jack had been messing around with a new project, sizing it up, when I walked downstairs the next morning and found him in the backyard. When I walked up and spoke those four words to him, he looked up at me, and though his cheeks gave him away, he tried to look annoyed with me. I just grinned at him until he broke. Finally, a small smile played along his lips, and he knew he couldn't hide it. Though, he tried to lower his head and go back to examining his new project.

The yard under my feet felt like a shag carpet, the grass soft and supple, the ground softened from the deluge we'd had. Rustling in the wind, my hair caught the soft, cool breeze the storm had brought back to town. The August sun overhead seemed muted by the cool earth underfoot and the breeze that had returned.

"I saw that."

Jack swatted a hand at me.

"Are you...*in loooooooove*, Jack?"

He looked up at me, trying to appear angry, but he couldn't keep that smile off of his face. The man had it bad.

"Is she your new squeeze, or what, man?" I asked.

Jack rolled his eyes and gave me what looked like a salute.

Don't know.

He stood there for a minute, concentrating, then he brought his fist up to his chest, palm facing me, and bobbed it back and forth like a miniature head nodding. Next, he held both hands out and open, palms pointing to the sky, and raised and lowered his hands back and forth like a scale.

Yes. Probably.

I grinned at him.

His next sign was one I'd never seen before, but it was so expressive, that I got the gist of it. Apparently, he felt that I should go do something with myself that was physically impossible. He wasn't being mean, though. He made his laughing face when he signed it, so I laughed with him.

"Fine," I said. "I won't talk about it."

He signed "thank you."

"But are you gonna ask her out on a date and get smooooooooches?" I teased. "Take her to Samuel's for a sundae and ask her to wear your class ring?"

Jack's head snapped up and he glowered at me.

"Okay, okay," I waved him off. "I'm done making jokes."

He signed "thank you" to me again.

"She understand sign language?" I asked.

Jack lifted one hand and tilted it back and forth while tilting his head back and forth. I was pretty sure that wasn't official sign language, but it translated well enough.

"That's good," I said. "You have your notepad for the stuff she doesn't understand, right?"

He nodded. I had told Jack I wouldn't make any more jokes, so I hoped he wouldn't take my next question as such, but I had to get it out.

"I guess your letters worked," I mumbled quickly.

Jack tilted his head to the side and frowned at me. He signed "what?"

"Oh, come on, man," I kicked at the ground with a smile. "The Shirlene letters. You have it bad for Sofia and the letters have been going to the post office. Also, I hear you going in and out of the house at night. You've been slipping letters into the post office slot, haven't you?"

Jack looked at me like I was the craziest person he'd ever met, then slowly began shaking his head. He signed "not me."

"Come on."

Seriously, he signed.

"Oh."

Jack began signing, and when he saw that I didn't quite understand, he signed a second, then third time, then looked at me. He was indicating that he did something, ending with his two index fingers pointing up and down side by side above his head.

"Sky?"

Jack repeated the sign.

I thought about what he was trying to tell me.

"You look at the stars?" I asked.

He nodded happily.

"You come outside at night to look at the stars?" I asked, disappointment settling in my gut.

Again, he nodded.

"You don't leave at night to send letters?"

No. Sorry. He smiled at me as he signed.

"Well, shit," I grumbled and kicked at the ground. "I thought I'd solved one of Possibly's unsolved mysteries."

Jack made his laughing expression before signing "sorry" again.

Disappointment that I wouldn't be able to give Auggie an answer to the Shirlene letters pulled at my gut.

"It's all right," I said. "I guess I just…well, I saw you two the other night. Then again yesterday. I guess I just assumed?"

He started to sign something, then stopped himself to dig his notepad out of his breast pocket. Apparently, whatever he had to say was too advanced in sign language that he didn't think I'd understand. Jack jotted down a note and then held his pad out to me to read.

It was a good theory, but it was wrong.

"Yeah."

He jotted another note.

I think the Shirlene letters are from Starbuck.

"Oh, yeah?" I grinned. "Why him?"

Jack held up a finger before jotting another, longer note on his pad, before holding it out to me to read once again.

I think he's sweet on Levi Lee. He could practically be the boy's father, but to each their own. Levi Lee lives with him, you know?

I gasped in shock, then laughed uproariously. Jack turned red, but he made his laughing expression, too.

"Do you really think so?" I asked.

Jack shrugged with a goofy grin.

I don't know why, but I decided to share some gossip with Jack as well.

"You know," I started slowly, "Levi Lee asked me if I wanted to *get coffee* with him yesterday…"

Jack froze and stared at me, his expression blank. After a moment, he jotted a note and held his notepad out to me.

What did you say?

I wanted to be offended that Jack had felt the need to ask, but then I realized that there was no reason to be offended. Besides, he was only asking the logical question for someone who—though he was my stepfather—didn't know me all that well yet. How was he to know how I'd feel about a guy asking me on a date?

"I said 'no.'"

Jack nodded as he wrote another note.

He's a nice kid.

Again, I found myself saying a thing out loud that shocked even me.

"Yeah. He is. And it's not like it wasn't, like, a *maybe* at first. But…I'm not interested in Levi Lee," I said quickly. "He's really nice, though. He's a good friend."

Jack smiled. We stared at each other for a moment, unsure what to say or do next. We had both shared more intimate information about ourselves than we had in our entire lives. Information that, at first, felt dangerous to share. But, like everyone in Possibly, we allowed each other to just be who we were. It felt good. All things considered it was awkward. But not in a bad way. It was a first *real* step in getting to know each other.

Is there someone you want to get coffee with? Jack held his notepad out to me again after jotting down his note.

I looked up at Jack and smiled shyly. He reached out and nudged me in the arm.

"Well, yeah," I swatted his hand away. "But I don't think that's going to happen. I think I messed that all up."

Jack examined me for a few moments, and his gaze made me so uncomfortable that I had to fill the silence with something. The truth was as good as anything.

"Auggie," I said. "I…wouldn't mind getting coffee. With him."

He didn't react; he was jotting in his notepad quickly before holding it out to me.

Auggie is a really nice kid.

When I looked up from the pad, Jack was smiling at me. And it was genuine.

"He is," I said. "I guess I'm not always a great kid, though."

I slumped as my brow furrowed, conveying my frustration with myself. Jack reached out and gripped my bicep. Gave it a squeeze. When I looked up at him, he was smiling at me. He didn't sign or say anything. What was there to say when someone was throwing a pity party?

"I know," I said. "Suck it up."

Jack made his laughing expression again.

"I'm going to go see his art installation tonight, though," I said. "So…we're friends still."

Jack nodded.

"Anyway," I said with a shake of my head to clear my thoughts, "I'll get out of your hair. I know you want to work and stuff."

Chewing at the corner of his lip, Jack examined me for a few moments, then he was jotting in his notepad again. Finally, he held it up for me to read.

I think I'll give myself a break today. Do you want to help me start a new table tomorrow?

The grin on my face was immediate and felt like it would split my face in two.

"Seriously?"

He nodded.

"Yeah, man," I said. "I'd love to help."

Jack gave me a grin and a wink and moved to grab his tarp to cover up the bits and pieces he had been examining when I'd found him in the yard. Suddenly, he stopped, and waggled a hand at me to make sure he had my attention. When it was clear I wasn't going to rush away, he started jotting in his notepad again. It was a quick note, so he was holding his notepad out to me within seconds.

You're a nice kid, too.

"Thanks, man," I said, looking anywhere but at Jack.

My cheeks were growing warm as Jack returned the notepad to his shirt pocket and signed to me once again.

I mean it.

"Okay," I said. "Let's…let's move on?"

Jack smiled, but relented with a nod. When he made no indication that he had anything else to say, I turned, intending to head back into the house. Leaving Jack to cover up his project for the day so that I could go have breakfast was my goal. However, at the sound of the plastic tarp being dragged over the wood and other supplies in the yard, I turned back to Jack. I hadn't intended to discuss so many serious topics with him when I'd first set out to tease him about Sofia that morning, but I'd learned one thing for certain while staying with Jack. When he feels like talking…talk as much as you can.

"Jack?"

He looked up at me.

"Do you think I'm like everyone else in town?" I asked, chewing at my lip. "Can I be an artist? I mean…will I ever find what art I'm good at?"

Jack turned up his mouth in concentration and looked upwards, thinking over my question. I was left to worry about what answer he would sign or write down on his notepad. For longer than I felt necessary, especially since I was anxiously awaiting what he'd decide, Jack contemplated the question. Finally, Jack returned his gaze to mine.

His fist came up and nodded like a tiny little head again.

"Really?" I asked.

Jack dug his notepad out of his pocket and flipped pages, but didn't actually write anything down, before holding it out to me.

Is there someone you want to get coffee with?

"I already answered that, Jack," I answered nervously.

He nodded, held up a finger, then went about jotting down another note to me. When he held the notepad out for me to read, my breath caught in my throat.

Start living the way you want. Because you're starting to understand your art.

I thought this over, then raised my eyes to his.

"Life is art," I said, nodding along as I stared at the message.

It was so obvious. I, along with everyone else in town, had said or acted out that belief a million times since I'd arrived in Possibly.

Jack shook his head with a small grin and jotted down another note. He gestured at his pad as he held it up for me to read.

No. YOU are art.

INFINITY AND US

*Y*ou know, Possibly isn't so bad. It's weird, but it's actually pretty cool. I'm happy here. I'm happy. I'm good here. I'm okay. Sorry for ignoring your texts. But I'll be okay. I'll see you whenever it's time to see you. I hope you're happy, too.

Shooting off a message to Mom that night just felt right. I'd ignored her texts for so long, I'd almost forgotten that she had actually texted me a few times. She hadn't specifically asked me to let her know that I was doing well, but she hadn't said she wasn't interested, either. So, I decided to let her know not to worry about me—in case that was a thing. Letting her know I was happy was more for myself. To let her know that even though she'd thrown me out on the side of the road on Two-Mile Trail, things had worked out.

So, there.

I'd had nothing else to do as I sat on my bed that night, waiting for the time to arrive to walk over to the barn. Reading would have been a great way to pass the time, but I found myself staring out at Possibly, thinking over the last few months. Thinking about the future. Smiling. I smiled a lot as I stared out at downtown Possibly in the dark.

When the fairy lights—which no one had bothered to take down—came on just after dusk, I grinned even more. No one knew who had put them up, but a new tradition had been made. There was no reason Liberty Lane—and the rest of Possibly—had to be so dark in the early evening. They weren't left on all night, though. Amos switched them all off before he ventured to bed each night. Just in case anyone wanted to stargaze without light pollution.

The fairy lights were a remembrance of the town's celebration and Lilly and Amos making up. They also served as a nightlight—a beacon—for everyone until bedtime.

It was a good new tradition. A nightly appreciation of what the mysterious hanger of lights had done for the town.

When eleven-thirty approached, I slipped my jeans and t-shirt back on, pulled on fresh socks, and slipped into my sneakers. Sneaking downstairs through the darkened house, the living room was aglow with electric blue light. Jack had fallen asleep in his recliner in front of the T.V. An old *Scooby Doo Where Are You?* episode was playing, the sound so low I could barely hear it.

I took a second to grab the old crocheted afghan off of the back of the couch to lay over Jack, somehow not rousing him from his slumber. Then I snuck out the front door, shutting it quietly behind me.

I took my time, strolling along the dark roads of Possibly on my way to Auggie's barn. The utter darkness no longer bothered me, sent chills up my spine. The shadows that seemed to move of their own accord as I approached Bend of the Road Graveyard didn't unsettle me.

It's funny, what one becomes accustomed to once they've grown used to their home.

The Possibilian breeze whispering across Susurrus Creek and through town felt like a beloved older relative running their fingers through my hair as I approached the fork in the road by the graveyard. If I concentrated, I could still smell

Starbucks' treats baking in his ovens, though the café had been closed for hours. I could nearly hear the chimes from Windchime Hollow tinkling on the breeze. My mind imagined Wyatt was firing off a round somewhere near Lovelorn Pass Bridge, though I knew that to be some sensory memory repeating itself in my brain.

It all made me smile, not cower.

Possibly, like all towns in America—maybe the world—had its quirks. When a person first arrives in a town, it takes some adjustment. Change can be scary. Most of us find ourselves intimidated by the new; the strange and unusual. Over time, if we are patient and take time to try and understand—even if we can never find it in ourselves to fully comprehend the differences—we learn appreciation.

We learn that change is fascinating.

Soon, those things that once felt strange and unusual begin to feel like home.

I stopped at the north end of Bend of the Road Graveyard, standing on the pavement at the border of the grass as I stared at the large headstone that I'd seen the night Auggie and I had seen our ghosts. A smile came to my face as I stared upon it again, though I wasn't sure if I was happy, sad, or just acknowledging yet another quirk of my new home.

The breeze picked up, sending my hair flying everywhere, and I found my eyes drawn to the large tree behind the headstone. Shadows are one thing, but the dark figure standing beside the tree was no shadow. For some reason, I didn't find myself startled at the sudden appearance of Malia.

She said nothing; made no move to communicate. I stared deeply into the darkness of her hood before glancing back at the headstone. My smile grew and I looked back to her. With a slow nod, which she returned, I carried on down the road. I didn't look back

1234 by Feist was playing on Auggie's radio at the barn. I was barely past the south end of the graveyard when I heard it on the breeze. Auggie seemed to be playing his music louder than usual that night. Maybe he was getting jazzed up in anticipation of finally achieving his goal with his installation art. He'd been working on it before I'd arrived in Possibly, and a few months later, it was possible his end goal was in sight.

Couldn't blame the guy for going a little overboard with the volume.

As I approached the barn, I spotted Auggie at his worktable through the barn doors, which were cracked and shooting a blade of light out across the walkway leading up to the building. I thought to knock, considering that I wasn't sure where Auggie and I still stood, but I knew he wouldn't hear me over his music. Of course, the doors were only cracked for one reason—my arrival. There was no reason to be overly polite.

I pulled one door open just enough to squirm between the two doors, and let it shut softly behind me blocking out the rest of Possibly. It wasn't immediate, but Auggie seemed to sense the change in the barn and turned to find me standing just inside the closed doors. He gave me a careful smile as he leaned, nearly laying on the worktable top, to lower the volume on his radio. Once the volume was at a reasonable level so that we could hear each other, he spoke.

"You're late," he said simply.

I grasped at my pocket, searching for my phone before I realized I had left it on my bedside table.

Did I cause Auggie to miss his chance at another go in the maze?

When I looked back over at Auggie, prepared to apologize profusely, he was grinning at me.

"Turd," I said.

"Your timing is perfect," he said. "Just like last time."

"Oh," I said, smiling cautiously, "good."

"We've got a few minutes, so…"

I nodded. "Yeah. So…"

"How's Jack?" Auggie asked quickly to fill the silence between us that the music couldn't quite fill. "I haven't talked to him in a few days."

"He's good," I lightened. "He's really good. He asked me if I'd help him with his next project. We start tomorrow. We'll see after that if he wants my help anymore."

Auggie chuckled.

"Him and Sofia kind of have a thing going on," I said, to which Auggie's eyes grew wide. "I saw them at the dance the other night. Then again today at the post office. They—"

"So…Jack's the letter writer? Shirlene's mysterious admirer?"

I shook my head. "I thought that, too. But no. Jack promises it isn't him. And I didn't check to see if there's a new letter today."

"There was," Auggie said.

"Crap," I kicked at the floor playfully and ventured further into the barn, closer to Auggie. "Did you read it?"

Auggie looked at me like I was crazy, which made me laugh and walk over to finally join him at the table, though I gave him space.

"Something like, '*I release my love as it cannot be, and hopefully, we meet again as friends one day*', but I'm paraphrasing, obviously," Auggie said with a sigh.

"Yikes," I said. "Do you think that means the letters will stop?"

He shrugged. "It's not like the letter writer will tell us. And Shirlene is pretty quiet. Only one way to find out, right?"

"Right," I chuckled.

Auggie looked up at the skylight, then checked his phone. My eyes followed his up to the ceiling, wondering if we would have to continue filling the silence or if the time for the maze had come.

"So," Auggie said, "do you think you'll beat me at my own maze again tonight?"

I grinned wickedly. "Only one way to find out, right?"

"Right." Auggie laughed. "Are you...are you ready? It's almost time."

"I've got my maze crawling shoes on," I lifted each foot in turn, the sneakers I'd arrived in Possibly no worse for the wear. "And I love to win."

Auggie gestured at the other side of the barn.

"You want to start on that side again?"

"Up to you," I offered.

His mouth pursed up in thought. "Yeah. Same places. I'll beat this side of the maze if it kills me."

The two of us chuckled and stood in awkward silence for a moment, before I flicked my head towards the other side of the barn. Auggie gave me a nod, so I left the table to head to the other maze entrance. Auggie turned the music up a little louder—probably so we could hear it in the maze and the silo after—and put away the few tools he'd had out. When I got to the second entrance, I turned to find Auggie standing by the lever that would start the maze's mechanism.

There was no preamble or pomp and circumstance.

"Ready?" Auggie hollered across the barn, his hand gripping the lever tightly, ready to pull.

"Good-a time as any!" I replied.

Auggie gave me a nod.

"One…two…three! *Go!*"

Auggie jerked the lever on the side of the silo down, released it, then ran for his entrance as the skylight overhead began to roll open all the way. I waited until he was at the opening of his tunnel before ducking into mine. The darkness swallowed me up and the music became muffled by the steel tube around me. Thoughts of spiders and other creepy-crawlies didn't enter my mind. The duct work seemed just as clean as the first time I'd crawled inside to try the maze.

Unlike my first go at Auggie's art installation, I didn't wait for my eyes to adjust, nor did I hesitate to begin crawling through the duct work. From experience I knew that my eyes would adjust fairly quickly and my shoulders and head could easily guide me while my eyes were catching up. Nothing in the tunnels was hard enough to actually hurt myself on, and time was of the essence, so I crawled ahead at full steam, smiling, hoping that I would not just beat the maze once again, but also Auggie. Though, I found myself hoping that Auggie would be a bit quicker than our previous go.

Through the walls of the duct work I could hear the radio playing and the sounds of Auggie banging around in the distance, desperately fighting his own creation. Grinning, I took a turn when I hit a dead end, fairly certain that I remembered the path I'd taken through the maze before. I couldn't be absolutely sure, but listening to the way the sounds outside of the tunnel were muffled or louder clued me in on the right path. If I saw too much light, I was circling around to the entrance once again, or I was close to the silo opening. However, I knew that outside sound was muffled in the silo, but not near the entrance, so that helped me tell the two apart.

Even after two tries at the maze, I still wasn't clear on what Auggie's art installation was supposed to mean—what it was supposed to accomplish for him as an artist—but I knew it inspired me to try. No matter how many times my shoulders bumped into corners or my head slammed into dead ends with a hollow metallic "thunk," it made me want to crawl faster.

I'd seen the moon and stars before. Thousands of times. But I'd never seen them from inside a silo. And never with…*a friend.*

After what seemed like an eternity of crawling on my hands and knees through the metal tunnel, the sound of the radio seemed to be getting louder. I stopped, wondering if I was winding back to the entrance or if I was near the silo exit. Straining to hear the words of the radio, the words sounded muffled, and I smiled.

The silo.

Full steam ahead, I crawled along as the tunnel grew lighter. When I turned a final corner, I could see the exit ahead of me—a ring of warm light that only Christmas lights could produce. The Christmas lights that hung from the rafters and ceiling of the inside of the barn. Moments later, I was scurrying out of my metal tube and onto the floor inside the silo.

I leapt to my feet and whipped around in an excited frenzy, looking for Auggie. Once again, he was nowhere to be seen. When I stopped and listened, I could hear him banging around in his tunnel still. It suddenly occurred to me that I should have brought my phone with me. I could have set a timer so I would be able to tell how much time was left. With nothing to go by—except the fact that it felt like I had been crawling around in the maze forever—I had no idea if Auggie still had a chance of making it to the silo in time.

Looking up through the skylight at the full moon staring down at me, I raced to the lever on the interior wall of the silo. I wrapped my fingers around it tightly and positioned myself so I could watch the tunnel exit on Auggie's side. I had no intention of pulling the lever until he popped out, but I wanted to be ready in case it came down to the wire.

Seconds—*maybe hours?*—ticked by as I watched the dark hole that led into Auggie's side of the maze. No matter how hard I concentrated, I couldn't tell if the sounds of Auggie crawling through the tunnel were getting closer or further away. I had no idea if he was doing well in his quest to beat his maze, or if we were once again going to fail. Sweat beaded on my forehead and between my shoulder blades, and I couldn't think of a worse time for it to start trickling down my back to lower places.

This is not the time for Swamp Ass, I thought to myself.

It wasn't even all that warm inside the silo, but my nerves were getting to me as I listened to Auggie's struggle within the maze. Once again, I was faced with making a decision. Of course, Auggie and I hadn't promised to wait for each other to pull the lever like we had the first time, but I felt that it was a rule that didn't change with each try. Even so, I wondered if I should pull the lever and hope Auggie wouldn't get mad, but simply be happy that we could look at the moon and stars together, or if I should honor our promise.

As much as it pained me, I tightened my fingers on the lever…and decided to honor that promise.

If we missed the moon and stars, they'd be there the next night. And the next. And every other night. We'd just have to keep trying until we got it right.

I could live with that.

Auggie inspired me to keep trying.

When the banging in the tunnel grew louder and closer, I gasped with happiness, knowing we still had a chance. As Auggie's head popped out of the tunnel, his eyes immediately found mine and he grinned so widely I thought the corners of his mouth would split.

"*Hold on!*" He scurried out of the tunnel and leapt to his feet.

Itching with expectation, my fingers turned white as they gripped the lever. Auggie raced across the width of the silo and joined me at the lever. Together, we looked up. The skylight was still wide open. When I felt Auggie's hand wrap around mine on the lever, I looked down at our fingers touching, then over at him. He gave me a cautious smile and a nod.

"Together?" he asked.

"Together."

We both hooted and hollered in triumph, and then we jerked downwards on the lever. Darkness so thick it could practically be felt slithering along my skin enveloped us. A mechanical "*CLANK!*" sounded from somewhere outside the silo.

We had beaten the maze.

A gasp from Auggie's direction startled me, but when his hand tightened over mine on the lever, I realized he was simply excited. Looking up at the silo opening that looked out of the skylight, I could only stare in awe and wonder at first. With the lights off inside the barn and the lack of light pollution in Possibly, the sky was infinite.

We weren't just looking at the swollen and heavy moon looming down upon us, but the universe laid out beyond a place only the greatest minds could measure. Swirls of stars twisted through the sky, blankets of pinpoints of lights and clusters of fireflies shone in my eyes as I stared up in wonder.

The universe wasn't some intangible, obscure place that only esoteric science and mathematics could give meaning.

It was *right there.*

If I reached up, I knew I could touch it. I could scoop up a fistful of stars, slide them into my pocket, and keep them for myself for when the world felt dark. I could grab the moon with both hands and have it lift me into the sky, weightless and carefree, unconcerned with the trivialities of life. It wasn't the universe out there and Auggie and me inside the silo. We were with it and it was with us. We were all part of an ever-expanding, unimaginably beautiful, intricately intertwined organism that was alive from one end to the other.

We were the universe; the universe was us.

Auggie's hand squeezed mine again and slowly slid away. I'd been focusing too much on the silvery blue orb in the sky and the fireflies that hung unmoving around it to notice, but my eyes had adjusted to the dark.

How long had we been staring up at the sky and holding the lever together?

The silo wasn't a cylinder of darkness any longer. The moon had filled it with a calm blue light, just bright enough that I could make out Auggie's form as he walked to the center of the silo. He was staring up at the sky, a beatific smile on his face. My hand finally slid from the lever and I couldn't help but smile as I watched Auggie admire the result of all of his hard work.

He was speechless. Even he hadn't imagined how beautiful the universe would look from the center of his creation. There was something about his smile, the result of seeing his reaction to his work paying off that made my breath catch in my throat.

I didn't know how to explain it—even to myself—but something deep inside of me, a question I never knew I'd asked of…whatever is out *there* that could reply…was answered. I felt complete.

I was no longer the desert tortoise staring up at the moon, asking it to be my friend. To give me someone to share myself with. Though, it had heard my request. It had simply taken liberties with the delivery.

So…the moon took away my status as a desert tortoise. *Maybe I'm…a Fennec fox?*

"Auggie," I felt myself breathe out.

He turned to me; his smile unfaltering.

"Yeah?" he asked.

"It's beautiful."

"You're not even looking," he chuckled.

"Yes. I am."

Auggie gave me a curious grin and cocked his head to the side. After a few moments, his smile melted away and he averted his gaze.

"No," he said, though his voice was shaky. "I can't do that."

"Why not?"

"Not with you."

"But why?"

"I can't do that with someone who is embarrassed by me," he said softly, his voice even shakier. "Or who doesn't know what they want."

"I was never embarrassed of you. I was embarrassed by me. But I'm not anymore. And I know what I want."

"No, you don't," he said.

Without another word, he walked across the silo and his hands felt around on the wall for something. A second later, the hatch door popped open, a slightly darker oval of blue light appeared. The music poured into the silo. Auggie stepped through the opening and back out into the barn. I stood in the silo, wondering what to do before the interior barn lights came on again seconds later. Without another thought, determined to not talk myself out of what I knew to be true, I dashed across the silo and bounded through the hatch door.

A roll of thunder cracked overhead.

Auggie was at his worktable, his back to me. He had turned the radio off and his hands were gripping the edge of the table.

"Fine," I said, emotionless. "If that's how you feel."

"It is," Auggie said.

"I can't force you to believe me that I know who I am. That I think you're brilliant."

Auggie didn't respond.

"There's only one thing left to do," I said with a shrug.

Auggie tensed at the table, his hands slowly sliding from its edge. He turned to me, a concerned frown on his face. Another crack of thunder sounded overhead and lightning flashed through the skylight.

"What?" he whispered.

"Don't worry about it," I said. "I won't bother you anymore."

"Jordan—"

Lightning and thunder joined forces in the sky once again. Then rain began to pour through the skylight into the barn. Auggie jumped with surprise and ran for the controls to close the skylight. I could've stayed and helped him, but it was a one-man operation. Instead, I turned, gave a resolved sigh, and raced for the barn doors. As I approached the barn doors and gripped the handles to throw them open, Auggie screamed from behind me.

"Jordan! Wait!"

I ignored him and threw the doors open. When I raced outside, the rain greeted me, slapping against me, soaking me to the skin immediately. I didn't stop running. Pumping my arms, unconcerned with watching my steps, I ran away from the barn, headed south. I crossed Liberty Lane, nearly slipping on the wet pavement as I tried to put distance between Auggie and me.

Across the tram tracks I fled, then across the patch of grass and trees that separated Starbucks and the post office. When lightning flashed overhead, my eyes landed on Lovelorn Pass Bridge. I continued to run, racing to the wooden bridge, concerned with nothing except one thing.

"*Jordan! STOP!*"

Auggie's screams from behind me were barely audible over the rain and rolling thunder, but I knew he was racing after me when I heard him.

My feet slapped along the pavement as I turned on the road to make my way to the bridge. Resounding hollow "thunks" met my ears as I ran onto the bridge. At the center, I stopped and turned to the railing, my hands reaching out and gripping it tightly. I looked up to the sky, rain dropping into my eyes, my hair plastered against my forehead and skull as I watched the lightning dance through the sky. There was only one thing to do.

Auggie's feet were clomping hurriedly on the bridge when I lifted my foot to the first rail so that I could climb.

"*Jordan!*" Auggie bellowed as I raised myself up. "*Stop it right now!*"

Ignoring his pleas, I climbed the railing, being careful to not lose my footing and ruin the ritual. After a few false stars and near slips, I found myself standing on the railing, my back to Susurrus Creek. Precariously, I wobbled on the railing as Auggie ran up, sliding to a stop in front of me.

"Jordan!" he cried out over the thunder.

"It has to be done," I said with an emotionless shrug. "I don't want to obsess over you like Amos was with Lilly. That's not fair."

"You...you've obsessed over me?" he looked up at me, a shocked look illuminated by the lightning.

"It doesn't matter anymore," I said, the rain slapping against my back.

"Jordan!" Auggie shook his head. "This is dumb."

"Then why do you not want me to do it?" I asked, looking down at him.

Auggie screamed over the thunder and rain.

"It's just an old wives' tale, Jordan!" he demanded. "It's not real!"

I snorted with amusement, though I was certain he couldn't hear.

"You really have to find something to believe in, Auggie," I said.

He glowered up at me, though a hint of a smile played at the corner of his mouth. I threw my arms out wide.

"*AUG—*"

I didn't have time to finish my exclamation. Auggie's arms were suddenly reaching up and wrapping around me. His actions caught me off guard and I startled. And one foot slipped from the rail like I'd stepped on a banana peel. A blink of the eye later, I was falling backwards from the bridge. I had just enough sense about me to realize that Auggie was spilling over to the creek below with me, dragged over the railing by my weight.

I've never jumped from a bridge before. For any reason. I'd never jumped from anything if I wasn't certain there was something there to keep me from certain doom. So, it was curious to me that the short fall from the bridge to the creek below seemed to last forever. As if I was falling in slow motion, my arms and legs flailing wildly as I waited for the impact with the water. To see if, like everyone else before me, the creek would safely catch me.

When I felt my back connect with the water's surface, and then the creek gushed up around me in a tidal wave of water kept warm by the summer sun, my breath was ejected from my body. If I'd known when to expect the impact, I might have held my breath in better. The suddenness and shock of it all sent me under the water with no safety net. No way to make sure that I would be able to kick to the surface before I was gasping in lungfuls of water, sealing my doom.

Surprisingly—though it shouldn't have been—I popped to the surface seconds later. The fall, though it felt infinite, wasn't nearly far enough to push me too deep under the surface. Then again, I'd landed on my back—like a reverse belly flop—that had probably helped, even if it had stung. Immediately, I began spinning in the water, searching out Auggie.

Lightning ripped through the sky and the thunder purred like a cat, illuminating the creek around me. Auggie was bobbing in the water a few yards away, glowering at me. I couldn't help it. I began to laugh. Uproarious, uninhibited laughter poured forth as I bobbed up and down in the creek, treading water with my swirling arms and legs. It took him a second to find the humor in it, but Auggie's laughter finally pealed through the air.

Once again, lightning flashed, bright, but weaker than before, and the thunder sounded—though it seemed to be coming from much further away. Auggie and I continued treading water and laughing until our eyes met again, and a silent agreement passed between us. Simultaneously, we spun in the water and began paddling towards the western bank of

Susurrus Creek as the rain eased up, turning into a light sprinkle as we made our way to the shore.

By the time we had reached the western bank and were crawling up it in tandem, the rain was barely a mist and the thunder that rolled through the sky sounded like it was coming from a million miles away. When we reached solid ground again, out of breath, but still laughing, Auggie and I plopped down on the muddy bank of Susurrus Creek, our legs dangling over. When our laughter finally died off, and both of us were catching our breath, soaked like drowned rats, I turned to look at him.

Auggie was already turned to meet my eyes.

"You're brilliant," I said, though I'd had no idea what I was going to say until that moment. "You're absolutely brilliant. That's what I think. And I'm not embarrassed of you."

Auggie started to look away, but stopped himself. His eyes came back to mine.

"And I know what I want," I said. "It just…took me a while."

"Jordan—"

"I'm not like you," I said. "I'm not always so sure of myself. But when I figure things out, I don't change my mind."

Auggie stared into my eyes, a small smile on his face.

"I guess I'd never thought that I'd feel this way about a boy, but—"

"You know," Auggie said, chewing at his lip, "I'm not a boy."

I stared at him for a second.

"You're not a girl," I said, stupidly.

"Exactly," Auggie's smile broadened a bit.

For a few moments, we stared into each other's eyes. The rain stopped and thunder sounded a final time in the distance.

"I can work with that," I grinned goofily at them.

"You're not weirded out by that?" they asked, though they didn't avert their eyes. "You're not going to call me weird?"

"Of course, you're weird," I nudged them. "But that's not the reason."

Auggie glowered at me for a moment, then they were smiling and nudging me back.

They started to say something to me, but as soon as they opened their mouth, a hollow whistling sound whispered down Susurrus Creek from the north. Just like on the night of the Fourth of July. I turned to look up the creek, then I spun my head back around to Auggie.

"Reed whistles," they said, simply. "Years ago—not sure exactly when—some of the kids in town carved whistles into reeds. When the wind blows right—hits them just right—they make that noise."

I grinned at them.

"Some things have a simple explanation around here," they shrugged.

"Just some things?"

"Not everything is simple," they said with a shrug, their smile faltering.

Before they could say anything, or get inside their own head, I reached out and laid a hand on their cheek. Auggie's eyes stayed on mine as I leaned over and placed my lips against theirs. I knew I should have asked if it was okay, but something told me it was. When my lips touched theirs, I waited a second, making sure they wouldn't pull away or push me off of them. When their hands came up to cup my face, I let my arm fall down and leaned into the kiss they were returning.

By the time they pulled away from me, the rain, thunder, and lightning were all but a distant memory. Only the protesting grasshoppers and the no longer mysterious reed whistles kept all of Possibly from being as silent as a tomb. As we stared into each other's eyes, Auggie kept their hands on my face, as if examining something.

"I wrote the Shirlene letters," they said.

I smiled, but I didn't respond.

"Love's not easy to come by," they continued at my silence. "I never thought...I've always felt that wasn't a thing that would happen to me. So...I decided to write to a love I had convinced myself didn't exist, but desperately hoped did. It was just a thing to make me feel better at first. But then everyone began to expect them. Everyone was excited for a new Shirlene letter each day. So, I kept writing them. I had plenty to say anyhow."

I grinned at them in silence for a few moments longer.

"Why 'Shirlene', though?" I asked.

They shrugged. "It's a grown-up, old-timey name. No one would expect a teenager to use it."

"Clever."

"I'm brilliant."

"You are."

"It taught me to sneak around at night. So," Auggie grinned sheepishly, "hanging up the lights and playing the song the other night wasn't that difficult to manage."

"I kind of figured," I chuckled as Auggie's hands hesitantly slid from my face, though we didn't move to part.

"Really?"

I nodded. "No."

Auggie laughed loudly.

To let me know that I hadn't overstepped, Auggie leaned closer and pressed their lips against mine. It didn't last nearly as long as our first kiss, but it was just as perfect.

"So," I asked, licking my lips slowly as Auggie pulled away, "the ghosts. How'd you pull that off? Who was under the sheets?"

Auggie slowly shook their head with a grin.

"I had nothing to do with that."

"Right," I rolled my eyes with a laugh. "I'm sure."

"I didn't," they said with a playful nudge at my arm.

"How can I be sure you're not lying?"

"There's only one way to find out," they said playfully.

I chuckled as I stared into their eyes, nearly made blue by the moon that was now peeking out from behind the clouds.

"It's a date," I said.

Auggie's happiness at my statement was apparent in their expression.

"Auggie," I asked, "why haven't I met your parents?"

They looked into my eyes.

"They'll be around one day," they said. "You'll meet them if you stick around long enough."

After enough time in Possibly, that made perfect sense.

ENCORE

*O*ne *Night at a Time* by George Strait was possibly an unwise choice for AMOR, considering Amos' and Lilly's history. However, as Jack and I worked on his new table all morning long, I never once heard Lilly screaming downtown whenever it played. Apparently, love songs were okay for Amos to play, as long as their understanding held true. It was very *Possibly* of her, to let Amos do what made him happy as long as he wasn't trying to influence her.

All morning long, Jack and I had worked on his new project, prepping the wood, sanding and trimming and cutting. We joked and signed, sometimes I read notes from him on his pad. A temperate August day made our work easier than it typically would have been. Though I had learned plenty about woodworking from Jack throughout the morning, I wasn't sure we had accomplished much. He'd assured me that the prep work was the most important part of the project, I still felt we hadn't done much. Of course, I was going to trust him. He was the expert.

When lunch came around, we had leftover chicken fettucine alfredo from the night before—one of my favorite dinners. It was just as delicious reheated the next day. Especially with the buttery, garlic-y bread we decided to make on the fly. After lunch, the two of us worked together to clean the dishes. Jack washed and scrubbed while I dried and put away. It was impossible for Jack to sign or write while we worked, so I did all the talking.

I'd let him know that since lunch was over, and we weren't going to do anymore work on the table for the rest of the day, Auggie and I were going to hang out. He smiled teasingly at me at the announcement—and I deserved it after I'd heckled him about Sofia—but I merely bumped him with my shoulder and smiled back.

"We're going to go ghost hunting again," I had explained. "We have to walk around town backwards thirteen times again."

Jack made his laughing expression at that explanation. I laughed with him.

Yeah. Maybe it was silly.

Then again…maybe it wasn't?

Is something pointless if you do it with someone you care about deeply?

Once the dishes were done and Jack was drying off his hands, I told him that I was going to head out, since I knew Auggie was probably already waiting on me. Jack gave me a stern look—quite unusual for him—before signing one request.

Be careful.

"Ghosts aren't real, Jack," I said with a wicked grin.

He cocked an eyebrow at me.

"I know," I said. "We'll be careful. Always. Promise."

His expression softened and he smiled before signing "be careful" to me once more. I looked down at the floor to keep my rosy cheeks from being on full display, and Jack pulled me into his chest. He gave me a squeeze against his chest and released me. He didn't prolong the saccharine sweetness of the gesture.

"All right," I said, stepping away from him. "I'll be home for dinner. Gotta do something before midnight, right?"

Jack nodded, amused. Then he signed once more.

Invite Auggie.

"Will do," I nodded to him as I headed for the door. "See you in a little bit...Jack."

He gave me a wave and then I was dashing out the door and down the front steps as *All the Pennies* by Mindy Gledhill began to play on AMOR. I jogged across the yard as Wyatt's gun exploded in the direction of the post office. I could only imagine Levi Lee in the middle of a Pirouette when Wyatt had decided to fire off his gun. Not that I wanted it to have happened, but Levi Lee stumbling at the shock was just comical.

Though I hadn't worked at Starbuck's that day, I could tell what was on the menu. The smell rode along on the Possibilian breeze and tickled at my nose as I jogged down the street to Bend of the Road Graveyard.

Blueberry muffins.

I could practically taste the juicy, tart berries. The sugary, cinnamon-y crumble topping. I could feel the light, fluffy cake dissolve like cotton candy in my mouth and the cream cheese icing filling coat my tongue and stick to the roof of my mouth.

Heaven. Or the closest thing to it.

I was halfway to the graveyard when I spotted Auggie standing by the north corner, their back to me. Two metal water bottles, one gripped in each hand, hung at their sides. I picked up my pace and raced towards the graveyard, my excitement for our first date swelling inside me. Auggie heard my feet on the pavement as I approached and turned to grin at me as I slid to a stop in front of them. Without a word, they held a bottle out to me.

"Hey," I said as I took the bottle.

"Hey."

"Am I late?"

"Your timing is always perfect," they said. "You always seem to be in the right place at the right time."

"I'm finally good at something!" I crowed to the sky comically.

Auggie laughed at my display and reached out to nudge me in the bicep. I looked down at them and stared into their eyes, my smile growing.

Auggie sighed. "You think we'll see our ghosts again tonight?"

"One way to find out, right?"

They nodded resolutely.

"Did you know Levi Lee is into ballet now?"

I chuckled. "Yeah. I talked to him the other day."

Auggie leaned in to whisper.

"The tights might need a pair of shorts over them, right?"

Grinning, I said: "I don't know. The view isn't so bad. Usually."

Glowering at me for a moment, Auggie couldn't help it, they burst out into a grin.

"Okay," they rolled their eyes. "I'll allow it."

We both laughed as we stood there at the north end of the graveyard, and I found my eyes wandering to the large headstone at the edge of the grassy area. There'd been stifling hot days in Possibly over the summer—and Auggie and I should have been sweltering. Typical of Possibly, I found that the weather was perfectly pleasant there beside the graveyard. The town could throw a person for a loop once in a while, but Possibly was usually a pleasant place to live. More than pleasant. Enjoyable.

I found, there beside the graveyard, that I felt a feeling I hadn't experienced in a long time—and rarely, if ever, on the road with Mom. I felt happy. I wasn't sad, I wasn't overjoyed. I was happy. I was content. And, when I really thought about it, I'd been content in Possibly since almost the first day I'd arrived. It wasn't Possibly, its citizens, or the unusual way things worked that had made me have sporadic periods of anger and unhappiness.

All of that had been on me.

Instead of leaning into a good thing, I'd rebelled, refusing to adapt for a time.

But the happiest people, the ones who thrive, are the ones who adapt. And if you have a quirky, peaceful town like Possibly to do it in, you're kind of an asshole if you don't jump on the opportunity to change.

I Gotta Feelin'—The Cleverlys version—began to play on AMOR.

"You know," I said, prying my eyes from the headstone to look at Auggie, "happiness is kind of an art."

They gave me a goofy smile. "Yeah?"

I shrugged. "Takes practice."

Auggie said nothing; they stepped up and gave me a soft kiss on the lips. When they took a small step back, a content smile on their face, I knew Possibly was where I belonged. I'd see Mom again one day—that was for certain. But she would have to come to Possibly. I was going to stick around. Why mess with perfection? Why not just be content?

"Ready?" Auggie asked.

"Ready."

So, Auggie came to stand beside me, turning around as they did, so that both of us were facing the graveyard. And we started to walk backwards, beginning our first of thirteen laps around downtown Possibly. I smiled as the Possibilian breeze ruffled my hair and I watched the large headstone grow smaller in the distance we created.

And, just like the night I'd seen Malia under the tree, I wasn't unnerved by the fact that "Jordan" had been etched above "Burke" upon it.

I was a Possibilian, after all.

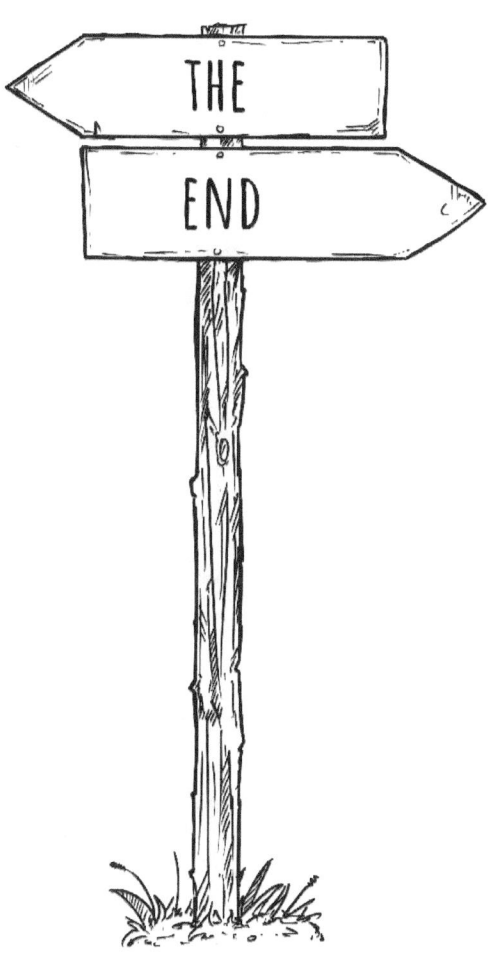

About the Author

Chase Connor spends his days writing about the people who live (loudly and rent-free) in his head when he's not busy being enthusiastic about naps and Pad Thai. Chase started his writing career as a confused gay teen looking for an escape from reality. Ten years later, one of the books he wrote during those years, *Just A Dumb Surfer Dude: A Gay Coming-of-Age Tale*, was published independently. Now with The Lion Fish Press (and 20 books later), Chase has numerous projects in various stages of completion lined up for publishing. Chase is a multi-genre author, but always with a healthy dollop of gay.

Chase can be reached at
chaseconnor@chaseconnor.com
Or on Twitter **@ChaseConnor7**
He can also be found on Chase Connor Books
https://chaseconnor.com
or on Goodreads
https://www.goodreads.com/author/show/18055910.Chase_Connor

SIGN UP FOR THE CHASE CONNOR BOOKS NEWSLETTER AT **CHASECONNOR.COM** or
shorturl.at/vDL03

He does his very best to respond to all DMs, emails, and Twitter comments from his reader friends and loves the interaction with them. Chase has several novellas/novels for sale in e-book, paperback, hardback, and audiobook formats wherever books are sold.